The Scientific Marvel Fiction
of the French H.-G. Wells

A MAN AMONG
THE MICROBES

I0634761

*The Scientific Marvel Fiction
of the French H.-G. Wells*

A MAN AMONG THE MICROBES

by
Maurice Renard

translated, annotated and introduced by
Brian Stableford

A Black Coat Press Book

ISBN 978-1-935558-16-3. First Printing. March 2010. Published by Black Coat Press, an imprint of Hollywood Com-
ics.com, LLC, P.O. Box 17270, Encino, CA 91416. All rights
reserved.
Printed in
the United States of America.

Table of Contents

Introduction

This is the second volume of a set of five, which includes most of the "scientific marvel fiction" of Maurice Renard, and some related works. It includes translations of the novel *Un Hommme chez les microbes*—the first version of which was written in 1907-08, although no version was actually published until Crès released one in 1928—and the entire contents of the collection *Le Voyage Immobile suivi d'autres histoires singulières* (Mercure de France, 1909).

The first volume of the series, *Doctor Lerne*, includes translations of the novella "Les Vacances de Monsieur Dupont," first published in *Fantômes et Fantoches* [Phantoms and Marionettes] (Plon, 1905), the novel *Le Docteur Lerne, sous-dieu* (Mercure de France, 1908) and the essay "Du Roman merveilleux-scientifique et de son action sur l'intelligence du progrès," first published in the sixth issue of *Le Spectateur* in October 1909.

The third volume, *The Blue Peril*, comprises a translation of the novel *Le Péril bleu* (Louis Michaud, 1911).

The fourth volume, *The Doctored Man and Other Stories*, includes translations of four stories from the collection *Monsieur d'Outremort et autres histoires singulières* (Louis Michaud, 1913), the novella "L'Homme truqué," first published in *Je Sais Tout* in March 1921, and a miscellany of later articles and short stories taken from various sources.

The fifth volume, *The Master of Light*, comprises a translation of the novel *Le Maître de la lumière*, which first appeared as a *feuilleton* serial in *L'Instransigeant* between March 8 and May 2, 1933.

The introduction to the first of the five volumes includes a general overview of Renard's life and career in relation to his scientific marvel fiction, which I shall not reiterate here, confining the remainder of this introduction to the specific works featured in this volume.

Un Homme chez les microbes, here translated as *A Man Among the Microbes*, was the novel with which Renard intended to follow up *Le Docteur Lerne, sous-dieu* (tr. as *Doctor Lerne*), making further inroads into what he considered to be the undeveloped imaginative terrain of "scientific marvel fiction." Although the version translated here was published in 1928, advertising itself as the "fifth edition" in order to give some hint of the tribulations preceding that publication, the "prehistory" of the work can be vaguely sketched out from a series of hints, including the one dropped in the prologue to the published version, in which it is revealed that "Doctor Prologus" has been working on his masterpiece for 20 years, having started on July 30, 1907 and concluded his final revision on October 28, 1927 (although, if the implications of the prologue can be taken at face value, he still had to type out a fair copy for the publisher, and only started that work on November 6).

Evidence of a less oblique character is provided by the number of occasions on which Renard advertised the imminent appearance of the book during that interval. It is mentioned in the prologue of *Le Péril bleu* (tr. as *The Blue Peril*), in a list that includes all of his previously-completed scientific marvel stories, and then began to be advertised in lists of works "*en préparation*" [in preparation] or "*à paraitre*" [forthcoming], including books issued by Louis Michaud and Edition Française Illustrée. In the spring of 1923, he was interviewed by the Belgian writer Jean Ray and optimistically informed him that the book, "awaited for nearly ten years," would be published in October of that year—the back-reference presumably being to the planned Louis Michaud edition that never actually appeared.

Adding all of these hints together facilitates the deduction that the four "editions" preceding the first printed version were probably produced in 1907-08, 1913, 1919 and 1923, with the published version being completed in 1927. Renard—unusually, among writers of the day—was known to be an inveterate reviser who was never content with one draft of his works and rarely with two, and the intricacy with which he links up the multitudinous and disparate details of his longer works reaps the benefit of this assiduity, so it is entirely conceivable that he wrote the second draft of *Un Homme chez les microbes* purely and simply because he was dissatisfied with the first—having taken time off in the interim to produce *Le Péril bleu*—but the others were certainly written with a view to publication, presumably with increasing desperation as he tried to find a version that a publisher might find acceptable.

At least some of the difficulty that Renard had in publishing the novel must have been to do with its startling originality. When it was written—although not by the time it was published—it was the first "microcosmic romance" to feature a voyage into the subatomic microcosm. The fifth version is able to make fleeting use of an analogy based on the Rutherford-Bohr model of the atom first proposed in 1911, which likened an atom to a tiny solar system, in which electrons orbit a central nucleus much as planets orbit a star, and the first-published literary development of that notion, R. A. Kennedy's *The Triuneverse*, had duly appeared in 1912. By 1928, the latter had been followed up by Ray Cummings' "The Girl in the Golden Atom" (1919), which—although it stubbornly clung the obsolete model of the atom itself—eventually became the parent of a curious subgenre of atomic solar system stories in the American pulp magazines. Renard, however, did not have the benefit of that analogy when he first elected to send his hero on a microcosmic odyssey, and drew his inspiration from much earlier sources—to which he conscientiously gives credit in the printed text.

A second difficulty that Renard must have faced while persuading a publisher to take the work was the sarcastic spirit in which the novel was written. All of his early scientific marvel fiction mingles black comedy and melodrama, but in very different proportions; in general, the longer the work, the greater the preponderance of melodrama tends to be, but *Un Homme chez les microbes* is a striking exception to that rule, offering much greater preponderance to comedy even in its mock-melodramatic passages. While both *Le Docteur Lerne* and *Le Péril bleu* bear strong resemblances to currently popular forms of fiction, *Un Homme chez les microbes* harks back to much older models that were widely considered—at least by commercial publishers—to be obsolete. Although it does have an obvious "Wellsian" aspect—while *Le Docteur Lerne* is Renard's *Island of Doctor Moreau* and *Le Péril bleu* is akin to chimerical cross of *The Invisible Man* and *The War of the Worlds*, *Un Homme chez les microbes* is patterned on *The First Men in the Moon*—it is much more obviously framed as a Voltairean *conte philosophique*, and the single previous work to which it owes far more inspiration than any other, as acknowledged within the text, is Voltaire's *Micromégas* (1752).

It would be inappropriate to give too much away in advance, so I shall leave a more detailed commentary on Renard's extrapolation of ideas contained in Voltaire's satire to an afterword, but the particular combination of imaginative extravagance, logical reasoning, acidic humor and social satire resulting from that extrapolation was a combination that undoubtedly seemed bizarre to the publishers who balked at the earlier versions of the novel; they presumably deemed that it would pose too great a challenge to readers whose obvious preferences tended towards thrillers, mysteries and love stories with happy endings. It is probably no coincidence that *Le Péril bleu* very carefully includes all three of those elements, albeit in a conspicuously wry fashion, and that Renard never wrote another novel that attempted to draw as high a proportion of its narrative energy from novelty and irony, and as low a proportion from earnest melodrama and suspense, as *Un Homme chez les microbes*.

When Renard was invited to contribute a piece about *Un Homme chez les microbes* to a series of articles in *La Rumeur* on the topic of "*Pourquoi j'ai écrit...*" [Why I wrote], he made no mention of the trials he had undergone in order to get the book into print, or even that it had taken him 20 years to do so. In fact, he contented himself with four tersely disingenuous sentences:

"I was in need of relaxation, of an outburst of laughter. So, naturally, I was led to treat, among the ideas I had in reserve, the one that lent itself most to gaiety and fantasy—in a word, to a "*blague.*" I have never amused myself so much as by voyaging thus among the microbes. I hope that the reader will find it no more difficult than I did."

The word in quotes, which I have left untranslated, can refer to a joke, a mistake or a hoax. All three shades of meaning were presumably intended in this instance. Modern readers, of course, will find no particular difficulty in appreciating the novelty and bizarrerie of Renard's story, and are much better placed to appreciate the brilliance that must have gone into the original version. As to how the present version differs from that original, we can only speculate—but the likelihood is that it would have been considerably longer, filling in at least some of the lacunae noted *en passant* in the present version. The publisher obviously did not regret those cuts, but Renard almost certainly did.

Between the publication of Le Docteur Lerne and Le Péril bleu, Renard published his second collection of short stories, Le Voyage Immobile suivi d'autres histoires singulières, here reproduced in its entirety. Like his first collection, Fantômes et Fantoches, it consists of stories that are quite various in content and tone, although they are all "*singulières*" [strange] in one way or another. The preface to the collection, however, advertises the fact that they have been arranged in such a way as to illustrate a spectrum of strangeness extending from a pole at which the logical development of the strangeness is at its maximum to one at which the role of logic is minimal. It is for that reason that I have translated all the stories, including those which have no "scientific marvel" content at all.

As with *Un Homme chez les microbes*, it might spoil the reader's enjoyment of the stories if I were to discuss any of their contents in detail in advance, so I shall leave the few specific comments I would like to make to an afterword, and confine myself here to more general observations. The first story in the collection, "Le Voyage immobile," here translated as "The Motionless Voyage," has been translated into English before, for a pamphlet published by Hugo Gernsback, the publisher who founded American pulp "scientifiction" and later renamed it "science fiction" in the 1920s. That version is entitled *The Flight of the Aerofix*; it is considerably abridged, most notably by the omission of the last few pages of the story, and that major omission, although not entirely unjustified, means that the abridged version is not a true representation of Renard's intentions.

"La Singular destinée de Bouvancourt," here translated as "The Singular Fate of Bouvancourt," is a contribution to a subgenre that John Clute calls "Edisonades"—tales of brilliant scientists whose inventions usually do not work quite as anticipated—numerous examples of which had already been produced in Britain and America, often reacting, as this one does, to the surprising discovery of X-rays. When Jean Ray interviewed Renard in 1923, he bewailed the fact that Renard had killed off "the illustrious Bouvancourt" instead of preserving him for continued use, rather than limiting him to a single sequel (translated on volume four of the series), but there is only so much that can be done with radiations alternative to X-rays, and Renard obviously thought, after two such ventures, that he had done enough.

"Le Rendez-vous" is here translated straightforwardly as "The Rendezvous," although the unnecessary hyphen in the French title is significant, deliberately emphasizing the literal meaning of the portmanteau word in a way that does not translate; the second component of the imported double meaning might be rendered as "Come Hither." The story advertises itself as a homage to Edgar Allan Poe, and deftly combines the imagery of two of Poe's best-known stories, attempting the

12

difficult task of winding up horrific dramatic tension to a pitch that might surpass the master's own endeavors. Renard was by no means the first writer to make such an attempt, and must have been familiar with similar pastiches written by French writers such as Jean Lorrain and Marcel Schwob, but he probably had not read the American and English pastiches by such writers as Robert W. Chambers and M. P. Shiel; those included in the latter's *Shapes in the Fire* are the most exaggerated. Renard's story can compete with the best of those predecessors in terms of its content, although Shiel easily outshines him in stylistic bizarrerie.

"La Mort et la coquillage," here translated as "Death and the Seashell," is the slightest story in the collection, anticipating the skill in crafting ultra-short stories that Renard was to hone to a kind of perfection later in his career. Its primary interest is its preliminary deployment of a theme to which Renard returned twice more, in a more substantial fashion. The first of those revisitations was "Parthénope ou l'escale imprévue," here translated as "Parthenope; or, The Unforeseen Port of Call," which was evidently one of Renard's favorite stories, since he reissued it in three later collections—a status it fully deserves, given its complexity and the dexterous manner in which it appeals to both ends of the spectrum that it is helping to illustrate. The second revisitation was "La Cantatrice," a translation of which—as "The Cantatrice"—is included in volume four of the series, in order to complete the set.

"Le Statue ensoleillée," here translated as "The Sunlit Statue" ("The Insolated Statue" would be more accurate, but too esoteric), and "Une Légende chrétienne d'Aktéon," here translated as "A Christian Legend of Akteon," similarly have no relevance at all to the overall theme of the series; like "Parthénope ou l'escale imprévue," they belong to a category that Renard described as "Contes à la plume d'oie" [Goosequill tales], meaning that they are deliberately old-fashioned, in their remote settings if not their outlook. The provide a neat illustration of the fact that Renard's initial literary affiliation, before he became infatuated with scientific marvel fiction, was to the Symbolist Movement that had evolved from the *fin-de-siècle* Decadent Movement, many of whose writers delighted in redeploying Classical materials in a fashion that showed them in a new, and usually more cynical, light.

The version of *Un Homme chez les microbes* from which this translation was made is that contained in *Maurice Renard: Romans et Contes Fantastiques*, an omnibus published by Robert Laffont in 1990. The translation of *Le Voyage Immobile suivi d'autres histoires singulières* was made from the 1919 reprint issued by L'Edition Française Illustrée.

Brian Stableford

A MAN AMONG THE MICROBES
SCHERZO

To Georges de la Fouchardière.[1]

It is by means of fiction that men everywhere
are rendered attentive to the truth.
Bernardin de Saint-Pierre

Micromegas...
Voltaire
(*Micromégas*, Chs. I-VII)

Messer Lodoviso, dove mal avete pigliato tante cognlionere?[2]
Cardinal Ippolito d'Este to Ariosto

---

[1] Georges de la Fouchardière (1874-1946) was a journalist and occasional novelist, notable for his satirical and polemical assaults on contemporary bourgeois society and its particular brand of Christianity. If, as seems likely, this dedication was attached to the story when the first version was written in 1907-08, Fouchardière would then have been at the beginning of his career, having recently obtained his first regular appointment with *Paris-Sport*.

[2] "Where did you find so many stories, Master Ludovico?" is what Cardinal d'Este—who was Arisoto's patron, although the poet complained bitterly about the quality of his support—is alleged to have said when presented with a dedication copy of the *Orlando Furioso*.

Cinematographic (why not?) Prologue

The room is decorated in the colors of moonlight: blue and silver. It has the scent of a florist's shop. The armchairs welcome you with an amorous solicitude, so unparalleled is their flexibility. Everyone, my dear, is making a great fuss, given the prices charged by places that encourage smoking and call for the maximum state of undress. Finally, maddeningly beautiful young ladies are taking care of you, with distracted expressions; they're the usherettes.

But three strokes have sounded, so traditionally that it surprises and amuses you. Three strokes, it is true, of no one knows what, no one knows where. If it were a bell you might say: "The Angelus?" No one dreams of doing so, of course. Besides, the orchestra—which is invisible, in the Bayreuth style—suddenly unleashes one of those dissonances whose ambiguity leaves you aghast. And at exactly the same time—zing!—the lights are dimmed.

Another chord (if one might call it that)—zong!—and semi-darkness.

Darkness? No, there is the screen: a rectangular moon, a parallelogram of empty light. But it is now furnished and inhabited. Mons Prologus is stirring there.[3]

---

[3] Renard occasionally used "Mons" as an abbreviation of Monsieur, so this appellation can be simply translated as "Monsieur Prologus," but if the whole phrase were considered to be Latin, it would mean "Mount Prologue," slyly reflecting the fact that the Paramount logo was as familiar to cinemagoers in the 1920s as it is to their modern counterparts. By 1927, Renard would have seen the German movie version of *Les Mains d'Orlac*, which presumably influenced this version of the prologue, but there are hints within it that it might have cannibalized an earlier version, inspired by an initial wonder at the magical representations of early silent cinema.

(And off we go: the orchestra launches into a fantastic scherzo, a great reinforcement of mocking bassoons, muffled percussion and equivocal saxophones.)

Mons Prologus, the ancient character of drama and farce—it is definitely him. As long there have been actors, he has worn the toga, the smock, and all sort of masks. Today, he sports a frock-coat, made up as a bizarre old scientist; and he calls himself "Doctor Prologus."

In his hexagonal study, whose walls are covered from top to bottom with books, books and yet more books, Doctor Prologus is working. Two rotating bookshelves stand within arm's reach, one to left and the other to the right, and there is a third behind them; that one he can reach by making his mahogany chair pivot.

The table is also hexagonal, and also pivots. Laden with open books, boxes of cards and scattered notes, it whirls freely under the impulsion of the scientist, thus presenting him comfortably with the book, the card or the note that he desires to consult. Tricks of that sort were already known in the Middle Ages.

Doctor Prologus radiates cheerfulness, and there must surely be a powerful reason for that cheerfulness, for he has the look—oh, how he has the look!—of a very intelligent man.

That cheerfulness does, indeed, have a reason.

For 20 years, our man—have I mentioned that he bears a strong resemblance to Renan and Pasteur?—has been writing, unremittingly, one of those works that bring perpetual honor to their author, his fatherland and humankind. Title: *The Physiology of the Senses*. Now, observe this: Doctor Prologus is currently writing *the last page* of his conclusion. What a day! What an hour!

We see him, momentarily, in the full exercise of his genius. The rotating bookcases are spinning like tops; the doctor himself, transported by enthusiasm, enters into the gyration with his mahogany chair, without ceasing to consult the dictionary that he has just grabbed. Will he ever stop? Meanwhile a "close-up head shot" displays his vast artificial forehead and his actor's eyes, which are seeking to put on a profoundly scientific gaze, while cursing those damned mercury lamps. *Nothing like them for ruining one's sight*, he thinks.

Finally, one sees a close-up of his hand and a huge pen, which is tracing this so-called immortal sentence:

Given the present state of physiological knowledge, and, of course, taking everything into account, we are unable to conclude with anything other than diatheses and idiosyncrasies.[4]

And beneath it, in capital letters, the magic formula that signifies both *Victory!* and *oof!*—the words:

THE END

Then, it is necessary that we see how content Doctor Prologus is! He gets up, looks up gratefully into the sky, where God is, and—in order that the audience should understand everything necessary—he gathers up his manuscript, contemplates its title, *The Physiology of the Senses*, and then takes a calendar for the year 1907 out of a drawer, which bears beneath the date July 30 the following note:

"Today I began my *Physiology of the Senses*."

After that, Doctor Prologus directs a gaze charged with happy melancholy toward the tear-off calendar hung somewhere nearby.

OCTOBER 28, 1927

More than 20 years! What a day! What an hour! All in all, what a minute!

And now, thanks to a superimposition of images, while the physiognomy of Doctor Prologus reflects the ineffable daze of memory, we see the misty evocations of his labor succeed one another.

A beautiful feminine face appears, grave and mysterious, with a finger posed on the mouth. It is a portrait of Humanity.

---

[4] It is difficult to believe that any actual cinematographer would ever have confronted his audience with such a gnomic sentence. Diathesis is a now-obsolete medical term referring to a constitutional predisposition of some kind.

But within that face, the eyes first come into focus and then blur again. And the ear. And the nose, to which a rose is raised. And the mouth. And the finger...

Sight. Hearing. Smell. Taste. Touch. *The Physiology of the Senses*...

Iris and fade. Instead of the face, Doctor Prologus-in-memory appears. He is conducting an autopsy. He is dissecting a tongue. He is observing a night-bird with his eyes. He is leaning over an ants' nest. He is holding a snail beneath his magnifying-glass. He is following a dog, which is hunting with its nose in the air, over a fallow field. *The Physiology of the Senses*...

Everything disappears from view. The scientist has chased it away with the back of his manly hand. Taking up his manuscript again, he consults it. *Diavolo!* It's gibberish! Erasures, substitutions, insertions make it quite indecipherable, save for the author.

Come on! he encourages himself. *It's not finished! It's necessary to have this cryptogram typed up.* And, quite placidly, he takes the dust-cover off a splendid typewriter.

The action seems trivial—but the orchestra must know something, for it produces a tumult of strangely sensational and, so to speak, ominous Russian music. Those who know what Russia music means immediately have the impression that this typewriter...ah! Pay attention! It will have a role to play, that's certain, and no ordinary role. The little flute hisses like a Mama Cobra whose soft eggs the mongoose Rikki-Tikki-Tavi is about to steal. There are two muted bugles sounding discordant appeals in duo. But above all, there are violins—altos, basses and double-basses! To imitate the noise that typewriters to make, sarcastically interpreted, some of their players execute stifled *pizzicatos*, while others strike the sounding-boards with the wood of their bows. Ah! How satisfying, allusive and Hoffmannesque that is, my dear! How *avant-garde* it is, even more than Saint-Saëns once was...but let's pass on. When you were a child, did you ever play the game of searching for some object that your little playmates had hidden? Do you recall the concert of their young refrain, sometimes murmurous and sometimes strident: "You're getting warmer, warmer! You're getting warmer, warmer!" And then, all of a sudden, the fortissimo of that puerile Orphean chant, howling: "You're hot! You're hot! You're hot!"

Meanwhile, Doctor Prologus does not know that he is "hot," because he cannot hear the orchestra's prophecy, being merely, at the end of the day, a photographic image, a humbly conventional mime.

He limits himself to gazing down at the typewriter, without even sitting down at the keyboard. Ennui is painted on his features. *What!* he is thinking. *Just like that? Straight away? Get right down to that uninteresting task, having just finished a magisterial work? Aren't I entitled to some relaxation? A week's holiday? Yes—we'll get started on* The Physiology of the Senses *in a week's time. From now until then, let's live a little, damn it!*

He puts the cover back on the typewriter, a mortal unconscious of Fate, deaf to the premonitory explosions of that orchestra, which replaces the ancient chorus at this point, and becomes quiet, as if it wanted to say to Prologus: "You're getting colder, you're getting colder!"

In the shadow, however, through the metal of the dustcover, the typewriter appears, glowing brightly—O expressive prodigy!

Abrupt resumption, by the musicians, of the suggestive cacophony.

Doctor Prologus hesitates momentarily before putting his manuscript in the drawer. Once more, he looks in the direction of the machine, which immediately fades away, leaving nothing to be seen but the innocent and ordinary dust-cover. His eyes make a tour of his study. He opens the two shutters of a window overlooking a pleasant boulevard, through which the orchestra precipitates an invasive flood of the sonorities of Life…

Bah! Next week. Let's go.

The drawer closes again upon *The Physiology of the Senses*, and the door closes upon the determined Doctor Prologus.

Here he is again—very well-dressed, I must say!—with a knight-commander's rosette in his buttonhole. He is not at all ridiculous, being the complete scientist that he appears to be and the complete Prologus he still remains—which is to say, bearing within him that slightly impertinent self-confidence that always characterizes Prologuses when they are clowning on stage and speaking to the audience.

He is in Paris, like a gourmet at a feast.

All vacations pass like lightning. We recall this one in the "envisioning" that follows. Scarcely has a scene appeared than a mist absorbs it or another scene surges forth, with the effect that the two images are momentarily superimposed—which is rather disagreeable. Thus, we always see two Doctor Prologuses at the same time, one coming into focus and the other fading out. But the most curious thing is that all this emerges and retreats within the frame of a huge eye, a huge mouth, a huge ear, etc. Visual leitmotivs. No need to insist; you understand. And you will even know, exceedingly alert readers that you are, that the sonorous leitmotiv of the typewriter is continually cutting obsessively through the breadth of the music.

Doctor Prologus is striding through the Autumn Exhibition. Paintings. The sequence of rooms extends to infinity. Thousands of pictures go past in a whirlwind, as if glimpsed through the window of an express train. Sculptures do the same in the opposite direction....

But Prologus meets some friends. Polite, though lively, discussion on the subject of art: schools, color, aesthetic theory, drawing, personality, expression of nature, etc.

Ostentatious dinner at the home of the immortally beautiful Madame Dupont, nicknamed Dupont des Arts because she leads to the Institut. Succulent dishes. Gossip. Wit. Elegance. Exposed cleavages, occasionally deplorable. A few gigolos of letters, arts or science. Shot under the table: ladies' and gentlemen's feet, some of them in conversation (re-read *La Con-fession d'un enfant du siècle*).[5] Doctor Prologus smiles in a philosophical fashion, accustomed to imagining the basements of the planet and the wings of society.

Concerts. Doctor Prologus has his predilections. He par-ticularly likes worrks that have a hint of burlesque and a sym-phonic interpretation. *La Danse macabre, L'Apprenti sorcier* and *Ma Mère L'Oie* satisfy him easily.[6] He listens admiringly while the conductor of the orchestra dances intelligently with his arms, and attains the height of sensuality in watching *Pe-trushka* delightfully choreographed by male and female ballet dancers who have fled the Bolsheviks.

A walk in the Bois, chatting. Autumn, like an old blonde, exhales its odor of nuts. Many beautiful and well-heeled people of every sort. Not a few gigolos. Nature. The season. Paris entire. Amours and mundane trivia.

Afterwards: receptions, teas, literary and scientific sa-lons. Balls, and even dance-halls with negroes, jazz, twitching, laborious entrechats, saltatory epilepsies. A large number of obligatory gigolos, on holiday, go almost everywhere.

But what books does Doctor Prologus read while he waits to fall asleep at night? Those that have always delighted him—*Micromégas, L'Ile des plaisirs, Gulliver*—and it is Vol-taire or Fénelon that close his eyes when it is not that joker

---

[5] The reference is to Alfred de Musset's memoir of the early 19th century, first published in 1836.

[6] The *Danse macabre* cited is presumable the 1872 piece by Saint-Saëns. *L'Apprenti sorcier* (1897), which was not at the time of writing irredeemably associated with Mickey Mouse, is by Paul Dukas. *Ma Mère l'Oie* (1910) is by Maurice Ravel. A few bars from Igor Stravinsky's *Petruskha* (1911) were reproduced along with the quotes in the preliminary material of the novel.

Swift.[7] (This is very pretty, thanks to the poetry of appari-
tions.)

Following days: theaters, cinemas, circuses, music
halls...and ceaselessly galloping, cramed on to the screen,
men, women, gigolos, the entire retinue of the epoch.

Suddenly: halt! The vertiginous race comes to an end.
And the calendar takes over, enormous and peremptory, fixing
the date:

NOVEMBER 6

The week is complete.

Ah, with what triumphant fury the nasal theme of the
typewriter bursts forth in fanfare! What volleys of demonic
laughter the instruments make, to greet the entrance of Doctor
Prologus in his study! Great gods, what is going to happen to
him, to unleash such a musical sabbat, in which the damnedest
of arid drums crackle over a crippled rhythm, while the clari-
nets shout themselves hoarse, like so many mad ducks?

Doctor Prologus advances placidly into the tranquil
place.

And here he is, sitting down in order to type *The Physiology of the Senses*.

The typewriter experiences the touch of his fingers. It's a
sort of preliminary caress.

The manuscript is inclined upon a lectern. We read on
the topmost sheet:

THE PHYSIOLOGY OF THE SENSES

Introduction

It is regrettable that Cournot, in his treatise *De l'ordre et
de la dépendance des idées fondamentales dans les sciences et
la philosophie*, Bonnier, in his *Audition*, and Laures, in his

---

[7] As the list of authors indicates, the didactic tale *Voyage dans
l'Ile des plaisirs* (1687) is by the Abbé Fénelon.

Synesthésies, have neglected that which Descartes and Condillac had anticipated.[8] I mean…

Etc.

On a shelf neatly-cut blank sheets of paper are piled up and, beside them, sheets of blue carbon paper, which will permit Doctor Prologus to type two copies of his work at the same time.

Carefully, He interleaves a sheet of carbon paper between two white sheets. Snap! The three sheets are caught by the prehensile roller. And *tap! tap! tap!*… The ribbon glides. The keys are struck. The virgin sheet is imprinted…

THE PHYSIOLOGY OF THE SENSES

Doctor Prologus smiles broadly. He is daydreaming, about things and people that are reflected in the polished black surface of the machine: dinners, pictures, concerts, dances, Swift clad in a smoking-jacket, Voltaire in a waistcoat and suit…. And this mingles with the ideas of his *Physiology*, as he remembers his work, his observations. It is in an astronomical sky, where populated worlds orbit, that couples execute

---

[8] The cited work by Antoine-Auguste Cournot (1801-1877) is more usually known as *Traité de l'enchainement des idées fondamentales dans les sciences et dans l'histoire* [Treatise on the Linkage Between Fundamental Ideas in Science and History] (1861). Pierre Bonnier (1861-1918) published *L'Audition* [Hearing] in 1901. The rather obscure Henry Laures might only have made the list because his *Les Synesthésies* [Synesthesia] (1908) was a recent publication when the first version of the introduction was completed; the topic was of some interest to the Symbolists, who probably latched on to it immediately. The other references are to the great René Descartes (1596-1650) and Etienne Bonnot de Condillac (1715-1780), author of *Traité des sensations et de la logique* [Treatise on Sensation and Logic].

their Black Bottom. It is with the eyes of insects, formed in facets, that Prologus revisits the Autumn Exhibition…

Damn! he says to himself. *Pay attention!*

He smiles again, and continues his task.

Tap! tap! tap! tap!

Introduction

It is regrettable that Cournot…

The orchestra goes wild.

Distracted, without breaking any records, the physiologist nevertheless arrives at the foot of the first page.

The result isn't too bad. The sheet looks fine. Let's see the carbon copy; is it clear?

Stupor! What's this?

In a paroxysm of amazement, he reads:

A MAN AMONG THE MICROBES
SCHERZO

Part One

Marvel of marvels! The carbon paper has not copied *The Physiology of the Senses*, but something else! Doctor Prologus has just typed, simultaneously, the beginning of his austere treatise and, beneath it, what? The beginning of some sort of fairy-tale…

It's a dream, an enchantment!

Prologus starts laughing, in harmony with the violins.

A surprising phenomenon of spontaneous generation! he thinks. *Like Macduff, who, according to Shakespeare, was not born of woman, at least in the same fashion as everyone else, this story has not emerged from a human brain, at least in the same fashion as other stories!*

And quickly, quickly, quickly, he resumes his fabulous duplicate occupation. He laughs, he laughs, he laughs. His speedy fingers race. What a piano technique! It goes back to

Padereweski. His work makes the noise of a downpour on the roof. It progresses, progresses, progresses. The sheets pile up, the *Physiology* on one side, *A Man Among the Microbes* on the other...

Mons Prologus, you may now disappear. You have told us what we need to know. Quit the doctoral frock-coat, dispense with your borrowed face and go forth, in other disguises, to pursue your career as a prefatory mountebank. We know what *A Man Among the Microbes* is.

The reader is free to assume that the cinema, perservering, will show him the comedy—or, rather, that the irresistible usherettes will spread out through the auditorium to sell the little booklet that you have just insidiously introduced and which, as you have shown him, merely contains a fairy-tale.

The reader is no less free, while complaining, not to stay for your pantomime, if he thinks that the time for fairy-tales is past, and that candid fantasy can no longer be tolerated.

Part One: Fléchambeau's Engagement

I. A Chapter About a Hat

At the foot of the high mountain, the little sub-prefecture was reminiscent of an ancient avalanche that had become civilized over time.

There was an open square in the center, and in the center of that square a humbly monumental fountain sported a *République* with powerful breasts, the work of some Auguste Barbier of the chisel.[9]

Pons—the young Doctor Pons—lived there, between the wig-maker and the notary, in a typical Savoyard house, dressed up to the nines with a huge roof of old tiles and a façade costumed in wisteria.

A storyteller of old, in beginning this story, would doubtless go back to Doctor Pons' disappointment when he learned that from one of his masters on leaving college that his health would not permitted him to practice the art of medicine in Paris, or in any other large city, or even to work there, as he desired, in glorious clinical research—which had the result of sending Pons back to Saint-Jean-de-Nèves, the mountain town of his birth, where his only two colleagues held him in high regard because of the few cases that he handled.

A not-quite-so-old storyteller would be content to start the story by describing the arrival at Pons' home of his friend Fléchambeau, a trainee advocate at the Paris court, who had

---

[9] Auguste Barbier (1805-1882) was a poet whose *Les Jambes* (1831) is a stirring denunciation of the supposed evils of his era, inspired by the July Revolution of 1830. The *République* is, inevitably, represented in the fountain by its conventional personification as the lovely Marianne—hence the proud breasts.

come to spent a few weeks of relaxation at Sant-Jean-de-Nèves and was still there three months later, by virtue of an irresistible attraction—that of Mademoiselle Olga Monempoix, the beloved daughter of Monsieur Emile Monempoix, the president of the Civil Tribunal, and his wife, née Sanson-Darras.

We, being less pretentious, will jump into the dish feet-first.

"Good luck, old chap!" said Pons

They were in the hallway. Visible through the doorway that opened on to the square were the roundness of little acacia-balls, the busty Marianne of the fountain and, directly opposite, the house of Monsieur le Président Monempoix.

Fléchambeau shook the hand that his friend held out to him. As long as a day without tobacco, measuring a meter ninety-six from the soles of his feet to the top of his head, Fléchambeau was even more remarkable by the carroty color of his hair—hair *à la Crécy*,[10] Pons called it, jokingly. He was so tall that it took him 20 seconds and three-fifths to make the sign of the cross, and when he put his hat on his flamboyant head he looked like a candle snuffing itself out.

His hat, for the moment, was a magnificent shiny topper. A black jacket, sharply cut, was set atop his rosewood trousers. His immense feet reflected nature in the polish of their size 47s. His gloves, size 9¾, gave him hands of soft butter. Three carnations in his buttonhole seemed, by an effect of proportion, to be only one.

Having adjusted his monocle and rubbed his short moustache, brushed into red spikes, this quasi-giant grimaced like a swimmer about to plunge into cold water. "I'm shrinking in my skin, old chap!" he said.

---

[10] The culinary term *à la Crécy* means "with carrots;" it derives from the fact that the ancient battlefield was reputed to produce superior specimens of that vegetable.

Nevertheless, he went out and headed toward President Monempoix's house, slowly: so slowly that Pons saw him ring the President's doorbell from the window of his laboratory. The laboratory was on the second floor, and Pons had gone up the stairs thoughtfully, and hence very gently.

It was a large window, emitting a flood of light, in a state-of-the-art laboratory—for Doctor Pons had not renounced the idea of being talked about. He had sought some study capable of keeping him busy in Saint-Jean-de-Nèves, without their doing any harm to his retreat. He had discovered parasitology—the science of parasites, let us add, for the benefit of ladies and children.

But parasitology only offered modest satisfaction to his sterile zeal.

And yet, what a pretty laboratory it was, with its white cupboards, its clean shelves filled with blue, red, green, yellow and other variously-colored jars and bottles, and the three microscopes lined up like an artillery battery in the window-bay on three nickel-plated side-tables, provided with an arsenal of forceps, cupels, phials, little boxes and objective lenses, all arranged like soldiers on parade.

Pons, still daydreaming, patted the crystal bell-jars that covered the microscopes mechanically—on seeing which, Mary Stuart, his cat, who had followed him, rubbed her nose with her paws in order to participate in the distribution of caresses.

He took her in his arms.

A tabby, with languorously dull eyes, she had a slight squint, which was why her owner had named her Mary Stuart, in memory of the unfortunate princess—who was, as everyone knows, similarly afflicted. She had very nearly been called Gibelotte, the lucky beast![11] A stroke of luck having saved her from that posthumous disguise, she had taken refuge in Pons' house, where she fulfilled the functions of she-cat, which is

---

[11] A gibelotte is a *fricassée*, usually of rabbit or hare, cooked in white wine.

not quite the same as the job of tomcat, for—as Pons repeated to her tactfully, but with irritating insistence—to be a female cat is to be female twice over.

Thus, Mary Stuart dutifully earned her offal making a furry figurehead on the corners of bookshelves, striking those attitudes that we would like to see as expressions; showing herself, as was only right, to be myophagic and cynophobic—which is to say, eating rats and spiteful with regard to dogs—and keeping herself tidy and slim, like a working girl. There was no end to her work. Her furry coat was something on which one could warm one's hands. She purred—which is the interior smile of cats—and sometimes provided the spectacle of rolling right and left in a gracefully dolorous sensual fashion, with hoarse cries and veiled glances. She danced on her hind legs after flies. She disappeared on mischievous escapades, without warning the household—with the result that one grew anxious, then irritated, and one searched for her—before suddenly reappearing as if nothing had happened, just like that, as if by magic, rolled up in a ball beside the fire or curled up on the corner of the table, with her feet and tail gathered up, and her eyes narrow and somnolent. Then she populated the cheerful house with a horde of comical kittens, which made clownish entrances, one of them leaping on all fours, another advancing sideways with arched back and bristling hair like a Japanese warrior in a kimono, a third charging like a train until crashing into the wall, to make people laugh, a fourth following some mysterious invisible flight through the air with naïve blue eyes, and two more being inseparable, stretched out on the carpet side by side, each one playing with its hind feet buried, oddly, in the other's belly…

"Come on," said Pons, "you, who help me to live! *Muni, muni, muni*…"

And he was about to tease her, repeating, in the voice of an old lady, the ritual phrases—"Oh, what a funny rabbit! One might think it was a cat!"—when he noticed that she had been in the hairdresser's shop again. That neighbor was raising a litter of brats, who were infatuated with the cat, although no one could understand why. She frequently came back from there with a cravat knotted round her neck or dragging some trinket. The children dressed her up without her making any protest. Today they had put pomade on her head, in order to give her a streak. She was reeking of heliotrope.

In view of that odor, Pons put her outside, mocking her and promising, yet again, to have her stuffed once she was dead.

An eccentric, this Pons. He had a fine numismatic profile. He had a handsome face, too, but it was quite different. One was always surprised, when he turned round, to see an asymmetrical face, in which only the eyes remained similar: black eyes shining with a somber gleam from the depths of orbits so deep that they eyes seemed to be lying in ambush in the depths of the skull—a skull, moreover, marvelous in its amplitude, so that it completely filled headgear of the vastest compass.

Thus conceived, Pons came back to the window, which gave itself wholeheartedly to the sunlight. With a glance, however, he had verified that the clock had done its duty; with a flick of his thumb he had superimposed the mobile needle of the barometer over the indicative one; he had questioned the thermometer, consulted the hygrometer and even taken a look at the calendar. In his house, there was no taking things easy. Everything was regulated: the hour, the day, the temperature!

The purple berries of the wisteria were framing the Place de la République. The amorous flowers, young widows scarcely yet in mourning, suddenly quivered, jerkily, nervously and briskly, thanks to the take-off of two small birds, which flew away so quickly that they could not be seen.

Pons gazed at President Monempoix's house, at the window of Mademoiselle Olga, his daughter—the window that was within range of a kiss, and the door that had closed a little while before on the immense Fléchambeau—all of which was behind the bronze effigy symbolizing the French Republic.

"Fortunate, fortunate Fléchambeau!" chanted Pons, who loved to soliloquize. "That lightning-conductor has received

31

the thunderbolt. Monsieur and Madame Monempoix are in the process of granting his request to avail himself of the hand of their heiress. And as for me, I'm here in the midst of my parasites and my lice…and to cap it all, I, who aspires to be a physiognomist, am disgusted by my own face. Oh, to depart on a luxurious voyage in a sleeping-car, with a delightful little wife who would adore me madly because I'd be a genius and she'd know it! Or to depart again, but for Paris, the city of a thousand *tours-de-force*, with my glory in the bag, after a discovery of the first magnitude! To say to my lackeys: 'Quick—I'm off, with ink in my pen, fuel in my lighter and scent in my handkerchief! Paris! Paris awaits me!' And to telegraph ahead: 'Pass the pumice-stone over the obelisk, make the dome of the Invalides shine beige! Polish up the Eiffel tower! I'm on my way!' And you, wet-nurse République…"

He did not finish. Fléchambeau was crossing the square with vast strides. The doorbell rang violently. The stairs were mounted eight at a time. The door of the laboratory opened as if staved in by a Soviet commissar. Fléchambeau appeared, full of rage, and launched his top hat at full speed at a wardrobe that did not want it and let it fall, having crushed it.

Faced with Pons' stunned silence, Fléchambeau folded his arms, tapped his feet forcefully to the beat of exasperation—*allegro furioso*—and proffered this single word, which he bit into as it passed by:

"Failed!"

His red hair was alight now upon his high-set forehead.

"Pardon?" said Pons, not believing his ears.

"You're an idiot. I've failed, I tell you—rejected, sent away. They're two peasants, two pumpkinheads, two…"

"What reason did they give for opposing you?"

"What reason? Too young. Olga, that is—and she's been 18 since Septuagesima! Talk about an excuse! Bad faith! Oh, but it's not over, this business! Filthy republicans!"

"Pardon me but you're forgetting that I too…"

"You! I don't give a damn about you!" He started pacing back and forth like a caged bear, all more reminiscent because he had plunged his fists into the depths of his pockets, so vigorously that the cloth had audibly torn. He was pale and panting. One might have thought him a sentinel in winter, the way he was tapping his feet, tightening his elbows and pulling his head down between his shoulders.

Pons picked up the dented top hat and handed it to him. "Go on, finish it off! It's still breathing. For pity's sake…"

The hat flew away, sharply slapped.

"Do you want mine?" Pons asked. "I'll go and fetch it…"

Fléchambeau smiled in spite of himself.

"Sit down, you silly fool. And tell…"

A dimpled leather armchair received the despairing young man in its lap; he overflowed it like a two-meter rule. "Ah," he said, "you, who know how I love, don't know how I hate! For I'm in love! And yet, I'm beloved."

"That's profound," remarked Pons.

"Yes, Olga loves me, I'm sure of it. She swore her oath to me in the presence of the Moon, the night when we danced at the Godbillons'. It was in the kitchen-garden, at the back. I put my arm round her waist, and talked to her tenderly. The moonlight, which has genius, allowed us to see; the shadow of branches extended over the wall like English lace. I murmured…"

"Understood," said Pons. "I'm as familiar with Mademoioselle Olga's sentiments as with her beauty. And beauty-wise, she has nothing to fear. Her shapely body is softly molded, slender and nicely rounded. Her curvaceous figure has a delightful flexibility. She has a pretty little snub nose, not inconvenient for kissing. Her cheeks are like Normandy apples in spring; or rather, the texture of their skin, the plenitude of their flesh, which are her privilege, are those of a pink rosebud that is just opening. In consequence, she does not exhale a perfume so much as a freshness. Her fingers remind me of those of Aurora, whom I knew very well when I was a student. There can only be two Graces in Olympus now, since she has descended to dwell among us. In brief, Olga is a little

33

lady scarcely grown, who, by God, doesn't have the look of being born from a kiss on the forehead!"

Fléchambeau had listened in ecstasy to his shrewd friend, but he stopped on these words that carelessly reminded him of Monsieur and Madame Monempoix.

"Ah!" he said, in a discouraged tone. "Let's leave the parents alone, especially Madame Veto!"

"The daughter is above her mother's level," Pons observed.

"I'll write to her—to Olga! A very spontaneous letter…"

"In that case, I'd advise you to make a rough draft first."

"No, I shan't write to her! I shall see her!"

"A little calm and method," said Pons. "One know longer knows where one is."

"Or rather…or rather, Pons, it's you who must act now!"

"Me? What silly idea are you nursing?"

"This one. Olga's youth: nonsense. When they come to me singing: 'We want to keep her until she's 20,' I don't believe them."

"Why not?" asked Pons.

"Because! Let's see!"

"Eh? Go on."

"I don't believe an iota of it. No more do you. Nor anyone else. It's the traditional non-welcome. It's the old dilatory response! No, no: there's something else behind it, and that other thing is that these folk are Republicans, that they need to be, for the sake of their advancement…"

"Madame Monempoix is the great-granddaughter of the Conventionist Sanson-Darras. Why tarnish her with a slander?"

"So be it. *Roture oblige.*[12] I'm only what I am, and no less: Fléchambeau, for God and the king. I don't hide it. They know it. They don't want a son-in-law of that sort!"

---

[12] This phrase parodies *Noblesse oblige*, asserting that plebeian blood also has its obligations.

"Possibly," said Pons. "But...you're holding hard to your opinions?"

Fléchambeau waxed indignant. "I will not," he said sing the *Carmagnole* and dance the *capucine* to please a *sans-culotte* and a *tricoteuse*."

"Happy is he," Pons extolled, "who has lasted long, like a lily."

"Enough! I can't tell you how painful your mockery is. Your republic can't make men any happier than the monarchy. As for God, in whom, alas, you don't believe..."

Pons excused himself softly; "We're not in the same club, he and I. I only know his name, as do the majority of men. I've a good deal of sympathy for him, but..."

Fléchambeau cut him off. "But all that's just words, and I want to stick to the essential matter."

"Which is?"

"That you're on the same side as the Monempoix: the port side."

"So?"

"Go see them, my little Pons. You know them well. Try to make them see the real reason for their refusal, and if it's as I suppose..."

"Well?"

"Well then, you have sufficient political connections on the left, to have them put a word in for me with the Monempoix—député X, or minister Y..."

Pons stared into the space above Fléchambeau's head for some time, the latter having drawn nearer to him and set the most persuasive button on his waistcoat at his eye-level. "It's not enough," he said, eventually, "that skylarks fall into your mouth ready-roasted; you want them to be boned as well."

"Oh!" cried Fléchambeau. "You're taking advantage of the fact that I'm alive to annoy me!"

"Don't complain, you great spoiled child. There are no hardier amours than frustrated amours."

"Yes, my boy, you've attained wisdom—everyone knows that."

"The wisdom of passions! I have my own passion too: science!"

"A little science, and much ambition!"

"I simply have faith in myself."

"Well," said Fléchambeau, diplomatically, thinking it opportune to talk to Pons about Pons for a while, "you're one of those lucky chaps who'll live to be 100, never having succeeded, and saying all the same: 'I had something there!' But be careful! When you're in Hell, ambitious Pons, Pons avid for celebrity, your head will be the bowl of a pipe filled with burning tobacco, which some two-horned devil will smoke for centuries on end!" Then, returning to his own sheep: "Tell me, Pons, my friend, will you do it? Go to see the Monempoix?" He took hold of the other's shoulders, and looked down at him imploringly.

"I won't go!" said Pons, resolutely.

But he went, without delaying much longer.

II. In Which Hope Disputes With Dread

According to the clock, Pons' absence lasted 35 minutes. According to Fléchambeau, it was prolonged for the famous "two hours" of which the peevish, the impatient and all the other individuals who have a casual attitude to precision always speak.

Fléchambeau went down to his room, sat down, got up again, sat down again, readjusted his monocle a hundred times over, and shuttled back and forth between the window, where he watched out for the appearance of his ambassador, and the mirror on the mantelpiece, where he reviewed his cause despairingly, moved by the sight of a sympathetic face. There, he smiled at himself, urbanely, amiable showing off his teeth—which were very white, with the exception of the two upper canines, which were gold. That commanding smile could not penetrate his anxiety-saturated being, however; it was only a mask. Fléchambeau put on that deceptive mouth as if it were a false nose.

The view of the square attracted him irresistibly, along with the surveillance of the house opposite, where his destiny was at stake. His nervousness lent the dwelling a strangely monstrous immovable physiognomy, with confused features borrowed from human nature, and an indecipherable gaze in its rectangular eyes.

One of those eyes opened suddenly. The beautiful Olga appeared at the window. He could see her under the *République*'s arm, and he showed himself.

The poor thing must no longer be able to understand what was happening. What! Fléchambeau had come to make his declaration, and had gone away in silence—and now it was his friend, Doctor Pons, who was chatting with her parents in the drawing-room. Her entire being was questioning.

Fléchambeau racked his brains in search of a telegraphic means of explaining the misadventure. He was relived of the responsibility by the appearance beside Olga of the young and unbearable Bobiche. She was the Monempoix' second daughter, a damnable ten-year-old imp, who was otherwise normal but invariably turned up at the wrong moment. She adored Fléchambeau, because of the stories he told her and the dolls with which he enriched her collection—in spite of which, the innocent Bobiche was the most annoying feast of trouble that had ever been seen, and, without being aware of it, the sternest guardian of Olga's virtue.

There's the limpet! Fléchambeau thought.

The little girl held out a red object to her sister, which Fléchambeau easily recognized as the toreador that he had obtained for her from Spain. The irritated Olga responded distractedly. Finally, Bobiche looked to see what her sister was looking at…

Fléchambeau took cover in the shadows of the room, and started smoking one cigarette after another.

Pons found him there, lying on the bed with his feet sticking out over the end, champing at the bit.

"Well?" said Fléchambeau, contriving his elevation. "Aren't you going to say anything?"

"There are," said Pons, "silences in which the closed mouth smiles…but don't get carried away; I'm only reporting a hope—a faint hope!"

"What? Spit it out, then! You're martyrizing me!"

Pons calmly sat down.

"You've pleaded my cause?" Fléchambeau went on. "You've shaken their resolve? You warmed them up?"

"Bah! Be expansive with those stubborn rationalists? One might as well launch one's heart against a marble block. No, no, I didn't play that poor game. No, for myself, I look for noon at twelve o'clock. I've obtained…"

"What?"

"A truce. A delay. I got that for, not without difficulty. Thirty days. In a month's time, you'll be condemned without appeal, or covered in flowers. Between now until then, it's up to me sort things out."

38

"I don't get it. Come on, was I mistaken? About the politics?"

"There's no use interrogating me. It seems to me that I've done a good job—haven't I? It's already not longer the flat refusal that you met with. So congratulate your friend Pons, and let him be—since, I repeat, everything depends on him. As for you, young man, if I have one piece of advice to give you, it's to leave. Don't stay in Saint-Jean. Here, your situation is false. Go away."

"Where to?"

"How do I know? To a spa! Into the mountains! Distract yourself. Take up a sport. Go to the beach. Shoot pigeons. Play tennis."

"But what about Olga?"

"It's preferable, naturally, that you refrain from seeing her."

"And in a month's time...?" stammered Fléchambeau, in painful distress.

"In a month's time, without getting emotional, you'll find out whether or not you have to wait for Olga to come of age."

"Three years! Oh, no, not that! Not that! You have to succeed, Pons; you have to go to your friends without delay...but be merciful, tell me what happened. How did you do it? What arguments...?"

Mary Stuart had slid her fluid body through the partly-open doorway. "*Muni muni muni!*" called Pons, still like an old lady. With a vertical bound, the cat was on his knees, motionless, although her tail was quivering. Then she started rubbing her teeth against one of Pons' fingers, which was scratching her neck.

"Mary Stuart," said the teasing man, "I shall end up buying a dog, just you see. Not one of those delicate and distinguished little tremblers that court attention in a heraldic manner, with one paw raised—a forepaw, of course—but an adoring spaniel that will release clamors of fidelity when it sees me. I shall call him Amarunthos, after the favorite greyhound of Akteon the voyeur. Because you cats only think of yourselves—you mistake your owners for backscratchers, toothbrushes or sofas. Dogs are more philanthropic, Mary Stuart. I'm going to buy one."

"Pons!" begged Fléchambeau.

The cat, purring sonorously, was the image of wellbeing. Her harsh tongue was activated by urgent thrusts, putting a shine on her soft tricolor coat—not blue, white and red, of course, but black, white and yellow.

"You have as many hairs on your body as there are people on Earth," said Pons, "or very nearly. And a few fleas, to be sure—but that's no cause for alarm for a parasitologist. Besides, everyone is someone's parasite; the flea is yours, you're mine, I'm the globe's, the globe that of some vaster world…"

"Pons!" groaned Fléchambeau.

"Pack your suitcase," was the reply.

At that moment, Fléchambeau pointed into the square. "Hold on," he said. "There's deputy Bargoulin, that red-faced sot who aspires to Olga's hand. He's hideous. I hate him. That turkey will get busy during my absence. He'll take advantage…but what's this I see? Monsieur le Président Monemppix is coming out of his house. God, how ungraceful he is! Deputy Bargoulin's going up to him. They're chatting. Monsieur Monempoix is making so many gestures that he seems to be dealing with a deaf-mute. What are they saying? Oh, it's about Olga—it has to be. Pons! Pons! Pons! Olga! Thirty days! And the uncertainty, the mystery! Tell me what's going on, old chap! Perhaps, for my part, I can help you at a distance. How do I know? I, too, know some powerful democrats…"

Drawing stripes in the air, Pons marked out his response, putting each word between two immaterial hyphens: "Go – pack – your – suitcase – " he said, "and – hop – it!"

III. Which Is Aptly Named a CHAPITRE, As It Contains a CHAT and a PITRE [13]

Fléchambeau did not wait for 30 days to pass before returning to Saint-Jean-de-Nèves. No game or exercise could distract him from his thoughts. Although he knew that Mademoiselle Olga Monempoix had been informed of what had happened, thanks to Pons, the separation caused him to suffer cruelly. Such is love, and there is no need to insist on it; everyone is familiar with its effects, however much or little of it they have experienced. Love magnetizes lovers—the analogous words say as much [14]—and whoever is separated from the person he cherishes experiences an attraction that solicits him and turns him around incessantly. Their hearts charge one another with a sympathetic fluid. Fléchambeau had taken his with him, as a compass bears its needle, but the North Pole, for him, was in Savoy.

One evening, after three weeks, measured out in miserly fashion, Pons saw him disembark.

The traveler was not proud of himself. He feared a reprimand. His friend's jovial manner reassured him.

"Yes, I ought to tell you off," Pons said to him. "But be welcome. Things are going well. The main part is done. It's 95% certain that we'll carry it off, and if you promise to be reasonable, I'll explain why."

"Reasonable?" Fléchambeau queried.

---

[13] This wordplay does not translate, as "chapter" cannot be broken down into English words whose meaning resemble those of *chat* [cat] and *pitre* [clown].

[14] *Amour* [love] and *aimant* [magnet] come from the same root in French, although their English equivalents do not recognize any such analogy.

"I mean secret," Pons confirmed. "You mustn't say anything to anyone until it's certain, until the total elimination of the 5% chance that still threatens us."

Fléchambeau stepped back in order to stick out his hand without breaking anything. "I swear," he said. "I'll remain as mute as a carp's tomb. On the expiration of the time agreed, though, will you be able to obtain the consent of the Monempoix?"

"Undoubtedly. Within a few days of it, at least. If not, we'll be defeated—I won't hide that from you. Wait for me—I'm coming back." They were in Fléchambeau's room. Pons slipped out. He came back shortly afterwards, with a tiny cat on his shoulder.

"Hey!" said Fléchambeau. "Mary Stuart's had more kittens."

"And she won't reject this one, eh? Look at that little face. It's the spitting image of the mother! It squints, it's tricolored—the same patches, even the same predatory expression. An exact portrait of the mother, in miniature!"

"It's marvelous," said Fléchambeau, without conviction. "But I've got other things on my mind, and I confess that I'm impatient to know…"

"Imbecile! *You know*. You know everything!"

"What? What?" The disconcerted Fléchambeau drooled.

Pons, meanwhile, enjoyed his friend's discomfiture, his lips closed in one of those jocund smiles which all seem to have sprung from Da Vinci's brush. "Imbecile!" he repeated, cruelly. "*This is Mary Stuart herself!* Listen, you were right—Olga's youth was only a vain pretext. The Monempoix—especially Madame—refused you their daughter *because you're too tall*. That's what they didn't want to tell you, so as not to hurt your feelings. It's understandable, moreover. Olga's only 1.55 meter, my lad—you didn't think of that, you drum-major! But her parents, especially her mother, took exception to it. That difference in height of 42 centimeters seemed to them an unbridgeable gap. To tell the truth, it's a lot—admit it!"

"So what?" said Fléchambeau.

"So, they opened up to me, on my insistence. They revealed the depths of their hearts to me—and I suddenly glimpsed an elegant, not to say marvelous, solution. *To shrink you.* Already, even while I was with the Monempoix, a chaos of ideas was bubbling in my head. For form's sake, to begin with, I argued that your wife could wear high heels—that Louis XV heels weren't invented for dogs. Madame Monempoix wouldn't give up. 'He's not a man, your Fléchambeau,' she exclaimed, 'he's an Alp! He's a husband for a mountain-climber!' And privately, thinking about the woman you love, I said to myself: *No, the father's short, the mother's tiny—that girl won't grow; she won't get any taller.* And then again...I was tempted by the research.

"Finally, I made my proposal: 'What if I bring you, in a month's time, a suitor less tall than your humble servant? If that suitor retained all of Fléchambeau's other qualities, would you accept him?'

" 'Gladly, provided that he pleases our daughter.'

" 'Very well,' I replied. 'On those conditions, would you permit me to ask you to wait for a month before accepting another offer?'

"They burst out laughing. 'It's bizarre,' said the President, 'but if you insist, my dear Doctor...why not? So be it. Is your other friend also an advocate? Well-educated? Good family? Nice fortune?'

" 'Exactly like Fléchambeau.'

"I was getting ahead of myself! But today, I don't think I was too far ahead, since...since, here we are!" Pons lifted up the tiny Mary Stuart in both hands. "I'm beginning to believe," he said, "that I'm on to something. Nice work, isn't it? It's a matter of the thyroid gland..."

Having released the cat—which was rather awkward, not having yet got used to her new stature—Pons took a little round cardboard box from his pocket. He opened it. It contained a number of pills, not much larger than number two grains of lead, scarlet in color.

43

"Two of these pills every morning, old chap, and Mary Stuart has become as you now see her. In six days. If my calculations are exact, the same treatment ought to reduce a man's height by two centimeters a day. I'm about 1.76 meter. To descend to my level, you'll only need 20 pills in ten days. Ten days, if, that is…"

"Show me!" said Fléchambeau. He took the box curiously, and rolled the red beads around. "Well I never!" he said. "I never heard anything like it!" Swiftly, though, before Pons could say or do anything, Fléchambeau picked up two pills and swallowed them.

"That's not very clever," said Pons. "My drug was effective on a cat, but that doesn't mean that it will act on a man. I hope so, of course—but at the end of they day, I can't be sure of it. I would have liked to carry out a few more experiments…"

"We don't have enough time," Fléchambeau pleaded. "The deadline expires in ten days. Then again, what am I risking? If I don't shrink, we'll soon know about it!"

"Agreed. But what if it makes you ill?"

"Is it dangerous?" Fléchambeau queried, his eyes penetrating. "Poisonous?"

Pons lowered his eyes in embarrassment. "I'd have preferred that you wait a little longer," he said, simply. "Tomorrow evening, my work would have enlightened me. Anyway, since it's done, let's leave it at that. What do you feel?"

"Nothing."

"No dizziness? Let me take your pulse…"

"In sum," said Fléchambeau, "1.76 meter is still honorable. Do you think she'll still love me as much?"

"No doubt about it. I've taken her into my confidence. Wait until you shrink, though—nothing's certain."

"As soon as she can love me forever, it will be."

"Your pulse is fine. No stomach ache?"

"No stomach ache, my friend. I'm starting a slight headache…but isn't there a height-gauge in the store-room? Let's go down, shall we?"

They went down to the store-room. Fléchambeau got underneath. He measured his 196 centimeters very precisely.

This happened at 8 p.m.

The following day, at the same time, without having suffered any ill-effects other than a few giddy spells and some
inconsequential nausea, Fléchambeau's height only measured
194 centimeters, exactly.

IV. Which Is the History of a Memorable Ten Days

Let us say right away, to reassure sensitive souls, that Doctor Pons' apprehensions were ill-founded. Everything went exceedingly well. There were no accidents, and no surprises. The extraordinary treatment, which had the objective of putting Fléchambeau within reach of Mademoiselle Olga, was not subject to any interruption or complication. The ten critical days succeeded one another harmoniously.

On the first evening, Pons had had a camp-bed installed in Fléchambeau's room, in order that he might sleep there. On that occasion, he had a brief but concise conversation with his factotum, in order to instruct him to maintain absolute silence regarding everything that passed before his eyes, until further notice.

This factotum, who answered to the name of Valentin, was, in any case, a trustworthy man, hard-working and taciturn, who did not go out much, spending his time indifferently, and of whom Pons was wont to say that he was indissoluble in the modern era. Valentin put the height-gauge in a more convenient location, and arranged various measuring devices brought from the laboratory on Fléchambeau's table, as well as numerous flasks, syringes, Bunsen burners, scalpels and bowls, designed to ward off any pathological eventualities.

With a thermometer in his armpit, Fléchambeau spent the greater part of his time slumped in a comfortable armchair. Pons took his temperature, monitored his blood pressure by means of a pneumatic bracelet, checked the rhythm of his heart with the aid of some sort of telephone, lifted up his eyelids to inspect his eyes, sniffed his breath—it reeked of tobacco, he said—made him read, at close range and from a distance, placards on which the same sentence was written in letters of different sizes, and tickled him on the soles of his feet; finally, he devoted himself to all sorts of chemical analyses, which you will forgive us for not enumerating or describing.

The only warning signs, in fact, originated from Pons himself. By virtue of interrogating the patient, asking him whether he was experiencing this or that, he caused him to lose his sense of reality. Asking the question *have you got a stomach ache?* six times in an hour eventually ends up purging the interrogatee as surely as rhubarb or senna. The first time, one answers *no* without thinking about it. Later, one interrogates oneself; one descends mentally into one's own belly, which is enjoying perfect bliss. Later still, though, one asks oneself: *Well, have I?* The harm is done—or the good. It is a symptom, or a prescription. Beware of it—or turn it to your advantage.

On the second day, Mademoiselle Olga Monempoix, secretly notified of the success of the enterprise, found a means to send Fléchambeau a few flowers and a note: *I love you. I shall be at the window at five o'clock.*

On the third day, in the morning, Fléchambeau observed that his signet ring was too large and that his monocle exceeded the dimensions of its orbit. He put them both in a box, promising himself that he would have the ring altered and to buy another monocle when he had attained his definitive height. In the meantime, he asked his friend to procure him a pair of spectacles. He ate with a healthy appetite, drank sparely, and displayed a very cheerful mood.

Every evening, at 8 p.m., he ingurgitated two red pills, after which he slept like a baby until the Sun rose in Valparaiso—which is to say, about 10 a.m. On the fourth day, however, he woke up much earlier. He had a bad toothache.

Pons was only sleeping lightly. He was anxious about Fléchambeau's sighs and restlessness. "What's the matter? There's scarcely any daylight to illuminate you and guide me…" He forced himself to laugh, but could not do so broadly.

"I've got toothache," Fléchambeau said.

"Which teeth?"

"I think…I think it's my two gold teeth…"

"Eh? Of course!" exclaimed Pons, reassured. "I didn't think of that. Your gold teeth aren't part of your anatomy. They don't have the same plasticity. My drug has no more effect on them than a cautery on a wooden leg. The more your other teeth shrink, the tighter your jaws gets…do you understand?"

"I understand that I need to have them taken out," said Fléchambeau, anxiously.

"No matter! You can have others fitted in six days' time—for we've only six more days to wait. Today, this evening, you'll be no more than 188 centimeters—you'll have shrunk by eight centimeters!"

Fléchambeau got up, clutching his mouth. He increased the tuck in the sleeves of his night-gown, as he did very morning, and, as he did every morning, cut a two-centimeter strip off the bottom of the garment. "Ah!" he said. "What an idiot I am! And my clothes! They'll have to be re-cut. I want it done properly…let's see, it's on Monday, isn't it, that the ten days finishes?"

"Yes," said Pons. "*Literary Monday, get up and go day/Replete with Sainte-Beuve and Alphonse Daudet!*"[15] He saw that Fléchambeau was slightly unnerved, and was counting on cheering him up by means of silly couplets, in whose improvisation he excelled. "But you can't go out to go to the tailor's," he went on. "Anyway, since we'll be the same height henceforth, I think I ought to adapt your so-called costumes for myself."

"Brilliant idea, Pons! Sort it out, so that I can present myself to my future parents-in-law properly dressed, on Monday. Ah, Monday! Great gods, though, how my teeth hurt!"

---

[15] In order to reproduce the spirit of the supposedly-improvised couplets of which Pons is so fond, I have routinely made small sacrifices of literal meaning in order to improvise suitably comical rhymes.

"I'll take them out for you," said Pons. "You can't keep canines that are too big for you. It won't do you any good. Your dentition would suffer a serious disorder."

"I didn't expect this," Fléchambeau admitted—and he wondered, not without anxiety, what other foreign bodies might yet do him a similar bad turn.

Pons collaborated in his research. They agreed, by way of conclusion, that apart from the teeth, the monocle and the ring, no other parasite could cause them any further annoyance, great or small.

It must be admitted, however, that Fléchambeau's pen seemed uncomfortable to him, being overly large, and that the young man's handwriting gave evidence of it. In the same way, the pipe that he lit in an attempt to soothe his dental pain weighed strangely upon his lips. "Ah! Ah!" he said, on perceiving that—and when he lifted his dumb-bells, he had to confess that he found difficulty doing so. "That's annoying!"

But Pons arrived, armed with a redoubtable set of pincers. Fléchambeau sat in the armchair, and the beautiful gold teeth came out, one after another.

The following days passed peacefully, in reading or conversation. Pons' anxiety dissipated, and joy got the upper hand—great joy; for, in sum, the most important thing about this entire adventure was that he had made a surprising discovery. What use might it be? He was not entirely sure; Fléchambeau's case was exceptional, and one didn't meet people every day, or even every year, who wanted to shrink. But that wasn't important. Applications were a secondary issue. The discovery was complete, that was the main thing. That was the pride, the celebrity. Goodbye, sad parasites: lice, fleas, acarians of every stripe! Saint-Jean-de-Nèves had now given birth to an illustrious man! And who could tell whether, one day, his statue might be raised somewhere?—in front of the college, for example, or even in the place of that *République* with the excessive breasts, which had been perched there for want of less allegorical and more individual illustrations.

The cat, indifferent to events, roamed around with velvet steps, now accustomed to living in a larger world and having to jump higher to reach the places where she took her siestas. It was different for Fléchambeau, who was *in the process* of diminution. He still bent down, even though it was now unnecessary, in order to go through the doorway to his dressing-room, which was low. His razor inconvenienced him by its dimensions; he shaved himself inexpertly. He lost his slippers 20 times a day. On the other hand, he did not notice that his hair, being finer, was becoming softer, because his fingers, thinner to the same extent, were endowed with a proportionately more delicate touch.

At meals, he ate less, cutting thinner slices. Three glasses of wine, instead of four, sufficed to make him merry. And if he had to stretch his arm further to grasp the bottle or the salt-cellar, he was compensated by the agreeable sensation of the wideness of his chair, and being able to tuck his previously-excessive legs under the table.

The most remarkable thing of all was that Fléchambeau shrank without any wrinkles creasing his face. He became, in fact, a perfect reduced-size version of what he had been before.

Finally, the tenth day arrived. The 20 pills had been swallowed. At 11 a.m., the height-gauge indicated a little under 177 centimeters. There as no doubt about it; by 8 p.m. that evening, Fléchambeau would measure no more than 176 centimeters. Fléchambeau and Pons would be equal in height.

The tailor brought the altered suits. The shirt-maker, the hat-maker and the shoe-merchant unpacked an assortment of articles that were the last word in fashion. A choice was made. He took care to select a pair of boots that were a trifle tight, a cape a trifle narrow, in anticipation of the half-centimeter that remained to be lost. Slightly cramped, the black jacket and the rosewood trousers molded the suitor, who was singing with joy. Pons put on his best clothes too.

At 5 p.m., the fateful moment when the 30 days was up, the two friends rounded the fountain of *La République*.

Monsieur le Président Monempoix had an electric door-bell, which was quite round, resembling a tiny archery-target. Pons' well-aimed index finger was right on the button.

"Bull's-eye!" he said.

"Dead center!" chuckled Fléchambeau, exceedingly happy.

V. In Which There Is a Superabundant Feasting

The Monempoix family's housemaid, a slattern with red hands and stout feet, did not notice anything. She was completely stupefied by her mistress's household requirements. "Come in," she said—and she introduced Pons and Fléchambeau into a Napoléon III drawing-room, which would have exhibited a certain charm had it not been for the profusion of table-mats, ribbons and Louis XV porcelain knick-knacks with which it was cluttered. On the wall, an exceedingly fine portrait of Convention-member Sanson-Darras, his attitude elegant, his gesture assertive, his mouth open to make some unanswerable assertion and his hair blowing in the wind of popular opinion, hung alongside a mediocre painting, made from a photographic print, representing Counselor Monempoix, the President's father, in a red robe. There was something neutered about the latter, whose nullity made the heart sink.

Pons turned his gaze aside in order to look at Fléchambeau, who was, to some degree, his own work—his scientific son—since he had retouched the work of his father. And he said to himself, proudly: *It's very good*—exactly as Elohim had done when He had created man.

Fléchambeau did, indeed, have a fine presence. Two carnations now sufficed for his buttonhole. The town's optician had sold him a spectacle-lens that provided a fair imitation of a monocle and did the same job. As for the unfortunate top hat, Fléchambeau did not regret having put it to death, since it is perfectly acceptable nowadays to go into another man's house empty-handed.

Monsieur Monempoix was the first to arrive. As soon as he reached the threshold he hesitated, looking alternately at Pons and Fléchambeau, uncomprehendingly, assuming that Pons had brought him some sort of reduced-scale double, experiencing a keen desire to be enlightened, and dreading being taken for an idiot if he could not enlighten himself.

Pons got him out of trouble. "Monsieur le Président," he said, "here is the suitor that you promised to receive favorably, on condition that he pleased Mademoiselle your daughter. Although it might appear rather incredible to you, it's my friend Fléchambeau in person. His tall stature constituted the sole obstacle to his happiness. I therefore sought a means of reducing it, and, as you see, I have succeeded. It's now up to you to keep your promise."

"Is it possible?" cried President Monempoix. Amazement and suspicion creased his face.

Monsieur Monempoix was a puffed-up bourgeois, rather insignificant if one took away his pale complexion. Did he not seem to have been injected with stearin?[16] Low on his feet, he had too much belly. His head offered the gaze a rotundity whose excessive baldness was vaguely suggestive of something indecent. In order to temper that—a vain exercise—he allowed his narrow crown of grey hair to grow longer than is customary, and that gave his soft, round, clean shaven face an appearance reminiscent of Béranger.[17] Imagine a bust of the famous songwriter—a bust made of wax, or rather of lard—which has been dropped, and has been deformed by its fall, with the nose flattened, the chin knocked sideways and bumps here and there. That was President Monempoix, momentarily alarmed, flabbergasted and anxious to the point of wondering whether he had gone mad.

But Fléchambeau spoke, certifying what Pons had said; and his voice convinced the President, even though it too was reduced, like an alto piece arranged for the violin.

The President opened the door and shouted up the stairs: "Darling! Come down to the drawing-room!"

---

[16] Stearin is a white fatty acid made up of esters of glycerol, a significant constituent of candle-wax and lard.

[17] Pierre-Jean Béranger (1789-1857) was a famous song-writer whose works became increasingly patriotic and political.

"Darling" arrived. That was Madame Monempoix. No one could ever have personified vermicelli or macaroni[18] in an end-of-the-year revue better than she did, insofar as the visible pallor and slightness of the woman's physique had something phantasmal about it. On seeing her, people whispered: "Her soul is scarcely materialized." Her caricaturish resemblance to a celebrated tragedienne encouraged the belief that a golden, or at least gold-plated, voice would escape her diaphanous lips—what an error! Nothing melodious or Racinian emerged therefrom. Her speech proved to be as bourgeois as can be; she pronounced her word in a raucous tone and punctuated them with singular grunts, as if there were a distant frog in her throat. That was supplemented by an insatiable desire to touch her interlocutors, to seize their hands, to lean on their shoulders, to look you in the whites of your eyes and speak into your mouth. More than one would have recoiled from such a mother-in-law, and nothing, perhaps, offers a more perfect testimony to Fléchambeau's love. Mademoiselle Olga could be proud of a passion that the existence of her mother had not discouraged.

"Look!" said the President. "I introduce to you our friend, Maître Fléchambeau, trainee advocate in the Parisian court of appeal! Doctor Pons has submitted him to a treatment. Look, darling! Isn't he admirable?"

"In truth," simpered Madame Monempoix, "I agree entirely. But how did you do it?"

"What does it matter?" said Pons. "The point is that it has been done."

"But will it last?" objected the President's wife. "Won't Monsieur grow again one day?"

"No, Madame—I guarantee it."

"In that case…"

The two spouses consulted one another with their eyes.

---

[18] *Nouille* [vermicelli] and *macaroni* both have double meanings in French, the former being used to refer to a silly or spineless individual and the latter to an Italian.

"Go on, then!" the President decided. "Go fetch your daughter." He turned to Fléchambeau. "You shall be our son, my dear boy. We give you the *amatur*." And he smiled delicately at his own cleverness.

In the meantime, Madame Monempoix let in Olga, whom she had discovered behind the door.

The lovers embraced one another. Pons bore silent and dignified witness to the familial scene of which he was the facilitator.

"Make her happy!" sighed the President's wife, with originality.

Monsieur Monempoix contemplated the betrothed couple, clasped in one another's arms, Olga raising her soulful eyes toward Fléchambeau's shining ones, and made the very personal remark: "You'll make a nicely-matched couple!"

"What about you, Pons?" said Fléchambeau. "Don't you have anything to say to me?"

Having thought about it, Pons timidly ventured: "I salute you, husband."

"Ha ha—how funny he is!" said Madame Monempoix, laughing.

"As witty as he is wise," Monsieur pontificated.

But Pons did better, placing a finger on his friend's chest and reciting: "*Love your fiancée, even to excess/You can't love too much, and you shouldn't love less*."

They burst into applause.

Fléchambeau was smiling all over his face. Delight piled up so extravagantly that he felt as if he were lifted off the ground, as if inflated by hydrogen or some other gas that was lighter than air.

"Be careful!" Pons said to him. "Don't be like that old man whose white hair turned black overnight under the influence of too much happiness."

There was general laughter, for each of them wanted only to laugh, and grasped the slightest opportunity to soothe that need for hilarity. With Pons present, there was no shortage of opportunities.

Meanwhile, the two fiancés could not draw apart. Monsieur and Madame Monempoix "Hmm hmmed" competitively, but in vain. Sitting on a settee, clinging tightly to one another, Fléchambeau and the charming Olga were devoting themselves to reciprocal acts of mutual tenderness—and it was, perhaps, merely to break into that truly interminable conversation that President Monempoix made a proposition.

"Dash it, though!" he cried. "Why don't both of your dine here this evening, with out most intimate friends? Darling, can't you improvise an engagement dinner? Digermal the caterer will send us everything necessary, along with a waiter or two. The Choderpils will come at short notice, with the Chabosseaus and the Dézormets…"

"Eh? Why not?" consented the Preseident's wife, who was not averse to making impromptu arrangements. "Go put on your smoking-jackets, gentlemen, and come back at 8 p.m. We'll celebrate this fine day with a fine soirée. Does that suit you?"

"Like a glove," said Pons.

Fléchambeau's response was merely to embrace Madame Monempoix, shake the President's hand, and favor his fiancée with one of those long, velvety and adoring gazes in which all the desire and devotion of a thousand generations of faithful lovers seem to be condensed.

On the stroke of 8 p.m., the two companions returned to the President's house—a house resounding with the noise of crockery and perfumed with a warm culinary odor.

Fléchambeau was exultant. That eighth chime marked the end of his diminution. His smoking-jacket, retailored to Pons's measurements, was not tight around his torso, and his trousers, lavishly ornamented with silken braid, fell neatly upon is patent leather shoes, neither too long nor too short. The physiological prodigy was complete.

There was no one in the drawing-room yet, but Olga made her entrance almost immediately, unfortunately flanked by Bobiche, who was clutching an entire carnival of dolls in her little arms.

Olga was wearing a sky blue dress, peppered with silver crescent moons not much larger than stars. The soft firmness of her vernal throat was quivering with enthusiasm, and her young breasts were as lively as two doves, which are venereal birds, Fléchambeau's gaze caressed her exquisite figure, the curves of her hips, modeled on waves, and the graceful broadening of a seat that Armand Sylvestre would have celebrated in song,[19] and certainly had not served as a template for the inventor of autobuses, which have been conceived for skeletons.

And the couple interlinked their twenty tremulous fingers.

This did not suit Bobiche. Not greatly surprised by the transformation of her friend Fléchambeau—children, growing incessantly, have only a vague concept of proportion—she intended to introduce to him, one by one, the dolls that she owed to his munificence and then ask him to finish an interrupted story: that of King Turbul and Prince Mirobol.

In order to liberate Fléchambeau, Pons took over. He inspected the dolls, and improvised conversations between the toreador and the Dieppe fisherman, the sailor and the Arlésienne, and then swore that he had the story of King Turbul and Prince Mirobol at his fingertips. "Where did Fléchambeau leave off?" he asked.

"When the fairies arrived for Princess Cuckoo's baptism. Some of them came in flying chariots, and some of them had angel's wings."

"Good," said Pons. "This is how it continues: But here comes Fairy Piane-Piane mounted on a camembert. She's fashionably late…"

---

[19] Armand Sylvestre was the signature attached to three collections of pornographic stories and verses published in the *fin-de-siècle* period, which achieved a curious shadowy respectability by virtue of their teasing wit and self-conscious delight in their own naughtiness.

Bobiche burst out laughing—but then the maid introduced the Choderpils, the Chabosseaus and the Dézormets in quick succession. Monsieur and Madame Monempoix arrived in the nick of time to welcome them.

Then there was a fine hubbub of exclamations, squeals and kisses. Everyone protested a joy and astonishment without compare. One might have thought that these ladies and gentlemen had only been living thus far in order to savor this moment of surprising felicity. One might have thought that they had never been preoccupied with anything but the destiny of the dear and dainty Olga.

Madame Choderpil proclaimed: "And now she's marring a phenomenon!"

They approached Fléchambeau with a certain repugnance, such as one experiences in confrontation with monsters at the fair in the museum.

Madame Monempoix exerted herself with a frenzy moderated by education. Her micaceous dress was a shade of mauve that would rather have been violet but could not quite achieve it. Pons tried to tell her that she resembled a *glycine*, but a slip of the tongue made him say "glycerine" and she thought it one of those medical gallantries that ladies can only take in small doses.[20]

Digermal's waiter interrupted these mundanities to announce that dinner was served. President Monempoix made a handle of his arm, which he offered to Madame Dézormet. Monsieur Dézormet, the prosecutor, with a compliment on his lips, escorted Madame Monempoix. Judge Choderpil followed with his wife, etc. Fléchambeau and Olga were like Paul and

---

[20] The wordplay in this sentence is impossible to translate, but I have improvised as best I can; *glycine*, derived from a Greek word meaning "sweet," is applied in French to various plants with sweet roots, including wisteria—hence the connection with mauve coloring. Where the word is used in the text to refer to the flowers outside Pons' window I have translated it as "wisteria."

Virginie when the banana-tree broke.[21] Pons, drunk with satirical joy, containing an outburst of laughter with great difficulty, brought up the rear of the prenuptial parade with Bobiche.

The meal was Pantagruelesque. Digermal, at short notice, had surpassed himself. That is always the way; only lengthily-prepared receptions misfire.

Monsieur le Président Monempoix enthroned himself as if in session, dominating the proceedings, to the great delight of our Pons. He was full of himself, and poured out his anecdotal autobiography without missing a mouthful. "One day, would you believe, when I was presiding at the petty sessions, the accused said to me: 'What about you, then, Monsieur le Président? Have you never committed anything?' 'Yes, monsieur,' I replied. 'Experts and police superintendents.' The public was in stitches."

He spoke humorously. To this same audience, he had always seemed to be parodying someone—no one could say who, but someone side-splitting, like one of those actors who make you laugh simply by being on the cast list. And while Fléchambeau was no longer anything but a heart, Pons was no longer anything but a dangerously-dilated spleen.

Yes, Fléchambeau was no more than a heart. He had been sat next to Olga, and he confessed himself incapable of eating or drinking anything. With its gentle but inexorable hand, Bliss was strangling him. In the atmosphere of her lovely promise, he breathed in a divine fever, the intoxicating languor of a chaste possession, and Olga's eyes fascinated him. It must be admitted that they really were exceptional eyes, incomparable in their softness, clarity and sentimentality. Every time the long thick eyelashes sank down and rose again, night fell and dawn reappeared. Indecipherable glances! Not so much glances, really, as wireless kisses.

"Oh, please, dear heart," said Fléchambeau, "turn down your eyes!"

---

[21] In Bernardin de Saint-Pierre's classic romance *Paul et Virginie* (1788).

But she could not, for lack of a dimmer-switch whose mechanism might command her heart, her head and her blood.

They were both serious, pale, tense and superlatively happy, the force of their satisfaction almost painful—and they were alone: quite alone, far from that noisy table, on an isle signed by Watteau.

"*Nunc est bibendum!*"[22] declared the President.

"Now is the time to drink!" translated Pons the Republican.

"He's priceless!" said Madame Monempoix. Pons had conquered her; the hungry eyes of the President's wife were nourishing themselves on him. She regretted that he was not sitting next to her, and her feet were agitating themselves in empty space.

"What are you going to do now?" he asked him. "Leave Saint-Jean? Tomorrow, you'll be famous!"

"I don't intend to do anything much: to give myself some time off, even pester the Muse. *Insouciant poet of yesterday and tomorrow/ Living with pen in hand, with time to borrow.*"

"Charming!" she sighed. And their dialogue continued, principally on the subjects of flowers and foliage.

As time wore on, the hot dishes succeeding one another, alternating with the cold ones, the merriment of the feast became *fortissimo*. Cheeks became pink. Remarks became spicy. The party became livelier and livelier. The noisy assembly became increasingly distant from the two lovers, plunged in their egotistical dream, like a festival on shore. But the others, milords! What a blow-out they had, those pre-eminent men, content to be able to set aside their praetorial masks for a while and rub their palms together to efface the marks of the hard and heavy balance in which misdemeanors, felonies and crimes are weighed!

---

[22] The quote—accurately translated by Pons—is from an ode by Horace, composed after the battle of Actium, in which Octavian (subsequently the Emperor Augustus) defeated Cleopatra and Mark Anthony.

And it did them good—let us say that word over and over again!—to see Emile Monempoix, divested of his magistracy, letting his proprietorial belly hang out, brandishing a large Louis XV carving-knife—surely sprung, Pons remarked, from the Damiens succession[23]—and cutting up a well-appointed leg of mutton into thin and juicy slices, with a gourmet expression.

But let us get on with the story, and not delay—we poor scribes with the empty bellies of lodgers—in order to stuff our imaginations narrating gastronomical delights of which we have only been able to sniff the memory through a air-vent. We are numbered among those wretches who gladly take their pens for forks and their sheets of paper for generously-filled plates. Let us break off there, Monsieur Historiographer. Your writing-pad is not a tablecloth, nor your writing-desk a dining-table. A little more, and you'll be drinking from the inkwell! *Presto! Presto!* Let's pass swiftly over the courses: entrées, roasts, venison, poultry, vegetables and salads (we're already way past the fish); let's race past the sorbet and the cheese, barely mentioning the Johannisberg, the Barsac, the Chambertin, the Pommery and the Samos. How swiftly the *petits fours* complete the cycle! Show, if you insist, Bobiche attempting to give the Dieppe fisherman a drink, Monsieur Monempoix recounting a dirty joke in a whisper, with a lewd expression, while the women cackle with delight and the men feel faint. Say that it's after 11 p.m.—what an alimentary session! Do your best to convey the slight confusion that reigns while the napkins are thrown away in handfuls and the warm-seated chairs, obliging quadrupeds, make farewell sounds as they are pushed back. And paint with a rapid brush the procession that heads for the coffee and liqueurs (there's chamomile teas for the sensitive.)

---

[23] Robert Damiens, executed in a particularly horrible fashion in 1757 after having tried to stab Louis XV, inevitably became something of a hero to anti-monarchists.

Fléchambeau got up, feeling—O delight!—a plump forearm slide beneath his own, and made up the tail of the binomial. Pons, in front of him, had the pleasure of walking in a crouch, as muzjiks dance, in order to make himself the same height as Bobiche, his other half.

"Forward, Mademoiselle Muzjik!" he said.

Now, something must have stuck to the sole of Flédchambeau's shoe—some crust of bread or other remnant of the dinner. He scraped his foot on the carpet...but nothing came off. It stayed there, hindering him...

Fléchambeau bent his knee, lifted his foot, and swiftly ran his hand over his heel...

He suddenly went pale—and Pons, turning round while laughing, could have believed that a breath of perdition had chilled his face. He straightened up, and released Bobiche...

"What's the matter?"

"It's my trousers," stammered Fléchambeau. "I'm walking on them. I...I'm continuing to shrink... Besides...my collar...my sleeves...look!"

"In God's name!" whispered Pons.

"Don't take it in vain," Fléchambeau told him. "Let's get out of here. Come on—take me away! Here's a turn-up for the books!"

Pons, turned into a pillar of salt, his expression tragic, was sweating.

They both withdrew, under the pretext of discreetly seeking a solitude which they were not, in fact, alone in desiring.

It is absolutely ridiculous that the night was serene, the atmosphere tranquil, the sky cloudless. What purpose, then, do thunder, lightning and all that trembling serve?

VI. Exit Fléchambeau

The moment was both ludicrous and dramatic.

As soon as they were indoors again, Pons sat down at his desk and composed an excusatory note to Monsieur Monempoix, informing him that they were obliged to take French leave by consequence of Fléchambeau's illness—a sudden illness, caused by the rigorous treatment he had undergone in order to make himself agreeable to Monsieur le Président.

Afterwards Pons went to wake Valentin and instructed him to transmit the note to its destination, without forgetting to recover from the President's residence the hats and overcoats they had left there.

When Valentin had gone, the two men looked one another in the face, Fléchambeau anxious and Pons perplexed. A formidable silence reigned: the silence of three pianos that no one is playing. Pons told himself that it was necessary to do something, at all costs. Fléchambeau, adrift in his smoking-jacket but straitjacketed by distress, was wearing an other-worldly expression.

"Why are you making that face?" Pons asked him, with a constrained smile.

Fléchambeau put all his violence and contempt into a shrug of his shoulders—and he began to wander back and forth distractedly, with his mouth set in stone and his eyes vague, like a bewildered mariner roaming through the interior of a submarine at sea.

"You look like a guide-dog that's lost its blind man," said Pons. "Why are you in such a bad temper? There's a remedy for everything. I once knew a one-eyed man who drank in order to see double; once drunk, he was just like you or me."

Fléchambeau used *le mot de Cambronne*.[24] Then he said: "The height-gauge!"

They went to his room. He took off his shoes and socks and set himself against the apparatus. The height-gauge indicated 173 centimeters and a half.

Pons furrowed his two eyebrows, for want of any more; he would have needed a hundred, like Argus of old, to express his annoyance.

Mary Stuart, odiously tranquil, squinted at them. Fléchambeau groaned.

"It's your fault too!" snapped the mortified doctor. "I didn't give you permission to swallow the pills. You began the treatment without my authorization. I told you: my experiments weren't concluded; my discovery wasn't complete. With regard to cats, animals, I was sure of myself and my drug. You can see that Mary Stuart isn't changing any more, can't you? She's stabilized—but you aren't. It's evident, therefore, that my drug doesn't have the same effect on humans as on cats."

---

[24] General Pierre Cambronne (1770-1842) commanded one of the last remnants of the Old Guard at Waterloo, where he was wounded and captured; while he was incapacitated, a rumor was put about that when his command was surrounded by enemy forces and called upon to surrender he had replied: "*La garde meurt et ne se rend pas.*" [Guards die; they don't surrender.] A sarcastic counter-rumor was launched alleging that what he had actually said was "*Merde!*" [Shit]—a stronger expletive than its English equivalent. Cambronne's indignant protests that he had not said either only added to the notoriety of the double-edged anecdote. When Victor Hugo wrote *Les Misérables* (1862), *merde* was still unprintable, but Hugo, in order to convey the fact that his character had no scruples about using it, stated that he used "*le mot de Cambronne*" [Cambronne's word]—a precedent that many other authors gladly followed. Everything Cambronne actually said during his doubtless-colorful life has been completely forgotten

"You're not telling me anything I don't know," said Fléchambeau. "But what's terrible is that I've shrunk two and a half centimeters in less than four hours!"

Pons, no longer able to find words to translate his consternation, uttered a belch of ire and impotence.

"Do something, damn it!" cried Fléchambeau, suddenly beside himself. "Do something! Don't stand there like a cretin! Give me a potion to drink, a bath in which to immerse myself. How do I know? There must surely be a remedy! Inject, massage, bleed, purge, sound, medicament away! At least take my pulse; consult, if necessary! Would you like to see my tongue?"

"That's not injured, at any rate," riposted the victim of this abuse. "There, there! Gently does it! Let's get a grip! First, I'll remind you that our abrupt departure deprived us of coffee and liqueurs. Coffee seems to me to be contraindicated, in view of your tone of exasperation, which is getting on my nerves—but liqueurs…"

He went in search of a bottle of cognac, whose three stars shone like Sirius, Altair and Vega…and they drank several small glasses of old Charentais alcohol, one after another.

Silence had fallen again, but the noise of hurried footsteps was audible outside in the Place de la République. A few moments later, Olga, breaking with all convention, came into Fléchambeau's room. She preceded Valentin, who was carrying the recovered items of clothing.

"Well?" she said, in an agonized tone.

By way of response, Fléchambeau contented himself with a demonstration. He took his new hat from Valentin's hand, and put it on.

It came down over his nose and ears.

"Has he gone mad?" the young woman's eyes inquired of Pons.

"Your fiancé, Mademoiselle," the latter replied, "is continuing to decrease in size. And I'm asking myself how to stop his descent. Be reassured, though: I shall succeed. You'll be the wife of an exceedingly handsome gentleman of medium height, that's all."

"Is that it?" said Olga, joyfully. "Oh, Fléchambeau, my love, it's *in spite of* your abundant height that I loved you. I adore short men!"

Ah, the good little soul! There are women who know exactly what to say, and exactly when to say it! And what's more, she had thrown the most enchanting opera-cloak over her bare shoulders!

Mollified, Fléchambeau embraced her as best he could. He attempted, in spite of his distress, to put on a companionable smile. His lips remained taut, however—was the cognac astringent?—and his smile contracted upon his closed lips.

Olga went away, fully tranquilized.

But Fléchambeau could not sleep at all—and all night long, Pons worked in his laboratory, consulted books, racked his brains, manipulated a great many dangerous substances, and ground up seemingly-abominable pastes.

At daybreak, Fléchambeau, who was shorter than he had been, made a lugubrious entrance. "It's still continuing!" he lamented. "No amelioration! I'm losing my mind. I just massaged myself with dentifrice and tried to hang the soap on the towel-rail…" Abruptly, he got carried away. "I've had enough of it, you know! Animal! You've got no idea! When one goes out in an automobile, one looks to see if it has brakes, you know! One doesn't open a tap without being able to shut it off! I…I…I jeer at you! I tar-and-feather you!"

"You frighten me," said Pons, quite placidly. "You're like policemen who can't say a word without seeming to be furious. But everything will sort itself out, you'll see! Here, drink this mixture."

It was a frightful grey syrup, with white streaks, in a test tube.

Fléchambeau swallowed it as quickly as he could, with the customary grimace. "But it's ipecac!" he cried.[25]

Pons shrugged his shoulders; it was his turn. "Well, to be sure, if you imagine that it's ipecac, there's no point drinking it. Although the idea that it's ipecac... Ah! What did I say?"

Livid and wiping his mouth, Fléchambeau let himself fall into the friendly dimpled armchair. The poor fellow, delivered of the beverage, was in a sorry state. The sleeves and legs of his pajamas had been folded back three times over. A garment that become much too large always looks somewhat deflated, and makes a sad sight, doesn't it? To cap it all, the weather was grim, the barometer was falling and it was beginning to rain on the town, which was already less luminous than usual because the gigantic presence of the mountain was blocking off the northern sky.

A church bell rang.

"Who's being buried?" aske Fléchambeau.

"No one—it's a wedding. *To those who don't feel well/everything sounds the knell.*"

"Oaf!" said the victim, feebly. And they shook hands, fraternally and sympathetically.

Fléchambeau contemplated the pharmacy behind the glass fronts of the cupboards. "Curse it! To think that the remedy is there, but secret! To think that some combination of those multicolored substances would be sufficient to put a brake on my..."

"Resorption," supplied Pons. "You're resorbing yourself."

"To think," Fléchambeau went on, "that nature surrounds us, with its rocks, its plants, *etcetera*, with all that's necessary to cure everything! To think that there are 'incurables' who commit suicide lying upon the very herb that might save them! My God! My God! My God!"

---

[25] Ipecac—short for ipecacuanha—used to be a popular herbal medical treatment, employed as an emetic.

67

And Pons bowed his head beneath the heavy hand of Fate.

He raised it again as if he had suffered an uppercut; Hope had struck him under the chin.

"Courage, damn it! Look: the Sun's appearing through the rain. And look again: *Pleasing the architect and the painter as well/The heptachrome rainbow rounds out its shell.*"

"Mercy, please!" Fléchambeau implored. "I'm in a bad way. My heart is hurting like a suppurating wound. Your *carabin*'s jokes, you see...ah!"

But Pons was no so easily disarmed. "*Carabin!*" he said. "That word brings back the pleasant memory of a brave little companion of the operating theater. She had a lover nicknamed Gastibelza, because he was a man with a carbine..."[26]

"I'd rather go than listen to this," said Fléchambeau—and did.

The Choderpils, the Dézormets and the Chabosseaus got their news from the morning paper. Those people certainly knew how to live! Pons and Fléchambeau were, however, visited by Monsieur and Madame Monempoix, accompanied by Olga; they only popped in briefly, the spouses being rather gloomy, and Olga desolate—but she obtained aauthorization from her parents to go back whenever she pleased.

It goes without saying that only the Monempoix family knew the truth. Everyone else believed in Fléchambeau's temporary indisposition. A few days later, however, the suspicion began to grow that something mysterious was going on in Doctor Pons's house and that Fléchambeau was the object of special attention on the part of Destiny.

---

[26] Once again, this wordplay—on *carabin* [a slang term for a medical student] and *carabine* [a carbine rifle]—is untranslatable. Gastibelza is a character in a popular ballad by Victor Hugo, in which he is characterized as "the man with the carbine;" Georges Brassens recorded a version of it.

There are stories that cannot be kept hidden, which spread with invincible force, whose strangeness is magnified as they pass from mouth to mouth, as long as no one has a very clear idea of what is going on. A statistician would have observed that many more people, especially women, were passing through the Place de la République, male and female citizens who were curiously distracted, apparently doing nothing, but who looked sideways at the house of mystery, to the extent that they sometimes bumped into one another, or got a jobbing carpenter's plank in the eye, or stumbled over the fountain's pavement, or fell head-first into the water-basin—as happened to old Baron Cormoranche, who only lived for rumor, gossip and slander.

In the meantime, the torture—or, more accurately, the passion—of Fléchambeau followed its course; for there are calvaries that one descends instead of climbing, and which are no less painful for it. Fléchambeau was descending now, without remission. The prospect of being a dwarf before the end of the month rendered him furious. He displayed an execrable temper. Let's not even mention his nights. His awakenings? The awakenings of a condemned man. And his days? Oh, his days! Also those of a condemned man—condemned, not to the guillotine, but the height-gauge. The terrible height-gauge! A construction that did, indeed, take on a certain resemblance to the scaffold: the height-gauge that executed Fléchambeau 50 times over, from dawn to dusk; the height-gauge that measured the progress of his disgrace and the march of his martyrdom; the height-gauge that decapitated him of a head every week!

Other tortures, though secondary, exasperated him no less, hurling him into mad rages—such as, for example, the question of clothing. At first, he was bought small ones from the ready-made racks in the department store. Pons had proposed borrowing them, but Fléchambeau hated that idea; the repugnant mold of someone else's joints gave him gooseflesh and made his hackles rise. In the meantime, he went from one

69

costume to another as a traveler goes from one hotel to another.

Olga came often. Her gentle presence retained Fléchambeau on the slope of his anger, but it aggravated his sadness and filled him with a somber irony. He could no longer put his arm round her waist without seeming ridiculous. One day, she wanted to sit on his knee; he was beset by a fit of fury then, so forceful that tears came into his eyes. And Olga heard him singing, with a sharp and jeering voice that would have wrung your heart: "*My father has given me a husband,/My God, what a man, what a tiny man!/My father has given me a husband,/My God, what a man, how tiny he is!*"[27]

He turned toward her, for he had retreated into a corner. "Tom Thumb!" he said, bitterly. "There you are! Tom Thumb!"

And what could be said in reply? Poor Fléchambeau!

The most bizarre thing was that he had continued to shrink quite properly. His proportions had not changed. There was still no wrinkling, and no shriveling. If he had been photographed, without including any object of comparison, the print would not have revealed anything of his general diminution. In reality, though, he was a dwarf: a dwarf with the proportions of a giant, the physiognomy of a giant, the gestures, the gait and even the habits of a giant. That was, in fact, truly extraordinary. If you imagine an elephant the size of a pony, a basilica the size of a maisonette…anything you like! It's funny. You don't know why, but it's funny. And there's nothing more sinister than wanting to laugh at something sad.

Olga's role was delicate and difficult. Every woman is maternal toward those who, being small, resemble children. It's not funny being small in any case, but when one has previously been large, what a disgrace it is!

In addition, Madame Monempoix was beginning to look sullen. She came more rarely, pinched, discontented and gla-

---

[27] The lines are from a popular children's song, which goes on interminably in the same vein.

70

cial. Olga was only able to care for Fléchambeau as she wished by virtue of a rebellion.

As for Monsieur Monempoix, he had become presidential again, making brief appearances and repeating tirelessly: *Capitis deminutio, capitis deminutio*,[28] thinking that deputy Bargoulin enjoyed a normal and fixed stature, and that deputies are, after all, created in order to deputize. "Never," he said to himself. "Fléchambeau will never grow again—and I don't want a son-in-law as tall as my boot!"

To grow again! Pons, meanwhile, was making every effort, in every way, to find the formula that would relaunch his friend heavenwards. Boxes of old books were arriving continually from Paris. He grew pale poring over treatises in histology, osteology and physiology. He grew thin. He lost sleep, his appetite for food and drink, his sense of humor, and even his sense of being alive. His profound eyes sank even further into their orbits; one might have feared that they were going to pop out of the back of his head.

As for Fléchambeau, he experienced all the terrors of his unfortunate fate, prayed ardently to the Lord his God, fervently repeating: "Fulfill me, Father, by granting my wish!" And—something worthy of note—he continually recovered impressions of childhood, having become so small that he was overwhelmed by the effort of moving a chair and had to climb on to a stool to look out of the window. These particularities did not give him any pleasure, even intellectually. Every day augmented his terror. At the outset, he had only feared the shame of being a dwarf; now, dwarf that he was, more frightful problems posed themselves to him. *How will all this*

---

[28] Like most of the remarks M. Monempoix makes, this is a legal phrase, wrenched out of context but ironically apt. The Latin *Capus* [head] was also used metaphorically to mean "life" or "status;" in Roman law, *Capitis deminutio* referred to a legally-recognized a loss of status, of which there were varying degrees, ranging from loss of the headship of a family and exile to enslavement.

71

*end? Where will this diminution stop? Will it not simply pro-
ceed to annihilation? Will it not go on until death?*

A day came when the height-gauge, that gibbet, was un-
usable; the cursor did not come down low enough. Instruments
of measurement are only constructed to accommodate that
which is reasonable, not the creations of an insane hazard.

Fléchambeau measured 25 centimeters. He was so small
that he had the look of having been born under a Brussels
sprout. For some time he had gone to bed in the cradle that
had played host to the earliest expansion of Olga and Bobiche.
It was from the latter's playthings that a doll's bed was extracted, a sort of oaken Moses-basket, in which Fléchambeau
had to resolve to spend the most agitated nights that any mortal had ever had to endure, until now. No human garment was
sufficiently Lilliputian for him; Olga, weary of incessantly
reducing those she had made for him, undressed Bobiche's
dolls one by one. Thus the pygmified Fléchambeau donned the
uniform of a colonel of hussars. A living doll, he had only
been wearing his red trousers and braided tunic for an hour
when Pons caught him attaching a thread to the armrest of a
chair in order to hang himself. That had a profound effect on
the brave man, who recovered his verve momentarily.

"Suicide, then? Declaring bankruptcy! Have you gone
mad? Come on, come on! You know very well that we'll get
out of this!"

"The only reasonable thing that one can do in this
world," cried Fléchambeau, "is to dispatch oneself into the
other! The man who kills himself is exercising his most basic
right, which is to get out of a place to which he did not ask to
be admitted."

"But his first duty is to do nothing about it," Pons retorted. "Your religion, moreover, forbids you to leave us. Then
again, we shall save you! You'll grow again. You'll marry
Olga, and you'll have lots of children, who'll be very happy!"

"The best way of ensuring the happiness of one's children is not to have any."

"Nonsense! Your duty…"

72

"That rhymes with *fruity*."[29]

"*Zut!* You're discouraging. Listen Fléchambeau: once upon a time there were two twins. They resembled one another so perfectly that one day, the wife of one mistook the other for her husband. The confusion was such that the mistaken wife perpetrated he treason without realizing it. The deceived spouse found out. Indignant, he wanted to kill his brother, but the fatal resemblance was such that, being deluded in his turn, it was himself that he shot, believing that he was shooting at the guilty party, his fraternal double. By chance, he survived. Fortunately, the bullet had gone through his skull without injuring the vital organ. Well, you…"

"Leave me in peace!" said Fléchambeau. "It's understood, I won't make any more attempts on my life—but leave me alone. Go away! Turn round!"

The colonel's uniform procured him a military soul, and incited him to command. He sometimes talked like a tiny phonograph whose amplifier has been removed in order not to annoy the neighbors. The next day but one, he became a toreador. After that, he was a Dieppe fisherman. Finally, he dressed himself in miniature togas, sewn by Olga, which assimilated him to the Romans, and beneath which he was as naked as a gymnosophist.[30]

No more monocle: consequence, poor vision. No more pipe, no more cigars (too large): consequence, bad temper. But these privations were nothing, compared to certain perils. Mary Stuart chased him, with the intention of devouring him. *The cat has taken him for a mouse!/My God, what a man! What a tiny man!*

---

[29] In French, *devoir* [duty] rhymes with *poire* [pear]. English is not quite so obliging.

[30] This term, whose initial reference was to an ascetic philosophical sect discovered in India by Alexander the Great, is sometimes applied—in English as well as French—to nudists.

Completely out of breath, standing on Pons's hand, which the latter put close to his ear, he demanded aid and protection.

Then the homunculus was taken into the laboratory. A dolls' house that Bobiche had been given for Christmas was set up on a table. It was furnished with the miniature items of furniture that had come with it, and a loudspeaker that amplified Fléchambeau's voice admirably. To finish the job, a wooden border was nailed around the table, for it only needed a window to be left open by mistake for the wind to carry the slight creature away as he walked in the enclosure.

That was not sufficient. A wasp, and then a large spider, nearly took possession of Fléchambeau and put an end to the story. A birdcage replaced the dolls' house, Valentin reinforced its metallic roof and sides—regardless of which, as a precaution, Pons armed Fléchambeau with a powerful sharply-pointed needle with a head of blue glass, which could serve him as a lance and permit him to defend himself against a fly, if it happened that a fly should insidiously penetrate that sort of food-cover…

The recluse was fed on scraps and crumbs. He was now the same order of magnitude as crickets and beetles. One evening, Pons felt a thrill of fear; he could no longer see him and, at the same time, a hairy caterpillar was climbing over the cage, like an errant moustache. False alarm! Fléchambeau was asleep behind a breadcrumb.

In order to communicate with him, a tube was now necessary. One put an ear to one extremity of the tube, and Fléchambeau spoke into the other—an instrument that was improved by the addition of an amplifier when the little voice became too thin.

Eventually, no microphone could any longer succeed in rendering Fléchambeau's murmur perceptible. The magnifying-glass with which people looked at him was then abandoned, being too weak. One of those monocular lenses that jewelers use to repair watches was substituted for it, and the sole means of communication thereafter consisted of reading what Fléchambeau wrote on extra-fine paper with the aid of a hair dipped in fine ink. It was, of course, a long time since he had been able to shave, so he wore a full beard, which changed him greatly. He devoted himself to a great many desperate and angry pantomimes, becoming smaller and smaller all the time, no longer being dressed in anything but the air around him, save for a parcel of some unknown substance, which was held on by some unknown means, and hid his you-know-what.

Pons had abandoned his research completely. To interrupt the diminution of Fléchambeau appeared to him to be quite impossible. The very smallness of the subject seemed to be an obstacle to the majority of medical treatments. Furthermore, Pons was now too unhappy, too grief-stricken, to be able to work lucidly. He never left the table that was Fléchambeau's domain—a domain that became more spacious for him with every passing day—and Olga spent many hours there, morning and evening, both of them contemplating through their jeweler's lenses the tiny, delicately-chiseled face of the figurine, whose red hair did for him what phosphorus does for the head of a match.

How would it end?

Fléchambeau, disheartened, made his will.

Whatever the cost, he wrote, *I want a Christian burial. Arrange it!*

"But you're not ill," Pons said to him. "Why are you talking about dying?" He took care to lower his voice and directed a small acoustic funnel made of paper at Fléchambeau, whose large opening was turned toward his own mouth.

"You're looking very well, my dear," said Olga.

I can't keep shrinking indefinitely!

"Why not?" said Pons, who had hesitated to pronounce those terrible words.

Fléchambeau's face expressed the utmost gravity. All three of them had been thinking about the same things for a long time, without saying anything.

"What has happened to you," Pons continued, "demonstrates that living tissues are far more plastic than anyone supposed, at least in the direction of reduction. Given that you have suffered no ill effects thus far, I don't se why your organism can't support a much more considerable diminution. Instead of thinking of yourself as shrinking, imagine that you're moving away, and the experience immediately takes on a different appearance..." Oh, how tight his throat was as he said that!

Going away, then, Fléchambeau traced.

"Yes, going away without moving..."

And without any hope of return!

"Do we ever know?" said Pons—but he felt tears coming. Olga's lens misted over too, and she took it away from her eye to wipe it.

You should have taken the pills too! Fléchambeau wrote. *Leaving me alone is cowardly!*

"I thought that I'd be more useful in another way," Pons said, by way of self-justification. "If I had shrunk too, who would have kept you safe? Who would watch over you...?"

That's true. I beg your pardon. But where am I going? What will happen? Alone! Without weapons. I can't take anything with me, since everything becomes increasingly disproportionate!

"Obviously. But a resourceful type like you will always get himself out of trouble—and Fléchambeau...you're undertaking a marvelous exploration! I've always maintained that the greatest adventures unfold in one place, that the greatest voyages are not effected geographically. I never imagined that my idea would take on a form as prodigious as that of your adventure!"

Fléchambeau appeared to meditate.

Pons, I know that the world isn't limited by the range of our senses. I know that our senses, themselves reduced, are limited. There are many things in the universe that they don't perceive naturally, some because they're too large, others because they're too small. Some of these things the progress of science has enabled us to discover: stars and microbes. So tell me, Doctor, what you know about the world into which I am going, involuntarily. First, do you think that we know about all microbes? We don't, do we?

"I believe in infinity," said Pons. "In the infinitely large and the infinitely small. The universe has no bounds in any direction. The Earth is only a ball of clay at a single point in endless space. What we call an atom measures a ten-millionth of a millimeter in diameter; now an atom is a solar system analogous to ours, a solar system in which the planets, 50,000 times smaller than the atom, rotate around a central star as the Earth turns around the Sun; and these infinitesimal suns, smaller than their planets, are a thousand million million times smaller than a millimeter. And everything leads us to suppose that these minuscule worlds contain others, which themselves contain others, inexhaustibly.

"It's probable that our Solar System is only an atom in relation to the great infinity, so great that the light of certain stars only reaches us after ten million years, at a velocity of 300,000 kilometers a second. It's probable that the great All is only an infinity of rotating systems, contained one within another, the dimensions of which, by their immensity or their smallness, escape, for the most part, not only our senses but also our understanding. As Nordmann[31] has said: *Reality surpasses dreams, and overwhelms them.*"

Olga discreetly withdrew. Fléchambeau followed her with his eyes, an inaccessible giant of whom he retained within him an image proportionate to his own height. When she had gone, he asked: *But what about the microbes? The microbes!*

Pons realized the extent of his friend's anxiety. Alas! Was it really necessary to instruct him as he desired? Would he not die before disembarking, so to speak, in the land of bacteria? Must he give him an education in microbiology, as

---

[31] Presumably the Finnish zoologist Alexander von Nordmann (1803-1866).

one informs a traveler about the mores of the populations he is going to visit?

I'm listening, traced Fléchambeau, with an impatient hair.

"There are," said Pons, "many more animals in the zoo-logical Noah's Ark than even the lynx can see..." And he launched into a description of the microscopic fauna and flora, softening anything that might frighten Fléchambeau. Correcting in accordance with his intention, he introduced him to the malevolent customs of various tiny worms, road-bacteria, algae and fungi invisible to the naked eye of ordinary humans. By chance, he possessed a few preparations, which he enabled him to observe through the microscope. Fléchambeau, clinging to the ocular lens at the very top of the instrument, was reminiscent of an astronomer afflicted with dementia who had made the mistake of looking through his telescope the wrong way. But Pons, although he told him that to cheer him up, had no joy in his heart. On the contrary, Fléchambeau reminded him of an explorer condemned to depart for the Moon, and who was examining the distant world on which he feared that he would soon run aground.

After that, Fléchambeau was replaced on the table, with a thousand precautions, and the lesson went on, for a long time.

When Olga came back, opening the door unhurriedly to avoid any displacement of air, she heard Pons saying: "In a gram of hydrogen, according to the method one employs to count them, there are 650,000 or 683,000 billions of billions of atoms. If there were only 500,000 billion billion, the sky would be green, but if there were 700,000, the sky would be violet. With regard to hydrogen, though, I should perhaps inform you of Prout's Law..."[32]

---

[32] The "law" proposed by William Prout (1785-1850) in 1815—nowadays known as "Prout's hypothesis" because it had proven faulty long before Pons made this statement—suggested that the atoms of all the other elements were "com-

"Ahem!" said Olga, fearful of some breach of good manner.

"Ah, Mademoiselle—you're here!"

"Yes," she whispered. "It's stronger than me; I've come back. I'm always afraid that some catastrophe will occur during my absence. But Valentin wants to see you, Doctor. A parcel has just been delivered..."

"I know what it is," whispered Pons. "It's a hypermicroscope, Mademoiselle—an ultra-violet microscope with quartz lenses and prisms. It provides magnifications of 400,000 diameters. With that, we might perhaps be able to follow him for a longer time..."

"Who, Fléchambeau?"

"Of course. Who else?"

"It's frightful! Frightful!"

Pons was amazed that anyone could be as pale without having died first.

An ordinary microscope sufficed, to begin with. We cannot say that the vision was perfect. These items of apparatus are not made for such uses. Even so, Fléchambeau was finally installed underneath the objective lens and, by ingenious miming, contrived to make himself understood.

It was at this point that the pathetic episode of the itchmite, *Sarcoptes scabiei*, occurred.

A damnably dirty creature, this mite. It isn't a microbe, as you know, but an exceedingly villainous little monster, an acarian, a tiny louse that adores darkness and takes a malign pleasure in burrowing into the skin of people or other creatures, multiplying there with a depressing rapidity—a single

---

pounds" of hydrogen atoms, and that their atomic weights ought, therefore, to be simple multiples of that of hydrogen.

pair can produce a million females and half a million males in three months[33]—and makes you itch in no time.

Pons was never able to explain how the mite had escaped from his tiny experimental menagerie, or by what sequence of incidents the animal found itself in the very last location where it should have been: on the thin glass slide that bore Fléchambeau and his fortune. We can only assume that it had remained there—or, rather, on one of its supports—after some parasitological observation. All that one can say, based on that hypothesis, is that the acarian had a durable life.

While Pons was taking a hygienic stroll, Olga, left alone in the laboratory, was on watch at the microscope. She perceived her fiancé—as she nobly insisted on calling him—as one distinguishes passers-by from the height of a sixth story. In order not to hurt Fléchambeau's eyes, the microscope's mirror only sent him a minimal amount of light. It was, in consequence, relative dark beneath the objective.

Suddenly, the mite appeared, monstrous and white, bristling with sharp spines, antennae and feet equipped with sucker, opening a beak whose two mandibles were reminiscent of a lobster's claws, and agitating all its redoubtable appendices with an unparalleled frenzy. Deprived of eyes but endowed with a very appreciable sense of orientation, it advanced gropingly toward Fléchambeau.

Now, by this time, Fléchambeau had diminished to such an extent that a female mite—for it was a female, four times as voluminous as a male—towered over him as the mammoth towered over our prehistoric ancestors. The comparison cannot be taken much further, given that our ancestors were dressed in furs and armed with flint axes, while Fléchambeau was unarmed and his only clothing was a layer of fine oil specially developed for miscroscopic examinations—a coating that preserved him from cold and might, strictly speaking,

---

[33] In fact, the female scabies mite only lays two or three eggs per day, which is why scabies sufferers are not totally consumed in a matter of weeks.

have given him an advantage in hand-to-hand combat because of the slipperiness of the oil.

Olga uttered a piercing scream. Fléchambeau raised his head on hearing that racket, which must have seemed to him to be a kind of sharp thunder. Fear was legible in his face.

What can I do? Olga asked herself.

The situation was, indeed, critical. The elephantine louse hastened its blind but sure progress. Would Fléchambeau seek salvation in flight? The mite was advancing rapidly. My God—so rapidly!

The young woman then altered the articulation of the mirror—instinctively, because the first concern of human beings and other creatures endowed with sight, when there is something that ought not to be happening, is to see clearly.

It was certainly a bright idea. An intense light was suddenly projected on to the two adversaries. The scene lit up violently. No more was required to deter a mite, since these tiny creatures, strangely enough, blind as they are, flee from light as from the plague. The mite abruptly turned tail, activating its four pairs of legs, and disappeared from the dazzling disk in which Fléchambeau, saved, was restraining the beating of his heart.

At that moment, Pons came back in. Olga told him what had happened. He was so accustomed to dealing with parasites that he was easily able to find the formidable dragon—smaller than the most derisory of aphids—without delay, even on a glass side, and slay it.

The mite episode thus had a happy ending, thanks to Olga's intervention—but it put into sharp relief the perilous aspect of a shrinkage that would soon expose Fléchambeau to all sorts of similar attacks. What would become of him, alone among the microbes—as alone as a castaway on a desert island, uniquely haunted by mysterious creatures?

The days went by. The inexorable diminution followed its regular course. Fléchambeau became molecular, then atomic. Use had to be made of the hypermicroscope, the most powerfully reinforced eye that had so far been invented.

The Pons house was funereal. Monsieur and Madame Monempoix did not come any more. They would not have been allowed into the laboratory anyway. No one went in there except Pons, Olga and the faithful Valentin, who thwarted all the attempts of cunning journalists avid to know exactly what was happening.

As might readily be imagined, the gossips had, indeed, accomplished their task. The local rags had begun to publish rumors of the enigmatic disappearance of a young man staying in Saint-Jean-de-Nèves. An odor of prodigy was floating in the air. To all the questions he was asked regarding Fléchambeau, however, Pons replied that he had left on a voyage. Where? He did not know.

Truer words were never spoken. Finding a plausible explanation for Olga's extensive visits was not easy, however. These visits, in themselves, prevented the acceptance of Pons's affirmations. He would not be believed until they ceased.

The last one was genuinely moving, to the highest degree.

It would have been dangerous to expose Fléchambeau too frequently to the radiations necessary to the employment of the hypermicroscope. Pons had therefore limited the number and duration of observation sessions. One Sunday morning, he said to Olga: "Come back this afternoon, without fail. I think it will happen this evening."

The day of mourning! A day, alas, long foreseen and dreaded! She would see her beloved for the last time—the man who, because of her, because he adored her, had swallowed the disastrous pills and was now descending into infernal regions from which no one ever returned!

Did she see him? Did she discern the ultramicroscopic man among the swarming multitude of particles of dust and forms that moved within the lunar circle of the objective lens?

She was, at least, persuaded of it, basing her conviction on the immobility of a scarcely-visible dot.

For some time, Fléchambeau had avoided displacing himself. Pons was afraid that he might never move again—but how could one tell why he wasn't moving? Illness? A decision he had made? A plan? Might he be stuck to the glass like an animalcule? He wasn't dead, at any rate, since he was still shrinking.

Raising her head, Olga said to Pons: "I can see him." Then she resumed her contemplation, and said, tragically: "I can't see him any longer! Ah! Yes… No!"

Pons looked himself, and discovered nothing.

Fléchambeau had disappeared.

Olga dissolved in tears, and collapsed in the dimpled armchair. Pons said nothing. Oh, that silence saturated with dreams, which oppressed them!

A new horizon had hidden the ever-more-distant voyager from their eyes, as he drew away in an unprecedented fashion. In space, to be sure—but without taking a step! Without, in the final analysis, going anywhere!

"And he'll never come back—never!" Olga sobbed.

Pons let his arms fall, having raised them in order to do so. Olga watched him gently and piously—as piously as if he were closing the eyes of a dead friend—cover up the microscope with its crystal bell-jar.

"Tomorrow," he said, "I'll put little wedges under the bell, in order that the air can circulate freely."

Olga looked at him in astonishment through her tears, while putting on her hat.

"Voyages," he said, "are the making of youth."

She realized, by virtue of these words, that Pons was, so to speak, "in shock," and she was astonished that she had never noticed the troubling amplitude of his cranial cavity. But it was not for his sake that she was there, and she had no viable reason to remain there against her worthy parents' wishes. For a few seconds, therefore, she considered in a meditative fashion the pure reflections of the globe within which her fiancé had crossed the frontier of human and scientific sight…

Pons thought her worthy of happiness.

They shook hands, with a comprehensive grip—and she did it quite simply. It is often said, after all, that one should never be astonished by anything.

VII. Exit Pons

Doctor Pons watched Mademoiselle Olga Monempoix cross the Place de la République to go back into her parents' house. That graceful spectacle delayed the solitude that would now take about possession of his time, and his life...

The wisterias were fading. It was within a frame of yellowing foliage that the square was revealed, while the *République* disdained to gaze at her own profound image in the fountain—would she have been able to, though, with such a bosom?—and Mademoiselle Olga Monempoix went home with genteel dignity.

She's truly good! Pons said to himself.

It is not with impunity that a young man and a young woman can spend long, emotionally-wrought hours together, every day. When Olga had shaken his hand, had their eyes not gripped in parallel?—if Pons dared to express himself in such terms. He admired her, that Olga. With what relaxed poise, with what fine courage, she had braved the malicious gossip in carrying her duty to Fléchambeau through to the end, in coming to Pons's house every day, with the knowledge and in the plain sight of all the slanderers!

Why did Pons then think of deputy Bargoulin, without benevolence? Why did he ask himself what President Monempoix and his wife might think of him? Why did he regret not having maintained that fancy in the "darling" mother's soul which his amusing gaiety had engendered there one evening?

But Olga vanished from sight. The little prolongation had expired. And the solitude began.

Solitude? What about Fléchambeau, then? The microscope under the bell-jar?

Fléchambeau rhymed with *tombeau*.[34] A couplet sketched itself out, which Pons severely forbade himself to formulate. He had been so deeply "in shock" a little while before that he had now become extraordinarily lucid—and melancholy.

Fléchambeau! His absence took up more room than his presence had done. But was he not absent and present at the same time? A strange absence, at any rate! And a presence no less strange! To be *and* not to be! A paradox realized! An impossibility accomplished! Fléchambeau? No longer anyone, and yet someone!

Someone? Until when? Who would ever know the moment of his death? Was he still alive, even?

He was an orphan, with no family. That simplified things. There was not so much as a third cousin to inform. Anyway, for some months, he had been talking about that voyage abroad, no one knew where. Later, there would be time to call attention to the fact, to say that Fléchambeau had not written to anyone, that no one knew his fate. Judges would declare him *absent*. Absence is a legal status like any other; according to the Code, one is *absent* when one is a *minor, divorced* or *disgraced.*

And that would be the end of it.

Pons had reckoned without his contemporaries, his factotum, Valentin, and himself.

Pons grew bored. His work in parasitology had nothing new to tell him; he conceived an irrevocable repugnance for it. His laboratory, moreover, filled him with sadness by reason of the hypermicroscope and its bell-jar, which he saw as a sort of cenotaph. For a while, he disposed a crown of forget-me-nots around it.

His deception also left him steeped in an exceedingly bitter gall. The golden gates of Glory had been opened by a crack to his spellbound eyes, but it had not lasted. His discovery had

---

[34] Tomb.

simply made mock of him, jeered at him, tainted him and lampooned him—in brief, satirized him. It had left him with a great disgust for human beings, their stupidity and their malice. That is always the way. When one comes unstuck, it is the world's fault—even without taking its wickedness into account!

But let us pass on to the factotum, Valentin. The latter, very respectfully, brought it to Monsieur le Docteur's attention that he would be leaving his service in a week's time, having decided to take a wife and go to cultivate a few modest acres of land that he owned in the Aube, near Troyes.

Pons cursed the wife, agriculture and the département de l'Aube—but what could he do against Troyes?

Now, the contemporaries. The contemporaries became unbearable. They had not swallowed the lie about the pretended voyage so easily. They wanted to know where Fléchambeau was, and what events had unfolded behind closed doors in the dwelling that he had been seen to enter, but from which he had not been seen to emerge. Pons was assailed with questions, importuned with statements that had double meanings and carried sly insinuations.

He turned his back on them.

Oh, the day came when it would not have taken much to launch him in pursuit of Fléchambeau! He held a dozen of the red pills in the palm of his hand…

The thought of Olga came back to him. He was surprised by that, and pleased. But that did not alter the fact that it was necessary to go away—to go away for a few months; not, certainly, to the land of microbes, but somewhere on the planet Earth; to be a voyager in his turn—this time, really, without leaving a forwarding address. To wander anywhere at all: in Italy, where orange-trees flourished, or California, where golden ingots flourished. Alas, necessity always necessities a choice of paths, as they say. Anyway, a change of air would be good for him. Already, at the thought of new environments, exquisitely ingenuous couplets were singing within him.

Handsome page, saddle my horse of jet/My thoroughbred mare or my bicyclette.

On night—the one after Valentin's departure—Pons piled some clothes into a tourist bag and checked that the crystal bell-jar was covering the hypermicroscope adequately. He closed all the shutters, went out through a concealed door, straddled his bicyclette, left Saint-Jean-de-Nèves with his lights off, went to the next station, and took a train for the Americas under a false name.

VIII. In Which One Perceives That the Character of Pons Is Merely a Second Avatar of Mons Prologus

Pons returned to Saint-Jean-de-Nèves in the month of February.

The Americas had not given him any satisfaction, and he could not understand the renown of Christopher Columbus, not that—almost forgotten, in any case—of Amerigo Vespucci. It seemed to him that, although the adventure had revealed New York and Rio de Janeiro to him, he was bound, on his return, to sum up his journey with a loudly proclaimed: "Nothing new!" It was unreasonable, but that was the way it was, and we can do nothing about it.

Then again, he had not enjoyed the inner tranquility that makes the most banal exterior charming. He was plagued by ideas: the idea of Fléchambeau, lost in the infinitely vast world of the infinitely small; the idea of Mary Stuart, of whom he had made a gift to Valentin; the idea of his abandoned house; the idea of having slipped away like a guilty man. His mailbox must be overflowing! And the registered letters at the post office! And what must they think of him, over there? And Olga, for heaven's sake! And Bargoulin, the detestable Bargoulin...

He could have written, to be sure—but he had sworn that he wouldn't write, and to perjure himself would have been execrable.

That is why a certain anxiety compressed his stomach as he exited from the Saint-Jean-de-Nèves railway station and headed for the Place de la République.

It was snowing. There was almost no one out and about. The sky was as dark as a hangar roof. A stupefying silence reigned. The snow ground underfoot like a silky powder, and as they fell, the snowflakes made the only noise that is noiseless.

Pons thought, without pleasure, about his cold house, full of dust and sinister…

He went up the main street, trampling the thick whit carpet. Two or three carrion crows, cockroaches of the sky, perched in the tops of the trees of the avenue, launched mocking and pedantic gibes at him. Rooks were spiraling around the church of Saint-Jean, making scandalized exclamations. The bronze *République*, dressed by the snow in a mantle of ermine, had the majesty of a black queen.

"Eh?" said Pons, his brow more overhung than ever. He stopped short, his exhaled breath playing the winter pipe. "What can that mean?" he mumbled.

The shutters of his house were open.

He resumed walking at a hurried pace, fumbled over the two locks with a feverish hand, and went in…

Damnation! It certainly wasn't warm in there!

The doors creaked.

Ground floor: orderly, dusty and deserted.

First Floor. His bedroom: same appearance—but he thought he could hear a confused moaning in Fléchambeau's room. Pons had to summon up all his self-control, ignore the acceleration of his heartbeat and remain deaf to the internal voiced that was crying out: "You're dreaming!"

If the Unknown were locked behind a door, no one could have pushed it open with more terror, emotion and timidity than Pons experienced as he went through the doorway of that room.

Is it, by chance…?

No, of course not! He was about to find some intruder there, a vagabond, perhaps a thief, or some wretch who had taken advantage of his absence to install himself in his home…quietly. Some *Bicard dit le Bouif*…[35]

---

[35] Bicard dit le Bouif (*Bouif* is a dialect version of *Boeuf* [Ox]) was a character invented by the novel's dedicatee, Georges de la Fouchardière, initially as a malicious caricature of lower-class cunning, while he was working for the *Canard*

As for Fléchambeau, damn it… Come on, come on!

He was inside.

What struck him, first of all, was the "lived in" appearance of the place, and the two pans on the extinct stove. Immediately, though, the bed attracted his gaze. There was someone in it.

The dream fell flat.

That someone was an old citizen, on which one might have thought that it had snowed, so intensely did his hair compete in whiteness with the beard that devoured his face. That heedless old man was lying in Fléchambeau's bed. Very pale, of course, and with closed eyes. In spite of the cold, his night-shirt opened to reveal his white torso, decorated with tattoos.

Pons, however, noticed his feet—not because they were bare and greenish, but *because they were immense and stuck out past the end of the bed.*

Brought back from his illusions, but not daring to believe it, Pons, oppressed and breathless, called out in a squeaky voice: "Fléchambeau!"

The man opened his eyes and smiled, weakly. His two long arms reached out. "Pons!" he murmured. "Dear old Pons!"

"You, Fléchambeau! You! Is it credible!"

The revenant did not reply. His head leaned forward, further and further…

God! The man was about to die!

Remembering that he was a physician, Pons made haste. He examined the sick man immediately, convincing himself that Fléchambeau was presenting all the characteristics of very advanced age—90 years old, at least—and that he was simply in the process of dying of old age. Dying of old age at 25! A

---

enchaînée in 1916. Bicard won such popular acclaim, however, that he was transformed into the hero of a series of movies, beginning with *Le Crime du Bouif* (1922).

nonagenarian at 25! That's not commonplace. And where had all those tattoos come from? He had had none before!

Before interrogating this astonishing grandfather, however, he first had to render him capable of speech and to prevent him departing on a voyage from which no one has ever returned.

Pons climbed up to the second floor, ran to the laboratory, and came back down like an avalanche, having scarcely had time to observe that the crystal bell-jar was still on top of the hypermicroscope.

He made the required injection in the desired place. Caffeine, presumably, perhaps camphorated oil. What do we care? All that matters to us is the Fléchambeau began to sneeze—a certain sign of reinvigoration.

Pons lit the stove, and put some water on to boil.

"Listen," said Fléchambeau. "Come here… You see how…I've aged…"

"Oh yes! But how did it happen?"

"I was so tiny, so tiny…time, for me, passed…more quickly… A mayfly lives…an entire life…in a single day…"

"Indeed—but tell me…"

"I think," breathed the old man, with a disillusioned smile, "that I don't have time to say anything very much. My minutes are numbered…"

"Tut tut!" Pons protested. "What's that you're saying? Everyone's minutes are numbered from birth, and yours…"

Fléchambeau shook his head, and said: "For the music at my funeral, I'd like…"

Pons interrupted him, facetiously. "*My dear friends, when I should die/Sing in the cemetery where I'll lie…* We're not there, damn it! You'll live 500 years, like the parrot whose loquacity you have." He paused, then resumed: "Anyway, you'll do and say plenty—your old age isn't natural. Personally, I consider it to be a sort of disease, of which you need to be cured—and I shall cure you!"

"Not if I can help it!" Fléchambeau said. "Anyway, Pons, I've had enough of your treatments. You might perhaps cure my old age, but it would be the same thing all over again—I wouldn't be able to stop growing younger. And then, my dear chap, to be a babe in arms in five or six weeks...no, Pons, I'd rather not, you know. I prefer to hold on to...that which is..."

"But, my old..." Pons interrupted himself; that word "old" seemed incongruous now. He leapt from one idea to another. "Olga..." He began.

"She's not married—I know that."

"I was going to say: should I tell her?"

"Keep it to yourself! Since I came back, I've made every effort to avoid her. I could be her great-grandfather, my friend! My young friend! Olga is a youthful memory! A pleasant memory, but nothing but a memory!"

"And...how long is it since you came back?"

"Long enough to have been able to write down an abridged account of my voyage. Look—do you see that notebook on the chest of drawers? It's for you."

Pons picked up the notebook.

"Read it, Pons—read it now. Soon, I won't be here any longer to give you explanations."

"Nonsense! If your hour was nigh, you wouldn't be chattering away like this. But Fléchambeau, what are all these tattoos you're covered with?"

"Read the notebook and you'll know. Please don't put it off. It's warm; I'm comfortable. Read, I tell you!"

Even though he was convinced that his dear Fléchambeau would enjoy, thanks to his tender care, an old age that would still be long, and robust, and peaceful—but reckoning, on the other hand, that he ought not to contradict him for the moment—Pons drew nearer to the stove. He put on a cheerful face, tapped the notebook, and declared: "*What a pity it's a Frenchman's story!//It's bound to be the bookshop's glory.*"

Fléchambeau appeared to be suffering resignedly.

And Pons read what you are about to read.

Part Two: Fléchambeau's Voyage
to the Land of the Microbes

I. How Fléchambeau Obtained Admittance
to the Realm of the Microbe Mandarins

My dear Pons,

I've come back from the world of the infinitely small. I've re-emerged from the invisible that the majority of men call nothing. But the house in which I've reappeared is empty! You aren't here. Where are you? And will I still be here myself—will I still be alive?—when you return? It's an old man that you would have seen progressively emerging from nowhere and regaining his original height, with a rapidity that would have amazed you: an old man close to death.

Know, first of all, that I lost consciousness at the moment when my dimensions were about to mingle me with all the microbes known to some extent to our scientists, with regard to the appearance and behavior of which you educated me. At that point of my diminution, was I still visible to your eyes? If so, the immobility of my body must have given you considerable anxiety. The strange transformation of my physique, the difficulty I experienced in breathing air that had become coarse, and the defective alimentation from which I had been suffering for some while, were presumably responsible for my weakness.

The fact remains that, at the very moment when my environment took on a truly fantastic aspect worthy of attention, I felt myself deprived of the means of observing it. The ground of well-polished glass, which was an expanse as chaotic as a rocky plateau for me, seemed to capsize beneath my feet. Darkness hid the bizarre vegetation and the creatures that were moving about—which were atoms to you, but giants to me. I was forced to lie down in order not to fall. My eyes filled with darkness, exhaustion made my limbs leaden. I thought that I was dying, and from my point of view, it was as if it had all come to nothing.

All of a sudden, though, vague impressions were born within my profound torpor. I seemed to see the objective lens of the microscope above my head again, like an enormous darkly-gleaming disk; then there was the point of one of those fine needles that you employed to move dust-motes away from me, and which appeared to me as a rough mass, bristling with protrusions and hollowed out by caverns...

Dreams.

A murmur grew.

I opened my eyelids slightly.

I was still lying down, but on a spring-bed, in bare room bathed by violet light. Four men surrounded me, one of whom was leaning over me as I awoke.

What a surprise! Men! Men of my own stature! A dream was the only explanation...but had I dreamed the entire experience of my shrinkage, or was I dreaming now?

Without making any movement, I examined the men with half-closed eyes.

The one who was leaning over me was a relatively old man, wearing spectacles made from a material unknown to me. He had a kindly face and an air of benevolence, but with a sort of moderation that I found again in the faces of the others. One of those appeared to me to be a handsome young man with delicate features, whose lips was shadowed by a light moustache. The other two, who were standing slightly apart, offered the singularity of being completely green, of a pale bronze shade.

All four were dressed in Russian blouses, and short kilts like those worn by the Scots. They had bare legs and were shod in sandals or Oriental slippers, with their heels exposed. Their clothes were variegated, in various designs and in neutral colors—more neutral for the two green men. Their hair, cut like Jeanne d'Arc's—including the old man's—hid their ears. Strangely, some kind of living tuft was visible on top of their heads, faded red in color, mingled with silver for the old

95

man, periwinkle blue for the young gentleman, and brown for the green individuals.

Those beret-less pompoms intrigued me. Mounted on short stalks, they put me in mind of insignia, distinctive marks of rank, rather like the differently-colored buttons surmounting the hats of Mandarins. I was in the midst of Mandarins, there was no doubt about it. But how were the tufts secured to their heads? I couldn't tell.

I soon found out.

The old gentleman reached out his hand and lifted up one of my eyelids. I saw then that he had twelve fingers instead of ten. Prudently, however, I refrained from making the slightest gesture, contenting myself with remarking that each of the four men was provided with six fingers on each hand.

Meanwhile, my observer had established that I was not unconscious. He turned to his young companion, lowering his head slightly, which permitted me to see that the tuft emerged from his hair like a flower emerging from grass—and that tuft, that topknot, that flower, that sort of dahlia or chrysanthemum,[36] began to move in an undulating manner at the end of its short and powerful stalk, while these individuals, very miserly in matters of gesticulation, emitted a slightly modulated hum.

They huddled around, touching the edges of my bed, which was isolated in the middle of the room.

I opened my eyes fully, and saw a singular spectacle: four men with twelve fingers each, two of whom were green, curiously watching my return to life. I was, however, imme-

---

[36] The word *pompon*, which I have usually translated as "tuft," and occasionally as "pompom," is sometimes used in a narrow sense to refer to a particular kind of flower-head, characteristic of dahlias and chrysanthemums. Because the English usage of "pompom" is more specific than its French usage, in referring specifically to a kind of costume decoration, I have preferred the more general term, except where an analogy to clothing-decoration is explicit.

diately conscious of the fact that it was not so much their eyes but their tufts that were looking at me—or, rather, *perceiving* me. Those four protruding balls were indisputably part of their bodies; their stalks had stretched; they were aimed in my direction, simultaneously reminiscent of the eyes of lobsters, the horns of snails with their sensory organs at the tip, human pupils and sea-anemones. For that extraordinary tuft swayed, stood up straight, moved and undulated all its tentacles—or, rather, its beautifully colored antennae. It extended them, tangled them or directed them in sheaves toward some target. Their movements revealed, to some degree, a darker center, which the tentacles surrounded as petal surrounds the heart of a chrysanthemum, or the iris of an eye encircles the pupil. And like a sea-anemone, that curious Actinia sometimes retreated momentarily into its tube, with a graceful gyration, disappearing like an eye when it blinks, and then re-emerged to expand in a spiral and spread out beautifully.

For the moment, then, the four men were converging upon me, drawn by my amazement. The four faces were bizarre, and bizarrely inexpressive.

These men, who were not members of my own species, breathed in the air in my vicinity. They sniffed me desirously, shamelessly flaring their nostrils. They had large noses, small lusterless eyes, and ridiculously narrow mouths bordered by lips that were really nothing but thin rims. As for the ears, one of which I glimpsed thanks to a displacement of the hair, they seemed to be the ears of a very small child.

What I have written above, Pons, will enable you to understand why these faces were not accomplishing the play of the features by means of which we translate our sentiments. I already suspected that the tuft was the organ of a sense that we do not possess; I was certain from the outset that these people enjoyed a highly developed sense of smell, that they had weak eyesight, and that they must be half-deaf and half-mute.

I obtained some initial proof of this when I saw the kindly old gentleman, weary of contemplating me, take off his spectacles to rub them on his velvety blouse and, a moment later, do the same to a shiny metal sprig, which he withdrew from his red tuft, in which those silver streaks that I had assumed to be natural were mingled. That sprig played a role analogous to spectacles with regard to the old tuft, enfeebled by age. Its owner took advantage of the moment to take a small machine from a bag hanging from his belt, with which he sprayed something on the tuft. Meanwhile, the young man offered round an open box divided into compartments, whereupon each of them, taking a few pinches of various powders from various places, set about sniffing them, moving their nostrils in a fashion that was surely a nasal smile of the happiest sort. At the same time, moreover, the four tufts were executing vaults and somersaults in which one could not help seeing the combined expression of gratitude and sensual pleasure. It was to the tufts what a gaze is to the eyes. Their faces had cleared too.

All this had reassured me. I sat up. "Gentlemen," I said, "I salute you." With that, I sneezed several times. On the fifth occasion, my elbow bumped into some pharmaceutical jars that had been set on a table beside me. One of the jars fell and broke, spreading around an emerald liquid with a rather sharp aroma…

You might have thought that my four fellows had just received a thump on the nose; they jumped on the spot immediately, brutalized by the *odorous punch*, as if dazzled by a sudden bright light. The blocked their noses with their twelve fingers—with the exception of one of the green men, who threw himself toward the window and opened it wide; for the room, rounded in all its parts, possessed a small window, whose panes, being flexible, opened like curtains.

The green man's action had the effect of teaching me something about the violet light. I had thought that it owed its coloration to the panes themselves. That was not the case. A beautiful ray of sunlight penetrated the room, not golden but lilac. The heat of the day invaded the place at the same time, so strongly that an abundant sweat covered me. I passed my hand through my hair; its length, and that of my beard, left me nothing short of astonished.

My "Mandarins"—I shall conserve that name, for want of a better one—had recovered from their malaise. The old one, whom I shall call Agathos,[37] noticed how hot I was, and set his tuft spinning. Immediately, the second green man hastened to manipulate the taps of a radiator, and the first closed the window. Agathos extended his hands over the radiator—or, more correctly, the *refrigerator*—in order to cool them with its salutary emanations.

He had turned his back to me in consequence, but his tuft—how shall I put this?—he did not take his tuft off me! And I felt full of admiration for that organ, which overcame the distressing infirmity of the human *back*, the half of us that is our other side, our opposite, which is thus deprived of sensory perception, leaving us half-impotent and making each of us a sort of hemiplegic. For a human being is built to face forwards, and thus for pivoting; his back—the wretched back that he tows around all his life without ever being able to look at it—is like the obscure and miserable canvas behind a portrait.

"Gentlemen," I resumed. "Please explain what has become of me…"

They gathered around me again. Their faces indicated application. They uncovered their ears in order to hear me. Their eyes stared at my mouth. Their tufts adjusted all their stiffened petals…

What bad luck! I thought. *They don't understand a word! And, as I continue shrinking, I shall leave their world without having learned anything!*

---

[37] The names that Fléchambeau bestows on the Mandarins are derived from Classical Greek. *Agathos* signifies "good," in sense of "virtuous."

But Agathos addressed his tuft to the young man, handsome in spite of his big nose, and whom I decided to baptize Kalos.[38]

Kalos then covered his own tuft with an apparatus that served him as headgear: a helmet surmounted by a crest, which bore some resemblance to a lyre or an aerial for radiophonic reception. You would have deduced, as I did, that he was in *telecommunication* with someone or something, by means of the silent language of the tuft. You would not have been mistaken. A few seconds later, above a plate fixed to the wall after the fashion of a bracket-table, another apparatus appeared, which appeared to me to have been sent by the magic of some sublime invention, doubtless for the transmission of objects at a distance by means of their dissociation and reconstitution before the eyes of the recipient.

Agathos took this apparatus from Kalos' hands. Imagine a mysterious mechanism enclosed in a casing, from which two slender trumpets emerge at either end. Agathos placed one of these funnels against his forehead, the other on mine. And then...

Then Pons, I experienced the extraordinary sensation of hearing a speech without words, of perceiving the thoughts of my interlocutor directly, without the intermediary of any sonorous or visible language. All form and style were banished from that conversation, in the course of which Agathos and I conversed, so to speak, brain to brain.

Agathos informed me, by means of that strange and marvelous machine, that a prodigious mass had appeared in their sky one day, like a heavenly body out of all proportion, which drew nearer, becoming more compressed as it approached. "One might have thought that infinity were condensing; then the astronomers announced that it was a matter of a world in the process of retraction, which was 'falling' upon..." There, I could not grasp Agathos's thought, at least with any precision, but I shall immediately give the Mandarins' "planet" the name

---

[38] *Kalos* signifies "beautiful."

of Ourrh, which it was given at a later stage by Agathos, when I taught him, at his request, the rudiments of spoken language and of the French tongue.

But let us press on.

That "falling" world was me.

I had arrived on Ourrh like a Micromegas, but like a Micromegas who was shrinking. Until my apocalyptic appearance in the Mandarin's firmament, I had remained imperceptible, so far as they were concerned, in the great infinity inaccessible to their telescopes, in the same way that you had ceased to distinguish me in the infinite smallness that is the beyond of our microscopes.

It is evident that Ourrh's gravity had attracted me when I had reached a certain smallness, and when I came to Earth—or, rather, came to Ourrh—on the planet, I was no larger, in relation to the Mandarins, than a young poplar is in relation to us.

My fall, whose location had been anticipated, had been softened by scientific means. Agathos, who was something like the director of a medical school, had obtained authorization from the "Ultimate Minister" to study me. He had constructed a light building around my body, and had immediately set out to find a means of arresting my diminution.

As chance would have it, he had succeeded in doing that at the point at which I had the stature of a lanky but thin Mandarin—for I had had nothing to eat for a long time, and Agathos had been obliged to nourish me by injection. Once my reduction was halted, I had been transported to Agathos's own house, and it was there, thanks to the care of the director and his assistants, that I had just recovered consciousness.

Had human eyes ever opened on such unexpected visions?

II. The Tuft, and Other Curiosities No Less Admirable

Pons, you must not be annoyed because someone else succeeded in that fixation. The Mandarins' science is much superior to ours. I haven't the slightest knowledge of chemistry, as you know; I would not have been able to remember the formula that permitted old Agathos to bring about a halt in my strange flight through the microcosms. Thanks to an expedient that I shall explain in due course, however, that formula will, *I hope*, succeeded in reaching you.

Agathos, meanwhile, continued his narration—and every time my mind posed a question or failed to understand, Agathos, having perceived it, answered me or clarified the issue by the sole medium of the thought-transmitter. An ineffable dialogue!

That day, he did not question me much, and left me to think for a while about what he had told me and what I had deduced therefrom.

I recalled something that Leibniz once said to Bernouilli,[39] which you had quoted to me: "Personally, I do not hesitate to suggest that there are animals in the universe that are as much greater in size than our animals as ours are relative to

---

[39] Gottfried Leibniz (1646-1716) and Johann Bernoulli (1667-1748) entered into a long correspondence in the 1690s, most of which was preserved for posterity; it was sometimes argumentative but mostly supportive, both men being anti-Newtonians. Bernoulli gave his assent to the remark quoted above, which dates from August 1698, and added his own conviction that: "there is no corpuscle which is not a sort of world in an infinity of creations." Although Voltaire was not an admirer of Leibniz's *Theodicy*—as proven by the scathing characterization of Dr. Pangloss in *Candide*—it is not improbable that he found his inspiration for the central hypothesis of *Micromégas* in the passage that Renard reproduces here.

the animalcules that have been discovered by virtue of the microscope, for nature knows no bounds. Reciprocally, it might be, and perhaps must be, that there are within tiny grains of dust, within the smallest atoms, worlds that are not inferior to ours in beauty and variety."

While I was lethargic, therefore, I had doubtless passed unknowingly through the world of known microbes, without ceasing to diminish continuously, and I had arrived in a world of microbes even tinier, for which the former were so vast that the latter did not perceive them. And these unknown microbes, these microbes' microbes, resembled men! I wondered then, fearfully, what creatures—what series of worlds, each vaster than the next—might populate our infinite largeness. I shivered in fear, with sacred terror, as I looked at the innumerable minuscule dust-particles that were moving harmoniously in the beautiful violet beams of the Lilliputian sun. And I thought of you, Pons! Of you and my Olga, who might perhaps be there, right next to me, although I was so very distant from you, in respect of my dimensions—yes, very far away, even further away than the Orion nebula is from the human inhabitants of Earth!

What were my dimensions! By what figure would you have evaluated them? By what fantastic decimal? How many thousandths of thousandths of microns separated my head from my feet?

Among the Mandarins, however, I was like a man among men, and that vertiginously microscopic room was spacious. The red chemise—or, to put it better, the chemise that *seemed* red to me in that violet light—in which I was dressed, had been tailored from a fabric of the most remarkable delicacy.

My meditation must, I suppose, have seemed respectable, for my host and his assistants, so far as I could see, were observing a profound silence. Understand by that not only that their mouths remained mute, but that their tufts remained immobile. That was what I thought at the beginning of my sojourn among the Mandarins, not knowing then that the language of the tuft did not require any movement of the organ—

that the Mandarins understood one another, by virtue of it, by means of a sort of *radiopathy*, and only oscillated the fleshy chrysanthemum in order to orientate it, or to emphasize their radiated discourse with analogous expressions and assorted gestures.

Later, I discovered that there were Mandarins who misused these unnecessary grimaces. Others laughed at their ridiculousness, but they found it impossible to correct themselves. They reminded me of President Monempoix and his orgy of gesticulations, appropriate to bad orators who give the impression that they are undertaking an apprenticeship in optical telegraphy. Agathos, Kalos and the two green men were not like that at all. And I became increasingly fond of all four of them as time went by, for I had always thought that someone who gesticulates and grimaces can scarcely talk and cannot write at all, given that one cannot send winks, sniffs, pouts or any other pantomimes by letter. I don't have the honor of knowing anyone who is a member of the Academy, but I'm quite convinced that all those gentlemen are as cool and distinguished as Agathos, Kalos and even the two green men were.

At an invisible signal presumably given to them by their master, the servant couple rapidly attended to my needs. When that was done, in the presence of Agathos and Kalos, I found myself freshly-shaved, washed and groomed, with my hair cut like Jeanne d'Arc's, by means of instruments and accessories that I shall describe in an appendix, if God permits. And there I was, costumed like a Mandarin, with a very becoming Russian blouse in an exquisite shade of pink, and a Scottish kilt with a hint of a Greek fustanella about it. It was, I think, made of silk cloth, and the blouse of surah. On my bare feet were Oriental slippers, made of some unknown fabric as supple and precious as Russian leather impregnated with *crème Simon*.

Seeing me dressed in this fashion, Agathos and Kalos put on the first smile I had seen on their thin lips, and did something that astonished me at the time. Each of them extended his left foot, launched his slipper into the air, and caught it very skillfully with the same foot. Such is the Mandarins' salute; they know nothing of hats, because of the tuft. To put on a cap, for them, would be to go abroad with a gag over one's mouth and opaque spectacles before one's eyes. So, instead of baring the head, as we do, they bare a foot. It's logical. Have you ever considered the hypothesis of an extraterrestrial being—a Martian, if you like—constructed monstrously, like some mollusk or lump of coal, confronted by a gentleman who salutes with his hat? Oh, how the mollusk, or the lump of coal, would laugh to see that! It's like a chair, an armchair. No, but have you ever thought about what a chair or an armchair would be like, designed for the use of creatures made like a starfish, a conger eel, a cricket, a grasshopper or a cockatoo? Personally, I had never thought about it—but since I've voyaged *tra los hombres*,[40] lots of new ideas have occurred to me.

Chairs the Mandarins have, because they're human in most respects. Agathos sat me down in a veritably delightful seat, adjustable to the dimensions of the user. Then, putting the thought-transmitter to my head again, he held forth along the following lines in that "fluidic" language.[41]

"You're presentable now, my good friend; we shall therefore be able to introduce you into society and offer you the compliments of Ourrh. Our wife is very desirous of making your acquaintance—but before I introduce you to her, it is

---

[40] The "tra" in this Spanish phrase is ambiguous, but is here used as a contraction of *ultra* [beyond].

[41] As all the dialogue between Fléchambeau and the Mandarins consists of thoughts rather than spoken words, a case could be made for rendering it all in italics, or all in quotation marks (Renard, following different orthographic conventions, uses dashes). It seemed to me, however, to be more appropriate to render Fléchambeau's transmissions in italics while putting the Mandarins' transmissions into quotation marks, so as to emphasize that what is unusual to the former is quite normal to the latter.

indispensable that you know certain things, and that we take certain precautions. You are not organized exactly as we are; you have only ten fingers and are denuded of a tuft.

"Now, it is highly desirable that you do not become a phenomenal figure. That would subject you to many unpleasant experiences and might perhaps expose you to dangers—to which I shall return.

"Although I was able, thanks to the Ultimate Minister, to screen you almost immediately from the curiosity of my fellow citizens, your ten fingers did not escape their notice. It is unnecessary for us to be unduly upset about it. There are unfortunates among us who are afflicted with that infirmity from birth, and it is a sufficiently ordinary anomaly not to provoke anything but compassion mingled with slight disgust, without there being any question of amazement, horror or—above all—*malicious curiosity*.

"The absence from your cranium of the tuft that is the instrument of our primary sense is another thing entirely. To be sure, poor Mandarins who bear useless tufts on their heads—with which they can neither perceive anything nor express anything—are not unknown on Ourrh, some malformation, malady or accident having deprived them of the sense that you do not possess, in the same way that some among us lose their sight or sense of smell, become deaf or mute. It was for their usage, I might add, that the thought-transmitter was invented that I am using at this moment to converse with you."

Pardon me, I thought, *but doesn't this transmitter also render signal service in conversations between foreigners—people whose languages are different?*

"That doesn't exist among us," Agathos' train of thought continued. "Our tufts transmit pure ideas from one individual to one or several others, without any visual, sonic or other intermediary—exactly as this transmitter does. Pure ideas and, of course, sentiments—everything, in sum, that constitutes mind and soul. I understand that, in respect of the world from which you come, it is the noise of the mouth and the resonance of the ear that are employed for communication. You really must permit me to study that singular mode of liaison…but let's return, if you please, to more pressing matters.

"I was saying that some among us are, if these terms are acceptable, 'blind' or 'deaf' in their tufts—but take note: they still have a tuft. It might be an ineffective tuft, a paralyzed tuft, or even a tuft reduced to its stalk, but at the end of the day, however bad the state of the tuft is, some vestige of it still remains. But you have none at all! From my viewpoint, it is as if your face had no trace of eyes, or not the slightest projection of a nose, or no more mouth than I have in the palm of my hand!

"You cannot go out like that. So this, is what Kalos and I have decided. No one—outside the four of us, who are absolutely discreet—knows that you have no tuft. You need have no fear on that subject. I was the first to notice it and I immediately enveloped the top of your head in bed-sheets, with the excuse that they served as compresses. We shall, therefore, make you a false tuft, analogous to those which are sold to unfortunate Mandarins who have lost theirs in some catastrophe, or have been subjected to a necessary amputation, and who, by virtue of an entirely forgivable coquetry, fit an artificial tuft on to what remains of their stalk.

"This is the object in question. It is a clear blue, matching your eyes, as nature demands. It is here, under my own roof, that this appendage has been specially designed for your use—which is to say, elongated by a cleverly counterfeited stalk that has a sucker at its base. You will be given a small tonsure, so that its adherence will be possible; it will hold fast by itself, I promise you.

"Thus, you will pass for a cripple sensitive to appearances, and not for a truly unacceptable monster. You'll be received everywhere. Good care will be taken of you—but you will have to be careful not to leave the thought-transmitter in the house; without it, from your viewpoint, it will be as if Ourrh were a planet of deaf mutes."

I would have liked to interrogate Agathos about the extent of that sixth sense, and penetrate more deeply into the mystery of the tuft, for it had not escaped my notice that the tuft possessed a very remarkable perceptive acuity. How did it perceive? To what quality of matter was it sensitive? Was I familiar with that quality, as I was, for example, with light, sound, taste and odor? Or was I aware of it indirectly, like electricity or radiant energy?

I subsequently learned that I was not aware of it at all, that I could never be aware of it, and that, with respect to that quality for which I had no sense, I was like a man born blind to whom no one had ever mentioned light. And like that man born blind, without eyes, who could only detect by touch that certain creatures have eyes—inexplicable organs reacting to inexplicable influences—I would always be reduced, in confrontation with that sixth organ, that sixth sense and that sixth aspect of the external world, to the meager nourishment of supposition.

But Agathos was very eager to introduce me to the person that I named, "terrestrially" as Madame Agathos—and they had to set about naturalizing me completely as a Mandarin, by placing the fake tuft as required. During that operation, I observed an alteration in the violet light, but not that it was darkening as dusk approached. One might have thought that a yellow light was mingling with it, blending with it.

Was I hallucinating? Objects and people now had two shadows instead of one—and the yellow light was gradually overwhelming the violet light.

What's happening? I asked Agathos, through the medium of the thought-transmitter.

"What?" he replied. "Does that surprise you? It's the violet sun setting and the yellow sun rising?"

In opposition to one another? I thought, nonplussed.

"Necessarily. Every day brings that alternation."

But what about night? When does it get dark? Never?

"I'll explain later," said Agathos, benevolently.

The artificial tuft did not inconvenience me at all. Moreover, it was a typical Mandarin gesture to lift my hand to it from time to time—which gave me the opportunity to verify its adherence, while appearing to make a familiar and instinctive gesture.

We went into another room then, which had nothing of the laboratory about it. It was strangely luxurious. The atmosphere was delicately perfumed. The walls, so far as I could see when I first entered, presented variously-composed surfaces, reminiscent of series of large charm-less samples: samples of cement or concrete, spattered with filings. Hemispherical objects were hanging from the ceiling on ropes, their flat surfaces on top and their round ones directed downwards. These pendants seemed to be incrusted with a profusion of metallic particles, arranged without any harmonization of their colors or linear design. The sight was barbaric and inopportune, even painful and incomprehensible.

The two green men had not followed us. Only Agathos and Kalos kept me company. I never ceased looking around me, and I observed that everything in that eccentric drawing-room was arranged in threes: the pendants, the coatings on the walls, and the objects distributed on the shelves and the refrigerator. Some of the latter were statuettes, while some were bodies without apparent signification, but whose surfaces, curves, protrusions and angles delighted the eyes with their graceful perfection; others, in compensation, were merely little blocks of unknown substances, polished or delicately striated, with no more elegance than if they had been representations of some new kind of potato or a pebble smoothed by the waves. But everything, everywhere, was arranged in threes!

Don't the Chinese arrange everything in fives? I thought. *Besides, three is a submultiple of twelve, and the Mandarins, who must have started out by counting on their fingers like everyone else, will certainly have adopted the duodecimal system—a consideration that has always made me suspect that the English, at one time, also possessed twelve fingers...*

I was about to ask Agathos a thousand questions about that, and about the pendants, when a trapdoor opened to reveal two more Mandarins.

Like us, they were blithely dolled up in kilts and blouses. They wore their hair a little shorter than Kalos—whose own hair was not as long as Agathos' or mine. From their bare arms, their cleavages and their harmonious legs, however, I deduced that they were two Mandarines.

Agathos and Kalos each kicked off their right slipper— the appropriate one for greeting women. Seized by a fit of zeal, I tried to do likewise—but I had never been any good at playing cup-and-ball, especially with my feet, and I missed my shot, laughing in confusion.

Madame Agathos and her friend, who were both blonde, each caused their tufts—one of which was the color of coral, the other of amethyst—to describe a joyful and quivering conical revolution. Madame Agathos was preceded by an imposing nose. The other, whom I named Mademoiselle Kala, must have been considered ugly in the land of the Mandarins, for her nose, cast from the same mold as Olga's, was small, dainty and, in my opinion, rather pretty.

Each of them was holding, and never ceased caressing, a small batch of those things whose shapeless appearance and substantial delicacy I had noticed—from which I concluded that there was a tactile sensuality on Ourrh, and an artistry of touch.

Although I was startled by the fact that the two ladies had emerged from a trap-door—a banal entrance that was, however, the last word in originality there—I did my best to deploy a measure of seduction. Following the example of the handsome Kalos--that splendid Cherub, that Russo-Scottish Raphael Sanzio—I showed off the pleats of my blouse and inflated the folds of my kilt: a blouse and kilt that had changed color in the yellow light. It's gallant to talk to women about fabrics, so I said to Agathos' wife, through the medium of the thought-transmitter: *Madame, I come from a country that has only one sun at its disposal. How difficult it must be, here, to find materials that sometimes support violet daylight and sometimes saffron daylight!*

"Oh," she said, with a slightly disdainful joy, "it doesn't take long to change clothes. Dual-purpose dresses are rare!"

I could understand why the two ladies were not wearing any make-up.

Color... I began.

"Oh, color, Monsieur, is nothing. But *chiendent* is..."[42]

I understood that Madame Agathos wanted to talk about the charm that arose from the tuft sense: the charm of the quality that I was prohibited from perceiving, and which I designated by the feminine noun *dounn*, along with the sense that perceive it, in accordance with the rudimentary language that the worthy Agathos was obliged to jabber in order to keep me company, like a scientist who has taken it into his head to educate a monkey. Except that it as the other way round, since the Mandarins only have rigid throats and clumsy tongues, good for nothing but humming, burping and yapping—which Mandarins perforce did no abundantly that sometimes, from a distance, the noise of their receptions somehow reminded me of Paris...perhaps of a visit to the Jardin des Plantes.[43]

---

[42] *Chiendent* [literally dog's-tooth] has a double meaning in French, referring both to couch-grass and, metaphorically, to a snag or hitch. There is also a weaving-pattern known in English as houndstooth, once employed in fashionable sports jackets.

[43] The Jardin des Plantes in Paris was not merely a botanical garden but a zoo—but that is only marginally relevant to the malicious sarcasm of the observation.

III. Look Out! Here Comes the Enemy!

Please excuse the incoherence of my narrative, Pons. It's just that I can't recall with any exactitude a sequence of events that happened some 65 years ago, if I reckon in Mandarin years. That scene in Madame Agathos' drawing-room has now retreated into the depths of my memory, since I've lived an entire lifetime since then, within a few months—a life full of days. My exile made it appear to me even longer than it was.

I have a clear enough memory of several things that made an impression on me, though, and I can still see Madame Agathos and her friend Mademoiselle Kala gently stroking their playthings, as one does with soft-furred little cats or smooth-haired lap-dogs. Agathos and Kalos were also caressing some on them. I didn't imitate them, for fear of drawing attention to my hands, in case anyone might be unpleasantly shocked by the fact that they only had ten fingers.

The temperature was noticeably cooler, the yellow sun radiating less heat than the violet one—the result of which is that on Ourrh, a midsummer day is regularly succeeded by a late autumn one. The Mandarins know no other summer and winter than that succession; they have only two seasons, which are daily. I was amazed by it, and I went to the window to see the effect of the yellow light on the external world. Kala followed me, moistening her tuft with the aid of a very pretty vapor-spray that she wore suspended around her neck. Only having darted a raid glance, for politeness' sake, at the almond-green sky and the street, whose spherical architecture seemed rebarbative to me, I breathed in the Mandarine's perfume delightedly, and divined that I would soon get used to the singularity of the twelve digits and the tuft.

Kala's arms and legs were adorned with a few jewels, remarkable more for their form than for their brilliance or their color. The upper part of each of her charming slippers was embellished with a little dial set with jewels. One of them, she told me via the transmitter, was what we call a chronometer. She took off her slipper so that I could get a better view of it. There was a superlatively black granule inside it, which never ceased rolling around the dial. The latter was graduated in a manner that would have seemed fantastic to you. I asked the beautiful Kala how the foot-ornament was wound, for I could not see any winder. She was astonished by the question. "But it isn't wound!" she said, finally. "It's time itself that makes watches go."

That confused me. The Mandarins had "isolated" time, then! They had located it, captured it! They owned it, like space! Like water, fire and air! And they made it turn this watch as water turns a mill-wheel. The granule rotated under the pressure of time, as a magnetic needle obeys the attraction of the north!

What about that one? I enquired, pointing to the dial on the other slipper.

Alas, Pons, although old Agathos tried to explain it to me, I was never able to comprehend—even in 65 years—what that other indicator-jewel divided and measured. To me, that sort of apparatus was always an enigma wrapped up in a mystery!

The green men reappeared. They brought trays loaded with bowls, in which could be seen, as in a confectioner's showcases, twenty sorts of bonbons, sugared almonds, pralines, *petits fours* and chocolate drops. These slender sweets were proportional to Mandarine mouths. Each of us took one—only one, carefully selected—and swallowed it. That was the meal, which I had taken at first for less than an appetizer.

Scarcely had I ingurgitated the little ovule, whose chocolate color had seemed promising to me, than I felt fully satiated. Meanwhile, the fondant had tasted of foul petrol; I had to conceal the fact in order not to invite questions. My Mandarins and Mandarines gave no sign of gastronomic pleasure as they ate their bonbons. They were taking chemical nourishment, and that was all there was to it.

The green men immediately passed around various powders, which we all sampled, but I must confess that, for my modest nose, the majority of those sophisticated snuffs had the same scent.

Why is it that those men are green? I asked Agathos.

He answered, as I had expected, that there were green Mandarins, who made excellent servants for white Mandarins, save for their innate laziness, which could only be corrected with a few blows with a stick—an extremity to which no one ever resorted unless it was to their own advantage. "But the green Mandarins," he added—still, of course, via the transmitter—"are primarily prized for the odor they give off. Their skin smells very nice, especially when it is moist, and according to the little that you have already told me about your world, or what I have presumed, it seems to me that you might compare our 'greens' to the amiable servants who, having accomplished their tasks, constantly play the violin or some other musical instrument. Our own music is that of perfumes."

With regard to that, in order that they might sweat and become odiferous to an appropriate degree, he politely asked the two greens—he thought "a green" as we would say "a black"—to perform their ethnic dance for us. They launched into frenetic entrechats at an ever-increasing pace, as if they were getting drunk on the very effluvia of their artistic sudation. Personally, I opened my eyes and nostrils wide without seeing anything more than a green tribal dance and without respiring, by way of music, anything but a few rather rancid odors.

I said that. I said "rancid" by transmitter to Agathos.

Agathos started. "Keep that to yourself," he told me. "You'd immediately become a lost cause in the public mind! Don't you know that everyone treats as imbeciles those who do not smell as one smells oneself?"

Rather discomfited, I wanted to change the subject, and I was about to ask Agathos about the particularity that arranged everything in threes, like Cadet Roussel,[44] when the arrival of a visitor was announced.

At this news, Agathos' tuft darkened and retreated. "Look out!" he instructed me. "Be wary. The Mandarin you are about to see is a nasty fellow. He's the director of the Museum. A 'luminary,' but an eccentric. I've been expecting him. You interest him prodigiously, and if I were not so well in with the Ultimate Minister, it would be him who would have taken possession of you—unfortunately for you. Be careful, I tell you—and do your best to conceal the fact that your tuft is merely a vain ornament. Play the role of a cripple who has lost his *dounn* accidentally. Or, rather, no! Pretend to be someone whose tuft has been blind and deaf since birth."

He had scarcely finished when the director of the Museum came in.

It is a characteristic of races—and even more so of species—not our own, that we are led to think that the individuals of which they are composed are identical to one another. Thus, every European, and every Frenchman, appears at first sight to possess an indubitable personality with bursts forth in his features. We experience some difficulty in recognizing a particular Chinese among other Chinese, or differentiating between Senegalese individuals. As for our brothers, the animals, although there are some among them that are exceptions to the rule, the majority, in compensation, exemplify it absolutely;

---

[44] Guillaume Roussel, or Rousselle (1743-1807) was a bailiff in Auxerre during the Revolution of 1789. Gaspard de Chenu wrote a malicious comic song about him, fitted to a popular tune whose original words were effectively replaced when the new ones were exported to the rest of France by soldiers serving in the post-Revolutionary wars. The first verse begins with the assertion that the bailiff has three houses, and the others follow the same pattern, mingling items of which a man might well possess three (hats, dogs, etc.) with absurd examples (shoes, eyes, etc.)

very few of us can distinguish one carp, weasel, partridge, wasp or grass snake from another.

Now, the Mandarins, so far as the face is concerned, are quite different from terrestrial humans, not only because of their noses, which are very pronounced, and their mouths, eyes and ears, which are derisory, but also because of the lack of expression I mentioned above. It follows that I always had a tendency to confuse one with another—with the exception, of course, of my friends…or my enemies.

Well, straight away, at first glance, I was certain that I would always be able to identify the director of the Museum anywhere, even in the midst of a multitude of Mandarins—let's say 100,000. And even if Agathos had not warned me, even knowing that I was dealing with a foreigner, I would have thought: *Here's a nasty sort.*

Will it surprise you now that the frightful director of the Museum will henceforth bear the name of Kakos?[45]

An old greybeard, he came forward obliquely, leaving his curt greeting incomplete. His twelve fingers were perpetually agitated, moved by a desire to grip or grab…what? Or whom? There was no way of knowing, but it made everyone recoil. And what eyes! What a nose! What a mouth! What a bespectacled tuft! A graying, unhealthy, weeping tuft. Oh, what a thrice-damned villain!"

He latched on to me unhesitatingly. He set out to make a circular tour of inspection, taking short steps.

Hey! I thought. *Watch out for my tuft!* And I began turning round, holding my head up, so as always to be facing the

---

[45] *Kakos* means "evil," routinely being opposed to *Agathos*—or oxymoronically combined with it, as in the sadly underemployed English word agathokakological. The orthographical similarity of Kakos and Kalos is unfortunate, from the viewpoint of the reader (and generates several misprints in the Laffont text) but the Greek language is more to blame than Renard.

investigative tuft and eyes, as the Moon does with the Earth, a little game as mocking as it is astronomical.

This Kakos was a great scientist; he had founded a new scientific theory; it explained the universe, using *dounn* as a basis, much as Einstein had based his celebrated theory on light. He was as knowledgeable as anyone in *dounnology*, and with regard to tufts. He had, moreover, made a fortune in the manufacture of what I have improperly named "spectacles" for tufts—and if I had known that, I would certainly have noticed that the blackguard was looking at me scornfully, as a shoemaker looks at a man without legs.

Perceiving that he would not be able to learn anything at present regarding my tuft, Kakos resigned himself to it, chose a seat, and joined in the conversation—but not without my sensing covetousness and avidity radiating in my direction with every passing moment. Everyone treated him very pleasantly. I don't know how long he would have prolonged his visit if the five people who were able to do so had not suddenly struck the attitude of those whose ears have just heard an alarm bell ring.

I had not heard anything. Kakos, however, immediately took his leave, as did the beautiful Kala.

When they had gone, Agathos said to me: "A bad business! He knows, or certainly suspects, that you have no tuft. Vigilance, my friend, vigilance! He wanted to talk to you; I told him that you were still too weak. But what does the future hold in reserve for us with an animal like that?"

He didn't see anything, I replied. *I didn't turn my back on him—which is what civility requires, thus ensuring that he couldn't take umbrage at my rotation.*

"What an error! Why do you think that it is uncivil to turn your back to someone?"

I bit my lip, Indeed, a Mandain's back has nothing disdainful about it, since the tuft ennobles it and establishes it as a front.

But what was that warning, I asked, *which caused Kala and Kako to leave?*

"It's the national broadcaster giving warning of artificial rain, in order that everyone has time to go indoors. We got rid of natural rain centuries ago, because it was much too capricious. Every few days, a short while after the dawn of the yellow sun, the official services make it rain for an hour. It's useful. Immediately afterwards, crews of road-sweepers clean the city; after that, night is switched on…"

Eh? Night is switched on? What does that mean?

Agathos wore a sort of smile. "Come," he said.

Pushed on to the balcony, I discovered a large city with innumerable terraces—but not a patch of greenery between the houses. On the other hand, the proximity of the horizon caused me a certain strange anguish. The planet Ourrh was obviously very mediocre in volume relative to the size of its inhabitants, the Mandarins.

"Look at those large towers," Agathos said, "erected at intervals, extending as far as the eye can see. It's from the tops of those towers that the pluviogenic prisms and the darkness-generators do their work. Look, take note of those glints: the prisms are being reorientated so as to decompose the atmosphere."

A short while afterwards clouds formed. The streets were animated by running figures, then cleared completely.

And the rain fell.

We went back into the drawing-room. These novelties had chased the obsessive thought of Kakos out of my head. Turing to Madame Agathos, I asked: *Have you really never been caught in the rain?*

"Artificial rain sometimes takes functionaries like us by surprise during our inspections of the planet," said Agathos.

That's fortunate for the umbrella-merchants! I hazarded, rather slyly.

As he was unable to obtain a very clear idea of an umbrella, I sketched its form in the palm of my hand with the tip of my finger—for there as nothing around us that resembled paper, or a pencil.

Agathos abruptly dropped the transmitter. I thought that he had despaired of understanding, and persisted with my explanation by extending a sheet of cloth over my head, disposing it by means of my raised arm.

Madame Agathos uttered a piercing scream. She pointed at my shadow on the wall, which a feeble ray of the darkening sunlight had just projected there, and which looked like the ludicrous silhouette of a giant mushroom.

I looked at the three of them, one after another, disconcerted as I was. Their pallor filled me with amazement.

Agathis, having picked up the transmitter, said to me with inexpressible anxiety: "You must never, never make allusion to the thing that you have sketched in the palm of our hand. Later, when I've got over my fright...later, after the darkness, I'll reveal to you the frightful, terrible secret that weighs upon Mandarinity. For the moment, please, let's not say any more about it! Let's go back on to the balcony instead; I need a little air after what you've just done to me. In addition, you can't fail to be interested in the switching on of the night, since I read in your mind that it's entirely new to you."

The rain had ceased. Strange machines were sweeping the streets. Others followed them, which were nothing but automatic spray machines; they produced a mist that flowed in all directions, hissing. It drifted so high that we received our share of it in the currency of crushing cold and chemical odor.

"Sterilization," Agathos told me, gravely.

I did not attach much importance to the word at the time, for, in the wake of the incited rain, a rainbow appeared on the backcloth of the bright clouds, and I admired the gradation of its colors, entirely different from our old solar spectrum.

Agathos understood my wonderment, and seemed to think it puerile. Replying privately to my mental questions, he told me that the violet sun and the yellow sun made up a double star. They orbited around one another. The planet Ourrh was maintained between them, immovably, except that it rotated on its axis, thus producing the violet daylight and the yellow daylight. I recalled the double stars of our firmament, thinking especially of Gamma Andromedae, whose couple is formed by one orange sun and one emerald sun, and then of Beta Cygni, an association of one golden sun and one of sapphire. Decidedly, everything was reproduced within the infinitely small.

"Pay attention!" said Agathos. "The national broadcaster is about to go into action. In a few moments, night will begin."

Indeed, the numerous towers, like so many lighthouses, began to project dark beams. They were shadow-beams. Under their influence, an unimaginable dusk gradually darkened. Night fell by degrees.

Fiat nox! I murmured.

Then I made use of the transmitter: *I confess, Agathos, that I don't really understand. Among us it's necessary to submit to the darkness of night, against which we struggle as best we can, with the aid of lamps—but on Earth, night is considered as a hindrance, a petty scourge…*

"There are caverns, mines and the insides of houses," Agathos replied, "that are similarly shadowed, which have informed us of the existence of obscurity and the benefits it provides—so we have sought means of spreading it everywhere, completely, at fixed times. Every two days, while our cooler sun lights the world—for we delight in warmth—a few hours of darkness are excellent for sleeping and for the health. But I sense that I'm only contriving a partial explanation. Don't think that the darkness is limited to blinding us with respect to our eyes, and, in consequence, providing relief for sight; that would be very little for us. The darkness also blinds our tuft, and blocks our sense of the *dounn*. Yes, there are a thousand things in darkness of which you have no inkling—and, reciprocally, in light…"

As he said this, a great silence descended on the city; the last remaining light was stifled by the dark tide. Before the night became as dark as a subterranean tunnel, I saw Agathos take out of his blouse what I shall call, without much reason, a "lighter" or a "pocket torch." He pressed a switch. A continuous grating sound became audible.

We were surrounded by the deepest darkness. Agathos took my arm and guided me back inside. He was not in darkness himself; his lamp-substitute permitted him to perceive things by means of his tuft sense, the *dounn*. The torch was not a lamp for the eyes, providing visible light for sight; among the Mandarins, the sense of sight is inferior to the sense of *dounn*, and luminous lamps are only for the use of those who have lost their *dounn*. Agathos promised to buy me one from the orthopedist.

You never see the stars, then, I said, *since your night, being so dense, hides them from your eyes as from your tufts*.

"Our tufts distinguish them quite clearly in broad daylight. Get out of the habit, my good friend, of always attributing to our tufts that which is appropriate to the eye. There's no relation between them! There are certain stars that 'shine,' if I might put it that way, for our tufts far more brightly than our two suns."

But I shall never see your stars! I replied. *That entirely new sky, which must be resplendent with an infinity of constellations—what is it like?*

"I'll give you a description," said Agathos, letting a certain compassionate sadness show through. "Besides which, at a particular point in time, when the violet sun is subject to a crisis, two or three stars are clearly visible to the eyes, as the yellow sun is rising and the violet one is setting. Having said that, we must get some sleep. Come…"

He led me from room to room in the dark, until we reached something that I judged to be a very satisfactory bed.

"Good night," he said to me. "Sleep well. When you wake up, you'll accompany me to a ball hosted by my friend, the director of the College of Judges. Afterwards, we'll visit a *radiure* exhibition; then I'll show you a few of our planet's sights. Good night. And don't dream about Kakos!"

I heard him fill his huge nose with an abundant powder, and sprinkle his old tuft with a vaporous pinch. I also heard him extinguish that *dounnic* lamp which only shone—so to speak—for him…

And you, I transmitted to him, merrily, *don't dream about umbrellas...or mushrooms!*

His teeth—the tiny atrophied teeth of a pill-eater—chattered, making a macabre sound. "Don't talk about that now! Especially in the dark...especially in the dark..."

Pardon me, I said. *There was once a tribe on Earth whose members, for reasons of decorum and superstition, never pronounced the name of Death. You remind me of them.*

"The name of Death..." said Agathos, in the darkness. "That's it. That's exactly it."

Sapristi! I thought, as I went to sleep. *Kakos...mushrooms...Ourrh isn't a place of complete peace! When I think, however, that I'm on a microscope slide, in the oh-so-tranquil laboratory of dear old Pons...! After all, though, Saint-Jean-de-Nèves, and Europe, and the Earth, and the Universe visible from Earth, are doubtless nothing but a miasma, perhaps a microbe among millions of others, in the veins of some gigantic creature, whose ephemeral fever maintains, through* our *centuries, that which we call* the eternal motion of the stars, *the ardor of our Sun and the life of generations...*

IV. See How They Dance...

Mandarin balls are always held in the light of the yellow sun, which is more flattering than the violet clarity—the word "clarity" being construed here in the sense of "light" and "radiation," since the Mandarins attach less importance to the purity of colors than to the perfection of the mysterious charm that they perceive with their tufts.

The yellow sun was, therefore, already very high over the horizon when the industrial darkness dissipated.

Agathos, his wife, the handsome Kalos and I climbed into an automobile that resembled a large bubble; to be exact, it consisted of two spheres one within the other; the external sphere rolled along the ground while the internal sphere maintained its orientation, by means of pivots, cardan joints or gyroscopes—how do I know? It was very comfortable inside.

We had dressed for the occasion in blouses and kilts of a finesse and softness so pleasant that I experienced a sort of modesty in not being able to take the pleasure of smoothing the folds of my garments in public. Agathos knew that, and was amused by it.

Quick to talk about a different subject, I asked him what the College of Judges was whose director would shortly be putting on a dance for us.

Agathos seemed troubled by what such a question allowed him to infer about terrestrial mores and the mediocrity of my intelligence.

"What!" he said. "I suppose that there are on your planet, as there are here, citizens that it is necessary to punish, and others whose job it is to apply the law! You see me stupefied as I read that which your memory recalls! What! You don't take the trouble either to select or to train magistrates, those men who, to do their job well, must be infallible gods! Your country does not possess a College where, for long years, judges are informed of all the complications of human nature?

There are no courses on the passions, manias, follies? On the influence of maladies? On the value of witnesses? But that's abominable! And what else? What's that you're trying to hide from me? No! Crimes are judged by various individuals selected at random? Oh!"

Agathos buried his head in his hands. He covered his tuft with a sash, as a sign of affliction—and I was ashamed to see that superior brother weep because of what men on Earth do.

Madame Agathos and Kalos undertook to console him, and put their bare arms around him. They were wearing jewels, which clinked—in particular, golden sheaths enriched with jewels which, fixed around the stalks of their tufts, might as easily be called bracelets as rings or necklaces.

My worthy old Agathos dried his eyes, his spectacles and his tuft-glasses. It was high time that he reconciled himself to our barbarism, for the bubble-automobile stopped. We had arrived.

The reception was in full swing. People were dancing furiously, amid a faint murmur that was not of conversation but of humming and interjections. Complicated perfumes succeeded one another. That almost total silence, above such a rhythmic and steady tumult, surprised me.

Instinctively, given the lack of music I looked for some master of the ball beating the measure to which everyone was so meekly submissive. Disappointment awaited me in that respect. In a corner of the room, green men were indulging in a thousand contortions as they manipulated devices that exhaled the most diverse odors. With rhythmic gestures—and without refraining from whimsies like juggling with corks, twirling long-necked flasks or cutting clownish capers on seats or one another's shoulders—these strange epileptic musicians were uncovering fuming pans, and corking and uncorking bottles or censers. One of them, who never ceased whipping his chair, as if it were trotting beneath him as reluctantly as some worn-out old nag, was running his 12 green fingers over the keyboard of an organ whose pipes contained odiferous substances.

It wasn't worth the trouble, I thought, *of making such a voyage to see this! In the 18th century Père Castel invented the ocular harpsichord and Abbé Poncelet fabricated his savory harpsichord—and our literature has been infested with such fancies ever since. It's true, though, that none of these paradoxical spinets has ever served to make anyone dance!*[46]

Agathos had not left my side. An old man attached to the bad habits of his youth, he bitterly deplored the odorous facetiousness of green jazz. "In my time," he sighed, "such savagery would not have been tolerated. The music of perfumes was fragrant and floral, as simple as nature—and so distinguished! Just breathe that *cacosmia!*"

Indeed, by means of a little concentration, I observed that the most vulgar odors were mingling with the sweetest. At times, effluvia of damp forests or enchanted gardens were cut through by the vile reek of culinary or pharmaceutical wastes. I can't remember without curiosity a certain inconceivably bold accord, in which roses, carnations, garlic, mutton stew, iodine and burning paper were in combat. But I was not equipped to grasp all the nuances of such an exhalation at close range; as for the rhythm, it escaped me completely.

On the other hand, what seemed to me fascinating was that I inferred from Agathos' comments on "modern" perfume music that odorous art had always been a representative art on

---

[46] The Jesuit mathematician Louis-Bertrand Castel (1688-1757), who earned a passing mention in *Micromégas* by virtue of his opposition to the Newtonian theory of gravity, published a proposal for a *clavecin oculaire* [optical harpsichord] in 1725 because he believed that "color music" was the lost language of Paradise, and might bring men closer to God. Various models were constructed by enthusiasts. Abbé Jean-Victor Poncelet (1788-1867) was not entirely serious when he offered his alternative proposal for a version appealing to the sense of taste (in the 19th century rather than the 18th), although there has never been any shortage of people who believe that good taste has brought them closer to God.

Ourrh. Every piece of that music was comparable to a landscape, or rather a portrait. The perfumer-composers worked like our musicians and our painters at the same time.

Agathos confessed to me that a humorist perfumer had made a caricature of him in which the personality of his typical odor had been rendered in the wittiest fashion. "Nothing more farcical!" he said to me. "On respiring that charge, everyone recognized me, in spite of the generic deformations. I ought to tell you, though, that the present school is excessively 'interpretive' and that one sometimes cannot tell whether one is sniffing a dead nature or if it's a marine one. The young are so audacious! But what do you think of our dances?"

I watched the undulating assembly. All those Mandarins and Mandarines with tufts and big noses, were waltzing. Yes, a sort of Boston-waltz, although they were not dancing two by two, but three by three. That gave the whole thing a ballet-like appearance that was not to be disdained. Sometimes grouped face to face, sometimes back to back, then side by side, with their hands interlaced, they were gliding harmoniously. I understood immediately, though, by studying the movement of their bodies, that the dance was terribly difficult, and I tell you straight away, Pons that, in order to dance it, it's absolutely necessary to be an expert in the integral calculus—a difficulty that isn't one for the Mandarins, for they understand all mathematics as you understand that two and two make four. They have a feel for it, so highly developed that it is truly, for them, a seventh sense. Haven't you observed, in fact, that mathematicians conceive things in the universe that remain in the unknown to everyone else?

"Would you like to dance?" old Agathos asked me.

Thank you, my dear master. I do have a gift for dancing, but I'm also very bad at maths. I'd prefer to converse with Mademoiselle Kala, who appears to be a wallflower because her nose is too small for the canons of Mandarine beauty. Pass me the transmitter.

Mademoiselle Kala was evidently charmed by the gesture. The Boston-waltz having come to an end, I was the object of general attention, and it counted for something to be seen to be in *dounnic* conversation via transmitter with the stranger from the great infinity.

I assumed that, in spite of the smallness of her nose, Kala would not think it in bad taste for me to discuss the music of perfumes with her.

"Does the powerful odor of the Mandarins astonish you?" she asked.

No, my dear demoiselle. On Earth, we have insects named ants, for which smell is the principal sense. Some of them are blind but have, as the saying has it, a nose at the end of every finger—and I'm certain that they perceive the world with their sense of smell as well as you with your tuft or me with my eyes. Everything, for them, is translated into odors: water; living creatures; ugliness, which smells bad; and beauty, which smells good. And they deem that anything odorless does not exist.

Kala's tuft shook. She moved it as a dog moves its tail, as an act of kindness.

"Do you think I have a pretty scent this evening?" she asked. A daughter of Adam would have said, with similar simplicity: "Do I look pretty this evening?"

Oh bizarrerie of universal Creation! That young woman with the little nose, ugly to the Mandarins, was almost seductive to me—and she was trying to please me in her own way, by courtesy of the charm of emanations that she doubtless knew to be pleasant, but whose seductiveness seemed to me merely accessory rather than a genuine principle of beauty or a genuine reason for love.

I saw that she was as happy as a hunchback, neglected in spite of her lovely eyes, with whom a young and famous blind man is politely conversing.

The dancing had begun again. In spite of the twirls and the choreographic leaps, the tufts of all the dancers were fixed on me. The Mandarins, still grouped in threes, were now executing a syncopated fake mazurka.

I revealed to Kala the astonishment into which I was plunged by this mania for the number three. She blushed violently, and the transmitter only showed me a great and fearful confusion in her inner being. Puzzled and surprised, I dropped the subject, and absorbed myself in the contemplation of the silent ball. It was then that I noticed something odd.

These numerous elegant Mandarins, who represented, in some, a substantial fraction of Mandarinity, presented three clearly-characterized types to my eyes, whether they were green or white—but let us leave the greens to their subaltern role.

Three types: men, women and cherubs, of a sort intermediate between the two sexes. Some of the latter resembled ladies dressed up as boys; others had the appearance of effeminate gentlemen. Although the costumes of all the Mandarins were similarly tailored, it was not difficult to separate the other two types from the hybrid type, to which the handsome Kalos certainly belonged.

I leave you to imagine, Pons, how amazed I was when I had observed this fact—which, however, would not have surprised me at all if it had been a question of ants, for instance, or many other small terrestrial creatures. When my suppositions were confirmed by the fact that every triad of dancers was composed of a man, a woman and a cherub, I confess that my ingenuity, basing everything on Earthly things, led me to think at first that these cherubs were, among Mandarins, merely what "workers" are among ants.

At any rate, Kala did not grant me the leisure to meditate any further upon the subject. She planted the transmitter on my forehead to inform me that she was about to introduce me to the master of the house. (On Ourrh, hosts have no expectations; if one meets them, that's all right, but if one doesn't, that's all right too.)

The director of the College of Judges was a grand old man with a funereal tuft, which assumed the attitude of a weeping willow on his bald head. He was deeply saddened because, on the previous day, the Omnipotent Chamber had done away with the punishment of tuftal execution, which consisted of cutting off the tuft of the condemned criminal. For the director, that was the cause of a profound affliction. He shook every hand as if he were wearing black gloves, and said to everyone: "Where are we headed? Where are we headed?"

I let him draw away, in a state of depression. The ball was being held, however, for the occasion of the marriage of his only daughter. Kala told me that, while laughing at the misery of the old killjoy.

In talking about marriage, Kala could not restrain herself from showing a certain fire, which made her seem more beautiful in my eyes. I put my hand on hers fraternally, without thinking about the six fingers of that trembling hand, or the amethyst chrysanthemum that was swooning into her blonde hair. God is my witness, and the memory of my Olga could not be offended by it: I did not mean to animate hope in the heart of that sweet Kala, who— because of her pretty little nose—risked remaining a spinster.

Are you going to marry too, Kala? I asked her, affectionately.

She closed her eyelids. The amethyst tuft retreated into its tube. Slightly pale, Kala squeezed my hands with tremulous force…then her eyes and her tuft reappeared.

"Thank you!" she said to me, with a long disillusioned sigh. "Oh, thank you! But getting married requires three!"

I stepped backwards so abruptly that I fell backwards. My fake tuft rolled over the floor with a noise of celluloid.[47] I replaced it swiftly, hoping that no one had perceived my complete "infirmity". But someone behind me started sniggering, and I saw—not without alarm—that it was the horrid Kakos.

---

[47] One of the first uses of celluloid was making billiard balls, but the practice was abandoned once artificial plastics were developed that were not occasionally prone to explode on impact (in those days, cannons sometimes really did sound like cannons.)

V. As Maeterlinck Put it: *"A Blind Man Seeking His Treasure At the Bottom of the Sea"*[48]

"Getting married requires three!"

Everything that is unusual in the eyes of men, Pons, seems to them to be monstrous. And yet, the very multiplicity of forms of terrestrial life informs us that the immense universe, in which there are worlds very different from our own, surely includes the most inconceivable forms of matter, and creatures very different from us, whose modes of life are beyond the scope of our imagination. There are, among the suns, planets and moons of the infinitely great and the infinitely small, multitudes of living beings that have *nothing* in common with us. I know that, just as you do. And if the Mandarins gave me such an impression of monstrousness, it was less because of differences that separate us as because of resemblances that make us similar. A man who is not entirely a man surprises us much more than a totally distinct creature, acquaintance with which would nevertheless lunge us into an abyss of amazement and dreadful admiration.

Suppose, on the other hand, that one of those terrestrial organisms that multiply all alone, without the collaboration of any of its fellows, were endowed with intelligence, and tell me what it would think of the manner in which mammals reproduce. How repugnant and inferior humans would seem to that creature!

---

[48] Maurice Maeterlinck (1862-1949) was best-known as a Symbolist poet and playwright—he won the Nobel prize for literature in 1911—but his relevance to the present work, and to Renard's scientific marvel fiction in general, also extends to his quasi-sociological studies of social insects. The slightly-misrendered quote (the last word is actually *"océan"* [ocean], not *"mer"* [sea]) is from the play *Pelléas et Mélisande* (1892).

That is true. We can and ought to believe, however, that environments and worlds exist where life can only be transmitted by the common effort of a quantity of individuals of the same species, differently conformed. And after all, in creating the Mandarins, God has not created being so very original by comparison with humans. *One* more—what's that? Elsewhere, it might perhaps require a *thousand*! Moreover, the extra one or a thousand is not the great discovery. The great discovery—which does not seem to be a progressive step—lay in not confiding the care of perpetuating its race to a single unique individual. From the moment when Nature established collaboration, the number of collaborators became philosophically uninteresting. Whether there are two or whether there are a hundred, the principle remains the same, in the cold light of reason.

Except that I had not expected that novelty! And the thing had, so to speak, fallen upon me like a bombshell, with all the more brutality because I had misunderstood it and then mistakenly represented to myself not only the triple union of the Mandarins, but also the three categories into which they were divided in order to contrive a better union. My habits of thought, once again, had misled me. Yes, there were three sexes on Ourrh. Yes, there were "workers" on Ourrh. But the true males were those handsome, seductive cherubs. The Mandarins that resembled me, who resembled the true men of Earth—Agathos and Kakos—virile as they seemed, were merely "workers." It was they who worked, were the breadwinners of the household, and only played, truth be told, a subsidiary role in nuptial matters—a role of indispensable presence, but no more. They were similar, my God, to those chemical substances whose proximity—and proximity alone—is necessary to the combination of certain other substances; you scientists call them "catalysts," I think.

But Pons, even if I had known all that, don't you think that I would have fallen over just the same, and wouldn't you have followed my example, considering the very dissimilar state of affairs that is prevalent on Earth?

I was extracted from the embarrassment and bewilderment into which Kala's statement had thrown me by the arrival of the excellent Agathos. He had noticed Kakos' intrusion, had witnessed my unfortunate tumble from a distance, and had come running, making extraordinary semaphore-like gestures.

From then on, though, those names—"Agathos" and "Kakos"—were no longer appropriate to them. Those individuals were neuter, and their names should have been rendered as "Agathon" and "Kakon."

Der, die, das. Masculine, feminine, neuter. *Bonus, bona, bonum*! Oh, those foreigners, those Ancients, with their three genres, what singular perspectives they open on things unknown, or on things no longer known! Is it necessary to see in *agathos, agathè, agathon* a reminiscence of what humans were in the remote past? Did Plato not have his Aristophanes say, in *The Symposium*: "Once, human nature was composed of males, females and androgynes."[49]

---

[49] Plato, who had his tongue in his cheek more often than some commentators suppose, invited the famous comic dramatist to the *symposium* [banquet] in order to introduce a calculatedly absurd but wittily apposite fantasy about there once having been a time when humans were of three different sorts—males, females and androgynes—each having spherical bodies, eight limbs, and two heads facing in opposite directions, until Zeus split them in two as a punishment for rebellious pride and moved their reproductive organs to the newly-exposed fronts of their bodies. This division condemned the resultant individuals to yearn for reunion with their lost "other halves"—the components of the divided males for other males, the components of the divided females for other females, and the components of the divided androgynes for members of the opposite sex, that being the origin of lust. The other guests at the banquet—including the homosexual tragedian Agathon—offer similarly allegorical accounts of the role of the god Eros in human affairs before Socrates, in a more

Be that as it may, I did not change the names of Kakos and Agathos. I had already become used to them. Anyway, was that the first time that I had continued to call "men" men who were not really men at all?

"We have to go!" said Agathos. "That was a regrettable turn of events. Kakos is perspicacious. He is probably convinced, now, that you have never had a tuft. In any case, the violet sun is about to rise—the ball will soon be over. Let's go." He turned to Kalos, who had also hurried forward. "You will be good enough, won't you, to take our wife back to the house? Monsieur Fléchambeau and I are going to the *radiure* exhibition."

Kakos watched us leave with malicious eyes and a tuft that was surely full of treacherousness.

The *radiure* exhibition took up the whole of a monumental exhibition hall surrounded by clumps of trees sculpted in stone or marble.

Why not real vegetation? I asked.

"Sterilization!" said Agathos. "This is decorative—but real trees…that would be too dangerous!"

His vague and evasive response betrayed an unease that I had already remarked. Without making any further observations, I allowed myself to be drawn into the interior of the building.

But it's an exhibition of suspensions! I thought.

The brightly lit, high-ceiling halls succeeded one another in parallel. A large number of hemispherical objects hung down from the ceilings, analogous to those I had already seen in Agathos' home and that of the director of the College of Judges. Large or small, they were always half-spheres turned to the ground, whose roundness, well-placed for examination by tuft, seemed to be spattered with various filings, but scarcely colored and devoid of any plastic or graphic interest.

---

tedious frame of mind, undertakes to analyze the conundrum of sexual attraction rationally.

A humming crowd was circulating beneath these pendants, their tufts widely expanded. There were crowds beneath certain suspensions. Some individuals were groaning audibly, others uttering cries of ecstasy.

Excuse me, I said to Agathos, *but I don't understand your exhibition at all! If you're making fun of me…*

"I wanted you to see this, my friend, for my instruction and for yours. It's an admirable lesson in philosophy. For be assured, Fléchambeau, that there is nothing in the world more exquisite or more ravishing for a Mandarin who enjoys the *dounn* than these works of art, due to the genius of our most illustrious *radistes*.

I can't see anything, I complained. *I can't smell anything. I can't hear anything. And that's quite natural, since I have no tuft! Here, I'm like a man born blind in an art gallery, who can only touch the color-coated canvases and say; "This one's rougher than that one…" I want to go. I must look like an idiot.*

But Agathos, his eyes closed, was *dounning* the suspensions, above which I could make out some sort of electric batteries.

"Marvelous!" he exclaimed by transmitter. "Adorable! In this one, what power! In that, what skill! That interior study! That *profil perdu*![50] That 'reverie'! That 'wrath'! That 'uncertainty'! Oh, the classics, my friend, the classics! What masters!" He quoted, in thought, thoughts that were names. Then he added: "We're in the retrospective halls. The modern works, by young artists, are hung over there."

From that direction, in fact, came the sound of an altercation. There was jostling. Two highly-developed Mandarins with large hands and sullen faces were throwing out an exasperated Mandarine who had just destroyed a suspension.

---

[50] *Profil perdu* [vanishing profile] is a technical term used in commentaries on painting to refer to a subject facing obliquely away from the observer, so that all that can be seen of his or her profile is the line of the cheek.

"It's the famous Mademoiselle X," Agathos told me, laughing wholeheartedly. "She's broken her full-length portrait, which she considered insulting!"

Other Mandarins were arguing heatedly, partisans of one school or its rival. I was extremely ashamed, melancholy and incensed.

"What do you think of it, then?" Agathos asked me.

I think that 50% of my compatriots would answer you shrewdly, without letting you see that they couldn't understand any of it. That's the way people get out of things where I come from. A host of clever individuals look knowing when confronted with works of art in which they can distinguish absolutely nothing—professional critics among them, of course. I've known two or three who, not being able to read, rather than learning, prefer to proclaim that no one can read. And there are many among us who scrape paintings with their fingernails and search for definitive epithets to express how smooth or how scratchy it is, without realizing that they ought to be talking about design, color and sentiment. Once again, Agathos, I don't understand anything of your radiures. *I see nothing here but similar rounded objects, scarcely distinguishable from one another, and completely uninteresting. I have no tuft, and everything related to* dounn *is forbidden to me. There's nothing! I admit it.*

Jostled by a movement of the crowd, I felt an indiscreet finger reach out to the sucker of my false tuft and, abruptly turning my head, I was pained to see that the infamous Kakos was at my side and that was to him that I had, for several seconds, been confiding my intimate thoughts and the avowal of my tuftal disgrace. But Agathos was not in a situation to receive the news of my misfortune. He had just met a Mandarin upon whom he was heaping praise, and to whom he introduced me. It was a renowned *radiste*, secure in his reputation, who was petrifying his face in order to give it a certain eternal *je ne sais quoi*.

Agathos asked him if we might visit his studio. The great artist agreed, condescendingly. He worked in vast premises

135

whose windows, at that hour of the day, were streaming with shafts of violet light. The place was, of course, filled with suspensions and also of those panels, similarly spattered with metal filings, that I had noticed on the walls of Agathos' drawing-room. The panels were of the same nature as the suspensions. It comprised an entire collection of works of *radiate*—or, if you prefer *dounnic*—art.

In the middle of the space was a tripod, on top of which a hemisphere of some blackish substance was fixed, partially covered with filings and turned, as you will have guessed, round side down.

Agathos and the *radiste* placed themselves between the three feet of the easel and stood there for some time contemplating the sketch tuftally, while I occupied myself making an inventory of *radiure* equipment: a tray laden with a profusion of pincers and hammers, and large slanting racks divided into numerous pigeon-holes, in which little piles of metallic flakes were distributed in a mysterious order. These racks were, in effect, palettes.

At Agathos' request, the master consented to make a sketch of me. I intrigued him, by virtue of also being famous myself, in my fashion. He therefore placed a virgin hemisphere on the tripod, brought his presumably-electric engine to bear, lifted his arms, and began to insert into it fragments of metal that he took from various parts of the racks, each of which he clipped, twisted and curled with minute care before lodging it, not without much forethought and some affectation, at a selected point in the incomprehensible mosaic.

When the sitting was over, he attached the hemisphere to cords that were hanging down, and hoisted it up among the others, hesitating for several minutes more over the exact level that it ought to adopt. Then, more statuesque than ever, he allowed me to shake his hand, while the excellent Agathos, intoxicated with admiration, kicked off both his slippers, one after the other.

"The resemblance is striking!" he told me. "It's an incomparable masterpiece! What artistry! What artistry! What artistry, in sum!"

Alas, I could only see a banal object, which—humanly speaking—had nothing in common with anything human. Imagine a savage, an illiterate primate, looking at the sheet of paper on which some poet had just described how he had seen his face and penetrated his inner being!

That done, the master made us welcome in his lodgings.

My "portraitist", an extremely refined person who reached for new sensations even in the coarsest forms of primitive art, possessed a few painted pictures, and sometimes amused himself by painting, as one of our great painters might amuse himself from time to time by cooking.

Painting is not respected among the Mandarins, any more than sonorous music, because they have very poor eyesight and confused hearing. In addition, with regard to painting, the alternation of the two solar luminaries upsets all color technique. Besides, in the canvases that were shown to me that day, I saw that my Mandarin artist was still attempting in his painting, more than anything else, to satisfy the taste of the tuft rather than the joy of the eye, and that his pictorial works, which were his "Ingres' violin" were entirely impregnated with that concern, as certain Earthly paintings are entirely impregnated with literature.

I could no longer doubt, now, that beauty on Ourrh was first and foremost the beauty perceptible by means of the tuft, and I collected a great deal of further testimony to that fact during the 65 years I spent there, in seeing the most lively passions aroused by Mandarins, Mandarines and Mandarinas whom I, personally, found neither more beautiful nor uglier than the rest. Those who had small noses, large eyes, large mouths and suitable ears, however, were inevitably less pleasing.

The *radiste*, his wife and the household cherub offered us snuff. Agathos lavished praise upon a liquid for spraying on tufts that was the master's own invention. They wanted to

137

interrogate me about Earthly customs, but Agathos set himself in polite opposition to that, carefully managing the situation, because, fearful of Kakos maneuvers, he wanted to maintain secrecy regarding the lack of tufts with which all Terrans are afflicted.

As we left that hospitable residence, I asked Agathos: *Is Kala ugly, to your tuft?*

"Yes, although it's of no significance, my friend."

Poor girl! And what about me, Agathos—how do I seem? Still, of course, from the donnnic *viewpoint?*

Neither good not bad, to be frank. But the beauty, of a 'worker,' you know…it's not very important! And I'd rather you were taken for a 'worker'—you'll have less trouble, and we can protect you from indiscretions more easily."

Kakos knows everything, I told him, timidly. *He perceived everything I was thinking. He knows exactly what I am, from A to Z.*

Agathos was overwhelmed by disappointment. "It was bound to happen," he said. "Take care, my friend! That odious gentleman seeks your ruin. I know that. He'll never let up until he has opened your skull to look inside. I can't see any salvation for you but flight—departure!"

But where can I go, Agathos? Where can I hide?

"Oh! On Ourrh, Kakos will find you. He's powerful and malevolent. Listen Fléchambeau—I can unlock the brake that halted your diminution in a matter of days. Would you like to depart into the infinitely small?"

Never! I'd rather die!

"There's only one thing I can do, then," said Agathos. "Set to work, to find a means…"

He became thoughtful, manipulating his huge nose with a nervous hand.

A means to what, Agathos?

"Eh? To send you home of course! To make you grow again! It might, perhaps, take me a long time, Fléchambeau, but I shall succeed! From now until then, Kalos will take you on a tour of our planet—but be careful! Oh, be careful!"

Don't worry about that, old chap! I was mad with joy.

"The Gods will see to it that all this ends happily," said Agathos, anxiously. "May the Gods hear me!"

For on Ourrh, two twin Gods are worshipped, just as two suns shine upon it.

VI. As Pascal Said: "Let No One Say That He Has Said Nothing New…"[51]

Before setting to work, Agathos absolutely insisted on introducing me personally to the Ultimate Minister and taking me to visit the Institute of *adounns*, as well as the Museum.

What? I said. *The Museum directed by Kakos, my arch-enemy?*

"It's necessary. We'll take precautions. But if you don't acquaint yourself with our Museum, you'll understand hardly anything of our world—and isn't it appropriate for a voyager, on returning home, to have an abundance of stories to tell? True ones, if possible."

Oh, Agathos, I said, *is it possible, then, that I might some day see the skies of Earth again? That I might once again taste a bowlful of beef stew? That I might marry my Olga—just the two of us, if possible.*

"I shall at least try," Agathos replied.

The Ultimate Minister received us urbanely. I saw him merely as a Mandarin like all the others, except that his tuft was tricolored—but there was artifice in that. The audience only lasted a few minutes, and was purely official. His Excellency was only interested in matters strictly related to the planet, politics and, most of all, elections. What came from the sky and the infinitely large left him visibly cold. Several mi-

---

[51] The reference is to the posthumously-published *Pensées* of Blaise Pascal (1623-1662), which includes the following item (#22): "*Qu'on ne dise pas que je n'ai dit rien de nouveau; la disposition des matières est nouvelle; quand on joue à la paume, c'est une même balle dont joue l'un et l'autre, mais l'un la place mieux.*" [Let no one say that I have said nothing new; the arrangement of materials is new; in a game of tennis, both players use the same ball, but one of them places it better.]

nisters and members of the Omnipotent Chamber were at his side. Their tufts were tinted red, for the most part; two or three, merely pink, were fading into the middle-distance.

"What a charming conversationalist!" Agathos said to me. "He's an old friend of mine. If you had perceived everything he said to me, you would be intoxicated! He belongs to a race of Mandarins that once lived near the Equator. They've veritable virtuosos of the tuft. I tell you, Fléchambeau, to perceive them is an enchantment—so the Ominpotent Chamber is almost entirely made up of these Equatorials, whose music has conquered the electorate. That doesn't matter—besides, some of them don't always demonstrate intelligence, so we are all the more grateful that that it is rare in persons who make a profession of climbing on to the podium to debate this or that and offer themselves for the admiration of the public."

Let's go visit the Institute of adouuns, I said, *which is, I suppose, the Institute in which Mandarins deprived of* dounn *are brought up—individuals deprived of the kind of sight or hearing that I don't possess, and also deprived of your power of speech. Is that really what it is?*

"That's correct."

There were 200 or 300 young Mandarins of all three sexes there—no more.

"Don't you find that they resemble you?" said Agathos. "That was how I counted on deceiving Kakos!"

To tell the truth, among those born *adounn*, unfortunate Mandarins with damaged tufts, there were some whose large eyes, ears and mouths reminded me of my compatriots, but as their noses had been subject to the same compensatory increase, I did not judge them as favorably as Agathos. They were trained to improve their sight and to speak a sort of crude language. Their sense of smell was so marvelously developed that they were expert perfumer-composers, and I was introduced to one young woman for whom her professor—a perfumer-organist in the National Orchestra—entertained high hopes.

141

As we were going through the establishment, a bubble-automobile ambulance brought in a Mandarin whose tuft had just been cleanly severed in a factory. Although the wound was bandaged, the Mandarin was staggering about; no longer able to walk straight, he put out his arms like a blind man, opened his eyes wide in alarm and uttered heart-rending lamentations.

One of the residents had died that same morning, having abused strong snuff. He had given up the ghost in a terrible sneezing-fit. The asylum's chief physician was preparing to carry out an autopsy of his head, in order to discover the underlying causes of his *adounnism*. I saw that as an admirable opportunity to inform myself as to the anatomy of Mandarins, with regard to the tuft, and I asked to be allowed to witness the operation.

Imagine my emotion when I established that the Mandarin organ that I call a "tuft" was nothing other than a development of the *pineal gland* that every terrestrial human possesses in the bosom of the brain, whose mysterious structure is that of an atrophied eye! Yes, Pons, yes! And you've already realized that, in order to expand above a Mandarin's head, the pineal eye emerges from the skull through…yes, quite simply, one of the *fontanelles*, those gaps which, among us, only close up and ossify as we grow older, and sometimes never harden completely.

I explained this to Agathos. I told him how troubled I was by this affinity between the gigantic Terrans and the microscopic Mandarins. My discovery delighted me and terrified me; it gave rise to a singular exaltation. I glimpsed, in a mist, the most curious hypotheses regarding the past of the human species, over millions of years. Since our pineal gland seems to be a vestigial organ, and since the fontanelle is a vestigial orifice, might our prehistoric ancestors have possessed the Mandarin sixth sense? Had they known the pleasures and the power of the tuft? How and why, then, had they lost them? Had the Mandarin microbes been large, in the remote past? Had humans been microscopic? I interrogated myself ardently.

I questioned my vaguest memory, my very flesh, in the hope of discovering some sort of trace of ancestral memories, transmitted to me across the millennia...

Agathos, initially enthused, suddenly became gloomy. "If Kakos were to suspect that!" he said. "I shiver with horror at the thought! I'm hesitant, now, to take you to the Museum."

Come on! I want to see everything before going away, Agathos! Don't go back on your courageous decision.

"All right. But the time has come, Fléchambeau, to reveal to you the mystery of which one never speaks."

The mushrooms?

Agathos nodded his head affirmatively. Later, when his poor little dry and shriveled tongue tried awkwardly to speak my language, he could never pronounce "mushrooms," but he said "ooms", and that word was so perfectly fitted to the cryptogams about which he told me, Pons, that I ask your permission to retain it.[52]

Now, this is how old Agathos expressed it. "Ages and ages ago, when the Mandarins were not yet masters of the planet Ourrh, they had to struggle mightily against the other species that aspired to supremacy. Among these species, the most obstinate and the most redoubtable was that of the Ooms. They were invasive mushrooms, which propagated with disastrous rapidity: hideous giant mushrooms. They were vanquished, but such was the horror of the struggle in which the Mandarin species was almost wiped out that our ancestors resolved to purge the surface of everything that might give rise to similar adversaries. The sterilization of Ourrh was decided. Today, you will not find a single animal on the surface of the

---

[52] In French, the word that Agathos cannot pronounce is "*champignons*" and the infantile abbreviation he contrives is "*hons;*" although I thought it appropriate to substitute English equivalents, the reader might care to bear in mind the vague phonetic similarity between "*hons*" and "huns," and the fact that this version of the story was written after the Great War, in which Renard had been fully engaged for its duration.

globe capable of improving itself by mutation, nor a single illicit vegetable. We have only conserved national forests, indispensable to the chemical exchanges on which our existence depends; furthermore, these forests are supervised to such a degree that nothing that can grow there but what we desire.

"The memory of the Ooms remains with us, however. It haunts our generations, one after another. Each of us hides the fear, but we live with that hereditary anguish—for alas, since our biological victory, our age-old triumph, the population of Ourrh has been reduced to a mere handful of Mandarins. The innumerable populations of early times melted into nations, and the nations themselves became agglomerated. One day, there was no more than a single State. Births then became rare, without any moral, fiscal or other measure, however insidious it might be, being able to provide a remedy. Today, Fléchambeau, of all our superb cities, one alone survives: this one. The others have disappeared, for want of inhabitants. Let us not mention villages, suppressed for centuries by social hygiene, for fear that peasant negligence might allow the deadly seeds of our enemies to grow in some dung-heap.

"Don't forget, however, that we venerate nature and life. That's why you shall soon see an immense garden and an immense Museum, in which we piously preserve a few specimens of animals and plants that it was necessary to destroy everywhere else."

Alive? Or stuffed?

"Alive, except for those that did not survive into our era."

But what about the Ooms, Agathos? I can't believe that you cultivate them!

"Never!" cried Agathos, with an old-fashioned grand gesture. "Never! Except…"

Except what? You surprise me…

He raised his head proudly. "The Mandarins are noble creatures," he said. "Do you understand me, Fléchambeau?

We only recognize the right to defend ourselves—not the right to annihilate."

That's exactly what we think where I come from, I told him.

"You will not be astonished then, that we conserve a small quantity of mycelium—the germ-plasm of Ooms—in the Museum, in order that the Gods cannot accuse us of having exterminated that which they have created."

Direly dangerous! I said.

"No. It's Kakos who jealously watches over all the treasures of the Museum—and Kakos is an inflexible servant of Mandarinity, ready to do anything for the cause of science, as for that of national progress—to the extent of opening your skull to enrich the sacred patrimony of our forefathers with new knowledge!"

You talk like a member of the Omnipotent Chamber, Agathos. So this Kakos is... likable?

"He is a vile, cruel, intractable villain—but, I admit, a pure Mandarin, who would not recoil from the greatest crime, or the worst sacrifice, for the glory of our endangered species! We shall go to see him. Politeness demands it. I cannot visit the Museum without his demanding to accompany us. Moreover, incessant avoidance would make him think."

Believing that I would be able, on my return, to tell the people of Earth everything that I had seen on the planet Ourrh, and especially in the Museum, Agathos had no suspicion that it would take him more than 60 years to discover the formula for my "re-enlargement" and that, having returned to my peers, I would only have a brief residue of life at my disposal. To waste time in detailed descriptions would be to risk not being able to finish the essential story. If I have time, Pons, I shall come back to my visit to the Museum, but I feel the progress of a deadly weakness, and I want to make haste to tell you what is indispensable.[53]

In brief, the Museum was a national park augmented with huge buildings in which the Mandarins conserved all possible relics of extinct animals and vegetables: a present world and a past world; an entire Nature exiled and reduced to specimens. Imagine that humans had scraped the Earth clean, that they had sterilized it, and that there was no longer a plant or an animal to be found outside the Jardin d'Acclimation.[54]

I shall leave all nomenclature there. Know only that I saw a thousand sorts of birds, fish and other animals, some of which were only inconsistent phosphorescences an others merely murmurs deprived of all appearance. The aviaries, the aquariums and the various enclosures presented all the natural resources. The animals were small. Some of them were ferocious. Almost all—of the more advanced species, at least—were organized in triads and possessed tufts.

A high wall surrounded the enormous enclosure. Sentries mounted guard on all sides and sterilizing boundary-fountains were erected at intervals, each with its flexible hose and its jet.

---

[53] Some text seems to be missing from the first sentence of this paragraph, which must originally have comprised at least two sentences; I do not know whether the fault is specific to the Laffont edition, or whether it was also present in the Crès edition. At any rate, I have had no alternative but to leave it as it is rendered in the former.

[54] The Jardin d'Acclimation was the Parisian equivalent of London's Kew Gardens, where plants from distant parts of the world were grown in order to find out which of them might be susceptible to cultivation in colonial plantations. Experiments were also conducted into which kinds of livestock might be most appropriate to intercontinental transplantation. Such work in applied botany and "ecological management" was a key aspect of the determined colonial and imperialistic enterprise in which Britain and France were engaged between the late 18th century and the early 20th century.

At the slightest alert—I mean, as soon as the tiniest suspect mushroom appeared—the critical location was copiously doused in a pitiless liquid.

We went along the pathways, perched on a slow vehicle that Agathos drove himself. Then we came back to the buildings and were received by Kakos, after having gone through several antechambers and explained ourselves successively to a dozen ushers, some of whom were more suspicious than others.

"Above all," said Agathos, "don't leave my side."

I've no desire to do so, I replied, sufficiently impressed by all that we had to go through to get close to Kakos—and to get away from him.

On seeing me, the Museum director could not suppress a fugitive expression of scientific concupiscence. Even so, he forced himself to by courteously amiable, and willingly accompanied us through the halls in which the marvelous collections were organized. I made the acquaintance of fantastic fauna and flora of previous eras. I even admired a few survivors that had been retained by virtue of ingenuity. And I went through the interminable galleries that sheltered the most miraculous conservatory that one could imagine—which is to say that there were striking photographs of every plant or animal, phonograph disks preserving their cries, calls, growls and songs, depository apparatus for various scents, from the perfume of flowers to the musty odor of buffaloes, other apparatus rendering the tactile impressions of scales, pelts, feathers or fruits, and others, even more precious, which delivered their conserved memories by means of the tuft.

We descended into the depths of cellars containing the evidence of everything that had been destroyed as being harmful. These cellars were veritable sealed blockhouses, with doors like those of strong-boxes. I could not go into the without shivering, but Agathos held my hand and never ceased reassuring me by giving me all sorts of explanations.

Receptacles enclosed dubious broth-like cultures. The most terrible maladies, the most murderous epidemics that had once decimated Mandarinity, were to be found there, vanquished, imprisoned, relegated to a dungeon, condemned to perpetual detention. Relative to that subject, Agathos told me that excessive sterilization had almost caused all the Mandarins to perish, because of the benign microbes that are necessary to maintain life—which are, perhaps, life itself. They had been obliged to react promptly, a few centuries later, against the excess of hygiene.

I don't know what surprised me more: to hear that microbe talking to me about microbes, or the strange and mysterious nobility that prevented the Mandarins from obliterating the worst enemies of their race completely.

Eventually, Kakos informed us that we had seen everything, and I released a sigh of relief on recrossing the threshold of that tenebrous inferno, which *dounnic* lamps brightened for the Mandarins but which I could only make out by the light of a sort of photophore designed for the use of *adounns*.

"But he hasn't shown us the Oom mycelium!" Agathos said, via the transmitter. "Where the Devil is it hidden now? I'm going to ask him."

They exchanged silent words. Then Agathos told me that Kakos had decided that he would no longer reveal to anyone the hiding-place of that frightful powder, the seed of calamity. I regretted that. I would have liked to drink my fill of the sight of that historic entity, still a potentially devastating scourge.

Agathos had seen the sacred deposit when the celebrated treasure was in the deepest cellar, where privileged individuals, under the guidance of Kakos, had been able to enjoy the intimidating spectacle. From what he told me, I concluded that it must be something like a handful of flour, in something like a black sweet-jar marked with a red circle and a white circle.

All the same, I said, shaking my head, *in your place, when you had the Ooms under your bootheel, I would have exterminated them. I wouldn't have left the smallest spore.*

Shaking his head in his turn, however, Agathos replied: "We have too much heart for that. We believe too firmly in the splendor of the world and its diversity. I'd rather not talk about those damned mushrooms any more, but, since we are talking about them, it's necessary that you understand, Fléchambeau, that they have left the memory of a deadly but magnificent cohesion, being one of those species in which the individual is submerged in the mass, obedient to the instinct of the collective, to the specific mind, being only a cell in the bosom of an organism, living only for the multitude of which it is a part. Their invasion was, to us, like an invasion of bacteria to blood corpuscles.

Ah! I thought. *On that note, I remember that I really am among the microbes—for where could one find a similar bizarrerie on "the human scale"?*

Kakos brought the tour to an end. He escorted us to the main gate of the Museum. I did not see that as an effect of politeness. His tuft never turned away from mine. The abject fellow regarded me broodingly with the tuft and his eyes. He trembled with feverish curiosity. He had all the trouble in the world tearing himself away from me. His bony hands squeezed upon an imaginary capture—and when we bid him farewell, in the Mandarin fashion, he launched his slipper with such an impulsive movement that it disappeared into the branches of a stone tree. He forced himself to laugh, while the concierge went in search of a ladder to recover the slipper.

That demonic laugher is ringing in my ears again.

*VII. In Which A Few Other Novelties Are Revealed,
Including Where the Frightful Kakos Hid
the Terrible Black, White and Red Sweet Jar*

Kalos put himself at my disposal as soon as Agathos had begun his scientific research. Together, we went through the city and across the world, escorted by robust and vigilant green men. The bubble-automobiles traveled as easily in the air and on water as they did on the surface of the ground.

The city of the Mandarins, austere and rational, extended for a long way. It was vast, about twice the size of Paris: the combined result of centralization and the planetary depopulation. As for the planet itself, I don't think that it was much larger, proportionally, than our Moon. Its complete sterilization reminded me of Alfred de Musset's "pumpkin."[55] It was an arid globe, streaked with hygienic forests, planted with pluviogenic lighthouses and guarded by innumerable surveillance-posts, powerfully armed with antiseptic reservoirs and sterilizing pumps. Nothing seemed to me more desolate that

---

[55] The reference is to de Musset's verse dialogue "*Dupont et Durand*" (1838), one of several gloomy pieces he wrote in which he argued that the world's future would be dire if materialistic technological progress were to supersede or crowd out spiritual development. The relevant lines of this particular vision are: "*L'humanitairerie en fera sa gamelle,/Et le globe rasé, sans barbe ni cheveux,/Comme un grand potiron roulera dans les cieux.*" [The humanitarium will come unstuck/and the shaven globe, beardless and hairless/will roll through the skies like a giant pumpkin.] "Humanitarium" is a term borrowed from the Utopian social philosophy of Charles Fourier (1772-1837), one version of which anticipated that the people of the future would live collectively in rationally-ordered "phalansteries" rather than in family homes, ultimately combining them together into a vast humanitarium.

those grey, bare and miserly landscapes, in which neither the twitter of a little bird nor the discreet call of an insect was to be heard.

On that subject, Kalos told me that the birds had disappeared in a matter of weeks. Dangerous propagators of all sorts of seeds, they had caused the Mandarins great anxiety. A means had been found of infecting them with vertigo by poisoning grass-seeds; they had spread that vertigo via the wounds that they had inflicted on one another in their epizootic fury. Once they became disgusted with flight and preferred to run rather than suffer air-sickness, they were easily massacred, and they expired while opening their futile wings one last time.

My new companion could not help feeling the immense sadness of these deserts deeply. His heart was vehement; emotion engendered harmonious transports within him. He sometimes sang poems to me in thought that I judged far more admirable for being grasped at their source without having been deformed by any language whatsoever.

Nevertheless, Kalos always inspired a slight aversion in me by virtue of the nonchalance, typical of every cherub, with which he allowed himself to live at Agathos' expense. I once told him so—to which he replied that he was only obeying the laws of Mandarin nature. "Furthermore," he added, "I shall grow old, and I too will become a 'worker', unless, by exception—which is not desirable—I remain a cherub and drag out the horrible old age of a decrepit ephebe. May the Gods spare me that lamentable destiny!"

So, I said, strongly intrigued, *you evolve...*

"Naturally! There are Mandarins who are 'workers' from infancy and remain so throughout their lives. Others are cherubs, but do not remain so, when they reach maturity, except by a freak of chance. As for our women, they are subject, after pupation, to changes different from those you have told me Earthly women undergo..."

After pupation? I interrupted. *What's that?*

It was then that Kalos took me to the most extraordinary establishments imaginable, at least for a Terran.

The Mandarins are not born Mandarins. They are born in a larval state, demanding, stupid and awkward. These larvae bear no resemblance at all to Mandarin adults—who, however, always exhibit an extravagant affection toward them. It is during the larval state that, delivered into the care of oft-facetious functionaries, they are submitted to certain treatments, the objective of which is to direct their growth, at the behest of their parents of the State, along particular lines. Thus, they are forced to develop their hands, their feet or their skulls according to whether the nation requires manipulators, marchers or intellectuals, or whether their fathers and mothers desire one thing or another. The future guardians of order, for instance, are encouraged in muscular development; surgeons fashion them a harsh and peremptory face; their fists are firmly clenched in order that they will never, never be able to open.

It is also in this first phase of Mandarin life that determination is made of who will be a cherub and who will be a "worker"—but the pupa often thwarts the plans and falsifies the prognosis. There is a period of subtle and mysterious metamorphosis. Strange and unexpected creatures frequently emerge from the split shell in which the Mandarin nymph has lain dormant for several months; the generic specialization is found to have been disrupted—which is rather fortunate, Kalos told me, given that the specializing functionaries sometimes have a tendency only to work on the head, neglecting to work for the profit of their own caste, which, being poor, is revolutionary.

I found it very strange that these forgers of humans, these sculptors of living beings, were badly paid, since, all things considered, their task was to carry the work of the Creator further forward, doing nothing less, in truth, than "manufacturing" the Mandarins.

Indifferently, Kalos stuffed a rare snuff into his nasal fossas, and checked that his hair was properly curled. "When I was a larva," he said, "it seemed to be the intention that I should be steered toward medicine, made into a specialist in diseases of the tuft. You can see where that got me…here I am, a cherub. That's much better!"

For how much longer, Kalos?

"A hundred years."

Oh! Do the Mandarins have a long lifespan, then?

"The average is 200 years."

That explains, Pons, why the worthy Agathos, who was no longer young, was able to work for 60 years before finding the formula that he was seeking, without becoming a valetudinarian who shakes his head in saying: "Once upon a time…"

Every evening—I mean every time the hour approached for artificial night to fall—I asked Agathos what progress he had made in his work. One day, he replied to me, dejectedly, that he was absolutely certain of eventual success, but that the calculations he needed to carry out would take 60 years, even though he was exceptionally strong in mathematics and that ten Mandarins were to assist him, compared with whom our Inaudi was a mere dullard.[56]

I greeted this bad news courageously, and did my best to be content at having to prolong my sojourn among such charming friends to some degree.

It was decided that I would live in a little house adjoining Agathos' own. My aged protector organized my existence. To ensure my safety, he gave me very devoted green men and volunteered to pay all my expenses. I turned a deaf ear to that and learned to make decorative slippers; they were not very beautiful, but the singularity of my person soon caused them to be sought out by the most elegant.

Thus I lived for six times ten years, as a chaste dreamer replete with memories of another world, with the friendship of

---

[56] Jacques Inaudi (1867-1950) was a celebrated "lightning calculator," although not particularly gifted in other ways; his peculiar talent attracted a good deal of attention from psychologists, and from such popularizers of science as Camille Flammarion.

Agathos Kalos, their wife and the lovely Kala—for whom I felt an affection sometimes enriched by contained surges. I was homebound, by prudence. Adapting gradually to Mandarin customs, I forgot the divine pleasure of the pipe, the delights of epicurean dining and even the marvelous joys of love. My principal amusement consisted of giving lessons in speech to Agathos when he took an hour's rest. I also read a great many books—Mandarin books, which presented themselves in the form of recorded matter placed in a box. It was sufficient to attach a small funnel to the box and to activate a mechanism to change it into a thought-transmitter. Thought-writing was affected by the inverse procedure.

Meanwhile, I never became disinterested in Mandarin civilization. I continued to display the greatest and most legitimate curiosity about the world in which I was exiled, while waiting for Agathos' science to provide me with a passport to the Earth from which I was so distant, *without ever having left it*! And every day, some new oddity plunged me into amazement.

I would, therefore, have been quite happy, had it not been for nostalgia for the Earth, regret for our friendship, the pain of having lost my Olga forever and the tenacious fear of Kakos.

The latter led me a merry dance. There was no trap he did not set for me. He had long fits of covetousness, during which I was given no respite. At such times there was nothing but ambushes, stratagems and pitfalls, one after another. I no longer slept, save for a nightmare-laden semi-slumber; I saw Kakos imprisoning me in the depths of cellars, between seething liquid cultures and the terrible black-white-and-red sweet-jar before trepanning me alive in order to examine my brain.

Then a time came, after many long years, when Kakos, seemingly discouraged, ceased to persecute me. That happened as the time fixed by Agathos for the discovery of the formula approached. For a few months, the problem had been simplified. Having required billions of solutions at the outset, it was now reduced to a few thousand QEDs, and the day, hour and minute were approaching when it might be expressed, entirely resolved, by a single line of symbols.

That day dawned; that hour chimed; that minute arrived.

Agathos, very old and bent, presented me with two pills, the blue color of washing-powder, and said to me, his voice trembling with an entirely understandable emotion: "Here, Fléchambeau, is the fruit of my most sustained labors. A single one of these pills will return you to your natural height. I've made two, in case you lose one of them."

I put the two pills in my snuff-box—for you'll understand that I had become accustomed to taking snuff, in order to be like everyone else—and said to Agathos: *That's good. We have time*. Indeed, now that I possessed my *exeat*, now that I could leave whenever I pleased, I was no longer impatient. Old age afflicted me with all its indignities. The thought of Olga no longer dredged anything from my memory but a pinch of ashes; I thought that she was now an old lady, emaciated or corpulent, unless she had passed from Earth to Heaven. As for you, Pons, would you not have turned into some unbearable greybeard? Besides, I had acquired my habits on Ourrh. When I thought about leaving, I discovered that strong links bound my mind and my heart to that world.

For a long time, I put off my farewells and my departure from one day to the next. There were people and places I wanted to see one last time. Incredibly enough, certain harsh and lugubrious landscapes in the sterilized countryside had conquered me without my being aware of it. Their forbidding gravity and their sullen despair gripped my soul. And as Kakos left me in peace, I often went to wander, all alone, in those sinister solitudes and to nourish my sadness with their infinite desolation.

I especially liked one desperately arid valley, because I felt that its reddish slopes and its greasy soil were crying out to be covered with grass and crops. It was necessary, one day, to say goodbye to it.

I climbed to the top of a hillock, sat down on a rock, and sank into one of those meditations in which one is conscious of reaching one's innermost depths.

Monstrous in the distance, the Mandarins' one and only city studded the horizon with its white cupolas. There was not a single branch to be seen swaying, nor a single blade of grass sprouting. A mortuary calm weighed upon the funereal valley.

So many things were wringing my heart, so many things whirling in my head! *Old age, are you the cause of it? Or is it you, my imbecile tenderness?* I let my forehead fall into my hands, and I wept for the microcosm in which my life had gone by, and which I was about to abandon for ever and ever...

Suddenly, my false tuft was brutally snatched away fro me. I stood up straight, my blood pounding and my nerves taut.

Kakos gripped my left wrist with a hand of steel, and turned the tuft over and over in the other, laughing—that same old laugh!

I punched him hard on his enormous nose.

He absorbed the blow.

I tried to free my wrist, but the fellow's hand gripped it like a vice! He threw away my false tuft, and took out a short trepanning saw.

Another punch, on the chin.

He tottered, but righted himself, sniggering. Then, losing my bearings slightly, I threw myself upon him, assaulting him with kicks, scratches, bites...

We fell down.

Kakos uttered the most frightful scream that could emerge from a Mandarin's throat—which isn't saying very much.

I thought he was seriously hurt. Astonished to feel him stretching out his arms beneath my weight, however, I ended up looking sideways.

Then, I saw to my horror that, in the course of the fight, a black-white-and-red sweet-jar had slipped out of Kakos' clothing and rolled away. A stone that it had encountered had opened it, and a powder similar to flour was spreading out over the reddish soil.

It was, therefore, on his own person that the old madman had kept the seed of the Ooms. Calamity of calamities!

Kakos took advantage of my amazement to strike me an exceedingly painful blow to the head. I was starting to strangle him, in order to make him repent, when the increasing pain obliged me to let go.

I could only see my inert adversary now through a veil that seemed liquid. A slight crackling was audible from the direction of the sweet-jar. That was my last sensation before darkness overwhelmed me. I contrived to take a few steps unconsciously, but was obliged to fall down, duly *knocked out*.[57]

---

[57] The final phrase is in English in the original text.

VIII. The Ooms

Had Kakos grabbed me again, taking advantage of my swoon? I was choking... I was choking... Ah! He was strangling me! He was weighing down on my breast!

Darkness. Paralysis. Asphyxia.

The sound of muffled detonations reached me, as if through padded walls...

Ah! Was I, then, in the process of being stifled in the depths of the Museum cellars?

A bitter, pestilential odor violated my nostrils.

The detonations were multiplying...

I made an immense effort to move. My limbs seemed to be encased in a sheath that was immobilizing them. I shook myself forcefully. There was no doubt about it: I was immersed in a dark, cold, fungal substance that was molded exactly to my form.

Maddened, I lashed out furiously, launching kicks and punches in all directions.

The substance gave way, caving in. My blows rang soft and dull, as if on rotten wood. I contrived to sit up, burying my head in the spongy matter again. I twisted around, pulling my arms back and using my elbows aggressively, enlarging the empty space.

Through a suddenly-opened hole, the light of day extended a dreamlike hand to me. I precipitated myself toward it like a madman, shoving aside and crushing the viscous and puffy fleshy substance in which I was shrouded....

I had just emerged from a colossal and disgusting mushroom that had grown while I was unconscious. Several meters high, it easily matched our most gigantic trees in its basal circumference. It spread out up above like a vast roof.

A dirty mist attenuated the yellow daylight. The sun, at the zenith, shone weakly, a poorly-gilded circle with no radiant halo. A cannonade was thundering all around. Other mushrooms were visible between the mighty trunks that surrounded me. *They* were growing visibly, with frightful rapidity.

Suddenly, at the summit of the giant that had absorbed me during its ascension, there was a veritable bomb-blast. The cap, torn away, flew into a thousand fragments; a cloud of white smoke was projected in swirls, falling back everywhere as fine powder. Immediately, a swarm of petty cryptogams, as livid and pustulent as mushroom-toads, began to grow from the ground carpeted by that impalpable snow, crackling as they did so.

All around, in the heights, more explosions followed; the ripe mushrooms were launching their seed-germs. The powdery fog thickened. The thunder of the cannonade rolled, continually nourished. I began to cough cruelly, to sneeze interminably, gripped in the throat by the nauseating acridity of that vehement reproduction. Then, almost immediately, I felt the commencement of asphyxia, and I saw that my hands too were covered in pustules, which immediately caused me to itch intolerably.

It was necessary to flee without losing an instant, to reach the city, to spread alarm, if that had not been done already. The noise of the explosions must have given warning to the Mandarins. Besides, was there not a sterilization post only a short distance away?

But the propagation of the Ooms was accelerating terribly. I saw that I was in the middle of an immense forest of white sticky columns, covered with abscesses from which stinking sap was oozing. And more columns were growing, growing, growing without respite, crowding together, sticking to one another, agglomerating, building enormous palisades, with increasingly thick walls, cyclopean blocks that welded themselves to one another, gradually forming a deep and destructive layer on the soil of Ourrh, like the inundation of a solid ocean.

I tried to get my bearings, for the city was no longer visible. My gaze made a tour of the circle of death. And it was at that moment that I perceived a man's arm projecting from a monstrous trunk, motionless, with a bony six-fingered hand whose fingernails were already blued by the pitiless lattice-work manicurist: a rigid hand still clenched upon a short tre-panning-saw.

I started to run through that thunderous forest full of whispering growths. I wove my way between the growths, coughing, weeping, my face and hands exasperated by itching. The city...I caught glimpses of it from time to time. My God! How far the Ooms had advanced! The further I went, though, bounding in spite of my advanced age, the mushrooms, being younger, diminished in volume around me. The sky was less obscured by the pulverulent spores projected downwards by the ancestors. As I ran, I crushed circular colonies of Ooms. As I went by, I knocked adolescents over with thrusts of m shoulders. Far too few!

With the noise of a cataract, a sheet of liquid descended behind me. I recognized the aroma of the sterilizing prepara-tion. The Mandarins were beginning their defense. At the same time, the lighthouses brought prisms into play with shot forth sparkling red fire, and artificial clouds of a coppery thickness began to condense.

A stormy rain the color of beer, smelling strongly of phenol, fell thick and fast upon the valley of the Ooms. That defensive procedure was new to me; no one had ever men-tioned it. It was one of those military secrets that one keeps for the hour of danger. Unfortunately I noticed that it was not working very well, doubtless for lack of testing; the fuse went out. The clouds became charged with electricity, and lightning flashed; the clouds were volatilized. It began again, but the lightning still broke the continuity of the action; besides, it struck three lighthouses, which it destroyed.

As I came into the city, the militia was setting up batte-ries of imposing antiseptic gas machines, and a regiment of sterilizer-artillery was setting forth with its pumps. These Mandarins had a martial bearing; they were being encouraged. A crowd had gathered on the outskirts of the suburbs and on the terraces, in order to watch the frightful Ooms, of which they did not even dare to speak, emerging from the distant valley.

I arrived at old Agathos' house in a sad state, breathless, streaming with sweat, with my clothes soiled by the repulsive contact of the mucilage that had enveloped me.

Assembled there, funereally, I found Agathos and Kalos, their wife and Kala. I gave them a faithful account of the catastrophe, and told them that the guilty party, Kakos, had paid for his mad imprudence with his life.

"We're doomed," said Agathos. "This time, there's nothing we can do. The population of Ourrh had declined too drastically in the thousands of years since we defeated the Ooms. You were right, Fléchambeau—we should have destroyed them! We acted out of sentiment. Tomorrow, we shall no longer act in that way, I assure you—for tomorrow we shall no longer exist! I saw these Ooms just now, from the top of the terrace. It's a force of Nature that is advancing upon a little troop of Mandarins."

They're Lycoperdaceae, I said. *On Earth, they're commonly known as "wolfweed,"*[58] *begging your pardon. We possess giant species that attain the height of a child, whose heads are more than two meters in diameter. I recognized their resounding maneuvers. But the Ooms are redoubtable by virtue of their extraordinary mass, their swiftness and that fashion of uniting into a compact whole, gaining ground visibly.*

"We're done for!" Agathos repeated. "But you, Fléchambeau, you'll survive. There's no more time to hesitate or dawdle, my good friend. Quickly! Swallow one of my pills, and quit this world, where the Ooms will reign henceforth! The Mandarins are dethroned!"

How much time do I have left? I asked, my throat dry.

---

[58] In England, *Lycoperdaceae* are commonly known as puff-balls, but I have translated Renard's *"vesces de loup"* literally, even though no such term appears in the English dictionary.

"In six hours, at the most, they'll be in the city—but you'll be out of reach in less than an hour."

At that moment, Kala—who was lying on the carpet, more dead than alive—began to moan hoarsely. Standing up again, she pointed with a trembling hand to a few tiny mushrooms that were sprouting on my slippers with a virulent crepitation.

At this sight, Kalos grabbed a sterilizer hanging on the wall and, without further delay, doused me from head to toe.

I started to undress. Agathos followed my example. When I was entirely naked, he remarked that there was no point in my getting dressed again, since my clothes could not grow with me. It was then that I lamented the impossibility of taking away any concrete souvenir of the Mandarins and their planet.

"Yes," Agathos replied. "You can take a few photographs."

How is that?

"I solved the problem a long time ago—and, thank Gods, we can put my plan into execution before the city is invaded. I shall rub your body with a compound that will sensitize your skin. We shall imprint interesting images on it, with the aid of a photographic apparatus that is constructed to apply itself to your skin by suction. I shall develop each 'snapshot' one by one, as soon as I've sensitized each living film on each little rectangle of your surface. Your skin will grow, and the negatives will grow too—and when you have become a man of Earth again, you will only have to take as many proofs from the negatives as you desire."

That was done. Three hours later, my very skin was covered in photographic documents. A portrait of Agathos is next to one of Kala on my left breast, next to the heart. And you'll find, Pons, disseminated over all the parts of my person, something akin to a documentary album, as well as the two chemical formulas, which are inscribed across my torso just beneath the collar-bones. I only regret the haste with which Agathos had to work, which did not leave us the leisure to select the subjects.

When I was entirely tattooed, I briefly put on my favorite kilt again and tearfully took my leave of Kalos and the two women.

A continuous rumor was coming from outside. The Ooms' cannonade was drawing nearer, punctuated by the Mandarins' sterilizing salvoes.

Kala, sobbing, hid her beautiful aged face behind a cushion. Kalos put his arms around the other woman. Agathos and I went down into the garden. I opened my snuff-box and I took the two little blue pellets from the odorant tobacco.

Agathos! Agathos! There are two pills—and one alone will be sufficient, you said, to restore my dimensions. Agathos! Come with me, my old friend. Swallow the other pill!

"Oh!" said Agathos, looking at me affectionately. "I don't think that will be possible! You, Fléchambeau, have been large; for you, it's merely a question of becoming so again. But as for me...my tissues aren't compacted, like yours; they don't contain, potentially, the faculty of resuming a former development. Oh, I'd gladly go with you, Fléchambeau. Here, you see, everything Mandarin will doubtless perish...and then...and then, it isn't funny, deep down, to be a 'worker' all one's life, to work one's entire life for women and their cherubs...but what good would it do to try to leave? That pill can only procure me a different death from that which seems to be reserved for me..."

To die making an effort, Agathos, is a fine thing! And who knows? Who knows? Let's go, Agathos! Have some guts!

Without saying another word, Agathos rotated his tuft so as to perceive everything around him. He seized one of the two pills between his thumb and index finger; I picked up the other in the same fashion.

Hurry! I said. *The Ooms aren't far away.*

I undid my kilt. Old Agathos undressed completely, to the displeasure of my eyes.

Your good health! I cried

We stuck our pills in our mouths and swallowed them at the same instant.

Immediately, I felt myself rising up like a rocket. I saw the army of Ooms that was progressing invincibly toward the Mandarin city. I saw that, as a last resort, the darkness-generators were spreading night, in order that no Mandarin should witness the spectacle of the final cataclysm. My snuff-box, which was still in my right hand, seemed to shrink incomparably more rapidly than Balzac's piece of shagreen.[59]

By my side, Agathos rose up, also growing enormously—but as his amplification progressed, I saw him become diaphanous and transparent, and despaired. Soon, he was no more than a shadow on the point of vanishing.

I perceived, in the immensity, the vague silhouette of a vaporous arm—which, heroically, made a gesture of fare-well…and I found myself alone in the midst of a universe in which some stars grew, while others drew away until they became imperceptible dots that soon disappeared.

Like an express train traversing a region, I traversed worlds full of movement and populated with incomprehensible creatures. Then I recognized, titanic at first and subsequently negligible, the infinitesimal creatures and minuscule vegetables of which our science is no longer ignorant, and which cause our diseases simply by following the course of their destiny.

Finally, within the clouds, the overwhelming round form of an objective lens appeared to me. Beneath my feet, the chaotic ground gave me a reference-point on the surface of a glass side. The microscope re-entered the sphere of my senses. Upon that microscope, I rapidly became what a man is on Mont Blanc.

---

[59] The reference is to Honoré de Balzac's allegorical novel *La Peau de chagrin* (1831), in which the eponymous talisman, acquired by virtue of a diabolical pact, shrinks as it grants the protagonist's avid appetite for luxury, which he cannot ultimately restrain.

There was daylight—imperfect, because you had closed the shutters. I realized, however, that the microscope was underneath a bell-jar—a bell-jar raised up by means of wedges. A thread of spider-silk permitted me to descend on to the table. I got out of the bell-jar by passing underneath…

Two days later, I had become your old Fléchambeau again. Ah! The height-gauge measured no more than the 196 centimeters of my youth. I was back to normal. "The years are responsible for that!"[60] But happiness swelled my bosom. The escapade was over. I had come out of it safe and sound. My fatherland was restored to me! But I had been so frightened that someone might have moved the microscope! How could I know where I would find myself? Might not a man or an animal have swallowed the dust in which I was confined? Oof! I was in your house! I had not killed anyone by growing inside a body!

I was, however, astonished to find everything so exactly similar to that which I had left behind. I opened the laboratory window…

Olga! Olga in the full flower of her youth, beautiful, so beautiful in being pretty and being young…Olga was going past!

Oh, Pons, my old Pons! Oh! This frightful old age! I understood, I understood…but what good is understanding? What is all the understanding in the universe, compared with a single tiny tear that all the intelligence in the world is powerless to hold back?

---

[60] The quotation, taken out of context, is from La Fontaine's fable "Le Chat, la belette et le petit lapin" [The Cat, the Weasel and the Little Rabbit]; the whole sentence, spoken by the cat, is: "Mes enfants, approchez, approchez; je suis sourd, les ans en sont la cause." [Come closer, my children, come closer; I'm deaf—the years are responsible for that.] The cat is using deception to lure a potential victim within the range of its claws, but that does not seem to be relevant to Fléchambeau's remembrance of the phrase.

Epilogue

Pons closed the notebook. He poured a bucketful of anth-racite into the stove, which was about to go out.

Fléchambeau made a gesture.

Slowly, Pons said: "There's one thing I don't get, Parrots are much smaller than elephants, and yet they both live to the same age..."

"I wasn't able to write the appendix," Fléchambeau murmured. "I was too exhausted. I had grown again too quick-ly, and my age, my great age...make me a hot toddy."

Pons threw the notebook on to the table, meditatively.

"Gently!" said Fléchambeau. "Think of the catastrophes you might be unleashing in the infinitely small!"

While Pons was heating up the water for the toddy, he continued: "The compatriots of Micromegas had a thousand senses. In spite of that, Micromegas said: 'We still have a kind of vague desire, a mysterious anxiety, that informs us inces-santly that we are of little account, and that there are beings much more perfect than we are...' Man, Pons, is a monstrous and pathetic animal. Of the hundred thousand facets of the world, we only perceive the five facets for which we have senses. The individual who perceived the hundred thousand facets would see God! We only divine God very confusedly, just as we divine infinity and eternity—which our senses are incapable of perceiving—in such a way that our minds cannot succeed in conceiving them precisely. You can't fly in the air, you can't live at the bottom of the sea; thus, your thought can-not wander freely in spaces that your senses do not know. I suppose that the Mandarins, with their tufts, perceive things that we might compare to infra-red or ultra-violet light..."

"Drink your toddy," said Pons, handing it to him.

"Aagh! I've burnt myself. The Mandarins never burn themselves; their tufts see to that..."

"Don't think about the Mandarins any more, Fléchambeau. Tell me how you've been living since your return."

"Poorly," Fléchambeau replied. "Poorly. No one has recognized me. I only go out, in any case, after dark. People are very polite to me. But that, I think, is because the society of Mandarins has made me much more indulgent, more....broadminded. The humans of Earth are a little like Mandarins, without being aware of it. Each of them is infinitely more different from us than we are inclined to suppose. To treat our fellows as creatures like ourselves is a gross error, an inexhaustible source of misunderstandings, injustices and sad disappointments..."

Pons took his pulse, anxiously. Fléchambeau continued: "Some of our senses have the reputation of being superior. We don't know why—but we attribute all excesses to them. One man is crazy about music, another about painting, as a consumer, or an artist...and because another has an exceptional sense of touch or an uncommon sense of taste, you consider him a sensualist or a gourmet. Deadly sins. Vices. Is that reasonable?"

"Tell me, instead, what you've been doing here while waiting for me," Pons persisted, trying to calm the invalid's agitation.

"I've been reading. I've re-read old books that I never understood before...there are many books that have been written by authors who could see the infinitely large or the infinitely small—which come to the same thing...there are many works that remain unintelligible, Pons, if we do not hold them up to the light of the mind, in order to make out the watermark..."

"You've been on a long journey, Fléchambeau. It's necessary to rest now."

"Yes, a long journey...in three dimensions at once. There is a true 'Motionless Voyage,' as some novelist or other put it.[61]Pons, Pons, are you sure that we're not under the bell-jar of some gigantic microscope? Are you sure that some formidable eye isn't observing us through the ocular lens?"

"An ocular lens in the form a triangle? That tale's as old as humankind."[62]

"Pons," Fléchambeau continued, who had lost his train of thought, "it would probably be as well if you were to marry Olga—but be careful! Women, you see, resemble us less than the Mandarins. There's more difference, Pons, between a woman and a man than between a butterfly and a pike…"

"Yes, old chap, that's understood. But you mustn't *think* any more, at present. Sleep. Go to sleep, Fléchambeau."

Fléchambeau went to sleep, serenely.

Pons, with his chin in his hands, remained deep in thought for a long time.

A high wind had risen, which was rattling the branches of the wisteria like dry bones.

"Puppets!" murmured Pons. "We're tiny puppets made of breadcrumbs, made to dance on a plate by some philosopher author. With a single puff of breath, he could send us to oblivion amid the dust of the void…"

The squall became tempestuous then.

Pons looked at the bed. Fléchambeau was no longer there. Everything was tottering under the force of the wind. The house flew away. Saint-Jean-de-Nèves and its mountain, borne away to who knows where, yielded like wisps of straw to the caprice of the squall. A mysterious mouth was blowing upon the setting, and the little men that a fantasist hand had previously shaped.

---

[61] Renard himself; a translation of the story is contained in this same volume.

[62] In Medieval and Renaissance Christian iconography God was often represented as an eye—the "all-seeing eye"—in a triangular frame representing the trinity. The image was adapted into the Great Seal of the United States in 1776, in a version co-opted some years later by the Freemasons.

Pons was confirmed in the opinion that he too was nothing. He wanted to shout: "What did I tell you!" But the author had already taken away his voice, and his powers of movement and thought.

Foreword to The Motionless Voyage

Reader,

If it is sufficient for you that my stories are singular; if you are content to ask from each one, in isolation, the pleasure that it gives you; if you do not require any linkage between them other than sisterhood, and no more than a family resemblance (inevitable, alas)—then dispense with reading this foreword. It is rather forbidding.

If, on the contrary, you require a guiding notion that will enable you to examine the persistent developmental thread that runs through the collection, and which makes my stories into something like chapters in which a single train of thought is pursued—then read it. And forgive me for being laconic, borrowing the dry and churlish language of mathematicians.

The following stories are not assembled at hazard; they constitute deliberately-disparate parts of the same whole, and are grouped in methodical succession. Their totality forms a study of what I shall call the *logical marvelous*: a study whose object is the recognition of the limits of the genre and a proof of its flexibility.

The problem arises in this way: given that a work of the logical marvelous is composed of two elements, the marvelous and the logical, it is to seek out the extreme points to which one of the two elements might dominate, without the work ceasing clearly to possess its combined characteristics of fantasy and reason; without escaping from its strange ambiguous domain and falling out, whether into utopian science or systematic divagation.

If I am not mistaken, the first and last of my stories determine these two opposite points. The last, "A Christian Legend of Acteon," only includes the indispensable minimum of logic. The first, "The Motionless Voyage," contains the maximum dose of science. (I say "science" and not "logic" deliberately, because, in this romantic context, it appears to me that

171

one must imagine science as being logic in action—applied, realized, materialized, visible, tangible, audible logic, available to *the senses*, and not merely to *sense*—and as being the most striking expression in which one might clothe pure, abstract and speculative logic for the reader's eyes; and because mixing science into the work that one is writing is to enter into logic superlatively.)

After having established these two limiting terms of the study, it was necessary to connect them up by means of intermediary stories, in which the logical tint could be seen gradually to fade and pale while, by degrees, the marvelous color intensified. Thus proceeding from a cosmological paradox to a reasoned fable, I thought I ought to arrange a series of temporal steps toward the final stopping-points of my journey—the last stages of my work, the terminal tales—on the grounds that the more fabulous a story is, the further it has to be moved back through the ages.

If anyone asks me why I have followed the reverse order of natural chronology, I shall respond that I prefer to depart from the modern era, as featured in the romance of engineering with which my book begins; that I prefer to cast off from a milieu of concrete, positive and prosaic precision in order to draw away into dreams, to go forth and lose myself, along with myth, in the evasive night of time. To adopt here the true order of the centuries would, it seems to me, have been as scarcely rational as to descend in an etheroplane to the ultimate depths of celestial space, without ever having risen upwards, save on the back of the Chimera.

M.R.

THE MOTIONLESS VOYAGE

For Charles Derennes[63]

At about 10 a.m., the man we had rescued finally opened his eyes.

I expected a classic awakening—feverish fingers passed over the forehead; "Where am I? Where am I" stammered in a faint voice—but there was nothing of the sort. Our debtor remained tranquil for a few seconds, gazing into infinity. Then his eyes lit up with intelligence and energy and he cocked an ear to the sound of the propeller and the lapping of the waves against the hull. He sat up on the narrow bunk and set about inspecting the cabin, as coolly as if Gaetan and I were not there.

Next we saw him turn toward the porthole to look out at the sea, and then examine us, one after another, without curiosity or politeness, as if we were as-yet-unnoticed items of furniture. Folding his arms, he fell into a profound reverie.

Going by the external evidence, we had assumed that the unknown man with the handsome face and the nice hands had been well brought-up; his clothes, soaking wet as they were, seemed to us to be those of a gentleman. His conduct, therefore, wounded my companion and surprised me—although Gaetan had long become accustomed to seeing rustic mock-

---

[63] Charles Derennes (1882-1932) was a popular writer, whose novel, *Le Peuple du pôle* (1907; tr. in a Black Coat Press edition as *The People of the Pole*) was cited by Renard as a key specimen of "scientific marvel fiction" when he attempted to define that nascent genre in an essay published 1909—the next development in the train of thought that began with his contemplation of the "logical marvelous."

nobility and sophistication ill-wed to insolence in the same individual.

My astonishment did not last long, though. *Come on!* I said to myself. *No reckless judgments! Shouldn't we put the victim's strange behavior down to a perfectly excusable mental disturbance in the wake of disaster? Oughtn't we to respect his meditation? Judging by the extraordinary circumstances of his arrival, the occurrence can't have been anything banal....*

Gaetan, however, on finding him looking so well and behaving so badly, became impatient. "Well?" he said to him, roughly. "How are you? You're better, eh?" He repeated the final phrase several more times without obtaining any reply.

The man seemed somewhat bewildered by Gatetan's aggression. He looked him up and down, doubtless finding his elegant dress ill-fitted to his language and manner, and, after a pause for reflection—calculated to annoy that coarse gentleman even further—he nodded his head to indicate that he was, indeed, better.

Good, I thought. *He understands French—perhaps a compatriot.*

"You've had a stroke of luck," Gaetan went on. "Without us, you know...well, old chap, you'd be dead, what!" He concluded with an angry gesture: "Good God, are your lips stuck together?"

"Are you ill?" I asked, moving my friend aside, more to shut him up than to enquire after the taciturn fellow's health. "Tell me...are you in pain?"

The other shook his head negatively and became thoughtful again. My fears were confirmed and I exchanged an anxious glance with Gaetan. I don't know whether the man noticed it, but I thought I glimpsed a smile in his eyes, although his face remained stern. "Would you like something to drink?" I asked.

He looked at me, and said, with a strange accent: "Doctor?"

"No," I said, cheerfully. "No, no!" And as his eyes continued to interrogate me, I added: "Novelist...writer...do you understand?"

He sketched an affirmative nod that was almost a bow, and directed an interrogative flick of the chin at Gaetan.

"I don't do anything, myself," the latter replied, with a snigger. "I'm a rentier." And he added, parodying my own terminology: "Idler...good-for-nothing...do you understand?"

I observed the effect of this witticism on our guest's face, and hastened to change the subject. "Monsieur is the owner of the boat," I said. "You're a guest of Baron Gaetan de Vineuse-Paradol, who picked you up. I'm Gerard Sinclair, his traveling companion."

Instead of telling us his name and occupation, however—as I was inviting him to do—the man reflected for a few moments more, then articulated, rather laboriously: "Can you tell me what happened, please? I've completely lost my memory, after a certain point in time." This time, the accent was revealed in all its comic impurity; it was an English accent.

"Well, it's quite simple," Gaetan replied. "The launch put out to sea; it was the sailors in it who fished you out..."

"Before, Monsieur. What happened before?"

"Before what?" my friend quipped. "Not before the explosion, I assume?"

The man seemed stupefied. "What explosion, Monsieur?"

I sensed that Gaetan was about to get angry, and I intervened again. "My dear chap," I said to him, in a low voice, "let me talk to this fellow. He's doubtless the victim of a sort of amnesia that's quite frequent following a traumatic experience, and can't remember anything about his awful accident. Stay calm and don't say anything." Then, addressing myself to the man who had lost his memory, I said: "Monsieur, I'll tell you everything we know about your misfortune. That, I hope, will sufficiently refresh your memory to allow you, in your turn, to give *your host* a complete account of the event to which we owe the honor of your acquaintance."

Although I had emphasized "your host" vocally and by my expression, my listener had not flinched. He knotted his arms around his folded legs, set his chin on his knees, and waited for my clarifications. I went on. "You are, my dear Monsieur, on Monsieur de Vineuse-Paradol's steam-yacht *Océanide*—captain, Duval; home port, Le Havre. And you're safe here. She's a fine ship: 90 meters; 2 184 tonnes; top speed 15 knots, with a 5000 horse-power engine. In addition to crew members and service staff, comprising 95 individuals, there were, before your arrival, two passengers aboard: the *patron* and myself. That's not many—the boat has 28 cabins like yours—but, by virtue of its duration, Monsieur de Vineuse's cruise did not tempt anyone except your humble servant. We're returning from Havana, where it pleased my friend to select, in person and on the spot, a few cigars. So…ahem…"

I had expected the remark about the cigars, mentioned as a negligible detail, to elicit considerable amazement; I took advantage of it to catch my breath. "So, Monsieur, our return voyage was proceeding in the most pleasant monotony when, three days ago, the engine broke down. We had to stop. It's now August 21, so that was August 18. The repair of the broken piston-rod was immediately undertaken, and the captain wanted to take advantage of the stop to patch up his rudder. We had broken down at 40 degrees north latitude and 37 degrees, 23 minutes and 15 seconds west longitude, not far from the Azores, 1290 miles from the Portuguese coast and 1787 from the American coast, two-thirds of the way across—and we only got under way again this morning, at dawn.

"On August 18, the air was calm and the sea smooth; there was no breeze or current, no movement at all. A sailing ship with all its sails deployed could not have made a fathom in twelve hours, and the *Océanide*, freed from the caprice of the elements, remained perfectly still. The episode was by no means pleasant. However, on the captain's assurance that the work would not take long, we accepted matters without getting overly irritated. Because of the extreme heat—which was no longer tempered by the wind of our progress—we decided to sleep during the day and spend the nights on deck. Breakfast would be served there at 8 p.m. and dinner at 4 a.m..

"Now, the day before yesterday—Friday August 19—between the two nocturnal meals, we were walking along the rail, smoking in the moonlight. The sky was swarming with constellations. All the stars, even the planets, seemed to be twinkling. Shooting stars rained down incessantly, and their white trails persisted so long against the dark background that you might have thought some mystical piece of chalk was drawing parabolas on the blackboard of the Heavens. I was not too tired to follow that mysterious and grandiose geometry lesson. Everything, moreover, concurred with the majesty of the spectacle. An absolute silence reigned. The crew was asleep; nothing could be heard but the dull tread of our rubber soles on the boards.

"We were making our tour of the deck for about the twentieth time when a whistling sound emerged from the depths of space to starboard. Almost at the same time, we saw a faint light appear high in the sky on that side. It was coming toward the yacht, and the whistling sound with it. The sound grew louder, increased in pitch, then drew away and vanished, while the light passed overhead, animated by a speed that was relatively modest for a celestial object, leaping from one horizon to the other like a lazy shooting star, at no great distance.

"We immediately concluded that it was a meteor. The man on watch agreed with us, although he had never seen one like it in thirty years at sea. The captain, drawn forth by the whistling, accepted the evidence that it was a bolide without further ado when he had heard our explanations, He wrote in the ship's log that at half past midnight on August 20, a faintly luminous aerolith had passed through the atmosphere immediately above the *Océanide*, describing a course directly from east to west, thus following the 40th parallel, where we lay at anchor."

At this point, I looked at the man intently. He tightened his grip around his ankles, closed his eyes, and waited for the continuation of my story.

"As you might imagine," I went on, a trifle disheartened, "the meteor became the topic of our conversation. Each of us offered and supported various conjectures. Personally, I concentrated on a certain relationship that had struck me between the speed of its passage and the duration of the noise it made. Monsieur Vineuse offered an opinion that as scarcely banal, but defensible; according to him, the bolide—which, we had assumed until then, had appeared over the horizon—might have emerged from the ocean; there was no proof of the contrary. It was very unlikely, but the more fantastic theories are, Monsieur, the more seductive they are. We tried to excuse the fear that had gripped us by attributing a supernatural cause to it. To be perfectly frank, the abrupt appearance of that mass, heading directly for the boat, would not have left anyone unmoved, and we had released a sigh of relief on seeing the projectile pass over at such a height. Even at that moment of deliverance, you know, its damned whistling made us duck our heads—what soldiers call *bowing to the bullet*.

"In brief, we wished from the bottom of our hearts never to indulge in such practical astronomy again—which did not prevent the phenomenon from being repeated last night, slightly later, at about 1 a.m., and with very dramatic complications.

"Yesterday, Monsieur de Vineuse, weary of that sojourn in the open sea beneath a dangerous sky, gave the order to work on the repairs all day and all night. Working two-hour shifts, one detail was devoted to the broken piston-rod, in the engine-room, and another to the rudder, in the launch. The latter gang had just finished work and was getting ready to come back aboard at the very moment when the peculiar periodic bolide started whistling in the distance.

"In darkness as fiery as the preceding night's, everyone saw the pale light appear, rise up and zoom toward us. Monsieur de Vineuse thought he perceived, however, that it was less rapid than the day before, while in my opinion, the whistling had a lower pitch and was les intense. At any rate, the asteroid was still traveling at a fair lick. In a few seconds it would reached the zenith—and from there, no doubt, it would plunge placidly down to the western horizon. The Earth possessed therein a new satellite, a night-light moon, ephemeral and minuscule.

"But all of a sudden, Monsieur, there was something in its stead, like a sun crossed with a lightning-flash; nothing continued westwards along the orbit commenced, and the whistling was interrupted by a frightful bang. I received a punch from an invisible fist in my belly; the unsettled air choked us; we felt the *Océanide*'s timbers tremble; a wind got up, only to die down again just as quickly, and waves rose up, only to vanish instantly.

"Then, quite distinctly, we heard a hail of objects falling into the sea. One of them splashed down very close to the launch, reappeared and floated. That was you, Monsieur, clinging to the bolts of a sheet-metal door—but a very strange and miraculously light metal, since it allowed you to float with it.

"You were fished out, but unconscious. Not knowing whether you were alone aboard the…aerolith…the captain sent the launch to cruise the area within a two-mile radius. It searched the field of the catastrophe, without encountering anything but bits of metallic wreckage. The sea was strewn with them; they shone with a sort of dull gleam, if I might put it thus, and bobbed on the surface like excellent buoys. There was no sign of any living creature.

"During that search, Monsieur, you remained unconscious, in spite of our best efforts; we undressed you, put you to bed and watched over you. I believe, though, that your unconsciousness changed into healthy sleep toward dawn, at about the time we set off again for Le Havre—where we shall arrive, I presume, within a week.

"And here we are! Now, would you care to tell us who we have the pleasure of dealing with?"

The man nodded his head, but did not reply. "What about the metal sheet?" he asked, finally. "The floating sheet…the debris…"

179

"Well," said Gaetan, "it's still out there where you came a cropper. Monsieur Duval, the skipper, judged that it was scrap aluminum, of such poor quality that it wasn't worth the trouble of taking it aboard."

The stranger smiled frankly. Seeing that, my friend chided him jovially: "So tell us your secret, then—no one will steal it. It as a balloon, right? It's your dirigible that went bang? A little puncture, old chap. Come on, tell the gentleman!" Becoming annoyed, he concluded: "Oh, the Hell with it—if you don't want to give anything away, that's your business, isn't it?"

The other then embarked on a long speech, in his solemnly clownish double Dutch, which I shall try to reproduce as best I can, once and for all. "Monsieur le Baron," he proclaimed, "the slight conveniability...er...desire...er...that I present...whom am here...without invitation...and how, and why. For now I...er...rememory everything *very well*. But before the story... Permit me, Monsieur le Baron...to...er... supper... *if you please*...I'm *hungry*...which is to say, famished...splendid! Have you any clothes?"[64]

Gaetan had underwear and one of his own yachtsman's costumes brought from his closet. "Your coat ain't dry," he said, at the risk of his argot not being understood. Besides, it's in no condition to wear. Here's your purse and watch, which were in it. What do you think of these blue trousers and this jacket with gold buttons? Is it OK?"

"Don't you have any black clothes?" said the man, grabbing his purse.

"No. Why? Yours were grey."

---

[64] This original of this passage is a mixture of mangled French and a English phrases—the latter italicized here—which is impossible to back-translate in any proper fashion, but the narrator is mercifully content to refine his subsequent translations of what the castaway says (although he continues to render Gaetan's slightly coarse speech in an eye-dialect that can only be faintly suggested in English translation).

"That's all right. It's a pity, though—I would have preferred it."

Meanwhile, Gaetan had opened his guest's watch, like the badly-brought up child that he still was. "I wasn't able to take a look in your purse," he confessed.

"No," the other replied, flatly. "It has a secret lock."

Vineuse burst out laughing. "As for your ticker," he said, "there are some initials here. The casing has a C and an A, intertwined. Your name must be—what? *Cachottier Anglais*?[65] Ha ha ha!"

"My name is Archibald Clarke, Monsieur—at your service—and I'm an American, from Trenton in Pennsylvania. The rest I'll have the pleasure of telling you in a little while, after breakfast. Would you kindly lend me a razor?"

We left him alone. Knowing his name gave me a considerable feeling of relief, of much the same kind that I experience now in being able to describe him by a single word, "Clarke," instead of having to string out various alternatives, such as "the unknown man," "the disaster victim" and other wearying subterfuges of rhetoric. Gaetan was angry, though. He fulminated against the manners of the intruder—Clarke, I mean—and only changed his tune when the American—Clarke, that is—came into the dining-room. Clad in Gaetan's reefer jacket, admittedly, the latter seemed to us to be a decent chap. His physiognomy was quite pleasing, his education perfect, his manner easy-going—a thoroughly nice fellow.

Archibald Clarke ate conscientiously and drank in the same fashion, without uttering a syllable. At coffee, he poured himself a little glass of scotch whisky, lit a dollar "cheroot"— that being the factory price—and offered us his hand, saying: "Thank you, Messieurs." Was that for the meal or the rescue? The question remains unanswered. Then he took a few puffs on his cigar in quick succession—at two cents a puff, at least—and began speaking slowly, searching for his modes of expression, and perhaps also for his ideas.

---

[65] "Secretive Englishman."

181

The reader will forgive me for have corrected, on his behalf, the most ludicrous and obscure French that a citizen of the United States could ever have permitted himself to elaborate. I have also thought it appropriate to translate into French the American measurements of distance, weight, volume, surface area, etc. and not to mention the innumerable pauses with which, for various reasons, Mr. Clarke's speech was punctuated.[66]

You've surely heard of the Corbetts of Philadelphia? No? That's understandable, I suppose. In France, people might not know of the existence of a distant couple who actually made all the great discoveries of recent years, but were unlucky in that they were also made simultaneously by other scientists who were quicker to publish them. Edison, the Curies, Berthelot, Marconi and Renard have found nothing that has not been discovered by my brother-in-law Randolph Corbett and my sister Ethel, except that they discovered them a little sooner—with the result that my unfortunate relatives were always on the point of accomplishing their work of genius when some unexpected rival proclaimed his own identical one. *Too late* seemed to be their motto. That's why you're not familiar with them.

At home, however, theirs is a famous household; quite recently, the newspapers over there were full of eulogies to their indomitable audacity. That was with respect to an experiment in submarine diving. For several months, in fact, they were said to have been obsessed with submersibles, aerostats and automobiles—in sum, all kinds of unusual or vertiginous locomotion. And then...and then...excuse me for telling the story so clumsily. Your language is difficult for me—it cramps my style. By the way, will you promise to be discreet?

_____

[66] I have translated the terms of measurement given in the text directly rather than substituting the imperial measures from which they were supposedly derived.

Shortly, we'll be getting to a secret that doesn't belong to me...

Good—thank you.

Then, a few days ago—on the eighteenth of August—just as I was leaving my office, a telegram signed Ethel Corbett arrived, asking *Mr. Archibald Clarke, senior accountant at Roebling Brothers, Cable Manufacturers of Trenton, Pennsylvania,* to come to Philadelphia immediately.

That invitation gave me pause. A slight disagreement, which had arisen between us regarding the paltry matter of an inheritance, had ensured that the Corbetts had not seen me for some time. What was the matter? What should I do? I weighed it up—but the address on the dispatch, almost excessive in its detail, revealed how determined my sister was that it should reach me without difficulty or delay. It must, therefore, be something important—and then again, family's family, isn't it?

An hour later, the Pennsylvania Railroad deposited me at West Philadelphia Station, and I took a cab to Belmont. That's where the Corbetts live, in the admirable Fairmount Park, on the bank of the Schuylkill River, so amenable to all forms of boating, including subaquatic navigation.

The cab passed through the western suburbs, crossed a bridge and went out into verdant countryside. Night had fallen during the journey, but it was so rich in stars that I was able to recognize my brother-in-law's house from some distance away. It was a humble little house, to be sure, which seemed even humbler and smaller backed by an immense workshop next to a monumental hangar, in front of the testing-ground for automobiles and aircraft.

I recognized it, Messieurs, and my heart constricted. In that whole imposing block of buildings, only one window in the living quarters was illuminated. Now, the nocturnal activity of the Corbetts is legendary in Pennsylvania; every night, the festival of labor illuminates the glazed roof of the workshop or the bays of the hangar. You can imagine how alarmed I was, that night, by so much dark and silent quietude.

Jim, their black butler, welcomed me without a light and took me to the Corbett's bedroom—the only one illuminated. I found my brother-in-law laid up in bed, feverish and jaundiced. My sister came in immediately. For four years, I had only seen pictures of her in magazines. She had hardly changed at all. Her dress was cut in a boyish fashion, as before, and her short-cropped hair was hardly showing any grey in spite of her respectable age.

"Hello, Archie," Randolph said. "I never doubted that you'd come right away. We need you…"

"I imagine so, Ralph. What can I do?"

"Assist…"

"Don't tire yourself out," my sister said, interrupting. "I'll tell you quickly, Archie, for time's pressing. We've built…no, don't worry, Ralph's not in danger…a simple bout of flu, but he's under strict instructions to stay in bed…please don't interrupt me again. We—Ralph, Jim and I—have secretly built a very interesting machine, Archie. And for far that someone else will anticipate our discovery yet again, we've promised ourselves that, in future, we'll try out every new machine as soon as it's finished. Unfortunately, the flu took a hand in our affairs. Today, just as the goal was attained, Ralph was laid low. It's impossible to postpone the test, but the machine needs three people to operate it. Who could replace Ralph? Me. Who could replace me? Jim. But who could replace Jim? I thought of you. Your role doesn't require any training or presence of mind; it only requires a little discipline during the trial and a great deal of discretion afterwards. You can help us better than anyone else. Will you?"

"All right. Let's forget all our differences, sister mine. I've come to make myself useful."

"Be warned that we're running some risk."

"Bah!"

"There's also—how shall I put it…? In sum, this…sport…that we're going to try out, appears to be rather strikingly and exceedingly abnormal, bizarrely exaggerated, almost monstrous…"

"It's all the same to me. I've come to make myself useful. Show me the room where I'm to sleep. I'll go to bed immediately, in order to be in full readiness tomorrow morning."

"Tomorrow!" Corbett exclaimed. "It's not tomorrow, it's right now. There's 11 p.m. chiming. Go, my dear friend, go! Don't lose a minute!"

"What? The trial? In pitch darkness?"

"Yes. It has to take place outside—and if it were daylight, I ask you, would it remain secret from the jealous and perspicacious engineers who are spying on us incessantly?"

"Outside? Fine. So what is it, then?"

Ethel was agitating impatiently, though. "Since it's agreed, come on—let's go!" she cried. "Everything's ready. The functioning of the apparatus will enable you to understand its purpose better than any description. What? Change clothes? Put on overalls? There's no need for disguises—we're not in the theater. Come on!"

"Goodbye, Archie," said Randolph, "until tomorrow evening!"

What? I thought. "Tell me," I asked my sister as I followed her, "does 'tomorrow evening' mean that you intend to take me on a voyage that will last until tomorrow evening? But Ralph said that it's necessary not to show ourselves in broad daylight. Are we going to stop off somewhere before dawn? Where shall we spend the day? In sum, where are we going?"

"To Philadelphia."

"Excuse me? To Philadelphia! But that's where we are!"

"To be sure, my idiot brother. We'll make a circuit and come back here."

I shut up, sensing that she wasn't going to tell me any more and fully occupied in groping my way through the darkness. Ethel didn't want to attract the attention of unwelcome intruders of spies, which moving lights would have done.

My sister preceded me along an interminable corridor, and then through the workshop. There one could see clearly. Through the glass roof, the stars and the rising Moon were

185

shining on a chaos of strange shapes. To reach the other side of the room, we had to zigzag back and forth amid the most fantastic disorder, stepping over barriers of armed beams, suddenly hostile, avoiding singular creatures of steel squatting on their four wheels, and also moving around inexplicable windmills with helically-twisted arms.

Ethel threaded her way through the midst of these bizarre items without bumping into them. As for me, I had first to escape a certain round tire on which I trod, but as I gloried in having shaken off that cowardly trap, I was caught by the snare of a slyly unraveled rope. Then, after my victorious struggle against that hempen boa, there was a sort of spider that caught me in its web; a thread entangled me in its tight mesh, and I ended up getting bogged down in a marsh, which was the envelope of an imperfectly-deflated balloon. By clinging on to the fins of some kind of iron shark, however, I freed myself—only to bump into some kind of wooden bird. Doubtless the Spirit of Invention had put my valor to sufficient proof, though, for I found myself suddenly face to face with Jim in the hangar.

The hangar was as large as the nave of a cathedral, and served as a garage for aerostats, which occupied its periphery. The moonlight made their more-or-less inflated envelopes glisten. All those spherical, fusiform and ovoid balloons arranged against the wall seemed to be standing deferentially aside from a sort of shining partition that ran along the middle of the hall. Ethel pointed at it and said: "Here's the machine." Then she and Jim began conferring in low voices.

Aha! I thought. *That's it, the machine. Hmm! An automobile... colossal... Unless...perhaps a boat?*

As far as I could tell in the dim light, in which electric bulbs hung down stupidly and impotently, the thing resembled the blade of a gigantic knife, not sharp but exceedingly pointed. I can't think of a better comparison. It was about forty meters long and eight tall, and only a meter broad from the rear end to the middle. The forward part tapered in order to cut through…the air or water? At any rate, it tapered like a dagger.

I made out a triangular rudder at the stern. *Aha!* I thought. *It's a boat…no, it's an automobile!* In fact, the enigmatic vehicle was resting on squat wheels. They were fitted with rubber rings and mounted on unusually powerful springs. Beneath the apparatus, set between them, were black blocks that I could hardly make out. As I've said, the whole thing gleamed; it was, however—if one many couple such antonyms together—a dull gleam.

Ethel kicked away a few tools strewn on the ground and opened a door in the flank of this titanic blade, approximately in the middle. An electric bulb, abruptly lighting up inside the object, showed me that there was a cabin accommodated in its narrow base. It made up an exceedingly cramped retreat, four meters long, two high and only one broad. This habitat contained three seats, one behind another; they were comfortable automobile bucket-seats. In front of the first two a whole system of sparkling levers, knobs and pedals was installed. Behind the third were two handgrips at the ends of rods, which I took to be the rudder's tiller-shafts.

"That's your place," Ethel told me. "You're the helmsman. I'm in front of you, Jimmy's in front of me. Oh, no false modesty! We don't need you to be a qualified helmsman, my lad. You'll scarcely need to steer. The rudder only comes into play in exceptional circumstances. You probably won't even have occasion to touch it."

"Good—but what the Devil is all this machinery for?"

Ethel did not hear; Jim had called her to the prow, and she left me in a daze in front of the cabin. What a cabin it was, Messieurs! What a command-post! What a confusion of taps, graduated circles, quadrants, shafts, cords, screw threads, keys, wires, buttons and dials! And other mysterious instruments too! There was nothing resembling Christian furniture apart from the three armchairs—and perhaps also the pitch-pine clock standing against the forward bulkhead.

All things considered, it looked like a fine example of precision clockwork—but why was there a geographical globe under the dial, half-embedded in the chronometer's casing and capable of pivoting about a vertical axis, as if to demonstrate the alternation of day and night to young dunces? Why was there a curved needle fixed to the pitch-pine, negotiating the roundness of the terrestrial globe, whose tip was presently pointing to Philadelphia?

Powerless to deduce the answers to these questions, I continued my inspection. A basket filled with bottles and food-supplies intrigued me considerably. Were there no inns, then? Could we not spend the day in some solitary hostelry beside the river or the road? Oh, of course! There was a danger of running into some annoyingly indiscreet person there. In truth, though, the precaution seemed excessive. But what about windows? There were no windows.

"How are we going to steer?" I murmured. "How shall we survey the road, if it's an automobile, the watery depths, if it's a submarine, the mountains, in the improbable case that it's an aircraft? And first of all, in fact, what is this machine? Where's the engine? At the front? The rear? Above the cabin? Within the apparatus, that cockpit occupies a quarter of the height and a tenth of the length; it is, therefore, if I might put it that way, like the stomach in the belly of a whale. What's inside the rest of this artificial cetacean in which we're to become Jonahs?"

At that moment, my sister's voice rose up, trembling with pleasure and intrepidity. "Jim! Open the hangar doors. It's time to get the horsey out."[67]

---

[67] The term I have translated as "horsey" is "*dada,*" that being a French term for a child's toy horse—and, by extension, a metaphorical hobby-horse. Renard could not have known in 1909 that it was soon to be adopted as the title of a movement in *avant-garde* art, although the machine, its function and the story's comic tone are somewhat akin to the spirit of that movement.

The butler burst out laughing. I confess that I'm not at all fond of black people and their guttural language. They always talk to you as if they had sore throats. But Jim, with his adenoidal laugh…no! You can't imagine how much I disliked him…

Anyway, he slid back the immense doors on their rollers, and a starry slit widened from the top to the bottom of the edifice. The flat fields appeared, white in the midst of a circle of silvery hills. A little lake sparkled beneath the ruddy sky. Our mighty sword seemed to be on guard in front of all that. What frightful hidden force was about to move that crushing arm and get that rolling monument. Seemingly as heavy as a grounded ship, under way?

My sister switched off the light. "Let's get going," she said. "I want to set off at midnight exactly. What's the matter, Archibald?"

"You…aren't you going to start the engine?"

"Ha ha!" cried Ethel, as if I had just cracked the funniest of jokes. "Well, that'll be hard work, won't it, Jimmy?"

"Yes, yes," the nutler gurgled, with a grating laugh. "Does Ma'am recall the accident with the scale model?"

"Come on, Archie, lend a hand!" my sister went on—and she braced herself against the rear of the enormous mass, as if to push it. In spite of my bewilderment—I was about to help her, along with Jim, when we saw the metal colossus, moved purely by the simple effort of a female shoulder, advance smoothly toward its unknown destiny.

"Oh, it's well-balanced today!" Ethel remarked, simply. "I thought that it would take at least two of us to get it moving. No, no—leave it to me. It's child's play." Turning her back on the Schuylkill River—which killed off any nautical hypothesis—she pushed the vehicle into the middle of the field, in a westerly direction.

I escorted her. Jim followed us, brimming over with excitement and prancing about to a fandango rhythm.

"Excuse me, brother mine—I'll explain the mechanism to you once we're under way. For the moment, I've too much

189

to do..." Oh, what emotion vibrated in those words! How many months of laborious anxiety had my companions been waiting for this sensational moment?

For the time being, diminished by the amplitude of the surroundings, the machine seemed less terrible. Seen from the front, in fact, one saw no more than the blade of a saber viewed from the point. Having stood to one side to see it in its entirety, I discovered a few slight protrusions on top, which had been invisible under the hangar. There were also several that extended from the walls to the right and left.

Ethel checked the blocks between the little wheels. "Perfect weather," she said. "Not a breath of wind. Let's get aboard!"

We went into the blade. Jim carefully sealed the door behind us, and the rumor of nature—so faint that I had taken it for absolute silence—was abruptly cut off.

I thought at first that the cabin was completely dark, and I was beginning to think that ours would be an incomprehensible expedition of blind prisoners when my gaze was attracted by a patch of pale light above Ethel's seat. It was a sort of large lampshade glowing inside. I can only describe it as a large hemispherical funnel, hanging down, with the widest part at the bottom and the neck embedded directly in the ceiling. The neck was extendable at will, like the barrel of a telescope. By that means, Ethel brought the funnel down so that it surrounded her head, illuminating it with a lunar lividity. Then she made me sit down in her place.

Imagine my amazement to find myself seemingly transported outside, as if by magic! In fact, an image of the surrounding area was projected on the surface of the funnel, including the sky—with the crescent moon, the Milky Way, the deep blue background and the twinkling stars—and the white plain with its silvery hills. I turned my head to the rear and I saw the silhouette of Philadelphia, surmounted by the statue of Penn and haloed by the nimbus of light that floats above large cities by night. Also visible in the funnel was the Corbetts' little house, where Randolph was thinking of us as he lay in his sick-bed.

Oh, what a marvel, Messieurs! The vision of that living miniature positively fascinated me! I can give you some idea of it by likening it to the inverted images photographers see when they look through the polished glass of the darkroom to see what the landscape will produce on the plate. In this case, though, the landscape was revealed without inversion, in its entirety, in the form of a panorama, with the particularity that the observer seemed to be perched eight meters above the ground—which is to say, as you will have guessed, at the spot at which the stem of that improved periscope emerged from the roof of our prison. That was what facilitated the steering.

I would have kept my head under that miraculous lamp-shade for some time if my sister had not reclaimed her post. "What's so magical about trickery with lenses?" she muttered. "Every submarine in our fleet has one almost as good! Are we lined up correctly, Jim?"

The funnel's bluish phosphorescence diffused through the cabin; one by one, all the instruments emerged from the darkness. Jim leaned over a compass; he was no longer laughing. "Yes, Ma'am," he said. "We're orientated lengthwise to the line from east to west."

"Good. To your rudder, Archie! Simply keep it straight, until further orders, as you would while rowing. Are you in position, Archie?"

"Yes."

"Are you in position, Jim?"

"Yes, Ma'am."

"Good. Get ready! Release the weights!"

The butler pressed down on two pedals at the same time. I heard two simultaneous clicks under the apparatus, fore and aft, and something fell heavily on to the ground with a dull thud. Then it seemed to me, all of a sudden, that a sickening force pressed me down into myself—my head into my torso, my torso into my legs and my legs into the floor; in brief, I experienced the nauseating sensation of compression produced, on departure, by the abrupt thrust of an elevator. It lasted no longer than was required to observe it, however. Now, nothing betrayed the slightest displacement of our vehicle.

"Hang on!" I cried. "What's that?" Something was shining at my feet.

I bent down. Suddenly—oh Lord!—I shut my eyes, and my fists clenched on the tiller-rods, under the dizzying influence of vertigo. The floor of that cell was made of glass, so transparent that it seemed that there was nothing there, and through that gaping hole I saw Philadelphia sinking...sinking...at the speed of a fall.

We were rising upwards.

Ethel took no notice of my exclamation. She consulted a dial and read out in a loud voice the information she obtained therefrom. "Three hundred...four hundred...six hundred...a thousand. Jim, check it on the statoscope! A thousand and fifty...eleven hundred...is that correct?"

"Yes, Ma'am."

"Drop 30 kilograms of ballast."

The butler activated another pedal. There was another click, and I saw one of the shadows that were interposed between ourselves and the abyss diminish in volume and become slack. This time, it was not a weight that fell; in view of the risk of striking down someone out for a late stroll, a mechanism permitted sacks filled with sand or bottles filled with water to be emptied out by remote control. For what reason had the Corbetts systematically prohibited any direct communication with the exterior? I would have given anything to know—but it was not the right time to interrogate my sister. She was hypnotically fixated on the barometric dial, counting: "Fourteen fifty...fourteen seventy-five...fifteen hundred meters! Finally! Ah! Fifteen forty—that's too much!"

She seized a hanging chain and pulled down on it. Above our heads, in what I shall call the loft, this action produced a susurrus of gas escaping through a valve, and the needle of the barometer fell back to the figure 1500.

"We're there!" Ethel proclaimed. Then, having consulted the clock over Jim's cap, she added: "Five to! Good. We'll set off at exactly midnight."

We'll set off? What did she mean? With a stupidly interrogative stare I studied her masculine hair-cut and the nape of her neck; I was so intrigued that its curls seemed to me to form a vague face, grizzled and mocking.

"We'll set off, you say?" I queried, unable to hold back any longer. "Haven't we already set off?"

"No."

"What more is there, then? What do you intend to do, Ethel?"

"Go around the world, Mr. Inquisitive!"

"Eh? What? Oh—you're joking! Around…"

"…The world. In one day. Is the apparatus equilibrated, Jim?"

The frightful prospect of a flight with a madwoman in the guise of an aeronaut blurred my vision, and it was through that mist of dizziness that I made out the accursed Zulu consulting a spirit level. It revealed that the machine was tilted forwards imperceptibly. A little ballast, dropped from the bow, rendered it absolutely horizontal, but caused it to climb up twenty meters. Ethel declared that, after all, that was of no importance. A compass, interrogated, gave her a satisfactory answer. She smiled and murmured: "Perfect; the heading is due west."

And when midnight sounded in the depths of the clock, my sister commanded: "Start the engine! Contact!"

Jim turned a large commutator. Immediately, behind the rear panel, the invisible engine started up with a very quiet but very insistent hum. It rumbled more and more forcefully, and as its activity increased a cooling breeze seemed to spring up around us, increasing to become a storm wind, then a tempest. A squall howled along the length of the aircraft, then changed into a simoom, and then a cataclysmic blast, and then something worse, unknown to human beings until then. Currents of air, as violent as never-ending javelins, flowed through the

193

joints of the doors in spite of their exactitude. An army of vipers could not have hissed any louder. A little tornado was generated, whirling within the cabin.

Meanwhile, the noise gradually increased at the surface of the apparatus, especially toward the forward cutting edge, where one might have imagined that an endless piece of silk was being torn. Under the force of the engine, our cell vibrated with increasing frequency, and I perceived, on touching the quivering wall, that it was less cold than I expected. In fact, the temperature was rising perceptibly, the thermometer-level climbing ceaselessly, and I could soon have believed that I was in some kind of extraordinary stove heated from without.

All this was evidence, as clear as daylight, of the displacement of our vehicle and its incredible velocity. So far as I was concerned, Ethel's dementia ceased to be a matter of conjecture and became a heart-rending certainty. In any case, my brave sister manifested no surprise, undoubtedly having anticipated every aspect of the vertiginous event. On her orders, Jim sealed up the doors and muffled the air-currents, by means of wadding driven in with a chisel. While this task was ongoing, Ethel consulted a long graduated scale along which a cursor was continually advancing, reading out a new set of figures. "Five hundred…six hundred…a thousand…twelve hundred…twelve fifty!"

I ought to mention that *twelve-fifty* was pronounced in a triumphant manner, and there's no reason not to tell you that, at that very instant, the cursor stopped on the scale and the column of mercury in the tube of the thermometer stopped rising, while the noise of the engine and the whistling sound of our progress became constant.

"Twelve-fifty," my sister repeated. "We're there, then!"

After a glance at the clock, fooled by a brief mental calculation, my sister gestured toward the terrestrial globe. "Jim," she said, "at three minutes forty-five seconds past midnight, put Thorndale under the point of the needle. *Thorndale*, right? We'll pass over it at that instant."

194

Jim waited for the moment, and rotated the globe by hand in such a fashion that the point of the fixed needle curving around its rotundity was over Thorndale. Immediately, he pressed a button and the sphere—doubtless activated by the machinery of the clock—began to turn slowly on its axis from left to right.

For myself, I recovered, with some difficulty, from a suffocating surprise. "Ethel!" I cried. "It's not possible! Already? We've reached Thorndale?"

"No," she replied, keeping watch on innumerable small instruments. "We've passed Thorndale. At present we're crossing over the railway between Valley and Siousca. Watch the needle on the globe, and watch this too." Ethel pointed at the graduated scale, whose indicator was still stuck on the number 1250. "That," my sister went on, "is a tachymeter, which measures velocity. It indicates a displacement of more than 2.8 kilometers a minute, which is approximately 1250 per hour."

"Damnation! We're moving at...."

"No, my friend, we're not moving."

"Oh! Explain, damn it!"

"We're not moving. It's the air that's rushing past all around us. Our vessel is motionless in the liberated atmosphere—and that, Archie, is why I've baptized it the *Aerofix*."

"Oh!"

"Yes. Wait a second...then I'll be content. Just this tap to shut off...there! I'm all yours. Let there be light, in your mind and in the cabin!" And my sister created electric daylight, whose glare obliterated the moon and the stars in the depths of the periscope.

"It's the air that's rushing past us?" I repeated, in a fit of curiosity.

"Come on, brother mine—wire merchant as you are, have you never thought how ridiculous people are in their manner of traveling? How ridiculous it is to displace themselves, by a tremendous effort of steam, gasoline or electricity, *on a moving ball*, when it's sufficient to remain stationary above it for all the points on the same parallel to file past before your eyes, one after another, with the opportunity to land there?"

"Damnation!"

"That is, however, the idea that Randolph and I have had and realized. The *Aerofix* is the proof of it. Yes, the air is moving around us, and the Earth beneath us. With respect to them, it is motionless. Gravity, to which our balloon remains subject, maintains it at a constant distance from the center of the Earth, but it possesses an engine that frees it from the drag of the globe rotating on its axis. It's in that sense that it's not moving, for our old planet continues to transport it in its journey round the Sun, and the Sun to transport the planet in its own infinite sidereal revolution. Except that, as the Earth continues its axial rotation from west to east, we shall effectively travel around the world from east to west, in 24 hours—or, to be more precise, in 23 hours 56 minutes and four seconds, just like the Sun."

After scribbling a few figures on a piece of paper, I hazarded: "I recall, though, that the Earth is 40,000 kilometers in circumference. In that case, since it takes 24 hours to rotate on its axis, it ought to be displacing this apparatus at...slightly more than 1666 meters an hour!"

"Not bad, for a cable-hawker! The cashier's showing his mettle! But mind-numbingly stupid, my delightful companion—it's at the equator, and there alone, that the circumference is 40,000 kilometers. If we'd taken off at Quito, for example, the tachymeter would indeed indicate 1666.6 recurring. Unfortunately, Philadelphia, from which the *Aerofix* rose up, is on the 40th north parallel, which only measures 30,000 kilometers, since it's nearer to the pole. Thus, the terrestrial sphere only rotates there at 1250 an hour. And what do you think would happen if the ascent had taken place at one of the poles, which remain as sedentary as all the points on the axis? We would have the same spot incessantly beneath our feet, and our décor would be a circle of ice, spinning around the polar center like a gramophone disk.

"Take note of this, too. The further the balloon rises into the bosom of the mass of air drawn into the terrestrial dance—an elevation that only slightly increases the circle we appear to be describing—the greater is the rapidity of the fluid that surrounds it, since that would take us further away from the center of rotation. That particularity would increase the effort expended to maintain it in immobility against a more vigorous current if the gas that we encounter in ascending were not rarefied as the torrent accelerates. The more furiously the wind blasts into us, the less dense it is. The dividing spur still has the same facility; the two phenomena counterbalance one another."

"But why stop at 1500 meters?"

"Because the highest peak on the 40th parallel doesn't quite reach that altitude—and we need to avoid a collision with the Rocky Mountains, don't we?"

"We're following this 40th parallel strictly, then?" I said.

"Strictly. Perhaps, one day, our machine will be able to vary its fixity by means of the gravitational attraction of the stars, or even with the aid of the Earth's progress in its orbit. It will then be a matter of immobilizing itself relative to the Sun, in order to make oblique journeys around the Earth—apparent journeys, at least. But we're a long way from that! At present, we're forced to follow the parallel of our choice as if it were a railway track. The rudder is merely an accessory designed to line the aircraft up and to combat harmful winds during the descent. We're obligatory globe-trotters, brother. Look at the compass; its needle won't oscillate by a millimeter in 24 hours, with no declination, provided that the magnetic pole is also the axial pole. We'll have north perpetually to starboard."

"So we'll get back to Philadelphia tomorrow," I muttered, wonderstruck, "after having circumnavigated the fortieth parallel. That's the *circuit* you mentioned."

"You've got it. Look at the globe on the clock—it's both an indicator of our successive positions and a representation of reality. The motionless point of the needle represents the *Aerofix*. Every 24 hours, the same places pass sequentially beneath it. Philadelphia will be there tomorrow—but we'll be a little late, because of the time required to come to a halt when the terrestrial drag resumes. These two maneuvers require an imperceptible progression; if I were to stop the engine abruptly while we were absolutely stationary—which, moreover, is impossible—the airflow would immediately grip our vessel again, and the front wall would hurtle toward us with the force of a shell."

I felt sweat beading on my forehead and moistening my palms. "This accursed heat!" I grumbled. "And that damned whistling! I can scarcely hear what you're saying, even though you're shouting."

"Yes, all that's caused by the friction of the air. Don't you find it stifling?" She unmasked the little openings that perforated the doors, which were connected to the outside by tubes slanted toward the stern. These ventilators were well-designed; a delightful coolness spread forth. "What trouble we had finding a remedy for the excess of heat!" my sister continued. "Ralph discovered a heat-resistant plaster, with which the hull is coated—an insulating layer."

I was about to voice some judicious reflections on the subject of air and the contradictory faculties it has, of chilling the body at high speed and setting it on fire at prodigious velocities, when my sister switched off the lights again. Once the immediate effects of darkness had eased, I could see Ethel helmeted by the periscope, very pale in its milky light.

"Their Highnesses the Rocky Mountains!" she announced. "Look at them, Archie!"

The sky tinted the magic funnel blue. Clouds were floating there now. The most distant seemed to be crawling without haste; the nearest were flashing by like fluffy lightning. Others, which we passed completely through, vanished from sight in the blink of an eye. Emerging over the horizon—I mean the edge of the lampshade—a patch of darkness climbed rapidly toward the stars. It was bizarrely outlined, white light playing about its tips, and I saw that it was the redoubtable mountain chain, heading toward us "full steam ahead."

The racing glaciers produced opalescent trails in the moonlight, like the tails of comets; a fugitive pallor illuminated our transparent floor; ridges leapt up and peaks loomed. One might have though that a mountainous herd was stampeding. Then it all died down. The summits fell away, back into the invisible zone, and the firmament, free of clouds, filled the periscope with its magnificence. The glass floor seemed to glitter in innumerable facets, and became a window of diamond, with the emotion of a living gem in its moving fires.

The butler was seized by a fit of idiotic gaiety. His throatiness increased in proportion to his joy and at was as if he were subject in the meantime to a hysterical diphtheria. He choked, arched his back, and coughed up a few interjections in honor of the Pacific.

"Yes, that's the Ocean," Ethel confirmed. "Three twenty-two—dead on time."

I let out a scream. "What if we fall?"

"There's nothing to fear, you old coward my dear little brother. The *Aerofix* is solidly built."

"Hmm!" I said, offended by her disdain and wanting to put on a brave face. "It is, indeed, a fine heavier-than-air craft, a superb…"

"It's a balloon, Archibald, an authentic gas balloon. Neither fixed wings not helicopter rotor-blades could sustain themselves or maintain rotation in the atmospheric avalanche, the point of support being too fleeting. It's a balloon. But you'll appreciate that, with respect to aerofixes, the gondola—in which the engine is located—has to be absolutely contiguous with the envelope; otherwise, the latter, in accompanying the movement of the Earth, would stretch and break its cords, if they were not broken at the outset. Thus, our apparatus has a single hull, the metal of which is an alloy of aluminum and another substance that weighs no more than cork but is unfortunately slightly lacking in resistance. That hull is divided into two levels by a horizontal partition. The upper section, above us, is filled with a gas known only to us, which possesses an ascensional force six times that of hydrogen. The 'ground floor' is divided into three compartments—in the middle, the cabin, wherein I have the pleasure of talking to you; forwards, a very narrow receptacle containing Corbett accumulators, a light but almost inexhaustible source of electrical energy; and finally, in the rear, the engine-room.

"Ah, the engine! That's our glory! Perhaps you're imagining a million-horse-power steam-engine? Not at all. The Aerofix is no steamer struggling against a fluvial current, whose power, just sufficient to prevent it from being driven back, maintains the boat in place. If that were the case you could say that the Corbetts hadn't invented anything at all; their balloon would simply be the fastest contemporary aerostat, capable of traveling at 1250 kilometers an hour—and capable, by virtue of that fact, of seeming to be motionless relative to the center of the Earth, on condition that it's following a parallel. Oh, that's possible, in theory, and the idea might occur to anyone, by virtue of a simple multiplication of current speeds and the force they engender...but in practice, that's like enabling a fly to travel with the force of a locomotive. Then again, it would be a poor result anyway, devoid of elegance—a crude invention...

"I repeat, our engine is not *driving* the *Aerofix*, but freeing it from the Earth's drag. It's a *generator of inertial force*. Do you understand? And although it produces the same effect as a flying factory hurtling from east to west, it only employs an insignificant force in doing so."

"But what is it?" I asked. "What principle..."

"Ah, that's it! I can't tell you. Don't ask me to. Corbett would be displeased..."

"You know how discreet I am..."

"Hold on, Archie—I'll point you in the right direction. Don't ask me any more. Do you remember those toys called *gyroscopes*, which amused us when we were children, and which turned on an extended filament without falling over, in any position? They adopted the most incredible angles relative to their supports, appearing to defy the principles of equilibrium and gravity. Do you also recall their recent application in England, where the engineer Louis Brennan[68] adapted a set of them to his two-wheeled tram, in such a way that the vehicle, as ill-balanced as a bicycle at rest, sustained itself, motionless and unshakable, on a single rail or a rope thrown across a precipice? In brief, any object fitted with gyroscopes remains stationary in unstable equilibrium, as if it were animated by high velocity. *The effect of the gyroscope replaces that of acquired speed.*

"That's the power that a special device permits us to amplify. Behind you, six gyroscopes—six improved flywheels—are rotating in empty space."

"Lord! What if they were to stop unexpectedly!"

"That would require an unimaginable catastrophe. Brennan has demonstrated that, from the moment one stops activating them, gyroscopes continue to rotate for 24 hours, of which eight are useful—a more than sufficient delay to revert to the thrust of the atmosphere without suffering any shock and find an appropriate place to land. An accident could only be produced by the destruction of the...well, the special device...and unless it were done deliberately..."

"Ethel! Ethel! I'm amazed!"

"You can well imagine," my sister continued, "how I was able to push the apparatus so easily. Lead weights, attached to the underside, are equilibrating the ascensional force thus neutralized, with the result that the balloon only weighs the few pounds necessary to support it on the ground. These compensatory weights can be uncoupled from the cabin automatically. It's the best way of 'casting off.' Oh, we've thought of everything. First we experimented with a scale model, the

---

[68] The Irish-Australian engineer Louis Brennan (1852-1932) patented his gyroscopic monorail in 1903 but had not yet demonstrated it when Renard wrote this story; although the apparatus worked perfectly during the demonstration he mounted in November 1909, Brennan could not persuade anyone that the system was safe to use, and it faded into the margins of the history of technology.

size of a canoe, but the engine was inadvertently switched on in the workshop; the little aerofix then departed unceremoniously. Breaking through the wall, it ended up burying itself in a Belmont hillside—it's still there."

"But isn't there a chance that the heat will ignite the gas?" I asked.

"Don't worry. The enormous explosive bubble can only be detonated by a spark or a naked flame in contact with it. A chimera!"

"Good, good…that's all right. I understand your system perfectly, Ethel…although, to begin with, I took your *autoimmobile* for an authentic motor car!"

"Because of the wheels, I bet? Sprung wheels—they're simple shock-absorbers that function during landing. We go down, land without a shock, and momentum causes us to roll forward a few meters before stopped. The most vulgar airplane is provided with them."

"God, good," I babbled. "Oh yes, it's very fine!" But the stupor of living such a paradoxical dream blurred my hearing, and I couldn't take my eyes off the rotating globe, whose slow and regular revolution described our passage along the fortieth parallel.

Ethel noticed my condition.

"I think I know why you're dumbfounded," she said. "Unexpected discoveries always seem, at first, to be contrary to the Laws of Nature and infractions of the Universal Order. When any great invention is made, the world proclaims it a miracle for a week, with a sort of terror—and certain victims of Science have the false appearance of criminals justly punished for flouting the law. Archibald Clarke suspects that he's witnessing something darkly indecent!"

I had no desire to criticize, though. The psychology of crowds confronted by scientific results left me cold. "Frightful, frightful!" I murmured. "All that water, and no end in sight! What's down there, beneath our feet, eh? How deep is the sea, do you think?"

"Between 1000 and 2000 meters. We're somewhere between the 140th and 160th meridians."

"That's true—it's nearly five o'clock."

"Five o'clock in Philadelphia! But not in the place we're visiting. Here, it's still midnight. We *are* midnight, very nearly. Today the *Aerofix*, motionless in terrestrial space and human time, is accomplishing its midnight voyage…"

Anguish gripped me by the throat. "That's true," I remarked. "The Sun isn't rising."

"Of course! It's still on the far side of the Earth. The apparatus is playing a sort of hide-and-seek with it. Noon is reheating our fugitive antipodes, since we form the heart of the darkness seemingly moving round the globe. Archibald, we'll have lost one day's light and lived, on the contrary, one night too many! Later, when the discovery is put into commercial development, when everyone has an aerofix, it's probable that people will much prefer diurnal trips—and the enemies of darkness will be able to live in an eternal noonday, confront innumerable dusks or bathe in the glow of an endless dawn. Look at the sky in the depths of the periscope; the cupola of the one is immutably reflected in the skull-cap of the other. Nothing moves—except the moon! The constellations are no longer advancing in our perspective. One might think that the celestial pendulum has stopped!"

"There's one of them that still works admirably," I relied. "It's in my stomach, and it's signaling that it's dinnertime with redoubled chimes. I haven't had any dinner, sister mine!"

We dined.

You will be able to judge, Messieurs, from the manifestation of my hunger, that your humble servant's morale had recovered somewhat, however slightly. It is always better after a meal. Ballasted by excellent conserves and a large glass of brandy, I found myself no more uncomfortable in that narrow blade than in the corridor of a sleeping-car—except that a general ache testified to the nervous tension recently experienced, to which it was the reaction. In the bosom of that lukewarm half-shadow, however, good digestion made my eyelids heavier. They closed, to the monotonous lullaby of the whistling air and the humming gyroscopes. As if in an auditory fog, I vaguely heard the clock chime and Ethel mutter that we had completed a quarter of the journey. Then I fell completely asleep.

"Hey, hey! None of that, brother mine! You're asleep, I think. Come on! Come on! I might have need of you at any moment. You have to stay awake. You have to be vigilant."

"Humph!"

"Think about the delights of Japan, over which we're passing," she said to me.

"To the Devil with Japan!" I retorted. "It'll be as black as if it were snowing soot!" Jim seemed to find that very funny. "And you can shut up," I said to him, as I stood up. "You don't have any right to split your sides when one mentions soot, chimney-sweep that you are!"

"Peace, peace! Archibald! Stay in your seat."

The butler bent down, arching his back. His shoulders shook with repressed joy. I thought I could detect a thick-lipped smile through his thick skull—but Ethel's imperious voice had calmed me down. "Where are we?" I asked her, in a dry tone in which there was still a hint of anger.

"A few leagues west of Peking. There's the Ala-Shan desert."

"Still 1500 meters above the ground?"

"No—1500 meters above sea level. The mean altitude of the desert brings us 500 meters closer to the ground."

Then silence fell again. In truth, I may call the perennially similar racket of the air and the engine "silence." I could no longer hear them, any more than the thousand murmurs that make up the tranquility of our worst solitudes.

For a long time, I struggled against drowsiness. In order to do that, I tried to take an interest in everything: the attitudes of my companions; the ballast released at intervals; the uncertain physiognomy of Ethel's hair; all the lethargic countries in which peculiar folk were lying in strange beds beneath two-pronged roofs...but imagination doesn't make up for know-ledge, and I knew nothing about all those dark lands, in which I couldn't make out a single tree! I was reduced to inventing the world, in the fashion of a child riding an inert wooden horse, pensively contemplating the road traveled for long pe-riods of time.

Two alarms, however, shook me out of it.

The first was caused by an impact—a very feeble one—at the prow of the aircraft. Something soft had been in our path. My sister calmed the terror that erupted within me with a single sentence. She had perceived, through the telescope, "two large wings" that had been instantly eclipsed.

The second alarm I owed to Jim. He suddenly got up, fearfully, demanding to know whether we were still on the same heading, affirming that it would be terrible if we had gone off course, because of the mountains of Kashmir, 3800 meters high, and that he was too tired to take account of it himself.

A glass of brandy revived him. Having recovered his self-possession and his lucidity, he returned to his post in front of the clock.

Finally, my sister cheerfully announced, in the manner of a steward in a dining-car: "Luch-time! Take your tables for the first service! It's noon!"

"Noon!" I repeated, checking the darkness. "Noon at midnight!"

The Chinese firmament constellated the lampshade with its cosmographic dome, like those maps of the sky vaulted in imitation, which are knows as uranoramas.[69] The darkness of

---

[69] This Greek-derived term (signifying "sky-view") seems to have been sparingly used in 19th century French with refer-ence to celestial globes and orreries, but not to describe the kind of projected display to which Renard is here applying it—although that is surely a more appropriate usage. The word could have been usefully adopted into English to describe the

the night seemed to me to have a greenish tinge. Clouds like our cumulus clouds were masking and unmasking the same astronomy. The sole change was that the crescent Moon had enlarged its watermelon slice and had departed south-eastwards on its own initiative.

Breakfast had had the appearance of a supper, and lunch resembled it; no one did any great honor to it. The nocturnal afternoon passed by, indefinitely. The Caspian, Turkey, Greece, Calabria, Spain and Portugal succeeded one another, invisible and devoid of interest. An insurmountable irritation made me tap my feet on the transparent floor through which nothing was visible. I became restless, and moved about the narrow cell.

It was with childish pleasure that, at about quarter to twelve, I received the order to return to my post. My sister added that she was about to stop the engine and put the brakes on the gyroscopes, in order gradually to recover the terrestrial drag, so that we would be able to descend once again to Phila-delphia.

The stubborn glow of the electric lamp flashed on. Jim turned the large commutator and tripped several switches. In the aft chamber, brake-shoes could be heard grating on the flywheels; the hum became deeper; the air whistled less and less forcefully, and the tachymeter-needle began to retreat.

I gripped the tiller-shafts in my febrile hands. My sister had ordered me not to make use of them until I received her signal. Occasionally, beneath my feet, the lights of some At-lantic vessel left a double wake of red and white light mirrored in the water.

This situation lasted for an interval of time that seemed to me to be excessive. Leaning over my sister's shoulder, I perceived an extreme annoyance in her features. In reply to my questions, she relied: "It's just that we're not slowing

---

displays mounted in planetaria, but does not seem ever to have been used in that context.

down quickly enough. I'm afraid of overshooting Philadelphia."

The clock showed half past midnight, and the air was still whistling furiously. I mopped my forehead nervously. "Do you think we'll be able to land in the vicinity?" I asked. "If it were more than a hundred kilometers from the city…"

The butler shook his head.

"No, Jim? That's a no, isn't it?" said my sister "There's no point persisting—I've started too late."

"But there's no problem!" I exclaimed, suddenly. "Once we've stopped, you can put the machine in reverse!"

"You're an ass, Archibald. The balloon, as you so judiciously remarked yourself, isn't an automobile but an auto*im*mobile. To turn back in its flight, it would require the Earth to rotate in reverse—and that little fantasy would be followed by the end of the world, because of the repercussion. No, no…we're well-supplied with gas, ballast, electricity and food; the only reasonable thing to do is to make a second tour of the world and to decelerate sooner. Get the engine going again, Jim, and take your brakes off!"

As she came to this exasperating decision—which was immediately put into action—a vaporous accumulation of dots, like a swarm of fireflies, spread out in the depths of the abyss; Philadelphia was passing by…

"Poor Randolph!" Ethel sighed. "He'll be worried!" And without drawing breath, she launched into a loquacious and fast-paced little speech, in the manner of someone who fears a reprimand from her interlocutor and does not want to let him speak. She thought it her duty thus to inform me of the best way of reaching Belmont after the next day's descent. According to her calculations, the apparatus should not touch down more than twenty kilometers from the city, and from there, some horse or other would haul it back to the hangar, to which we'd return before dawn. In spite of her verbosity, that final word unleashed my lamentations.

"Alas, the dawn! What are you saying Ethel? I feel nostalgic about the dawn! It seems to me that the Sun is extinct forever...permanently! I came wanting to be useful...I'm resigned—but you promise me that we'll be in Philadelphia tomorrow, without fail?"

"I swear it. Tomorrow, a few seconds after one o'clock. We've lost 60 minutes in necessary and mistaken maneuvers."

Jim put back the clock's globe by 1250 kilometers.

This time, Ethel took care to provide her crew and herself with the necessary rest. She and Jim were to stand watch in turns. As for me, being a stray layman on the expedition, I was granted the unexpected liberty of doing as I liked. I thought that our captain was now anxious about the nervousness that I had betrayed by my agitation and my invective against Jim.

Worn out by fatigue, I lay down on the glass floor, with the foot of my armchair between my legs; in the guise of a taking a siesta, I surrendered myself to horrible nightmares for long hours. No dream, though, was equal in its extravagance to the fabulous reality, so my awakening seemed to me to be the start of a nightmare more horrible than the rest. When I realized that it was really necessary to go through that delirium again, all the aggravation of the situation descended upon me at a stroke. The periscope was projecting its skylight glow into the cabin; Ethel, her face blanched by the usual lividity, was fast asleep, reminiscent of a corpse; Jimmy was at his post, earnestly standing guard, like a bronze sculpture—and all around us reigned the implacable night.

I felt frightened, and made a despairing gesture—and in the process, my hand bumped into something smooth and cold, which turned out to be a bottle of brandy. Three seconds later—the time for one serious draught—the fear had been put to flight! What am I saying? In human memory, it had never taken possession of my valiant heart! That sinister visitor, however, returned to the attack; in order to exorcize it, it was necessary to take frequent gulps of courage. Besides, the courage in question tasted good.

I ingurgitated it boldly, without reflecting upon all the consequences of a bravery assimilated in that fashion, incorporated in a liquid form, in that minuscule cabin, unequipped with modern conveniences, in which I shared the sad lot of a mocking negro and a well-brought-up lady. Pardon me for mentioning this, Messieurs—it will attest to the veracity of my story, and cast some light on the extent to which the tales of Jules Verne and other armchair tourists differ, at first glance, from an authentic voyage. In any case, my intemperance was amplified by more important consequences, which I shall explain in due course.

It was seven o'clock, and we were over the Balearic islands, when Ethel ordered the decks to be cleared. "Come on, Archie, get up! Enough sleep. Get hold of your tiller-shafts."

"Aye aye, Mrs. Corbett!" I said, with a gracious smile. "At your disposal, Mrs. Corbett!"

Having abruptly switched on the electric light, my sister looked me up and down. During the entire day, she had shown me the back of her head; she had not even looked to see whether I was asleep or not. The jovial expression on my face only revealed an intense and entirely legitimate satisfaction at finally landing in Belmont.

The brakes groaned. The wind softened. My busy companions never ceased manipulating, one after another, the infinite series of regulatory controls. I was ashamed of my inaction—but a noble pride swelled my bosom at the services that I would render with my tiller. They would see my talents as a pilot! Oh yes, for sure! I was going to amaze that brave fellow Ethel and that cretin of a chimney-sweep! One, two—helm to port! One, two—helm to starboard!

And "just to see," I hauled alternately on the tiller-shafts.

It goes without saying that the rudder did not flinch. Gripped by the vice of the air-current, to which our speed provided solid resistance, it was prevented from pivoting on its hinge. I ran out of breath; my rods seemed to be welded to something immovable—and that made me hopping mad! *You'll come around, old chap*, I said to the recalcitrant rudder, privately. *You'll come around, if I have to skin my fingers!*

After that, I hauled harder, so furiously that one of the rods broke away from the infernal apparatus. Impelled by the effort, I pulled a considerable length of it through the partition wall. *Aagh!* I said to myself, suddenly cooling down. *Just as long as no one saw anything!*

There was little to fear; the other two were only thinking about their maneuvers. Perhaps the damage could be repaired. So I groped about with my rod, in the hope of re-attaching it—but the shaft, which traversed the entire engine-room, had come free of the opening by which it exited from the balloon at the rear. It was sheer folly to attempt to put it back in without going into the engine-room, attempting to reconnect the tiller—whose mode of adaptation was unknown to me—at a distance. That is, however, what I tried to do, furrowing my brows.

Suddenly, I lost my temper. With all my might I thrust the rod backwards and upwards. Whatever it ran into gave way, slightly less easily than a piece of cardboard. The end of the shaft went through it. I felt the extremity of the road catch in the hole it had made, and I disengaged it with an abrupt movement. Then, a very distinct whistling sound became audible, above that of the atmosphere. Ethel pricked up her ears. Panicked, perceiving that the rod was still held by something supple and enveloping. I tried to tear the crafty liana away…

My sister and Jim, turning toward the suspicious whistling, saw me standing up, shaking the rod in both hands. They threw themselves forward…

Too late.

The supple knot had snapped in the darkness, and there was a sort of sputter outside, which sizzled and crackled…

"Great God, Jim!" cried my sister. "The gas is escaping! And I heard something like a spark! Quickly! Run!"

Jim ran toward the gyroscopes. And I, losing my head, opened a door into the void…but I did not have time to throw myself out. An instantaneous furnace…a deafening thunder…the impression of light exploding and sound at the maximum…I clung on to the door and lost consciousness…

The rest of the story, Messieurs, you know better than I do.

Archibald Clarke had stopped speaking. Open-mouthed, we watched him finish his last cheroot and his last glass of liquor. Thanks to him, the level of cigars had sunk within the box, and within the bottle, the cylinder of whisky, gradually flattened, had become a very thin disk, like a fluid washer. We had interrupted Mr. Clarke frequently with admiring *ahs!* and *ohs!* and I had been obliged, several times, to assist in the discovery of terms that escaped him. The honorable victim had taken advantage of these numerous respites to make excessive use of tobacco and alcohol, with a sort of bizarre ostentation.

Gatean opened his eyes wide and inspected the unique survivor of the incredible escapade, off-handedly. Mr. Clarke got up from his chair and leaned on his elbow at one of the portholes. Their little round windows were lined up in the wainscot of the dining-room like so many miniature seascapes, but they were pitiful canvases, circumferences that cut out the uniform sea and the empty sky, rendering them as flat geometric circles sliced into two segments—one green and the other blue—by the horizon.

"It's not pretty," the American declared.

"Well, old chap…well…" murmured Gaetan, ruminating upon the Corbetts' exploits.

"In consequence, Monsieur," I said to Mr. Clarke, after a momentary pause, "your sister and Jim are dead?"

"Almost certainly," he replied. And Mr. Clarke threw the butt of his extinct cigar into the Ocean, as if the fortune of Ethel Corbett, the fate of Jim and the destiny of the cigar-end all carried the same weight in his phlegmatic soul. "Oh, the blacks, you know!" he said. "As for my sister, hmm! The poor girl sometimes played dirty tricks. The business of that inheritance! You have no idea…but what good does it do to prattle on about it now? Bah!"

This plunged us back into silent contemplation of the individual.

"Monsieur," I said to him, eventually, "can you explain this? When the *Aerofix* passed through the atmosphere over the *Océanide*, I noticed a certain strangeness with regard to the whistling. On the first day, it began to make itself heard...I hesitate to say...after the appearance of the machine, whose light was invisible at long distance, but well after the probable moment when, invisible still, it had emerged from the horizon—and the *Aerofix*, on the other hand, had already plunged beneath the western horizon while the noise of its passage was still whistling. The second time, there was an approximate coincidence of duration between the audible sound of your apparatus and the heavenly arc that it would have described in its entirety had it not been for the catastrophe..."

Clarke, after due reflection, concluded: "It's quite simple, Monsieur Sinclair. The first day, when we arrived over the *Océanide*, we had scarcely begun decelerating, and our speed was superior to that of sound, which is 46.66 meters per second. Are you with me? On the second day, our more emphatic deceleration must have equalized the two velocities. Do you want the detail of the calculations?"

"No need."

"It's an elementary school problem, anyway. Given a train, etc..."

"Damn it, though," exclaimed Gaetan, "with your facility of comprehension, which doesn't seem ordinary to me, it's impossible that you aren't able to give us a few tips regarding the *Aerofix*. The light accumulators, for instance?"

"I've told you all I know," Clarke replied. "And I've only confided that to you—under the seal of secrecy—because you pulled me out of the water, and your insistence on knowing my story demanded satisfaction. Once again, the vital parts of the engine, its interesting components, were hidden from me. I had no opportunity to glimpse them or reach any conclusion regarding them. Perhaps a scientist or an engineer might have been able to deduce the contents of the sealed chambers and the particular combination of the gyroscopes from remarks made in the cabin, but for my own part, I'm incapable of it. I was only able grasp my poor sister's calculatedly-succinct lesson as well as I could by reason of its very simplicity and because, like everyone else in our century of sports, I'm familiar with the elements of mechanics. If I remembered a few figures with sufficient ease and certainty, don't attribute that to my scientific knowledge, which is negligible, but to my profession of accountancy, to the practice of which—with its homely but punctual pleasures—I'm in a hurry to return."

Having pronounced these wise words, Mr. Clarke fell silent once more—and in spite of our entreaties, he never consented to return to the subject of the *Aerofix*, claiming that it reminded him of uncomfortable situations.

It must be said that, until our arrival at Le Havre, where Mr. Clarke took his leave of us, he remained obstinately uninformative, not only with respect to the motionless voyage but on every other subject as well. We had the greatest difficulty extracting a few details from him concerning Trenton, the cable industry and his cherished employers, Roebling Brothers. Moreover, he spoke only to me. Gaetan displeased him—that was evident—and, to the extent that circumstances forced him to keep company with his host, Mr. Clarke treated him with polite gratitude, while remaining remarkably laconic.

As soon as the *Océanide* was accommodated at the disembarkation quay, Mr. Clarke, having refused the subsidies that Gaetan offered him to enable him to return to his fatherland, bid us an effusive farewell and went across the gangplank at a run.

The natural result of his departure was to relegate Mr. Clarke to the ranks of memories and ideas. An absentee is no longer anything but a thought, and as such, his being—simplified, schematized and essential—appears to us with his characteristics emphasized, in the manner of a theatrical character. It always seems that we are looking at dead men and voyagers from a great distance; their forms and nuances appear to us in a single dominant color, often in caricaturish silhouette. In our memory, Mr. Clarke assumed the aspect of an

213

extraordinary marionette. The fellow's eccentricity stared us in the face, as the saying has it. Now that he was no longer there, a palpable witness to the extraordinary adventure, his story seemed to us to be a dream, and he seemed a hallucination himself.

A little later, I proposed a shipboard enquiry. It went ahead, conducted without overmuch method, and only served to exasperate our curiosity. The only information with which it provided us related to tips—before leaving, Mr. Clarke had distributed them to the crew and the staff, and they were lavish. In itself, the fact that the accountant had squandered the contents of his wallet in nabob-like largesse constituted a vague charge against him in our eyes. That was not all, though! These gratifications he had paid out—he, an American arrived directly from Pennsylvania—in French banknotes and gold coins!

The Paris train carried me away, with my imagination full of the mystery, while Gaetan went by automobile to his Château de Vineuse-sur-Loire. Without employing more ink than the incident warrants, I ought to mention a stupid altercation that preceded our farewells and which, in making our temporary separation into an irrevocable breach, authorizes me to describe Monsieur le Baron de Gaetan de Vineuse-Paradol exactly as he is. If he does not like what I say, I am at his disposal...but let us leave the unfortunate aristocrat there and return to our subject.

A few weeks after my return, I possessed a little dossier concerning Mr. Clarke and the events preliminary to his fall into the Atlantic. Included therein, first of all, were cuttings extracted from newspapers and the bulletins of observatories, concerning the rain of shooting stars on August 19-21 and the passage of a bolide across the skies of Europe during the night of August 19 and 20.

After that, translated for my benefit, there were several witness-statements from Italian, Spanish and Portuguese correspondents resident on the 40th parallel, testifying that they had not noticed anything abnormal or head any unusual whistling sounds on the night of August 20 and 21. That they had seen nothing was quite natural; Mrs. Corbett had switched off the electric light over the continents—but what was one to think of the fact that they had heard nothing?

In the matter of these depositions, it is necessary to guarantee the absolute honesty of their signatories, so I shall register the source of my documents. One of my nephews receives a little global review printed in various languages; it is the organ of a highly-reputed international club whose polyglot subscribers delight in exchanging all sorts of things, from illustrated postcards to certain poems that no one will ever illustrate. I am obliged to my nephew for the reports from Italy, Spain and Portugal, and also for the remainder of the dossier's contents. These were also translations of letters, but letters sent from Philadelphia and Trenton. They formed a crushing collection of evidence against Mr. Clarke.

There was, indeed, a Fairmont Park in Philadelphia, and in that park, west of the River Schuylkill, a Belmont, with a plain surrounded by hills "very well suited for launching an airplane," according to the obliging informant—but the Corbetts did not exist. In Trenton, among the manufacturers of pots and the—less honest—fabrication of Egyptian scarabs, the workshop of the cable-manufacturers Roebling Brothers was familiar, and even held in universal great esteem, but no accountant at the establishment answered to the superb forename and succinctly luminous surname of Archibald Clarke.

Our man had become once again "the unknown man," "the disaster victim" or "the shipwreck victim." His long narration had merely furnished me, in his regard, with one further epithet with which to designate him, justly but imprecisely: "the liar."

Months went by without my learning anything new about the pseudo-Clarke. I had lost myself in conjectures in his regard when, the day before yesterday, the postman brought me the following letter. It was enclosed within two envelopes. The outer envelope, in addition to the address and the franking mark, bore a still-moist stamp from Post Office no. 106, Place du Trocadero. The interior envelope bore a second superscription traced in a different hand, which had written the whole of the letter.

To MONSIEUR GERALD SINCLAIR
Man of Letters
212 Avenue Armand Fallières
Paris (XVe)
Dear Monsieur,

I shall ask you, very humbly, to excuse my conduct aboard the *Océanide*. You must have known for some time that I was playing a part, and considered me, with good reason, as a boor. I would, however, have preferred to remain silent! Why did you oblige me to speak—you, and most especially Monsieur de Vineuse-Paradol, my saviors, who had a right to know everything and a duty not to demand it?

No, Monsieur, I am not the American accountant Archibald Clarke. I am a French engineer, and the apparatus I was testing, on the night of our fortunate encounter, was not *exactly* an aerofix. Oh, I would have been able to describe all its component parts, item by item, down to the least linch-pin, but my discovery is so important and so simple that I preferred to pull the wool *partially* over your eyes than risk my glory in reckless confidence. What sort of men were you? I did not know. Certainly, you had saved my life—but Monsieur, although the action of fishing one's peer out of the sea testifies to meritorious sentiments, it offers no proof of the discretion of the savior, or even his probity. Add to that the facts that the manners and tone of Monsieur de Vineuse are suggestive of a highway robber, that you might perfectly well have duped me with regard to your status, and that, even in the opposite case, no one is more inclined to gossip than a idle millionaire, and there is no one more talkative than a novelist in quest of copy. Isn't that so? Don't expect any more of my present frankness, Monsieur, than my former dissimulation. The latter is obliga-

tory, as the former was necessary, and they are equally justi-
fied.

If it surprises you that I put my little fable together so rapidly, in view of the short time I had available before relating
it, I should tell you how I was helped, in that matter, by the
considerable foundation of truth it contained. As for the rest—
the legendary part—it is difficult from me to clarify, in their
entirety, what tenuous chains of reasoning and trivial associa-
tions of ideas caused me to manufacture it. First, I believe,
there was the lucky chance of a meteor having passed over
your boat the previous evening, and the fact that the need to
generalize—so human, my dear Monsieur!—had caused you
to assimilate it to your conjectures regarding my arrival. The
repaired rudder of the *Océanide* engendered the broken rudder
of the *Aerofix*. Your sojourn at a point on the 40th parallel had
no less influence on the direction of my fantasy. Curiously
enough, though, It was the most insignificant and most inci-
dental of your statements that suddenly steered my toward the
wonderful idea of a voyage on the wing of night—I mean the
mention you made of your nocturnal meals, each of which
resembled suppers...

Let me confess to you, too, the assurance that I felt of not
being refuted on any point by the most knowledgeable people
aboard the *Océanide*: a writer of delightful but frivolous tales,
a fop, and the excellent Captain Duval, who treated the substance of my vehicle as scrap metal.

Localizing the single stage-set required a description of
its décor; I chose Philadelphia, to which my business often
takes me, and I claimed to be a native thereof in order to profit
from the hesitations and pauses expected of a speaker employing an unfamiliar language. At this point, you will ask yourself
how I detected your ignorance of English. My dear Monsieur,
in the presence of an unknown man who does not reply to
questions formulated in French, and seems not to understand
them, does one not use all the languages of which one has a
smattering? Now, you only interrogated me in French...

You see, Monsieur, that I was armed from top to toe—and I took the details of the scene-setting so far as to drink too much whisky, in order to lend more credence to the episode of the brandy, and to smoke too many cigars, with the effect of giving me a thirst…so my subterfuge succeeded. You believed me—but don't consider yourselves excessively gullible; the wariest individual would have heard me out without suspicion, for events happen every day that are impossible from the scientific viewpoint. Every time a cat, falling from a gutter, lands on its four paws, that cat is impertinently defying the theories of aeronautics. What it does cannot be done; Science forbids it, in the same way that Newton's formula relating to wind-resistance forbids birds to fly.

Don't hold yourself strictly accountable, therefore, for your credulity. And don't hold it against me, either, in spite of my sins! Consider that, in order to admit them, I have not waited until I am able to repair them entirely by means of total confidence. That will come. The reason that permits me to write to you today in none other than the completion of a new aircraft constructed on the same plan as no. 1, lost at sea. Indiscretions can do my now harm, now; the machine is ready to take flight. In a few days, you will learn, thanks to my triumph, who I am and what my balloon is! And when you read, in the enthusiastic newspapers, the account of my authentic experiment, then, Monsieur, you will be incredulous—FOR IT WILL BE EVEN MORE MARVELOUS THAN THE MOTIONLESS VOYAGE.

I shall reserve for you the gift of my true impressions. You will be able to make them into the most thrilling story—but between now and when you do me the honor of writing them, Monsieur, I gladly give you authorization to publish the little romance that I had the audacity to narrate to you, if you judge it worthy to divert your readers.

That I have done.

THE SINGULAR FATE OF BOUVANCOURT

To Paul Courtois.[70]

During my absence from Pontargis, Bouvancourt had got a new housekeeper. The new servant insisted that her master had gone out, but she was deceiving me, inasmuch as I could hear my friend's voice trumpeting in the laboratory at the end of the corridor, so I took the liberty of shouting: "Bouvancourt! Hey, Bouvancount! It's me, Sambreuil. Can I come in, in spite of your orders?"

"Ah, my dear doctor, what a pleasure it is to see you again!" the scientist replied, from off-stage. "I've never had such a keen desire to shake your hand, Sambreuil, but there's a snag. I'll be shut up in here for half an hour. It's impossible for me to open the door just now. So go through the drawing-room into my study, I beg you; we can chat through the door, as we can here, and you'll be more comfortable there than in the hallway."

I had been familiar with the layout of the little apartment for a long time. The residence was dear to me because of the resident, and, as the Louis XV drawing-room was the usual venue of our conversations, I took pleasure in seeing it briefly once again, even though the furniture was singularly pretentious in its banality. Bouvancourt, in fact, believed himself—quite mistakenly—to be first and foremost a master decorator. He spent his leisure time nailing, sawing and hanging things, and it was not, in the eyes of the great physicist, his slenderest entitlement to glory to have designed and constructed those

---

[70] Paul Courtois wrote lyrics for numerous musical pieces, now mostly forgotten.

chairs and bracket-tables "to complement a set of authentic fire-irons."

With an affectionate glance, therefore, I honored the horrible imitation furniture, the woodwork sculpted with a stamp, and the specious tapestry cynically pretending to be an Aubusson[71]—and it never even occurred to me to be shocked, so familiar had that ugliness become. Bouvancourt's ridiculous pretension, however, was vividly recalled to my mind once I was in his study. He had brought the most frightful embellishment thereto.

In order to make the room seem larger by means of a *trompe-l'oeil*, he had set a large mirror against the wall separating the study from the Louis XV drawing-room. It was a simulacrum of a door, and matched the actual door; it was a mirage of sorts, reminiscent of the booby-traps that one finds in the Musée Grévin.[72] The large mirror was supported by the floor itself and, in order better to deceive the eye, it was framed by large claret-colored plush curtains similar to those at the widows and other doorways. Oh, those curtains! I knew immediately whose hands had molded them into pleats, inflated them in billows, precipitated them in torrents, and which infernal upholsterer had tied them up with those tasseled cords! And I stood in front of that terrible lambrequin, whose cords twisted its fabric in a ferociously ingenious embrace, quite speechless.

"Well, doctor," said the laboratory door, in Bouvancourt's muffled voice, "are you there yet?"

---

[71] Aubusson is a commune in Creuse that was long famous for its rugs and tapestries (often showing hunting scenes), many of which were produced by Royal Appointment in the seventeenth century.

[72] The Musée Grévin at 10 Boulevard Montmarte, founded in 1882 and named after its first artistic director, Alfred Grévin, is a wax museum, the Parisian equivalent of London's Madame Tussaud's.

"Yes—but I was admiring your sense of decoration. You've got a mirror here—magnificent!"

"Isn't it? How do you like the drapery? It's my own work, you know. The study seems enormous, doesn't it? It's very fashionable just now. Isn't my study chic?"

In truth, the room did not lack "chic," certainly not because of the objects designed to furnish it, but for the reason that it served as an annex to the juxtaposed laboratory, and concealed a chaotic crowd of astonishing machines of all shapes, sizes and materials, for practical work and demonstration. Two windows, one looking out on the boulevard and the other on the street, illuminated the corner room, sprinkling glitters, gleams and flashes over the ebonite, the glass and the copper. Thus more-or-less lit up, various balance-pans, disks and cylinders were visible. Manuscripts were heaped up on the desks, as if thrown there in a glorious fever of genius. An algebraic problem whitened the blackboard. Science exhaled its chemical aroma in all sincerity, I exclaimed: "Yes, Bouvancourt, old chap—yes, it's chic, your study!"

"Excuse me for receiving you in this fashion," he went on. "It's Saturday today. My laboratory assistant…"

"Still Felix?"

"Yes, of course."

"Hello, Felix!"

"Good day, Monsieur Sambreuil."

"My laboratory assistant," Bouvancourt went on, "asked if he could finish early. He's going away tomorrow, and I can't put this experiment off."

"Is it very interesting, then?"

"Extremely, my dear chap. It's the final one of a series; it ought to be conclusive. I'll doubtless make a nice discovery…"

"What?"

"The free penetration, by invisible light, of substances that the Röntgen rays still have difficulty traversing: glass, bones and others. We're working in the dark. I'm trying to take a photograph. Permit me to remain silent for a few minutes—it won't take long. Come on, Felix!"

Then I heard the insectile hum that induction coils make. There were several of them going; the buzzers, according to their tightness, imitated the sonorous flight of bees or that of hornets, and their swarm sang in passable cacophonic harmony. That infernal pedal-note, humming amid the calm of a provincial town, encouraged drowsiness, and I would probably have dozed off if it were not for the trams, whose passage along the boulevard filled the first floor with a periodic racket. Their electrical wires ran close to the house at the level of the windows; there was even a bracket supporting the cables attached to the facade between the laboratory window and the study windows. Every time they made contact with this suture, the trolleys produce a spark. My idle waiting was enlivened thereby. The coils, meanwhile, continued their parody of a beehive.

Several trolley-shafts rattled past in succession. Ever-inclined to calculation, I counted them.

"Will you be finished soon, Bouvancourt?"

"Have a little patience, Monsieur Sambreuil," Felix replied, vaguely.

"Is it going well?"

"Marvelously. We're almost there."

These words gave me a furious desire to get to the other side of the door, in order to see the new phenomenon occur for the first time and contemplate the inventor at the moment of his invention. By means of his discoveries, Bouvancourt had already inscribed several dates in the calendar of Renown.

A clock chimed. I shivered. The moment was historic.

"Can't I come in now, Felix?" I lamented "I'm getting bored. That's the twentieth tram going past, my lad, and…"

I said no more. As it touched the suture, the 20th tram emitted a spark as crackly and as dazzling as a bolt of lightning. Then behind the laboratory door, there was a sequence of explosions, simultaneous with a series of assorted anodyne blasphemies.

Puff!

"Oh thunder!"

Piff!

"Dash it!"

Paff!

"A thousand million curses!"

Et cetera. Bouvancourt's anger was banal, but not sacrilegious. "When the fusillade had ceased, he cried: "We'll have to do it all over again! What a disaster! What bad luck, my poor Felix!"

"What's happened, then?" I said.

"My Crookes tubes[73] have blown up, of course! That's what's happened! It's not difficult to guess!"

Prudently, I shut up. A few seconds later, I heard Felix opening the door to the hallway and going out.

Finally, Bouvancourt appeared.

"Hello!" I said to him. "What have you done? What a state you're in!"

At first, I was nonplussed by his appearance. The cause of my astonishment gradually became clearer. The physician gave the impression of being surrounded by a very thin fog—a sort of violet tint, visually analogous to mildew, enveloped his entire body with a vaporous and transparent film. There was a strong odor of ozone.

Bouvancourt was quite unmoved. "Right!" he said, simply. "Most curious, indeed. It must be a residue of the accursed experiment. It'll go away, gradually."

---

[73] A Crookes tube is a primitive discharge tube developed by William Crookes in the 1870s, consisting of a partly-evacuated glass cylinder with an electrode at either end; it differs from subsequent cathode ray tubes in that the electrodes are not heated, so they do not emit electrons directly. Crookes tubes were usually operated, as Bouvancourt's are, by Ruhmkorff induction coils; it was this kind of apparatus that permitted Röntgen's accidental discovery of X-rays in 1895.

He offered me his hand. The colored aura that enveloped him in mauve was intangible, but I was astonished to find that the hand was extremely flaccid. Suddenly, the scientist snatched it away from mine and pressed it to his torso, under the evident influence of a palpitation.

"You're not well, my dear chap—you need to rest. Shall I examine you?"

"Come, come—no childishness, doctor! It will pass. In an hour, it'll no longer be visible, I swear. Then again, to the Devil with the disappointment, since here you are, back again! Let's talk about something else, if you please. What do you think of this novelty? Isn't it fine work, that lambrequin? And the mirror! A Saint-Gobain,[74] old chap!"

And while Ingres' violin[75] whined away in my memory, he led me to his masterpiece.

Suddenly, however, stupefaction immobilized us. We looked at one another interrogatively, not daring to say anything. Finally, Bouvancourt asked me, in a tremulous voice: "There's no doubt, is there? You can see it too—there's nothing there!"

"Perfectly," I stammered. "Nothing...nothing at all..."

There, indeed, the miracle commenced. I don't actually know which of us perceived it first. The certain fact is that, although we were both facing the mirror, *my image alone was reflected therein*. Bovancourt had lost his. In the place which

---

[74] Saint-Gobain, nowadays a multinational corporation, originated as a manufacturer of glass and mirrors, descendant from the French government's calculated development of a domestic alternative to Venetian glass in the 17th century.

[75] The great French painter Ingres played the violin for pleasure relaxation, so the phrase "le violon d'Ingres" became a popular 19th century nickname for any such secondary pastime. Renard could not know when he wrote the story that Man Ray would transform the significance of the phrase by producing a classic surrealist visual representation of it in 1924.

it should have occupied all that could be seen was the very distinct reflection of the desk and the more distant one of the blackboard.

I was bewildered. Bouvancourt started uttering cries of joy. Gradually, he calmed down. "Well, old chap," he said, "this is, I think, a discovery of the first magnitude…and one that I scarcely expected. Oh, how fine it is, my friend! There's nothing there! How fine that is, my dear doctor! I confess that I don't understand it, though. The cause escapes me…"

"Your mauve aureole…" I suggested.

"Shh!" said Bouvancourt. "Shut up."

He sat down in front of the glass, empty of his effigy, and began debating the issue, although that did not require him to stop laughing and gesticulating. "You see, doctor, I understand in part. For reasons that I won't confide to you—for fear of being roundly scolded—I've impregnated myself with a certain fluid, the tenacity of which I was far from suspecting. I'm presumably saturated with it, for that nimbus seems to me to be an excess of fluid, superabundant to that within me, which is leaking out.

"We recently discovered that this gas—that light, if you prefer—has an unexpected property. I only expected it to have the faculty of traversing substances already permeable to ultra-violet radiation—flesh, wood, etc.—plus bone and glass. A vague relationship is certainly discernible between the property that I supposed it to have and the unexpected quality that has just been manifest…all the same, I can't explain it. X-rays, its true, are unreflectable, but…"

"Optical science has not yet unveiled the secret of reflection, has it?" I asked.

"No. In reflection, optical science studies a set of results whose cause is not well-understood. It observes facts, without knowing the exact nature of their source, and pronounces the rules according to which they are routinely produced—then names these rules "laws" because, until today, there has been nothing to falsify them. Light, the agent of optical phenomena, is a mystery. Now, this mystery is all the more difficult to

225

solve because half of its manifestations, ascertained and studied intently for some years, are not directly perceptible, being not only impalpable, silent, odorless and tasteless like the others, but also cold and dark.

"Yes, only ten years ago, it was imagined that light was reflected by objects, more or less totally, but that it never penetrated into them." Bouvancourt raised his voice. "What magic! All these bodies, transpierced!" He tapped the mahogany of his armchair with his curved index-finger. Then, seized by a sudden idea, he leaned toward the mirror and tapped it in the same fashion.

That drew a fearful exclamation from me. His finger perforated the crystal as easily as the surfaced of a placid wave! Circles were born at the point of entry and radiated one by one, their concentric ripples disturbing the limpidity of the vertical lake as they were propagated.

Bouvancounrt shuddered and looked at me. Then, getting up and stepping resolutely toward the mirror, he buried himself entirely within it, with a slight sound like rustling paper. An eddy made the deforming images dance. When everything calmed down, I saw the violet man *on the other side of the glass*. He looked me up and down and laughed soundlessly, comfortably installed in the reflection of the armchair.

Beneath my own finger, the product of Saint-Gobain resounded solidly and impassively.

In the environment of the reflected study, Bouvancourt's lips moved, but no words reached me. Then he put his head through the bizarre partition that separated us, upsetting the vision again. "What a strange place!" he said to me. "I can't hear my own voice there."

"I couldn't distinguish it either—but couldn't you select another means of communication? Your immersions and emersions prevent me from seeing for some time."

"They stop me too; I perceive you in the study as you see me in its reflection, with the difference that I'm keeping company with your image."

His head plunged back into the extraordinary world. He moved about there without any apparent difficulty, touching objects and feeling them. As he displaced a flask on a shelf, a ringing sound made me turn my eyes toward the actual room, and I saw the actual flask rise up into the air momentarily and replace itself on the shelf. By this means, Bouvancourt provoked several movements in the actual study symmetrical with those he initiated in the apparent study. When he passed close to my double, he took care to go around him. Once, deliberately, he pushed him lightly, and I felt myself moved sideways by an invisible individual.

After a few experiments of this sort, Bouvancourt stopped next to the reflected blackboard. He seemed to look for something to his right, then slapped his forehead, and discovered the sponge to his left. Having rubbed out the equations and formulas, he made his own impressions with a nimble piece of chalk. He wrote in large characters, in order that I could read them easily from the threshold of the mirrored room that was forbidden to me. He often left the slate, hazarded an exploration, verified a suspicion or tested some conjecture, then returned to write the result of the experiment. Behind me, the actual piece of chalk tapped away at the real slate with a noise like that of a telegraph, extending indecipherable gibberish from right to left, in inverted letters.

Bouvancourt wrote the following account. I copied it out in my notebook, for the dimension of the characters quickly covered the board and necessitated frequent erasures.

I'm in a strange region. One can breathe here without difficulty. Where can it be situated? We'll think about that later. For now, it's appropriate to observe.

All these doubles of reality are flaccid to a supreme extent—almost inconsistent. The room in which I'm located ends suddenly where the visual field of the mirror finishes. On my side, the wall against which the mirror is set is a dark field pierced with a rectangle of light...a dark and impenetrable plane. It's distressing to look at, even more so to touch. It's

227

*neither rough, nor hard, nor warm, but simply impenetrable; I
don't know how to express it.*

*If I open the window, the same opaque night extends to
either side of the reflected landscape. It's that too, which constitutes the unreflected sides of images, including the back of
your own copy, doctor. Your phantom is divided into two
zones—the one facing the glass is similar to one of your
halves; the other is a silhouette composed of that frightful obscurity. The line that divides them is very precise and when
you turn round, the line remains immobile, as if you were
turning in front of a luminous hearth at night, always half-
illuminated and half in shadow.*

*The ammonia has no odor. Liquids have no taste. The
Ramsden machine is letting off apparent sparks, devoid of
energy, in the direction of the Leyden jar.*[76]

We were in the course of our correspondence when I
wanted to transmit to Bouvancourt my uncertainties regarding
what would happen in inclined mirrors, or those in the ceiling—or, even better, on the floor, and my opinion regarding
investigations of the weight imposed in these various hypotheses and even in the present case. With that end in view, I
sponged the slate myself. It took a few seconds.

I had just begun to write my proposal when the chalk
leapt violently from my hand. In awkward, tremulous characters, *going from left to right, as normal*—an indication that the
scientist was writing backwards himself, and wanted to make
me understand without delay, at whatever cost—it traced:
HELP! At the same time, a misty human form appeared next
to me, holding the white chalk.

I ran to the mirror. Bouvancourt ran within it to meet me.
His forehead was bloody. He crashed into the glass with all his
force, as if to break it—but a block of granite could not have

---

[76] A Ramsden machine employs a rotating disk to producing
static electricity by means of friction; a Leyden jar—a bottle
equipped with two electrodes, one internal and the other external—is a device for storing static electricity.

put up more resistance. It had become impenetrable, with an incomprehensible solidity, with respect to powers retained from the world beyond it. The scientist's head reddened from another wound, and I understood that, during my brief absence, he had attempted to escape. The mauve aura had dissipated, and the unfortunate man, abandoned by the fluid—doubtless vital in that unknown atmosphere—was giving increasing signs of asphyxia.

Several more times he charged, crashed into and bruised himself on the inflexible separation. The most frightful thing of all was seeing *his image* gradually reappear *on my side*, becoming a second bloody Bouvancourt, maddened and monstrous, with his dark half—and to see those two prisoners face to face, their lips silently twisting in howls and cries for help, continually throwing themselves at one another—hand to hand, forehead to forehead, blood to blood—and continually crashing into one another with the same savage gestures and the same impotent blows.

I tried—with what objective and by what intuition?—to drag the reflection into the laboratory. Having reached the limit of the mirror's visual field, though, the inconsistent being was arrested there, as if by the most immovable object. That frontier cut obliquely through the wide-open door, blocking it more solidly than a rampart of rubble with respect to the scientist's specter. With all my strength, I pulled him and pushed him against that immaterial barrier—which evaded my perception—without succeeding in getting him through it. He depended intimately on Bouvancourt's actual body, and that, as I had forgotten, was a prisoner in the fabulous region.

It was necessary to do something, though. The reflection was gasping for breath in my arms. What could I do? I lay him down on the floor—and there, in the depths of the mirror, Bouvancourt lay down spontaneously, red in the face, with his eyes closed.

I took a decision. In the drawing-room hearth there were those heavy 18th century fire-irons: I went to fetch one of them.

At the first blow, the mirror cracked from side to side. It was soon reduced to smithereens. The wall appeared, and the fire-iron scraped the thick wall.

I turned round. Bouvancourt's reflection was no longer there. Then a woman's scream resounded in the drawing-room. I found the housekeeper there, attracted by the din.

"Well? What?" I said to her, going back in. To my profound amazement, she pointed to her inanimate master lying on the parquet floor. The leg of a bracket-table, still in place, transfixed his thigh.

I declare here and now that a minute before, when I had gone into it to grab the fire-iron, that room had been absolutely deserted.

The physicist was alive, and he recovered consciousness after a few rhythmic tractions of the tongue and a few maneuvers of artificial respiration—but it was necessary for me to loosen the bracket-table and haul with all my muscular strength on the piece of wood before I succeeded in drawing it out. Its extraction left a singularly neat wound, piercing the flesh clean through and grazing the femur—a wound that, to tell the truth, did not really merit that name; it was more like a hole, whose edges manifested no sign of contusion. The weight of the table had not, therefore, been driven into the thigh. Besides, the fastening immobilized it. One might have thought—and perhaps it's the truth—that the limb had reformed around the table-leg, sealing it in like a mold.

I did not have time, though, to dwell on that subject; Bouvancourt's condition demanded all my attention. It was not his leg-wound that threatened his life, however, but the ulcers that covered him, and strange internal burns, from which he might never recover. It was the worst dermatitis that I have ever treated, accompanied by hair-loss and a malady of the finger- and toe-nails. In brief, he showed all the notorious symptoms of prolonged exposure to invisible light, which I had observed many a time in X-rayed patients before the introduction of instantaneous photographs.

In addition, Bouvancourt admitted to me that he had attempted to photograph an iron candelabrum through his own body and a sheet of glass—an experiment aborted in the manner I have related, which was the origin of this adventure. "I've composed the metal of my electrodes from a mixture of radium and platinum," he told me. He talked to me continually from his bed, directing innocent curses against the misfortune that had taken him away from his experiments, and hence from the solution of the enigma.

To calm him down, I informed him of the observations I had made, showing him the necessity of combining all our certainties in order to build logical suppositions thereon that would permit us to work more adequately. I devoted myself to an investigation of the relevant locations, in the hope that their examination might reinforce our documentation with further observations. I only discovered one thing: the bracket-table in the drawing-room was fixed, relative to the plane of the shattered mirror, at a point symmetrical with the one where I had set down Bouvancourt's image in the study.

I imparted this information to the scientist.

"Are you familiar," he asked me, "with the trick employed by makers of magic lanterns known as *melting views*?"

"Yes," I relied. "It consists of replacing one image projected on a screen by another. It's worked by means of two projectors; the first is slowly darkened while the second is gradually unmasked."

"There is, therefore, if I'm not mistaken," the physicist went on, "a moment when both images are visible together on the canvas, mingling their different subjects—the masts of a ship emerge, for instance, in the midst of a group of friends…"

"Well?" I said. "What does that have to do with…?"

"Imagine," the scientist cut in, "that the first view projected were my portrait, and that the second represented a Louis XV bracket-table. It seems to me that it gives a good enough idea of what happened to me at the moment when you broke the mirror…especially if the table had been photographed in my drawing-room and your humble servant in his study…"

"It doesn't explain anything."

"Indeed. On the other hand, however, everything that happened to us tends, in spite of reason, to justify a way of seeing that encourages belief in a space hidden behind mirrors…"

"But where do you imagine your—how can I put it—*temporary*[77] space to be located?" I retorted. "In the present case, the reflected study would have occupied the same space as the drawing-room."

"That's it—that's exactly it," said the professor.

"But at the end of the day, Bouvancourt, the drawing-room is the drawing-room! Two things can't be in the same place at the same time—that's crazy!"

"Ahem!" he said, pulling a face. "Crazy! First, there are melting views. Then again, we merely live in space and time, and do not know them. Immensity and eternity are inconceivable. Can you claim to know in detail the part of a whole that you do not know? Are you *certain* that two things can exist in the same time? Are you *sure* that they can't exist in the same place, simultaneously?" In a mocking voice, he added: "After all, the space of my body is, at the same time, that of an invalid and that of an elector of equal volume, not to mention other individuals…"

I was relieved to see that he was clearly joking, and the subject of the conversation changed. Besides, only experiments could satisfy us with regard to so extraordinary an

---

[77] The French *temporaire* can also be translate as "provisional," which might make more apparent sense in this instance, but as the word is subsequently contrasted with "permanent" I have used the direct transcription. There is an inevitable temptation, given the customs of modern usage, to substitute "virtual" and "real," but that would be stretching permissible translation too far.

event—which, I sometimes suspect, might not have happened as I thought I observed.

Scarcely convalescent, pale and limping, Bouvancort began his research. Fearing indiscretions, he sent Felix away—whom I replaced, as best I could—and set to work.

Let us state right away that *temporary space*—as we shall call it henceforth, by contrast with *permanent space*—never re-opened. The guinea-pigs that our prudence led us to utilize died of various afflictions, some of them hairless, other corroded by ulcers, some without claws, several of some unknown sort of fit. Three were struck down when, after many deceptions, Bouvancourt attempted to reproduce the trolley-spark artificially; one was killed by the scientist, who, in a rage, persisted in introducing it by force into a mirror. None, however, ever went to prance around in the world of reflections. Nothing could engender the famous violet transparency within them.

I gave up on the project. Bouvancourt continued it. "You're wrong," he told me. "I have a theory. There aren't just mirrors of glass...there are other substances endowed with reflective power, but more permeable..."

Poor old Bouvancourt! How stubbornly he pursued his chimera! What endurance and temerity! I had prescribed a strict program of treatment for him, under pain of death. Far from following it, he exposed himself continually to the terrible influences that had already nearly killed him. Every day, I saw his complexion become more jaundiced and his bald head slump further. The pathological symptoms reappeared. He became hideous, and he knew it.

After a little while, he told me that on the day of his discovery, he would probably be less delighted with the triumph than with not having to pore over mirrors any more.

"Patience, though!" he added. "Another week or two, and the Academy of Sciences shall learn something new!"

Yesterday, a dawn, a canal boatman noticed some unusual items of apparatus on the towpath. Taken to the police station, they were recognized by a sagacious inspector as "chemistry equipment." He went to Bouvancourt's house, in order to obtain fuller information. There, he learned that the scientist had disappeared the previous evening.

He was fished out of the canal.

"There are other substances more permeable than glass endowed with reflective power…"

Some people say that he drowned after having been electrocuted, in an excess of precaution. Others add, delicately, that "perhaps his housekeeper knows something about it."

"He committed suicide," affirmed the *Echo de Pontargis*, "suffering from an incurable malady occasioned by his perilous studies."

Someone once said to me, with a charming smile: "The cold light had burned his brain, eh!"

Only I know the truth.

I can see Bouvancourt on the edge of the nocturnal canal. He dips the zinc electrodes of his battery into the bichromate. Immediately, the Ruhmkorff coil emits its bee-like or hornet-like buzz; the bulb becomes phosphorescent. The scientist believes himself to be impregnated with mysterious clarity.

He looks into the liquid depths, at the inverted image of the restful landscape, snowy in the moonlight. He looks at that temporary space, into which the incorporated fluid ought to authorize him to descend into an even paler moonlight, an even brighter landscape…

And he descends, not knowing what laws of gravity govern that universe, at the risk of sinking into the gulf of the firmament open at his feet.

And he descends…but he finds nothing but permanent space—which is to say, in actuality, water: the weighty water in which human beings cannot live; the water of epilogues, whose silence is that which follows so many stories; the water of finality.

THE RENDEZVOUS

To the memory of Edgar Poe

Paris, Boulevard de Clichy
Tuesday, March 10, 1908
To the Public Prosecutor

Dear Monsieur,

Before reading this letter, you will have been informed as to how it was found, and you will have learned that I am dead. I will, in fact, have killed myself.

Nothing, doubtless, will contest the fact that I am my own murderer. I desire that with all my heart. I hope that the house will be found in good order, as it is now, and that I myself will be a very discreet, banal and obvious suicide. That is probable and rational—but not, alas, certain. For there is one thing capable of surrounding my end with tumult and mystery—so hideous a thing that one might die in order no longer to know that it exists. For no more than that, I can assure you!

That is not, however, the only reason for my death. If I kill myself, you see, it's also in the hope of killing *it*—the thing—with the same blow...do you understand? Except, you see, that I'm not *sure* of destroying it along with myself...so I thought it would be best to tell you my secret. It will explain any strangeness—if there is any—and prevent you from suspecting a murder.

Oh, above all else, don't accuse anyone! I've already done so much harm! Don't accuse anyone, if someone—someone bizarre—is keeping company with my remains. Don't accuse anyone of anything, even if the terror of a supernatural agony is recognizable in my features, and my crazed eyes are wide open, staring at the broken door. But no! Not

235

that! That's impossible—because, you see, at the very moment that I depart, I shall be saved! I shall kill myself before that, you see, even if I have to tear out my heart with my fingernails in order to die in time.

The clock marks half past one; that will, therefore, be in three hours time. My God! No more than three small hours! And so many things to say, so many long explanations to give!

To abridge the story, though, and to avoid describing the people involved, I've attached two photographs to my letter: one of a group of young people, and a portrait of a young woman. Would you care, please, to examine the former. That's not a battalion of lunatics. It represents the pupils in the studio of Montgény, the architect, in 1896. It was taken one Sunday in the courtyard of the school. It's a burlesque; everyone in it is showing off the key attribute of his particular talent, the emblem of his most characteristic habit, or making a gesture that symbolizes them. Very "Latin Quarter," as you can see, but also not very witty—and now so sad!

I call your attention to the group on the left. In the second row, the young man in spectacles, furnished with a palette and crowned with a diadem of turnips, is the watercolorist Guillaume Dupont-Lardin, whose name you will surely recognize. The turnips have been put on his head because "turnip" and "water-color" are synonymous in studio slang, and because good old Guillaume was already thinking of nothing but painting water-colors. His family, however, demanded that he should be an architect; he had given in, but he only worked hard enough to pass his exams and obtain his diploma, in order to set out subsequently on his chosen career. He is the best, the only friend I have ever had. I knew him there, at Montégny's, where he was student-treasurer in '96.

My turn now. I figure, with two comrades, in the scene of hypnotism that you perceive beneath Dupont-Lardin. I'm neither the little pale fellow who is sitting down nor the fat bearded one who seems to be sprinkling him with magnetic passes. I'm the tall dark one with the hooked nose. The other two, Juliot and Salpêtrier, really were a medium and a hypnot-

236

ist, and their exhibition was the principal turn at our parties. For my part, being a mere amateur in that kind of exercise, I had never been anything but Salpêtrier's assistant. I did it, moreover, without enthusiasm, and my master was disappointed in me, claiming that, with my gaze—"more hooked than my nose"—I might have been the greatest magnetizer in the world. It's possible, I suppose…but I've always found the process unpleasant. Those one puts to sleep flutter their eyelids so hectically, their faces are so utterly stripped of all expression, that it frightens me; it's as if one were crippling them…

Let's pass on to the second print. That one, Monsieur, I beg you to burn once you have studied it sufficiently. Do you place any credence in the religion of memory and the cult of objects? If so, I have no doubt that the poker will tremble in your hands when you mix the ashes of that photograph with the embers of a fire. I have never been able to separate myself from it since I stole it…

Oh, Monsieur, if things were worn out by gazes, if our tears were able to dissolve images and our kisses able to erase them, you would not have Gilette's portrait in front of you. Instead of that…she is no longer very elegant, my relic. One might think that it had rained on her all night long. Wretch! You were able weep upon a portrait every night; what more did you want? You possessed the sole sensuality that did not fade away of its own accord, and you have ruined it! You enjoyed indefatigable Desire, and you have satisfied it! Do you no longer know, then, where regret, repentance and remorse originate? Imbecile! There are ancient, rotten desires, which gratify as they decompose!

I've been stupid and criminal, it's true. But look at her! And yet, you can only perceive her as a silent, motionless form. You'll say to yourself: "She's a pretty girl, of the Scandinavian type." And you'll think about something else. Oh, if you only knew!

When I saw her for the first time, it was evening, in a twilit drawing-room. Suddenly, it seemed to me that a light emerged from the shadows. She was like a stained-glass queen coming toward me, so white and pink and blonde, with her young flesh as resplendent as a spring dawn! She looked at me quite frankly, her lengthwise-narrowed eyes full of grey light. I was dazzled.

An unexpected voice caused me to start. I had not seen Guillaume behind her, I heard him pronounce my name, then say: "This is my fiancée."

Then, Monsieur, I felt the Earth turn upside-down, and the stars appeared to me through the ceiling. I was lost. Oh, Gilette, Gilette!

That evening, I should have gone away, without wasting a minute—but it seemed to me that a precipitate departure would cast an equivocal shadow over the joy of the betrothed couple. I told myself that everyone would draw conclusions, and that it would be better to delay my flight until the day after the marriage. Was that the real reason? I wonder now whether, in staying, I was a hero or a coward.

Whichever was the case, I stayed. Then they demanded—oh, how reckless, how blind, they were!—that I built their house! Guillaume had bought an old property to demolish, in the Boulevard Clichy between the Place Pigalle and the Place Blanche, near the corner of the latter. It was their favorite quarter, and it was there that they wanted to live, in a house designed by me. You know what engaged couples are like—they brook no resistance. Anyway, how could I refuse? What reason could I give? That would have been to betray myself, wouldn't it? And then, of course, it suited me: to work for her, to build her home, to make her a house as one makes someone a dress, to create the décor of her gestures and the landscape of her beauty, to put my signature on the site of her life—I reckoned…well, was it not, so to speak, to complete her according to my own tastes, to couple her grace with my artistry, and to marry something of her with something of me…?

Nonsense! Silly talk! Words, words! Mere wordplay! So be it! So be it…

Meanwhile, I dreamed about that house, amorously. I didn't want it to be a temple for my divinity so much as an embrace around my beloved. I also wanted everything therein to be in accord with her northern splendor, and that the dwelling should become as an edifice what she was as a woman: a sort of emanation of her being. The ceilings in its rooms were to be appropriate to her height, and the dimensions of its doors in harmony with her passing and momentary silhouette. The walls behind her would require colors varied in accordance with the different rooms, but also as if a subtle painter had brushed each of them into the background of her portrait. I promised myself an orgy of attentions: the door-handles would bulge, beneath her hand, with welcoming roundness and immediate familiarity; the positioning of the furniture would be becoming to her poses, and each of the windows would seem the ideal frame for her to lean out on her elbows.

My task wasn't difficult, for Gilette was radiant everywhere, and her presence illuminated her surroundings with a mysterious personal light, the bizarre result of which was that everything seemed dependent on her, and embellished by her proximity. People and objects seemed to be effaced by her supremacy, and when she was there, the entire world seemed secondary.

No, no, my task wasn't difficult...pooh! What did I build? Go and see! Have yourself shown around the house! One might call it a Norwegian chalet, or Russian, or Danish, or anything else! It's banal and pretentious. My comrades nicknamed it " the isba."[78] Oh, *the isba*! Woe! Oh, our dreams, our dreams....!

But time's passing. I hear the ticking clock measuring it out behind my back. My hour is drawing near, and you don't know anything yet. Let's get on with it.

---

[78] An isba is a primitive Siberian hut made of wood and turf.

The construction of the isba was a cause of frequent meetings for us. The criticism of the plans, the examination of the estimate, the choice of details, and then the surveillance of the work multiplied our meetings and brought about an intimacy between Gilette and me, which the collaboration tightened. That didn't help to cure me. My lust was excited by it, until it became a sort of unbearable fever. When the house was finished, I perceived that it was too late to fight it, and that it could only be extinguished by death or satisfaction. Unfortunately, I did not want to die without having tried my luck.

Then I descended, one by one, all the steps of ignominy.

Far from going away, as I had previously resolved to do, I moved closer to the Dupont-Lardins, renting this apartment in the Boulevard de Clichy, 200 meters from the isba in the direction of the Place Pigalle. Guillaume and his wife rejoiced in my proximity. It was decided that we would see one another every day. A place was set for the "worthy architect" every morning and evening in the dining-room that he had constructed, on the table that he had designed.

They loved one another madly. Tell me—should that not have discouraged me, driven me to despair? Bah! Their affection only exasperated my desire, and filled my heart with jealousy. Furthermore, I was convinced that they were completely mistaken in loving one another, and clung to this absurd argument: "Nature has not fashioned them for one another. They're making a mistake. They're wrong to love one another. What right do they have to do so, since Gilette is destined for me alone? What other body could be more exactly adapted to mine? Her arms, I'm sure, would not be able to join together in empty space without designing the contour of my torso, and the adjunction of our lips would be the perfect kiss...."

In brief, never had there been two better spouses, in my view, than Gilette and me; we were truly two halves of the same whole. Stupid and banal, isn't it? "It's necessary, however," I said to myself, "that things should be as they are; how else could I suffer, because of her, this almost superhuman passion?" Is the violence of my lust an excuse for my sin?

Maybe. It's all the same to me. I leave it to you to judge, Monsieur. The fact remains that I loved Gilette in an exceptional, unique manner worthy of celebration, as Leander loved Hero, as Tristan loved Yseult…as everyone, doubtless, has loved his beloved, since the Lord created humans and created them male and female.

Three o'clock! Three o'clock is already chiming behind me! How quickly the hours rotate today! I haven't said anything yet. One might think that I'm retreating in the face of what must be said. Come on!

For more than two years, Monsieur, I was parasitic upon the Dupont-Lardins, and I had no other concern than to bring about intimate meetings with my hostess. They were rare, Guillaume working until nightfall in his studio and his wife staying by his side. After that, they went out together…

You can imagine all the stratagems that it was necessary to contrive to separate them, without seeming to. What villainies! What turpitude!

There was only one day a week, unless chance intervened, when I was assured of finding myself alone with Madame Dupont-Lardin for a couple of hours. That was on Tuesday, between five and seven. On that day, Guillaume had agreed to teach a course in the History of Art at a great institution for young ladies on the Left Bank. That tells you that Tuesdays were my true Sundays, and that I regularly took advantage of that godsend to go to the isba. Sometimes, there was no one there: "Madame has gone out." Sometimes, too, some unwelcome visitor came to disturb the charm—for me—of our solitude. But most of the time, things went as I wished, for Gilette had no reason to avoid my proximity, by virtue of liking to spend as much time as possible at home, and she received few visitors outside of her appointed day.

Yes, Monsieur, for 30 months I was only really alive for two hours a week, and not always then. For thirty months I was the ridiculous, odious, but unsuspected suitor of Madame

Dupont-Lardin. She and Guillaume, absorbed in their own happiness, didn't notice anything.

Oh, if only I had clearly distinguished Gilette's indifference, perhaps I would eventually have shaken off the yoke—but by virtue of wanting her to be well-disposed toward me, I gradually acquired the certainty that she would become so. And yet, I admit, to my shame, in spite of my expectations and assiduous care—which she did not even suspect—no word or movement ever escaped her that might have motivated an avowal on my part. In spite of that, I was the victim of a mirage, like so many other forsaken wretches. Soon, Gilette could not do or say anything without my interpreting it in favor of my covetousness. I translated her slightest gestures as good omens: a fleeting glance became a wink of connivance; any phrase whatsoever concealed an allusion; simple politeness became complicity. I was hallucinating, I tell you! And one day, a lovers' quarrel having come between her and her husband, I thought that the propitious moment had arrived.

It was a Tuesday—and I was able to converse with her in private.

I declared myself.

At first, she did not grasp what I meant. Then, when she had understood, she tried to laugh it off, pretending to think that it was a joke. Finally convinced of the gravity of my words, Madame Dupont-Lardin manifested as much sadness as amazement, and spoke to me very kindly and softly, but also quite categorically, without my being able to discover a single word of hope in what she said.

The mirage dissipated; it was as if there were a great darkness behind it. I listened to Gilette as one listens to a delirious individual. I had immediately made a decision to kill myself, that same evening, as soon as I had left the isba. I could no longer live in hope, you see....

She didn't know that; she read nothing in my eyes; she gave me advice, maternally. My God! We were sitting very close to one another face to face, in a tranquil manner. Her voice was almost unemotional. No one could have guessed that she was pronouncing my death-sentence. As for me, Monsieur, I looked at her...oh, I looked at her with all the strength of my existence. I was looking at her for the last time.

Vaguely, I heard her reasoning and moralizing: "My poor friend what you have done is not good, aesthetically or morally. It's not entirely your fault, however...I should have seen it...Guillaume too. But how could you suppose...? Oh, it's not nice, not worthy! You've been slightly mad, haven't you? But it's over? You can see reason now? Oh yes, when I think about it, it's obvious that you weren't yourself. Guillaume admires you so much—and you love him, too! What would he have made of this business? What were you thinking? Don't look at me like that. What would Guillaume have made of it?"

"Guillaume?" I replied, regretfully, knowing that my reply would make her indignant. "He would never have known anything, Nothing, therefore, would have caused him pain. I swear to you"—and this was true, Monsieur!—"that I would give my blood to spare him...even the slightest anxiety."

"But your cynicism and contradiction are frightening!" said Gilette. "Please my friend, say no more. I no longer recognize you. Listen: I don't want any rupture, any quarrel. No, Guillaume would be too upset, and might even conceive suspicions. You'll find, I hope, sufficient strength to stifle...your desires, without going away. Forget them, my dear, if they're not already forgotten. As for me, I no longer know what happened. Upon my word, nothing has occurred. I have no memory of your declaration; you don't recall my rejection; neither of us is aware that you have doubted my constancy. Isn't that the best solution? What do you say?

"Come on—let's resume our customary existence, me without rancor and you without bitterness. Except...if you recommence...then, what do you expect? Guillaume will be told. To listen to you twice would require your banishment and would be unworthy of his wife. You think so too, don't you? Well? Shall we forget? Is that a promise? Answer me."

243

On, Monsieur, how I pitied her plans! The future? The future was for others, not for me. I looked at her; that's all. I looked at her unrelentingly. She was the only light in the bosom of the great darkness. She opened her frightened eyes wide, which seemed to be magnified, and to be considering me with anxiety and curiosity...and I would never see them again! Never again!

"Come on!" she continued. "You're frightening me! You're not listening. Is it a promise? Swear! Give me your hands, honestly, as if I were a man. There. Swear to me never to speak to me again about today's subject. Swear to me that you'll cure yourself, that you'll no longer be unhappy or...dishonest. And, for my part, I swear to you on oath that..."

Monsieur! In the middle of that sentence, she broke off! Oh, it was extraordinary! In a matter of seconds, her voice had become lower and lower. She had become grave, voiceless and languid. Think of a phonograph whose spring is running down, about to stop—it was like that, odd and painful. At the same time, a stony indifference had frozen her features into the neutral appearance of ancient statues, the zero of expression. Her eyelids, having fluttered dolorously, had ended up becoming motionless, similarly petrified. She had arched them immoderately, revealing excessively staring eyes with enormous whites, like glass eyes...

And this was why Gilette, in the middle of her suddenly decelerated sentence, Gilette had fallen silent: I had looked at her too intently. She was in a trance.

I had noticed all that at once, you see. When her hands touched mine and her eyes began to allow themselves to be caught, I had seen it—oh, with alarm! But it wasn't my fault! No, not my fault! Open any manual of hypnotism: who would ever have the absurd idea of entrancing an unconsenting subject? It was an exceptional, almost miraculous case. I was fascinated by it—but I had perceived all the advantage that I might obtain from the circumstance.

The great darkness that enshrouded my soul had been il-luminated by an abrupt and diabolical dawn; nasal trumpets were blaring in my ears. And, instead of freeing the poor flut-tering eyelids, I had tightened the magnetic vice of my gaze upon them. Then, within myself, insistently, I had com-manded: "Sleep…! Sleep…! Sleep…! Sleep…!"

And now she was asleep, Monsieur, sitting in front of me, cold, pale and cataleptic, like her own marble stature.

And her entire future was at my discretion.

But it was necessary to act without delay; someone might come in unexpectedly, and then what a tragicomedy there would be! Rapidly, I sought to formulate the orders that Gi-lette was about to receive and would be clearly imposed on her mind. I wanted them to be brief, precise and complete, quick to deliver, easy to retain and exempt from all ambiguity, in-capable of giving rise to any misunderstanding by false inter-pretation.

After a minute, I believed that I had composed adequate terms, and I hastened to operate the suggestion, for fear was hovering over me—the fear of being surprised, and another….

I've already mentioned it: the company of the hypnotized frightens me. I have an aversion to their conversation. They're mysterious interlocutors. And the isolation in which I found myself, in a very perilous situation, with a patient whom pubic opinion would have labeled a "victim", redoubled my alarm.

I began with the traditional interrogation.

"Gilette! Are you asleep?"

In a blank and mechanical voice, she replied: "Yes."

"Are you prepared to obey me?"

"…"

"It's necessary. I wish it. Will you obey me?"

"…Yes."

"Good. Remember this: Every Tuesday, from next Tues-day on, at five o'clock, you will come to my home and"—I added in a hoarse tone, with a kin of sob—"you will be my mistress, as ardent and delighted as the most spirited, the most enraptured of mistresses. At seven o'clock you will leave, and

245

you will lose the memory of our rendezvous and our relationship until the following Tuesday. In the same way, when you wake up, you will forget that I have put you to sleep. Is that understood?"

"Yes."

"Repeat it."

She repeated the infernal orders word for word, without inflection, impassively and automatically, in the manner of a schoolgirl reciting a fable, and she articulated her promises of love as she had once intoned "holding a cheese in his beak."[79] An odious scene. I hastened to bring it to an end.

I woke her up. Fortunately, everything progressed normally. Beneath my transversal passes I saw the color and animation return to her cheeks, her eyelids fluttering and her eyes blinking, and Gilette's pose relaxed, while a low-pitched murmur escaped her lips, accelerated, rose in pitch, acquired cadence, and became her clear habitual voice, resuming in the middle of the interrupted sentence: "...I will never say anything to Guillaume. If not, I shall be forced to tell him the truth. Oh, come on, tell me that it's a promise!"

"Yes, I promise," I replied, cheerfully, my throat full of nervous laughter. "Yes, you're right: I was mad. But it's sufficient, to be mad no longer, to know that one is. And you have demonstrated that I was, Madame, in such peremptory fashion that I ceased to be, at the exact moment when you persuaded me. Oof! It's good to be able to joke about it a little! Ha ha ha! I'm now cured, permanently. Of course we should forget all about it. I agree with you—let's forget it. To hell with the nasty story! Let's never mention it again!"

---

[79] The full line from Jean de La Fontaine's fable "*Le Corbeau et le renard*" [The Crow and the Fox] is "*Maître Corbeau sur son arbre perché, tenait en son bec un fromage.*" [Master Crow perched in his tree, holding a cheese in his beak] It is one of La Fontaine's most of-quoted lines, thanks to the various metaphorical connotations that can be inferred from or imposed on the word *fromage*.

"Ah!" cried Gilette, in a triumphant tone. "Ah! Finally! You are, therefore, still the honest man that I was already mourning. What a nightmare you gave me, my poor friend! And what a relief too!" She took her head in her hands as she concluded: "But forgive me...such a shock...I ask your permission to take my leave, my dear; I've suddenly come down with an atrocious migraine..."

I spent the week that followed in a deplorable state of overexcitement. I don't know what terrors sometimes seized me by the neck and strangled me. Then there were crazy fits of joy and morbid hope, which shook me with an evil hilarity. Would she come? For a whole week, that was the only question I asked myself. Would she come?

Scientifically, I could not doubt it; but the hosts of the isba led so peaceful and joyful an existence that it would have shaken God's conviction. Mine was almost annihilated at times. An opportunist hypnotist, a sort of sorcerer's apprentice, I had played like a vicious child with something too immense, too scared, too mysterious...and now I remained confounded by my terrible work, to the point of mistrusting the most natural effects.

Gilette's insouciance in the meantime constituted a proof of my success, but I could only see it as evidence to the contrary, and I tried in vain to discover, in the depths of her pure eyes, the suggestion that I had implanted. I could not glimpse anything, any more than Guillaume could, with his husband's eyes behind myopic spectacles. The need to be certain haunted me. For that critical week, I established a calendar analogous to those the soldiers fabricate for the duration of their service, and just as they erase the days one by one, one by one I struck out the hours.

At the end of their litany, the Tuesday presented itself. It was October 1.

At hazard, I made my bedroom into a veritable hothouse, filled with precious flowers and rare foliage—and when the moment arrived, I went down to take up a position beneath the arch, in order to meet Gilette, if she came, and lead her to my second floor apartment without being able to make any mistake.

My belief that she would come had dwindled away by degrees, and I consoled myself as best I could by imagining all the humiliation of such a success. Even supposing that she would soon be there, what would she be? A simulacrum, a mannequin set up by me. What pleasure could an automaton of that sort provide?

When I saw her in the distance, though, clicking the pavement with her little heels, insubordinate and decisive, smoothing down her skirt with coquettish artistry, so white and pink and blonde, so light in spite of her furs and so graceful in spite of her haste—so alive, in sum; get on with it!—I could no longer think of her as an automaton. There was nothing jerky about her unconstrained gait, I can assure you!

She drew nearer. Her eyes were laughing at the escapade. They were not the eyes of a sleep-walker. As she passed me, she put her sleeve in front of her mouth and said: "Go back in quickly! What imprudence!" And she ran gaily toward the staircase.

Lord! One might have thought that she was springtime disguised as winter!

I rejoined her with a single bound, and I went ahead of her, taking her hand. Her perfume rose up in front of us, effluvia of orchards in flower and renascent gardens, filling the old stairwell.

On the threshold, Gilette enveloped me with all her crazed flexibility, plunged her gaze passionately into my eyes, and then whispered, through a kiss from which I thought I was about to faint, stammering with emotion: "At last, my love! At last! At last!" And desire made her lascivious pupils squint slightly. We slid toward the bedroom, interlaced.

Here I shall pause. What would be the point of accumulating all the superlatives necessary to describe all the maxima and all the apogees? The time passed like an Edenic breeze. Only a few vague reflections and attempts at analysis disturbed my blissful joy—but every time I questioned myself about Gilette, I was forced to recognize the naturalness to which her actions and language testified. There are things that cannot be contradicted. Furthermore, she manifested impressions that I had not ordered her to feel. On that day alone, her luminous young body awoke to prime delights. It struck surprised and confused attitudes; and, charmingly, she was glad that it was so profoundly astonished, and was agitated in spite of her in a scarcely modest fashion, which caused her to redden all over in rapture.

Such is the contradictory mind of man, though, that I started, abruptly, to think that it was *too* natural. A comedy, of course! It was by *feigning* being entranced that she had enjoyed it! Ah! Little poison! Little mask! She had wanted to keep the better part and the finer role for herself; to preserve for herself, in case of a possible scandal, the absolving excuse of suggestion!

Yes, Monsieur, that was what I thought. It's curious, is it not? Confronted by the enormity of my crime, I refused to believe in it, and did not want to admit my victory in the presence of its magical character and colossal dimensions!

Gilette took responsibility for calling me back to reality. Suddenly, she shuddered and said in a curt voice: "It's time. I feel it. I have to go." Then she got up.

I tried to pull her back with the end of a ribbon, but in order to detach herself she made a movement so sharp that the ribbon remained in my hand with a scrap of lace. And I observed an impulsive fatality in that retreat, which forced my respect and my credulity.

I helped her to get dressed.

Her farewells were tender and desolate. In tears, she repeated: "A week! A week without seeing you! How shall I be able to wait so long? But what can we do? It can't be helped. *Au revoir!* Until Tuesday! *Au revoir…*"

Her plaint weakened my firmness. That week of solitude, which had to be endured, appeared to me as a desert to be crossed, interminable and tenebrous. As I watched Gilette going down the stairs, I experienced a mortal anguish, like that of Hell itself.

She turned round on the final step and directed a broken-hearted smile at me. "Until Tuesday! Until Tuesday, above all…!"

Then, having studied my agony as I leaned toward her, she said: "Poor dear! It's time! It's time! Goodbye!"

She escaped.

I inhaled, until the last suspicion, the breath of April in which her presence lingered. And her absence commenced…a terrible and singular absence, in which Gilette was exiled as Madame Dupont-Lardin; in which the woman who loved me emerged from the other and went into the unknown, further away than anything else: nowhere!

I was not without anxiety, however, with regard to the consequences of our rendezvous. I feared that it might have left some confused vestige in Gilette's memory, and, the following day, I rang the doorbell of the isba.

I received the usual welcome there, cordial and informal. Guillaume, however, seemed worried. His wife, he said, had tired eyes and drawn features that presaged nothing good. He had found her thus after returning from his course the previous evening. And Madame Dupont-Lardin deigned to confide in me that she felt weary and languid, without being able to discover the reason.

Left alone with her for a moment, I took the opportunity to ask her, in the manner of a clownish magistrate: "What did you do yesterday, from five o'clock to seven?"

"Yesterday?"

"Why yes," I continued, in the bantering tone. "I came to offer you my compliments, and you weren't here. Who, then, deprived me of the pleasure of seeing you? The dressmaker? The milliner? Or the adulterer?"

Madame Dupont-Lardin burst out laughing. "Insolent fellow!" she replied. "You're overly curious. For your punishment, you shall know nothing!"

She had said these words in a very cheerful tone—but her forehead immediately became pensive, and she fell into an obstinate reverie from which I could not divert her. I understood that she was trying to remember how she had spent the time from five until seven, and that she could not.

Afterwards, I went home, tranquilized and without having extended my visit, for it was particularly disagreeable for me to converse with an indifferent Gilette, the stranger who, a week before, had snubbed, scolded and humiliated me, and considered me as nothing more than a camp-follower to be put back in my place.

The following Tuesday, my lover, faithful to her mission, re-emerged from nothingness and, delightful and punctual, brought me that weekly paradise of which I had assured myself.

I've just consulted the clock...it's five to four. Another thirty-five minutes to live! Oh, why didn't I write this letter sooner? I really need to collect myself somewhat!

So...oh, *I don't know any more! I don't know any more!*

So, that was how things stood at the beginning of October. And the weeks of darkness followed the dazzling Tuesdays.

The people of the isba saw less and less of me. I was reproached for that coldness. Madame Dupont-Lardin gently gave me to understand that my delicacy was overly reserved. She had "forgotten my indiscretion days ago, and took pleasure in chatting, as in the past, with Guillaume and his old friend." Oh yes! I too would have like to see more of her, but enamored, voluptuous, and not negligent! And I now deplored the scruples that had prohibited me from suggesting to her a pure and simple love, without intermittence, and a resolution to run away with me...and I cursed the fear that made me tremble at the thought of hypnotic sleep, and prevented me from putting Gilette to sleep again in order to be able to dictate a new law to her.

Oh, that frightful sight of a medium in catalepsy! Periodic acquaintance with the magnetized had not succeeded in vanquishing it. I shivered at the thought that, one day, an event would occur that would force me to plunge that woman into a trance again and intimate some command or countercommand to her. And now that I had sounded the psychic mystery, oh, ever since then, in that redoubtable shadow where thought treads on tiptoe, among the uncertain and formidable mechanisms that I had had the audacity to bring into action, everything frightened me! To obtain the results I had obtained, I had set in motion the most enigmatic machinery—and now I feared that the secret engagement of those gears might bring about unforeseen conclusions and irreparable consequences.

Now, the bizarrerie of the effects that I had brought about did not reassure me with regard to those that might yet be produced. The inexorable fatality of its phenomena is a terrible face of hypnotism. The obedience of the subject to the commands of the magnetizer has something blindly mathematical about it, which impresses you beyond all expression.

Several times, impelled by the genius of perverse frissons, I gave myself the squalid spectacle of Gilette reduced to the state of a magnetized thing. Once, as we were saying farewell, I said to her: "Stay with me. Don't go away again." And I placed myself in front of the doorway, with my arms extended.

Her face contracted painfully. She did not say a word in an attempt to appease me. She did not even try to duck under one of my arms. She simply went past. Wildly and impetuously, like a Herculean athlete, suddenly equipped with an irresistible force derived from who knows where. The shock knocked me down.

Another Tuesday—having premeditated this second test—I went to her house a little before five. It was the standard "old friend's visit." We chatted about frivolous things—

but Gilette, suddenly and without any formality, broke off our paltry duet and rang for her chambermaid.

"Give me my hat and coat, quickly," she said. Then, turning to me: "You'll forgive me…there's something I have to do. I'm absolutely obliged to go out. I'll see you soon, won't I? No, don't accompany me—I'm going to the Devil!"

Not knowing how to put it better, it was thus that she abandoned me in order to go to meet me.

Oh, what a strange mistress I had! Sometimes, Monsieur, remembering that it was my will that ruled over her, I experienced an abominable sensation of being possessed myself!

And yet, is love ever anything other than that? In every miserable pair of lovers, is not one always dominated, victim of the other's suggestion? And when it is the man who is fascinated, does that not seem to you to be monstrous, as if the woman were then usurping the prerogatives of the male? What do you say? In sum, our lusts—Gilette's and mine—were merely a transposition into the experimental domain of what happens in nature. I had done nothing but reproduce a natural phenomenon artificially, and my crime blends into a laboratory experiment. Perhaps it would not even have been a crime, if I had committed it in the name of humanity! What is it, all things considered? It's psychological serum therapy, that's all. I've inoculated passion, in the same way that one injects a virus.

God makes consumptives, just as he makes lovers; in the former instance, tuberculosis forced on rats and guinea-pigs replaces it adequately; personally, I have achieved the second replication. Replication? Get away! I have parodied it as a man might do. I have aped it in a burlesque fashion. And I was not long delayed in recognizing the inferiority of my work by comparison with His.

Gilette's health deteriorated. From one week to the next I followed its slow but inexorable decline. Always lively and radiant when she came to me, I heard from Guillaume, during one of my appearances at the isba, about the long unjustified meditations and the causeless depressions that took hold of her for hours at a time, while she sat huddled up in a savage mutism.

That day, Guillaume begged me to come back more often, to cheer them up…

I did nothing about it. I was perplexed.

One morning, near Christmas, Guillaume presented himself before me, causing me a keen apprehension. They had consulted the celebrated Dr. B*** with regard to Madame Dupont-Lardin's condition—but B*** had pronounced from the outset that Madame Dupont-Lardin was suffering from acute neurasthenia.

At that announcement, my fears dissipated.

"Well," I replied, "neurasthenia is treatable—and curable!"

"I know, I know. The doctor has prescribed capsules, wines, injections, douches. But the principal medication—would you believe it?—Gilette has refused. She refuses to submit to it."

"And of what does it consist?"

"Oh, it's nothing much. It consists of spending two months in the sun, in a verdant and pleasant country, by the seaside. Walks; rest; distractions…"

"Yes. But she doesn't want to?"

"She says that she can't; that it's impossible for her to leave Paris. And when I ask her why, she replies: 'I don't know, but it's impossible.' And then she resumes meditating, her eyes lit up, her cheeks on fire, and her head in her hands, as if she were hunting for the solution of an indecipherable problem! The doctor claims that this obstinacy is a further proof of the neurasthenia." Guillaume paused, then went on: "Listen, old man, help me, I beg you! Let's try to convince her, both together. She's followed your advice so many times! Her mother owns a villa near Saint-Raphael; if Gilette spends two months there, she'll be cured, she'll live. Otherwise…" He made a childish gesture of discouragement, sniffed, coughed, and ended up bursting into sobs.

"What?" I cried.

"The doctor…won't guarantee anything…"

Emotion made my reply tremulous. "You can count on me Guillaume! We'll convince her, I promise you. You did well to come. But she mustn't be left alone. Go now, old chap, for the time being. I'll follow you. I'll be there."

When the brave fellow had gone, wiping his eyes and his spectacles by turns, I tried to gather my confused ideas.

Without the permission of her "soul director" Gilette would not want to embark for the South. Now, her life being at stake, whatever the cost, she must go. Thus, the duty was incumbent upon me to put her to sleep and to grant her, if not her liberty, at least a few weeks of respite. The operation would be effected in my home, on the following Tuesday. Three days remained for me to simulate, in her husband's presence, the pressing objurgations that would legitimize, in his eyes, such a change of mind.

My program was completely full.

On the thirty-first of December, having gathered my courage in both eyes, I summoned Gilette to the hideous torpor.

A beautiful temptation offered itself to my consciousness: to say to her, "It's over. You'll never come again. Resume your independence."

That was the infallible remedy, the magic words! I did not pronounce them. I loved her too much. I preferred my pleasure to her happiness. And this, in its concise form, carefully prepared, was the decision of which I notified her, and which, by the same token corrected the faults of the earlier order:

"You will let nine Tuesdays pass without coming. On the tenth, at five o'clock, you will be here. After that, every Tuesday, there will be a rendezvous on the previous conditions— except that, if I happen to be near you, don't go looking for me elsewhere, and come to find me wherever I might be."

That same evening, she told Guillaume that she had decided to go and stay with her mother for two months, since he wanted her to go to the county so ardently.

Guillaume was exultant. He did not know how to thank the advocate of his cause enough. One thing, however, grieved him. Retained by the annual exhibition of his works, he could not leave Paris before the fifteenth….

He had the good sense not to avoid the issue, though. The decisions were taken; Gilette was to leave without delay, and he would join her in Saint-Raphael later.

On January 1, at 9 a.m., the Côte d'Azur express carried Madame Dupont-Lardin away.

It was the first time that Guillaume had been separated from his wife. It made him very melancholy and, dreading the desolation of solitary evenings, he pressed me to dine at the isba every day. Even sadder than him at the prospect of a longer separation, I accepted his offer gladly. At least, in that fashion, I would have news of Gilette, and someone who would talk to me about her. That helped me to endure the eternal days—especially the Tuesdays: those nine Tuesdays that were advancing very gently from the depths of the future; Tuesdays of fasting and abstinence, now as empty and black as the other days, like all those nights that all those days had previously seemed to me to be…

The first of them fell on January 7.

Tuesday, January 7, 1908! I expected it to be one of those ordinary, uninteresting days whose anniversary recalls nothing to make you weep…but it was a terrible day, Monsieur! And I know more than one person who will sob on the seventh of January every year of their miserable lives!

It was 10 p.m., or thereabouts. I was about to take my leave of Guillaume. He had received a letter from Gilette that morning, redolent of cheerful serenity, and, in order to celebrate what he called "his dear invalid's recovery," he had wanted to open a bottle of champagne.

That little orgy had dissipated my spleen and accentuated his optimism—and we were exchanging some rather roguish repartee, I can tell you, when a telegram was brought in.

He read it through. I saw him turn pale, and sit down heavily in order not to fall. At the same time, it seemed to me that my blood turned to cold water, and I felt my lividity like a glacial coating...

Guillaume was panting, as if he were out of breath.

"Bad news?" I said, in a strangled voice.

He began to shake his head, and stammered: "Very...bad news. My wife...very ill... I've been told to go...out there... without delay... without delay...." Rising to his feet with a single motion, he added: "She's dead! I'm sure of it. You know these cautious, circumspect telegrams. 'Come without delay' means 'you'll arrive too late.' Come on! I have to leave."

I reckon, now, that his calmness was more frightening than tearful and moaning despair, but I had so much difficulty mastering my own distress that I could not see it—nor could I measure how much more elevated his great and pure suffering was than my fear.

Perhaps he was mistaken, though. Why would the telegram not reveal the whole truth? I tried to convince him of that, and to persuade myself of it—vain efforts. Guillaume departed into the night with his funereal certainty, and I remained alone, facing mine—and the conviction that I was an assassin.

I strode back and forth in my room until dawn, covering league after league in an endless shuttle, which wore me out completely but achieved nothing. I had thought hard, to be sure, but had been unable to establish anything, save for useless suppositions. But Monsieur, the only evidence that imposed itself on my mind tormented it: Gilette, doing well until then, had fallen victim to a serious accident on the very day of our rendezvous and, to judge by the timing of the telegram, in the late afternoon—which is to say, at the time she was accustomed to spend with me.

Had I failed to efface from the tables of her soul the primitive injunction obliging her to come to find me between five and seven?[80] Was it a matter of a morbid accident, or a mental catastrophe? Or had she fallen under some carriage as a result of a somnambulistic precipitation? Had she been run over by a train?

To all these conjectures I raised thousands of objections. A bitter argumentative battle was fought inside my head; different voices launched their invective against my reason, my conscience and my egotism. I thought I could hear their altercation.

And that lasted until morning.

The light of the Sun gave me confidence. Doubt gradually equalized the good chances and the bad risks. Toward evening, I did not even believe any longer that Gilette was dead.

At 9 a.m., a telegram arrived:

All over. Guillaume.

No explanations. No details. No consolation. "All over." I knew neither the exact time nor the circumstances of the event. And I dared not telegraph to obtain the story…

Then the torture of the previous night began again—and this time, two dawns rose without brightening my interior life. I asked myself, with persecutory obstinacy: *How did it happen?* And while my interrogated consciousness could do nothing but confuse me, my questioned memory offered no worthwhile reply. I never left off repeating in every possible tone what I had instructed Gilette to do, turning my imperative formulas in every sense; no ambiguity revealed itself that

---

[80] I have left "tables" as it is rather than substituting the more immediately-comprehensible "tablets" because the Biblical phrase that Renard is echoing retains that term in the Authorized Version (2 *Corinthians* 3:3), where Christ's message is said to be "written not with ink, but with the Spirit of the living God; not in tables of stone, but in fleshy tables of the heart." The English terms "soul" and "heart," like the French *âme* and *coeur*, are to some degree interchangeable.

might indicate the solution to the mystery. As time went by, however, my guilt was affirmed by my judgment. The exact manner in which I was responsible for the calamity was something that still escaped me, but that I was its author, at the end of three days of anguish and insomnia, I could not doubt.

"You've killed her!" I shouted that at myself, Monsieur. "You've killed her! You've killed her!" And since then, I have been unable to impose silence on myself.

Beside the coffin that he had brought, however, Guillaume told me how Gilette had died. He told me about the absurd crisis of appendicitis that had come upon her like a thunderbolt, the necessity of an immediate and hasty operation, in the most unsuitable conditions, and her death under the chloroform at two o'clock in the morning. He told me all that, which should have soothed my soul. Well, do you know that I thought? "You've killed her! You've killed her!"

It was too late, you see. It was an obsession. "You've killed her!"

But no, it wasn't me. I'm innocent!

Go on! You know perfectly well, deep down, that it's you who killed her. You've killed her, I tell you. Ah! Ah!

Shhhh!

You've…

Silence!

…Killed…!

Oh! It's a curse!

It was at the exit from Montparnasse cemetery, following her burial, that I was subject to the first temptation to suicide. The state that Guillaume was in prevented me from giving way to it. To leave him in pain seemed to me to be deserting a post confided to me. I understood my duties as a consoler and I gave myself the task of accomplishing them before disappearing.

The widower's grief bordered on dementia. His fine initial stoicism had given way to the furies of rancor. He cursed love, fate and everything. He wished that he could believe in

God, in order to hold Him responsible for his distress and blaspheme against him effectively.

I succeeded, however, in putting his pencils and brushes back into his fingers, in bending him over his sketch-books from morning until evening, where portraits of Gilette soon succeeded one another, page after page, until the work exhausted him He resumed his Tuesday course. Round-shouldered, jaundiced, mute, darting fearful glances behind him, he was no longer the same man, alas—but at the end of the day, he was still a man, and had it not been for me…who knows? If it is not his life, it is, at least, his reason that he owes to my solicitude.

But how much trouble he had given me, at the beginning! The cemetery, too, was not far from the isba. It was such a quick matter to run to it! One crossed the Place Blanche, went along the boulevard, and the first turning on the right, the Avenue Rachel, was a short dead end on to which the gates of the necropolis opened. Three days on the run I found him there, in the little Dupont-Lardin family chapel. On his final escapade, he had lifted up the flagstone of the vault and was about to go down the stairway! I extracted a promise from him that he would only come back once a week, and that he would let the stone rest in peace.

He had the strength to keep his word. It was a good sign. After that, I was not long delayed in perceiving that he was getting better and better, and had no further need of a helper.

My role came to an end sooner than I had hoped. However brief its duration had been, though, Monsieur, it had been sufficient for me to live for one single month with my remorse to get used to its company. A crushing grief, an infinite sadness, rendered existence more sepulchral than death, but for the moment, the courage to get out of it had abandoned me. I was incapable of the slightest effort. My job as an architect disgusted me. Any labor exhausted me. I would have liked never to leave my bedroom, and that it should be carpeted in black, like a catafalque. The window remained closed. I held myself prisoner there to the extent that hunger did not drive me from it, and Guillaume, surprised by such an affliction—and perhaps suspicious—decided not to draw me out of it. I hated everything that interrupted my lamentable intercourse with the memory of Gilette. The joy of others offended me. A burst of laughter from a passer-by was sufficient to irritate me.

The Carnival, which produced a festival hubbub in the streets, brought my anger to the point of paroxysm. While it reigned over Paris, I tried to stop up the window by means of a carpet and a mattress—wasted effort; the rumor of the people in a jubilant mood filtered through the stuffing, albeit muffled, and also reached me via the neighboring rooms. Songs, howls of merriment and tunes played on toy trumpets escaped from it like rockets, and I understood, from ambulant music and explosions of noise that the floats of a cavalcade were filing along the road.

No longer able to bear it, I formed a determination to go in search of silence and peace in a more tranquil quarter. I went out.

The cavalcade was drawing away in the direction of the Place Pigalle. I fled in the opposite direction.

A scattered crowd disseminated its strollers across the entire width of the boulevard. The popular gaiety was reinforced by a plague of confetti. It was hurled energetically into every open mouth, but it only cut short obscenities and bestial cries, for the populace had borrowed the voices of herd of livestock, braying and lowing in pleasure. Paper whips, lashing out frenetically, outraged suddenly-frightened faces. Serpentine lassos seized necks and, for a second, linked up a group within the multitude. A few poorly-costumed people in masks were parading or performing imbecilic buffooneries. Oh, what a herd of donkeys! What a herd of goats! Idiots lecherous for *amusement* in that vale of tears! Joy! Misery! *Joy!* What an atrocious folly!

I hastened my steps.

It had rained that morning, but the day was ending in a fine winter evening, already mingled with lukewarm and perfidious languor. The setting Sun lit up the puddles with stained-glass gleams. A shabby Paillasse was stamping in the muddy pools in order to soil the citizens' Sunday clothes.[81] As I made a detour to avoid him, someone slapped me with a handful of sordid confetti. I became annoyed. The witnesses guffawed. I made off even more rapidly.

The boulevard became unbearable. Bordered by taverns with baroque shop-fronts—*le Ciel, l'Enfer, l'Araignée, le Chat Noir, les Porcherons*—fronted with misshapen and sinister statues, it was grotesquely ugly frame entirely appropriate to that proletarian masquerade.[82] I was on the point of taking refuge in Guillaume's house, but the dread of still being able to hear the howls of the Carnival there dissuaded me.

Everything grated on my nerves. *Le Moulin Rouge*, a few strides from the holy place where the dead lie, seemed to me to be the shame of Paris.

As I crossed the Avenue Rachel I saw that the gate of the cemetery wasn't closed. Should I go in? Alas, why? To hear rabble amusing itself beside Gilette's mausoleum! Such a prospect sent me back into the crowd, with my head bowed.

As I went on, the crowd thickened. I experienced increasing difficulty going through it. I felt that its *joy* was hostile to my despair, and its slowness opposed my progress. Gradually, I was forced to slow down. People looked at me

---

[81] Paillasse, the name of an old Neapolitan clown, was generalized for application to clowns in travelling fairs, and further adapted metaphorically to "men of straw" devoid of conviction.

[82] I have left the names of the drinking-dens in French, as is customary, but the sequence of names has some metaphorical significance, the first four items being Heaven, Hell, The Spider and The Black Cat. Les Porcherons was the name of a hamlet outside the walls of Old Paris—which had long been swallowed up by the expanding city in 1908—whose dives and brothels been a favorite destination of 18th century slumming aristocrats; its name is strongly suggestive of "swine" or "pigsty."

curiously. And in the Place Clichy, the mob—and especially the *joy*—became so violent that that I was obliged to turn back, jostling elbows and bumping shoulders under a deluge of confetti, streamers and invective.

I had to resign myself to it. The simplest thing was to return to the house. That was what I tried to do.

The flow diminished. The idlers were circulating with greater discretion—but I saw, without pleasure, that the masks were multiplying. The imminence of darkness was doubtless encouraging their wearers to venture outdoors, with their tawdry finery. They were pouring out of all the side-streets into the carnivalesque boulevard, dolled up in rags, made up with flour and ink, disfigured by ignoble painted grimaces—all pitiful and all *joyful*. They emerged from the gloomiest back streets, the darkest cul-de-sacs, and even from the Avenue Rachel, which led to the sepulchers! Yes, even there, people dwelt who wanted to dress up and claim their share of the *joy*, of the madness.

Two clowns came out of it in front of me. They had false noses made of cardboard, lustrous smocks parti-colored in yellow and blue, and were *joyously* singing the latest popular song. A woman, dressed as a laborer, with a pipe in her teeth and a moustache on her upper lip, followed them, laughing alone. Then came another, indefinable mask. Man or woman? Odalisque or Roman? Dirty toga or improper burnoose? It was impossible to tell what it was. But incontestably, its wearer was drunk, and had to lean on the walls in order to walk. In truth, it was a challenge! The most wretched wanted to rejoice today, in order to annoy me! This one's feet went *flip flop* on the damp asphalt; the peplum, which trailed in the mud, certainly hid nothing more than old slippers, but the filthy wretch was wearing a disguise and the brute was drunk! Oh, that *joy*, that *joy* everywhere!!!

I was indignant, and I swiftly overtook the drunkard, averting my eyes. That travesty of misery in a festive mood incarnated for me the unanimous revelry and the universal *Joy*, to such a point that it was odious to me to hear the drunkard's footsteps floundering behind me. All the sadness of the world had taken refuge in my soul. I aspired to solitude with an unhealthy ardor. A church bell, which slowly chimed the hour, seemed to me to be sounding a funeral knell.

I reached my house as one gains a place of sanctuary.

Relieved to have fled the enlivened throng, I climbed the staircase unhurriedly, and I had reached the first floor when a disagreeable sound made me go more quickly, attacking the climb. It was a halting *flip flop* on the floor-tiles of the hall-way, which soon died away on the stair-carpet.

Oh, damnation! The carnival mask that was now climbing up! *Joy*! The *Joy* was pursuing me!

In four strides I was on my doorstep, searching for my keys and not finding them, because of the urgency of my desire to find them and to hide myself from the view of that *Joy*, you understand: the *Joy* that was coming along the landing with its laugher and its hiccups, making fun of me!

Finally, the key slid into the lock—and I felt liberated, victorious, able to mock.

"May the Devil take Mardi Gras!" I said. "Hold on— Tuesday! It's Tuesday…it's today… alas! It's today that *she* was supposed to…"

And all of a sudden, Monsieur, my teeth began to chatter, and my bones began to dance the Dance of the Dead. I was in front of my open doorway, without being able to go through it. I heard the mask climbing up—the mask from the Avenue Rachel. I heard it stumbling against the walls in the semi-darkness. *An exhalation of the morgue preceded it!*

It surged forth, hanging on to the banister. It was not a burnoose, or a toga, but a parted shroud that enveloped it. What I saw, by the light of the setting sun, could not be described. It was neither masculine nor feminine, and it was not drunk. It was a creature of quicklime that was coming toward me…an obscure and slimy monster that touched me….

It embraced me with its cold and sticky rigidity. And this is what its death-rattle tried to say: "Come! Come quickly! Our two hours are curtailed; I had so much trouble getting out…I'm late. Come, my love! Oh, I'm suffering a martyr-dom…but I love you even more than I feel ill. Come!"

I allowed myself to be drawn, stupidly, uncomprehendingly—*and my late mistress dragged me to the bedroom.*

The blocked window created a precocious night there. Night was also falling inside my head. I was entranced by stupor. An abject kiss on my cheek suddenly woke me up. I stood up straight and pushed the amorous cadaver away, so brutally that I heard it fall over along with a chair. My hand sought a familiar object of its own accord; I turned something mechanically; an electric lamp lit up.

The dead woman had already got to her feet. Standing up, she rearranged the folds of her shroud. In the pitiless light, it was a sight to drive you mad, a spectacle to kill you, a horrible prodigy to which it was necessary to put an immediate end!

But how? What secret law of hypnotism had prolonged the effect of my orders beyond death? I didn't have time to think about that. Only one expedient offered itself to my confused mind: to put that thing to sleep and command it to return to its coffin and remain there, lifeless, until the end of time…yes! But was that material specter able to go to sleep? Were the dead magnetizable? Could those who were no longer awake become drowsy? Could someone asleep be put to sleep? And what about me? Could I be bold enough to plunge my gaze into those two ignominies…having not dared to do so when they were the stars in my sky?

I made a great effort.

"Gilette," I began—oh, these diminutive names do not suit the dead, and how false that one rang!. "Gilette…sit down. It's been such a long time since I last looked at you… No! Don't look into the mirror! I implore you! I forbid you…!"

Her death-rattle groaned dully. "It's abominable to know that one is dead…to feel oneself suffering thus…and f…"

"Mercy! Mercy!" I begged.

"Why ask for mercy? Are you guilty of something? I love you; that's all that matters. Come, my darling! Oh, I need so badly to be your mistress, as ardent and delighted as the most spirited, the most enraptured of mistresses…"

She pronounced the last words emphatically, and, with her arms raised in an atrociously coquettish pose, she extended her winding-sheet like a screen behind her miry nudity.

"Gilette!" I stammered, retreating to the doorway. "I told you...that I wanted…to look at you…for a while. Take this armchair…"

She obeyed meekly. Outside, a shrill steam-valve released an incessant incoherent shriek.

I tried to influence Gilette then, but I could not succeed in obtaining the condensation of my will-power, and my listless gaze vacillated. Besides, from a distance, without touching the patient, nothing can be achieved. Would it be necessary, then, to place ourselves hand-in-hand, knee-to-knee?

Just as I was preparing to submit myself to this new torture, a fortuitous occurrence plunged me even further into the gulf of horror. Someone in the antechamber exclaimed: "What! All the doors open! Oh, that odor! What a stench! Well, where are you?"

GUILLAUME!

What? Come again? *Guillaume was there*. It was Mardi Gras—a holiday; he had no class!

The scene that was about to unfold, Monsieur, unfolded in my imagination with a rare promptitude. I saw in advance, the satanic *flagrante delicto* in which the widower surprised his deceased wife in amorous conversation with the family friend—and I attained the depths of terror.

The cadaver stood up, tottering and bewildered, and went to hide behind the bed-curtains. With a flick of the wrist I put out the light and I ran to meet Guillaume, to grab hold of him, to drag him away, to take him downstairs so quickly that he only recovered his power of speech outside. I made no reply to his questions. I gripped him firmly and I forced him to run through the crowd, to run faster and faster. Where? I didn't know. We were going at top speed. At every moment, over his shoulder, I scanned the space that we left behind us—but, thinking of the vigor of the hypnotized and the injunction: "Come to find me wherever I might be," I stopped the first motorized cab that was free.

It took us to Montrouge, then to Vincennes, then somewhere else. It drove us through all the suburbs. I still kept silent.

At seven o'clock, however, I consented to go back to Montmartre, and, after having deflected Guillaume's insistence with the aid of a story I had invented and which he seemed to believe, I deposited him in front of the isba.

As I had expected, my bedroom was deserted.

As a precautionary measure, I shook the bed-curtains. No one was hidden there any longer. Besides, oily footprints were discernible on the clean carpet, in which the departure of the impure thing was inscribed, along with its impatient stamping and its arrival. But its sojourn in my home was eternalized in a nauseating fashion, and I had to air the place in order to expel Giselle entirely.

Then I began to reflect…

And I've been reflecting for a week.

"Every Tuesday, from five to seven, a rendezvous on the previous conditions" and "come to find me wherever I might be."

Thus, I have inflicted the haunting of a revenant upon myself! Every week, the dead woman will return, becoming more repulsive from week to week, for long years. I shall be visited at first by a filthy creature, then by a shapeless mass of little moving things; a skeleton will follow, whitening with age; and finally there will be a cloud of dust…but that cloud is a long time off…it will have to descend into to the depths of my own tomb, every Tuesday…*if the phantom is capable of surviving me…*

I could go far away…America. Nothing could rejoin me there, in two hours. But is it not necessary, by Divine Mercy, to attempt the impossible to in order annihilate that which I have formed? Can I allow that profanation of Death to continue without trying to put a stop to it? Then again, who knows? No one noticed Gilette because of the Carnival and the masks…but how can she pass unnoticed on other occasions?

It's necessary to put a stop to all that. Yes. However—even if the thing were practicable—I'll never be able to put her to sleep again. I'm too frightened. And do you know, I can't even see her again, or hear her, or…oh, no, no, no!

Tuesday. She'll be coming soon.

That's why I'm going to kill myself.

I'm going to kill myself, above all, because it's the only means of rendering myself blind and deaf, of separating myself from touch, smell, taste, memory and everything that allows us to perceive, to know, to recall.…

And I'm also going to kill myself—pay attention, now—because I have a definite hope of destroying, along with my will-power, that fragment of it which I slipped into Gilette's body and which, remaining alive, governs her on the appointed days and lends her, dreadfully, an intermittent and fateful soul.

I believe that. I'm not certain of it, for here I run into the unknown of science. Nevertheless, I shall kill myself before half past four, before she is reanimated, out there, before she can lift the li…

Oh! Who's ringing my doorbell? So forcefully? So persistently?

Who's knocking, so urgently?

My God, how dark it is! What time is it, then? Four o'clock! Still four o'clock! But…God in Heaven! The pendulum's no longer moving. The pendulum has been stopped since four o'clock! And how many lines I've written since!

The knocking's louder! The door's caving in! Oh! Oh! Oooooh! Gilette! One second! I'll open up! Wait a second!

Quick, my revolver! In the name of the Father, the Son and the Holy Spirit…

DEATH AND THE SEASHELL

For Jacques Pillois[83]

...and their form is of a malice so mysterious
that one waits to hear it...
Henri de Régnier, *Contes à soi-même.*

Put that seashell back in its place, Doctor, and don't put it to your ear like that in order to combine the rumor of your blood pleasurably with the murmur of the sea. Put it back. The very man that we have just buried, our beloved great musician, would still be alive if he had not carried out that puerile action of listening to what the mouth of a conch-shell had to say to him. Yes, your client. Yes, Nerval. You think it was a heart attack? It's possible. Personally, I doubt it—and these are the reasons. Don't repeat them to anyone.

On Friday evening, the day before the misfortune, I dined at Nerval's home. For 20 years, his intimate friends had joined him there every Wednesday. There were five to begin with; that day, for the first time, only two of us remained; an apoplexy, an influenza infection and a suicide left Nerval and myself face to face. When one is a sexagenarian oneself, such a situation is not to be taken lightly. One asks oneself: "Who's next?"

The meal was gloomy and funereal. The great man was taciturn. I did everything possible in the attempt to cheer him up. Perhaps, I thought, he was in mourning for other losses, all the more bitterly for being kept secret....

He was, indeed, mourning for other losses.

---

[83] Jacques Pillois (1877-1935) was best known as a composer of music, although he was also a poet.

We went into his workroom. On the open grand piano, the manuscript of a musical work was upside-down on the lectern, exposing a recently-started page.

"What are you working on, Nerval?"

Having lifted his finger, like a sad prophet advertising his God, he said: "*Amphitrite*."[84]

"*Amphitrite*! Finally. How many years have you been holding that in reserve?"

"Since my Prix de Rome. I was always waiting. The longer a work matures, the better it is, and I wanted to put the experience and dreams of an entire lifetime into it. I think it's time…"

"A symphonic poem, isn't it? Are you satisfied with it?"

Nerval shook his head. "No. This, however, this might do, at a pinch…my idea isn't deformed beyond all measure therein…"

And, skillfully, he played the prelude: a Neptunian procession. You'll love it, Doctor—it's a marvel.

"As you see," Nerval said to me, holding down strange, unexpected and brutal chords, "until this fanfare of Tritons, all goes well…"

"Magnificently," I replied. "There's…"

"But that's all," Nerval went on. The following chorus…misfires. Now, I feel impotent to write it. It's too beautiful. We can no longer…. It requires composition in the manner that Phidias sculpted, in building a Parthenon, simply, simply… We no longer know…" He suddenly raised his voice: "Ho!...and there I am, stuck!"

"Come on," I said. "You're one of the most famous, so…"

"So if I can't, what chance do the others have? At least their mediocrity is happy, though, simply because it is medio-

---

[84] Homer uses the name Amphitrite simply to refer to the sea, but in Hesiod she is a Nereid—a goddess—and the wife of the sea-god Poseidon (here called Neptune, Renard's usual preference being for Roman rather than Greek names).

cre and easily contented. Fame! Lovely glory, with all its griefs…!"

"It's always at the summits that the clouds gather…"

"Come on!" Nerval went on. "Enough flattery! And since the hour is decidedly lamentable, let's devote it, if you will, to more authentic pains. We have a duty to the disappeared."

On these enigmatic words, he took the dust-cover off a phonograph. I understood.

As you can imagine, Doctor, that phonograph did not play the medley from *La Poupée*, performed by the band of the Republican Guard, conducted by Parès.[85] The apparatus—much improved, sonorous and pure—had only a small number of rolls. It simply talked.

Yes, you've guessed it. On Wednesdays, the dead speak to us…

It's terrifying, that copper gullet and its voices from beyond the tomb! For, in its substance, it's not a question of a photographic or, even better, cinematic likeness; it's the voice itself, the living voice, surviving the carcass, the skeleton, oblivion…

The composer was seated in an armchair, next to the hearth. He listened, his eyebrows dolorously furrowed, to our dead comrades talking about sweet things from the depths of their sepulcher.

"Ah, science has done well, Nerval! A source of prodigies and emotions—see how closely it is approaching art!"

"Certainly. The more powerful telescopes become, the greater will be the number of stars. Certainly, science has done

---

[85] *La Poupée* [The Doll] is a suite included in *Jeux d'Enfants* [Children's Games] (1871) by Georges Bizet, originally composed for the piano. The *garde républicaine*'s orchestra, founded in 1852, became very famous, especially while it was conducted by Gabriel Parès (1860-1934)—which was why it made some of the earliest phonograph records commercially released in France.

well. But it's too young for us. Those who will profit from it most are our descendants—for, by means of these recent discoveries, they will be able to contemplate the appearances of our century, and to hear the sounds that our generation makes. Who can project the Athens of Euripides on a screen for our benefit, or release the voice of Sappho?"

He became animated, absent-mindedly juggling with a large seashell that he had taken off the mantelpiece.

Delighted with the lucky chance that was reviving his spirits, I thought that a development of the scientific theme— however paradoxical—might amuse him, and I took it up. "Don't despair. Nature is sometimes in advance of science, and the latter often does no more than imitate it. Look—what about photography? Anyone can see antediluvian tracks at the Museum—of a brontosaurus, I think—and can distinguish, in the ground, the imprint of the deluge that fell when the animal had passed on. What a prehistoric snapshot!"

Nerval had put the seashell to his ear. "It's pretty," he said, "the sound of this horn. It reminds me of the beach where I picked it up—an island near Salerno. It's old and crumbling."

I took advantage of the opportunity. "Who knows, old chap? They say that the eyes of dying men conserve the images of final vision. What if that spiral, formed like an ear, had registered the sounds that it perceived at a critical instant—the death of the mollusk, for example? And what if we could reproduce them, in the manner of a phonograph, with the rosy lips of its valve? After all, perhaps you're listening to the breaking of centuries-old waves..."

But Nerval had stood up. With an imperious gesture, he commanded me to be silent. His eyes opened vertiginously, as if upon an abyss. He held the little bicorn grotto against his temple, and seemed to be listening at the entrance to a mystery, held rigid by a hypnotic ecstasy.

On my reiterated insistence, he reluctantly passed me the object.

At first, I could only make out the bubbling of foam and, further away, the immense tumult of the open sea, scarcely perceptible. I sensed—I don't know how—that the sea was very blue and very ancient. And then, suddenly, the singing of women passing by…superhuman women, whose hymn was savage and voluptuous, comparable to the scream of a mad Goddess…yes, that was what it was, Doctor: a scream, but a hymn all the same. Those songs—those insidious songs. Circe advised not letting them take one by surprise, unless one is tied to the mast of a galley and the oarsmen have their ears stopped with wax…was that really sufficient to preserve one from peril…?

I was still listening,

The marine ghouls drew away into the utmost depths of the seashell. Nevertheless, from one minute to the next, the same scene unfolded, renewed, as periodic as on a phonograph, but incessantly troubling and never fading away.

Nerval snatched the miraculous conch from me, and ran to the piano. For a long time, he tried to notate the divine sexual clamor.

At 2 a.m., he gave up. The room was strewn with blackened and torn sheets of paper.

"You see, you see," he said. "I can't even transcribe the chorus under dictation!"

He went back to his armchair, listening, in spite of all my efforts to the venomous paean.

At about 4 a.m., he began to tremble. I begged him to get some rest. He shook his head, and seemed to lean over the edge of an invisible gulf.

At 5:30 a.m., Nerval fell, his forehead striking the marble of the heath—dead.

The seashell shattered into a thousand shards.

Do you believe that there are auditory poisons, akin to deleterious perfumes and toxic beverages? Since Wednesday's audition, I've been ill-at-ease. There's only me to go, now. Poor Nerval! You say that he died of a heart attack, doctor...but might it not rather be *from having heard the song of the Sirens*?

Why are you laughing?

PARTHENOPE
OR, THE UNFORESEEN PORT OF CALL [86]

For Charles Montaland[87]

Monsieur Vivonne's galleys had already been rowing across the open sea for several days when Monsieur de Beaufort set out for Crete in his turn, with a squadron of tall ships. Thus traveled, in the year 1669, the ten thousand sabers, pikes and muskets with which the army, under the command of Monsieur de Navailles, had orders to deliver Candia, for the triumph of Christ and the glory of the King.[88]

---

[86] Parthenope was one of several names cited by various Classical writers as those of the sirens of Greek mythology; a fugitive figure in Greek literature, she owes her particular celebrity to a legend associated with the city of Naples, which relates that her body was washed ashore there after she drowned herself as a result of her unrequited love for Ulysses.

[87] Charles Montaland was a *fin-de-siècle* composer whose fugitive fame was eventually outshone by a 20th century namesake, presumably his son.

[88] The Venetian city of Candia had been besieged by the Ottoman Turks for no less than 21 years when Louis XIV sent a French fleet in August 1669 to join forces with the Knights of Malta and the Venetians in an attempt to relieve the city. The fleet was commanded by his cousin François de Bourbon (or de Vendôme) de Beaufort, and included a contingent commanded by Louis-Victor de Rochechouart, Duc de Mortemart et Marquis de Vivonne; it carried an army under the command of Philippe de Montant-Bénac de Navailles. The expedition was a disaster; Beaufort went missing in action—his body was never found—and the army suffered such heavy losses that Navailles withdrew entirely, leaving the city to fall in Septem-

A courier was dispatched from Toulon to Versailles carrying the news of the successful departure. He had not covered six leagues when a gust of wind blew his braided hat off. That squall came from the sea. It was doubtless no more desirable to Heaven than to the Court, and surely emerged from the grottoes of Lucifer rather than the cave of Aeolus, for it had already maltreated Monsieur de Beaufort's ships off the Îles d'Hyères and broken the *Sirène*'s topmasts.

As soon as it was calm, the commander of the *Sirène*—who was then Monsieur Cogoulin—put his loudhailer to his mouth and asked for instructions from the Grand Master, whose vessel, thanks to the effects of the storm, had come close to his own—for one cannot pick up two fallen topmasts as easily as a braided felt hat. Monsieur de Beaufort himself, clinging to the *Monarque*'s rail with a furious expression, purple with rage, holding his wig down over his ears with his fist, replied to his subordinate that the damage was due to his own incompetence; that they did not have the leisure to delay the victory because of an incompetent like him; and that, so far as he as concerned, Cogoulin could go to the Devil.

Upon that, Monsieur de Cogoulin also went very red. He retorted that he would do his best to reach Candia on the same day, and at the same hour, as the Grand Master, provided that he was allowed to go by way of the Tyrrhenian Sea—that route being shorter and more sheltered than going by way of Malta, where the Knights' fleet was due to join up with the French squadrons.

The admiral seemed to reflect momentarily. Then his copper conch roared his reply. The general concentration of the combined forces would be at Cerigo. He would rendezvous there with the *Sirène* and two vessels that he would designate to escort her: the *Comte* and the *Princesse*.

Aboard the former, Monsieur de Kerjan, and on the other, Monsieur Gabaret, were commanded to haul in their top-

---

ber: a turning point in the waning Venetian Empire's long war against its bitter rival.

sails—thus depriving them of the same sails that their comrade had lost, to match her speed and remain in the same waters.

The three vessels were now sailing in convoy. Because of the damage to the *Sirène*, they maintained a short distance from the shore. The Tuscans, after the Ligurians, and then the Latins and the Campanians, saw the line of sails, white by virtue of their distance and swollen by a fair breeze, passing by on the horizon with the majestic grace which is both that of the swan and that of the standard.

A few islands, which they skirted, were able to observe the convoy at closer range. The hulls, high at the stern and low at the bow, were remarked upon. Their figureheads were admired, especially that of the second ship: a nude siren, who, with her head extended above the waves in the direction of the course to be followed, seemed to be towing the ship with all the strength of her taut arms, and drawing it toward its destiny—unlike the other two ships, which appeared to be pushing their inert statues, one of a bronze knight, the other of a silver queen. The eyes of the cannons were counted by the lids of the portholes; the rolling of the vessels, alternately putting them in light and shadow, seemed to be firing lighting-fast salvos from one moment to the next. Finally, as the marine passers-by drew away, turning their rumps one by one, people marveled at their castles, and how sumptuous they were, and how they raised up, in a dazzle of gilt, so many balustrades on so many caryatids.

These shining palaces could be seen from even further away. Every morning and evening, three cannon shots were sounded, and something pale rose up or came down there between the huge emblazoned lanterns. It was the fleur-de-lys flag, juxtaposed with the papal banner. And the shore-dwellers and islanders, wishing the Christian boats every success, anticipated a safe voyage in the restored good weather—for the azure sky, with its white clouds, flaunted the colors of the Virgin Mother, and the sea the blue of the King.

Four times the juxtaposed flags were hauled down in glorious twilight. But the fifth sunset, somber and windy, filled Messieurs Kerjan, de Cogoulin and Gabaret with anxiety. The night was diabolical; a cyclone whirled within it. The howling gale battered the ships, full of cracks and clamors, and the captains admitted defeat. All maneuvers were impossible, any command would have been ridiculous.

Monsieur de Kerjan prayed. Monsieur de Cogoulin took snuff. Monsieur Gabaret cursed. And each of them, on his bridge, awaited the dictates of fortune.

Never had their eyes had less work to do or their ears more, so much of a din was there in that darkness. Sometimes, however, lightning abruptly illuminated the chaos, and left their retinas with the persistence of a vision so brief that the agitation had not had time to make a mark on it.

The sea then appeared as a chain of sparkling mountains, in which the vessels, sometimes stampeding and sometimes rearing up, crowned some summit or littered some valley—and that spectacle, motionless by virtue of being instantaneous, suggested to Monsieur de Kerjan that mountain ranges were, after all, no more than enormous statues of the ocean. Monsieur de Cogoulin, for his part, was thinking about the nocturnal calm of Paris and the Marais—in the middle of which, in the warm and silent Hôtel de Cogoulin, his bedroom was asleep. Monsieur Gabaret was still cursing.

Finally, a livid-fingered dawn revealed, as if reluctantly, the neighborhood of a frigate to starboard and the proximity of three reefs to port. Behind the reefs, within a marine mile, a coast extended.

They avoided the rocks, with great difficulty. The *Sirène* even considered resting there, but Monsieur de Cogoulin, foreseeing the imminent wreck, ordered the intrepid thrust of the rudder that saved them. Unfortunately, the bound that the ship made threw four sailors overboard, and, as it fell back, its bowsprit collided violently with the frigate's stern-post. The smaller boat split open, and they had the pain of seeing it sink, without the fury of the waves permitting any attempt at salvation.

It was prudent, in view of the insufficiency of the rigging, not to persist in fighting against nature, and to assess the damage at leisure. A course was therefore set for land. They headed straight for it. They had passed the heights of Capri, facing the gulf of Salerno, and the three islets were the Petites Bouches.

An hour later, the three vessels were moored in a line in a placid cove, their prows turned toward the open sea, and their captains, having embarked in a launch, were able to make a tour of the *Sirène* and inspect its broken spur.

Only the painted wooden effigy had suffered from the accident. She had been decapitated, stripped of her left arm, bruised on her woman's torso and her fish's tail. Her human and animal wounds displayed dry fibers of beech-wood. The log was being reborn from the nymph.

Monsieur Gabaret, however, observed one sad detail: a bloodstain splashed the effigy's breast. One of the four sailors, presumably, had been clinging on there, but the collision had crushed him against the siren's bosom.

In spite of everything, Monsieur de Cogoulin smiled; that would not slow down the progress of his ship. He even talked about getting ready to sail immediately. Monsieur Gabaret dissuaded him, with the assurance that the sea would be mild the following day, and that they would resume their journey more advantageously at dawn, with rested crews.

Monsieur de Kerjan was of the same opinion. "Can we not spend the day on land?" he asked.

"Of course!" cried Monsieur Gabaret. "It might perhaps be the last time we touch the ground, and for my part, I won't be sorry on set foot upon it."

"So be it," said Monsieur de Cogoulin. "Anyway, the coast of Salerno is charming and curious, for the orange-groves grow among Roman ruins. I traveled there once. A few noble Neapolitans have villas there suitable to receive officers of His Majesty. Let's go dress more politely."

As the launch, rounding the *Sirène*, came in view of the shore, however, Monsieur Gabaret exclaimed: "*Sangdieu!* What's that *Bucentaur*? What's the Doge doing here?"[89]

A barge was coming toward them, trailing multicolored fabrics in the water, rather vainly. Its rowers were wearing livery and plying their oars in a very orderly rhythm. A handsome individual was sitting under an awning at the stern. Monsieur de Cogoulin noticed his shiny pink costume. *Five years ago*, he thought, *that costume would have been the utmost height of fashion. It's strange that such an elegant man should be so out of date—but I recognize that nose! Yes, it's Chambanne!*

The other was still coming forward. When he was close enough, he bowed and said: "Messieurs, permit me to...ah! Cogoulin! Cogoulin, here! What a lucky stroke of fate! Come alongside, then, will you!" And he leapt lightly into the launch, with the aid of a long cane.

Monsieur de Cogoulin introduced the two captains and said: "I would have sworn that you were in your barony in Nivernais..."

"The King," Monsieur de Chambanne replied, "did not want to impose a forced residence upon my disgrace. I live here, on the property of the Duc de Sorrente, to whom I'm related by marriage. I live in the midst of these ruins, in a house in the antique style, built on special plans derived from the ruins themselves. You can see it from here—in the cypresses, there...at the end of my cane. From my window I witnessed your annoyances, which afflicted me, and your flag, which caused me to deplore them even more..."

"Trivia," said Monsieur Gabaret. "The damage is insignificant."

"I bless the anodyne incident, then—which will permit Madame de Chabanne and myself to give you hospitality. I

---

[89] The *Bucentaur* was the gaudy and somewhat ponderous vessel employed on ceremonial occasions to carry the Doge of Venice through his watery domain.

have come to ask you to supper, Messieurs, and to offer you the use of my house according to your own pleasure."

"We're lifting anchor tomorrow, at daybreak," replied Monsieur de Kerjan. "Nothing, therefore, stands in the way of the pleasure that you have brought us so courteously, Monsieur."

"But, but…" Monsieur Gabaret stammered, studying the pink satin costume through his lorgnette, "I have nothing in my portmanteau but buff-leather and coarse linen…may I…"

"Please, Monsieur," proclaimed Monsieur de Chambanne, "don't shame me by talking about attire. You can see perfectly well that I'm dressed in the fashion of my grandfather!"

Monsieur de Chambanne's house was a trifle vulgar and gave evidence of whimsical tastes. Built on a hill, it resembled Roman temples that one no longer sees in their entirety, except in engravings. Monsieur Gabaret commented that it had the air of a brand new ruin.

The company went into the room where the meal was to be taken between the two valets who came to open the door. Monsieur de Cogoulin was immediately assured of eating well by the silver-plated dishes and of fine drinking by the Venetian glasses The table that had been set there, in fact, permitted the ultimate refinements of gastronomy. On a dresser, cedar and sandalwood kegs contained the wines, ready to flow from vermilion taps. In front of each cask, five crystal chalices, side by side, garlanded their transparency with festoons of fragile flowers.

Monsieur de Chambanne placed Monsieur de Cogoulin next to the Baronne, at the top of the table. Through the windows, beyond a marble terrace and behind the dark colonnade of the cypresses, one could see the sea. It rose up like a great blue wall, moving at the base, impassive at the crest. The three ships seemed painted in miniature there, and the three islets seemed quite close.

On the walls of the room, on a dark red background, frescoes—profane and sacred friezes—caused the capering dancers of some antique farandole to strike forgotten postures. The bare legs of the dancers beat out lost rhythms; the guests looked at them uncomprehendingly. Monsieur de Chambanne said that they were exact imitations copied from the palace of Tiberius. Monsieur de Kerjan praised them unreservedly.

"Why must these dances be forever foreign?" he asked. "How annoying it is no longer to know the melody with which those flute-players, muzzled with gags, drew from their double flageolets to punctuate them!"

Madame de Chambanne replied that each ballerina in the painting was executing a different step of the same courante—which became, by virtue of that fact, easy to reconstitute. "As for the music," she added, "is it not easy to imagine if one knows the steps that it is designed to elicit? It's simply a matter of discovering the cause by the effect. Listen…"

She made a sign.

The sound of a shepherd's flute rose up from the garden then. It whimpered an Oriental melody which was accompanied, bizarrely, by castanets and sistrums.

Monsieur Gabaret pulled a face.

The host confessed that all of this—the house, the frescoes and the concert—was the work of the Baronne, who was besotted with extinct things and their resurrection. "As for me, Messieurs, I profit from it in idleness, but I confess that this architecture makes me forget that of Monsieur Mansard.[90] He pointed to the ocean. "And here are God's great waters, which are easily the equal of Versailles!"

Monsieur de Kerjan listened to the flute while gazing at the friezes. When the piece finished with an evasive plaint and

---

[90] "Monsieur Mansard" was actually the architect François Mansart (1598-1666), whose name was misspelled when it was applied to "Mansard roofs," which maximized the living-space within attics at a time when Parisian houses were taxed according to the number of stories they had below the eaves.

a fading hum, he complimented Madame de Chambanne, and found her prettier than at first glance. In truth, that precious gem of a young woman had the eyes of a goddess: wide and limpid eyes that seemed always to be in contemplation before an immense and calm sea.

The lackeys, meanwhile, had taken away the soups and disposed the first course in an oval; it consisted of six entrées of fattened pullets and two hors-d'oeuvres of quail, with a broth of mixed meats in the middle. Beneath the plumes of their hats, the guests, in spite of their quality, assumed the kind of expression than an unexpected kindness procures.

"A flavorsome spectacle!" exclaimed Monsieur de Cogoulin.

"*Corbleu*, Madame!" said Monsieur Gabaret, whose épée was fluttering. "How fortunate we are to find you on our route—you and your victuals!"

"Why, Messieurs!" said Madame de Chambanne. "What a fine humor you are in, for men who are going where you are going."

"What is more natural?" explained Monsieur de Kerjan. "Firstly, battles are our lot. We go in quest of them without sadness—but, on my honor, without joy either! That is why, sailing to certain war, to possible death, not expecting to touch land for a long time—perhaps never—this evening enchants us in being an unforeseen port of call, of luxurious peace and charming life."

Monsieur de Cogoulin continued in the same vein: "Ah, Madame! You cannot imagine the pleasure of sitting down to these gold-braided tablecloths and carefully-prepared dishes like little apotheoses! The table and the chairs do not sway with the pitch of the sea: voluptuousness! The marine horizon, perceived through the windows, is not incessantly rising and constantly falling: intoxication! To tell the truth, I can still see our three vessels in the gulf, straining at their anchors, but their distant aspect assures us, at least, that we are not on board—for, having difficulty believing that, we look for every possible proof..."

"And then, Madame," said Monsieur Gabaret, "you are very comely, and there is—no offence—more than one hostess who could not be entirely welcoming to an ugly mug, like mine…which spoils many a reception, Madame, your reverence notwithstanding."

Madame de Chambanne bowed in recognition of the rustic madrigal. She pointed to the ships. "Is it so painful to live in those gilded châteaux?" she asked. "For myself, I never weary of the sea. It's so captivating!"

"Yes," sniggered Monsieur Gabaret, "one is sometimes more captive there than is reasonable. It's played me many a bad turn."

"Madame," said Monsieur de Cogoulin, with his mouth full, "Monsieur Gabaret has been shipwrecked a dozen times over; and he ate human flesh on the ninth occasion, just as I'm eating this capon-thigh."

Monsieur Gabaret obviously found that topic of conversation abhorrent. He became sullen, and asked for permission to dispense with his fork: "that Italian utensil scarcely used in France outside, perhaps, the Court." He added: "And you may take it for granted, Madame, that I'm no courtier, having eaten matelot with Father Adam's fork."

"In sum, Monsieur," the Baronne asked, "you don't like the sea?"

"Yes indeed, Madame! Like a mistress who is adored all the more the more she deceives you, and whom one curses when one is not kissing her on the lips."

"And you Monsieur de Cogoulin?"

"Oh, Madame, for me the sea is the upward path, and the star of Saint Louis is at its end; I like to imagine it as a wide ribbon of bright blue silk…."

"And you, Monsieur de Kerjan?"

"As for me, Madame, I'm attached to it for slightly…childish reasons, which render that country even more seductive to me than others. But you'll laugh at me if I tell you, so allow me to be silent."

"*Peste!*" said Monsieur de Chambanne. "Secrets?"

"Oh, tell us, Monsieur!" insisted the young woman.

Having gazed, in he vast and liquid eyes, at the reflection of the invisible ocean, Monsieur de Kerjan continued in thee terms: "Oh well, here it is: I'm from a land in which people believe less in History than in legend; korrigans caper over its heaths at midnight, and there are fairies gliding through its nocturnal fogs, Certainly, Madame, I cherish the Manoir de Kerjan, its crag, its pious and mulish vassals, and better still, undoubtedly, Mère Yvoël, who is the most loquacious of story-tellers—but more than anything else, I like those sprites that I have never seen and those ungraspable ladies. School-teachers have told me about Rome and Greece, the valor of Caesar and the wisdom of Pericles, but I remember Mercury or Pallas better—and if I still know a little Greek and Latin, it's not because of Plutarch or Livy, but Homer and Virgil, whom I still read for amusement.

"That's why, Madame, loving fable and not truth, it delights me to set foot on Cerigo, which was once Cytherea, on my way to Candia, which is in Crete—to visit, like the imaginary Ulysses of some phantom epic, the isle of Venus and the isle of Minos. Here, I shall gaze into springs to see if some blond reflection might still remain there; there I shall seek the antique labyrinth. Finally, lending myself to the soul of a god or a hero, I shall imagine myself, according to circumstances, as Vulcan or Jupiter, the Minotaur or Theseus, and I shall play the intoxicating game of reliving those lives that no one actually lived."

"Actually lived!" said Madame de Chambanne. "Who knows? Have your cruises not shown you surprising and incredible episodes?"

"Alas," sighed Monsieur de Cogoulin, "they scarcely resemble Aeneids, let alone Odysseys…" Then, suddenly, he protested: "Except for the present one! I don't know any more whether we're supping with Calypso or Dido!"

Madame de Chambanne wore a decidedly indulgent smile. "What, Monsieur!" she went on. "Can it be, after so many campaigns on the ocean, that you cannot report how sirens dress their hair? Or what fanfare the tritons sound on their seashells? Oh, you deserve that I should be Circe! Truly, have you never seen those famous creatures?"

"Yes, Madame: in dreams. A huge red triton swims in my nightmares. His wig is on sideways, and he blows insults at me through his copper conch, which blares: 'Incompetent! Incompetent!' all night long. That amphibian, Madame, is a nasty fellow."

"Don't blaspheme against the demigods," aid Madame de Chambanne laughing. "Neptune's hatred is pursuing you already..." But what about you, Monsieur, what do you think of sirens?"

"I've never seen one," Monsieur Gabaret replied, quite seriously. "But the sea is so mysterious! One often catches unknown and monstrous fish there. There are even some, I imagine, that are never caught, because they crawl along its very bed, without ever being able to emerge, like the clumsy bumpkins that we are said to be, on to land."

"Very true!" cried Monsieur de Kerjan. "For one may say this, Madame: that for birds and philosophers, the earth is merely the bed of the sky, and men drag themselves heavily across it, with the forbidden azure ocean above them, where clouds pass as well as surges.

"As for sirens and as for me, I am pleased to see their tresses in floating seaweeds; and whenever the waves have the suppleness of naked torsos, I am careful to search for other things there. Moreover, Madame, if by chance the sirens were more than curved waves with algal hair, it's *here* that one should be able to assure oneself of the fact. Look at those three islets. You name them Galli; we translate that as the Cockerels. Marines have baptized them the Petite Bouches—no one knows why—but antiquity knew them by another name: the Sirens. And I know the reason for that."

Interest was painted n every face, and everyone turned to the windows. Between the cypress-blackened obelisks, night was falling on the placid sea, still flecked with white. Lost in the mist, the three reefs could scarcely be distinguished; the most they could make out were the three patches of foam that the waves produced as they broke upon them.

Wax candles were now burning on the branches of candelabras set among the dishes of the second course, arranged in a diamond shape, and the maritime scene at which everyone was looking seemed even bluer in the reddening frame. The lackeys too were searching with their eyes for the blurred isles.

Monsieur de Kerjan continued. "I've undertaken the task—oh, utterly puerile, I confess—of tracing the itineraries of heroes on the map. Following the descriptions, I was able to situate the tales geographically and assure myself that, even if the exploits were false, or at least embellished, nothing is more authentic than their setting. This, Messieurs, is the place where, according to the winged words of Homer, the crafty Ulysses heard the sirens singing."

"It's rather curious," said Monsieur de Cogoulin, "that it's in this exact spot that my vessel, the *Sirène*, broke its figurehead, which had the form of the Homeric songstress…"

"The only one, doubtless, that our Heaven has ever seen!" replied Monsieur de Chambanne, shrugging his shoulders. "There are no sirens but wooden ones on the prows of ships and painted ones on heraldic shields. To my knowledge, three French houses bear them in their coats-of-arms—in so many sections—combing their hair and looking in mirrors, singly or in a pair, in flesh-tone or silver. But heraldry more often employs dolphin-women as supports for blazons, so…."

"Fie, my friend!" cried Madame de Chambanne. "Arid science applied to mythology!"

Monsieur de Chambanne shrugged his shoulders once more. "Pardon me," he said, in a different tone, "for interrupting such agreeable conversation, but I owe some slight excuse to Monsieur de Cogoulin." He pointed at an enormous fish on the principal platter. "That, Monsieur, is a porpoise, or I'm much mistaken. If the head is not close at hand, served separately at the top of the table, don't attribute that fault to my ignorance of current customs. I keep myself up to date in such matters, thank God! Because of the bad weather, though, the fishing yields are negligible at present, and the fish you see was thrown up on the sand a little while ago, still quivering, but headless. The freshness of its flesh and its rarity persuaded us—my chef and myself—to offer it thus."

"It's not a porpoise," said Monsieur Gabaret.

"What is it, then?" demanded Monsieur de Chambanne, sharply.

"It's a variety of porpoise."

"Oh, porpoise yourself, Gabaret!" chaffed Monsieur de Cogoulin, who had been drinking courageously. "You're very sharp, for an anthropophage! Another glass of burgundy, if you please!"

His Murano glass was handed to him, filled with red wine. He emptied it in a single draught and returned it to the valet.

Madame de Chambanne was showing signs of impatience. Her eyes never left the sea, which was getting darker by the minute. "We're very far from sirens," she sighed to Monsieur de Kerjan.

"That subject is dear to your heart, Madame! I didn't expect to find dreams so similar to my own here...."

"Oh, not similar: worse. For you only believe in sirens as symbols, and I believe that they exist, with their tresses, their voices, their scales..."

"May it please God that they do not, Madame! The three fabulous sisters devoured sailors, and of they existed they would be ferocious monsters, killing without mercy!"

"The three sisters...yes, according to the *Odyssey*, there were only three: Ligeia, Leucosia and Parthenope..."[91]

"That's right," relied Monsieur de Kerjan, a trifle disconcerted by so much knowledge, "but legend takes responsibility for getting rid of them. It's said that after they had heard

---

[91] Actually, Homer does not specify the number of the sirens, nor does he give any of them names.

the music of Orpheus, chagrin turned them into three rocks: those Galli that the darkness is now effacing entirely."

"They were not only three in number," Madame de Chambanne continued, "and—so the poets tell us—there were also river-dwellers among them. They live in the grottoes of the Rhine…"

"A little champagne," demanded Monsieur de Cogoulin. "This fish is famous. What, Gabaret, you don't have a high opinion of it? Are you feeling ill?"

Monsieur Gabaret did not, in fact, seem to be in the pink. His sun-bronzed cheeks had a greenish tint.

"Why, what's the matter, Monsieur?" enquired Madame de Chambanne.

But the rugged captain had recovered his color. "It's nothing," he said, smiling. "It's passed."

"Well then, eat!" urged Madame de Chambanne. "Is the variety of porpoise not to your taste? Would you like to add some spice? A few grains of fennel? A pinch of coriander?"

"Thank you—no, Monsieur, thank you…to tell the truth, I'm no longer hungry. A little sundew, if I may…"[92]

"You're very refined, for a cannibal!" said Monsieur do Cogoulin, bursting into broad laughter. "Two fingers of Bordeaux, if you please."

The venison dishes of the third course designed a circle on the damask cloth. A violent gamy aroma arose therefrom.

"Green truffles!" said Monsieur de Cogoulin, admiringly. "Are we still at Versailles?"

"Alas," said Monsieur de Chambanne, with a sigh, "Versailles had some advantages, after all. There are days…do you see…?" He raised the tip of his finger nervously to touch the corner of his eye. "Tell me, Cogoulin, what they're saying at Court; it still interests me, all things considered."

---

[92] *Drosera* [sundew] was once used for medical purposes as a diuretic and antispasmodic, but the fact that the parent plant is carnivorous is equally relevant here.

Then, while those two were making fun of the King and the *petit lever*, with all the affectionate ardor of a supper coming to its end, the two romantics, for their part, resumed their mythological subject-matter. Monsieur Gabaret wanted to join in. He did so shamelessly and clumsily, the sundew having developed an unfortunate natural disposition in his soul, and believing that the time had come to be witty.

"Would you like to tell me, Madame siren-lover," he said, "how they made love? Did they take men for husbands, or was it fish? For at the end of the day, my opinion is that those girls terminated in the wrong way, and ran a strong risk, like so many women, of never offering sacrifices to Cupid— for lack of possessing the temple, if I might put it like that. And if your naiads became profligate with sperm whales, ah, the naughty girls! You may think what you please about them, Madame, but *ventrebleu…*!"

"Calm down, Gabaret," said Monsieur de Kerjan. And with that, he kicked the captain's ankle hard. "The sirens, my dear chap, are immortal, and don't care at all about posterity. Perhaps the tritons sometimes amuse themselves with them—I don't know exactly how. Furthermore, they loved one another fraternally; the poets claim that they hardly ever parted company and that one siren could not perceive anther without going to cajole her; in operas, they're always singing trios, and painters delight in representing them as three marine Graces interwoven in a triple caress."

"Three fingers of Lesbos," demanded Monsieur de Cogoulin of the nearest valet.

"And Cyprus for me!" said the Baron, his cheeks flushed. "To the health of Athénaïs de Montespan!"

They drank.

The fruits had replaced the meat dishes, and their bowls, alternated with dishes of stewed fruit, were arranged in a square.

Madame de Chambanne was rather prudish, and fearful of licentious talk. She perceived that the conversation was increasingly tending in that direction, with a guard-room tone in Monsieur Gabaret's case and a foppish one in Monsieur de Cogoulin's. She therefore ensured that the desserts were dealt with very expeditiously. Then the company retired to the drawing-room; and Madame de Chambanne, having served the hippocras—which was made with white wine and the juice of red oranges—with her own hands,[93] thought it wise to leave the men free to tell their dirty jokes.

She slipped away.

The drawing-room was not at all reminiscent of antiquity. Its furniture was recent, and large flowing yellow curtains had been drawn across its windows. Monsieur de Kerjan parted them, but scarcely had he glanced at the blue landscape, where the golden poops were turning into silver châteax in the moonlight, when Monsieur de Chambanne whispered in his ear, in a voice tremulous with tears and perfumed with hippocras: "Leave them closed, Monsieur, I beg you! Let us imagine for a while that we're in Versailles! Look, blinking one's eyelashes like this, one might believe that one were in Madame's saffron boudoir; the laurel grove is on the left, there...and behind that curtain—*oyez*,[94] Monsieur, *oyez*— babbles the water-jet of the little octagonal basin!"

"But what about the sea, Monsieur?" replied Monsieur de Kerjan, slightly put out. "God's great waters?"

---

[93] Hippocras was supposedly a tonic beverage, made by spicing wine with sugar, cinnamon and fruit juice and straining it through a piece of linen known as "Hippocrates' sleeve." The French spelling is *hypocras*, whose similarity to *hypocrisie* [hypocrasy] completes the leavening of *double entendre* with which this suggestion-laden passage is replete.

[94] The Old French *oyez* [hear ye] has been largely banished from French dictionaries, but is still familiar in English as the traditional summons of town criers, handed down from Norman times.

"Ah!" said the other, tearfully, "the Pièce des Suisses is more redoubtable; my shipwreck is mirrored there.[95] It's more beautiful still, since it's not here…"

"Yes, yes," murmured Monsieur de Cogoulin. "Exile! Too much chagrin!"

"Yes, yes, drunkard!" muttered Monsieur Gabaret. "Too much Cyprus!" And without further ado he lit his clay pipe, black and stinking.

They went back to the hippocras; Monsieur de Chambanne had a water-jug full of it brought in. Then he begged Monsieur de Cogoulin and Monsieur de Kerjan to tell him about some antechamber intrigue or bedroom adventure. They brought him up to date with the latest scandals, while he listened blissfully, with his eyes closed, making occasional replies—and, from time to time, according to whether some sally plunged him into a dream or brought him back to reality, a smile came to his lips or tears to his eyes.

Meanwhile, Monsieur Gabaret, bored with hearing his fellow captains chattering like two flighty women, politely nodded off and started to snore.

They had been conversing and sleeping in this manner for some time when Monsieur de Kerjan saw the large closed curtains suddenly light up with a cold glare, and the windows projected the pale shadow of their lattices thereupon. The candle-flames paled.

"Look out, Messieurs! Here comes the dawn."

---

[95] The Pièce des Suisses is a pond at Versailles surrounded by bushes, so-called because it was dug by the Swiss Guards; the reader is free to speculate as to exactly how the pink-clad baron's fall from grace came to be mirrored there. Chambanne's nostalgia might seem a trifle overdone, given that Louis XIV did not move his court to Versailles until 1668, so he could only have been there for a matter of months before being banished.

He shook Monsieur Gabaret, who was groaning in a dream in his armchair, with sweat on his brow and one foot on his broken pipe.

The atmosphere in the dining-room was warm and heavy. They were feeling the discomfort of garments worn for too long, which sleepless nights leave behind. Monsieur de Chambanne rang a bell. No one came. The drowsy lackeys were slumped on the benches in the hallway. It was necessary to wake them up. Their mastered ordered that the barge be made ready. Afterwards, Monsieur de Chambanne and is guests went outside, clad in long capes.

A cold wind was moaning through the cypresses. It was keen and sharp, laden with sand, and stung their feverish cheeks, as irritant as a bellows. Reddened eyes blinked; clammy flesh shivered beneath the mantles.

They were soon on the beach.

During the night, the sea had thrown up its victims. The shore was strewn with bodies. Some of them were already some distance from the water-line, but others, still half-submerged, stirred as each wave came in, and the sea played with them like a cruel cat, obliging its cadavers to repeat, with mannequin gestures, the somersaults and hiccups of their dying moments.

The four men inspected their sinister ranks.

The crew and passengers of the sunken frigate were lying there, dead, including several women and a child; some were naked, others dressed in tatters; some were visibly costumed in gaudy finery, albeit in shreds—doubtless traveling circus performers. All swollen and turning green, their faces were contorted with passion, terror or rage, and some of them offered glimpses of unexpected masks, grimacing with expressions so monstrous that no living person, it seemed, would have been able to imitate them without dying.

Monsieur de Cogoulin, who was going from corpse to corpse, recognized two of his sailors. "There are still two missing," he said.

"They'll never be seen again," replied Monsieur de Chambanne. "It's too late. Here, the sea often keeps drowned men. Three fishermen disappeared last year. They went down near the islands. None reappeared. Truly, one might think..."

"Come here, Messieurs, look at this!" cried Monsieur de Kerjan. He had moved ahead of the others and was waving his arms wildly, leaning over a confused mass the color of the sand.

They joined him.

The thing was a dead woman, entirely naked—or, rather, the upper half of a woman, horribly mutilated. Some accident—the impact of two pieces of wreckage, presumably—had cut through her abdomen, at the requisite height to ensure that her trunk remained modest in spite of its nudity.

Silence reigned. Monsieur de Kerjan made two energetically-punctuated signs of the cross.

What was lying there before them was disconcerting. The creature was bizarre. Her narrow face emerged from strangely ill-kemp hair, as rough and wild as a mane, mingled with seaweed. Little round eyes were still lit by a yellow gleam which must have been astonishingly bright when she was alive. Beneath the nostrils, designed to draw in mighty draughts of air, a large mouth revealed the serrated jaw of a carnivore, whose exceedingly large canines were biting the lower lip. The cheeks were flat and the chin receding. There were no wrinkles; no pleat on the woman's forehead gave evidence that she had ever thought, nor any at the lips that she had ever smiled. The smooth face was ageless, and its serenity might have passed for bestial indifference.

It was, however, a human being. The muscular torso, elegantly hollowing out her figure, and her breasts, pretty in their smallness, proved that by evoking the idea of a Spartan virgin, skilful in physical games. The absent legs must surely have run and jumped! One imagined them lean, muscular and swift. As for the arms, they confirmed the athletic hypothesis. A coarse down covered their knotty tendons, and tufts of bristly hair sprouted from the armpits.

The most curious thing, however, along with the canines, was that the hands were webbed all the way to the fingernails, which grew as hard, long talons. Her entire skin was sun-tanned.

Monsieur de Cogoulin was the first to speak. "It's a savage!" he said.

"More likely," Monsieur Chambanne retorted, "some phenomenon exhibited on stage and embarked on the frigate with the circus-performers. I've seen hands like that in a jar in the apothecary's shop in the Rue Gilles-le-Queux. It's a birth-defect, apparently."

"No," said Monsieur de Kerjan. "That hair has never been combed, and those swan's-feet have never plaited it. I'll swear, too, that no chemise or wimple has ever brushed those shoulders—which are singularly beautiful for such a monkey-face. Otherwise, the body would be paler than the hands and the face."

"Those acrobats," insisted Monsieur de Chambanne, "must have been very badly advised, to take such poor care of their meal-ticket."

"She's extremely tall, for a cripple!" said Monsieur Gabaret. "She must have been a colossus, on her legs."

"If she ever had any," murmured Monsieur de Kerjan.

"My word," continued the other, "her slice matches the slice on that porpoise-variant you served last night. If one welded them together...." He interrupted himself abruptly. The idea that had crossed his mind presumably seemed baroque—or had he been put off by the expressions on the faces of the three gentlemen?

They looked at one another momentarily.

"Bah!" said Monsieur de Chambanne.

"Damnation!" added Monsieur de Cogoulin.

"Hmmm," coughed Monsieur de Kerjan.

"All the same, Monsieur, all the same," continued Monsieur Gabaret, "that variety of porpoise stank diabolically of human flesh..."

The morning wore on.

While Monsieur de Chambanne had the dead buried, the vessels gradually disappeared, in single file. First the horizon covered their magnificent châteaux, then hid their sails, whitened by the distance, one by one. The *Sirène*, the *Princesse* and the *Comte* moved on, and the naval statue whose heartwood had been reborn drew them along, bloodily, toward their destination—and toward defeat.

On board, the commanders were taking a nap.

They retained a strangely tenacious memory of that long day, considering the vanity and incoherence of its incidents, which were perhaps linked together by a secret knot. Messieurs de Kerjan and Gabaret were able to relate them, in every detail, to their grandchildren—who thought them ordinary and uninteresting. And if Monsieur de Cogoulin did not recall what has just been narrated two months later, it was because a slow-moving cannonball, fired from a felucca, had carried his memory away with his head.

THE SUNLIT STATUE

For André Vermare[96]

We had climbed the Lykabette[97] to look at the moonlight over the sea.

Phidias[98] loved the spectacle, and when the fancy took him to delight in it, none of his pupils would ever have failed to follow him, some by virtue of courtesy and others of taste. I was one of the latter, for I also love moonlight over the sea—and Phidias knew that. In the studio, Korebos was his favorite, because the servile Korebos affected to imitate his methods and even his manias; outside, it was the shoulder of Agorakrites that supported him as he walked, because of Agorakrites' beauty; but on the nights of the Lykabette, who did the master talk to most? To Kritias. And why, if not that he divined my soul, and sensed how much it rejoiced in moonlight over the sea?

---

[96] André Vermare (1869-1949) was a Lyonnais sculptor.

[97] As there is no consensus as to how Greek names should be rendered in English or French, I have only altered Renard's terms when he uses a French phrase (e.g. *Mont des Abeilles* [Mount of Bees]) or where there is a familiar English equivalent (e.g. *Delphes* [Delphi]), leaving all the rest as he renders them. The Lykabette is a hill long since swallowed up by the expanding city of Athens.

[98] Phidias (c.480-c.430 B.C.) was the most famous Athenian sculptor of his era. None of his works survive, although Roman copies give us some idea of what they looked like. The statues to which Renard refers—except, of course, for the one at the heart of the story—were all mentioned and praised by contemporary writers.

297

In truth, nothing else could enchant me like that—but it pleased me most of all to see Phoebe rise over a horizon of waves, born from the sea like Aphrodite herself. Now, that is a marvel of which the Athenians are deprived. Under the penalty of a long voyage, it is necessary for them to survey terrestrial space from the Pentelique to the Hymette if they want to watch the lunar dawn. Only the enthusiasts who climb the Lykabette discover a corner of the gulf, between the Mount of Bees and the hills of Salamina; and when the fleeting moon is already far from its departure-point, one sees the sea catch fire from up there, as if all the fish were wriggling on its surface, in the opaline dazzle of their scales.

That is why we had climbed the Lykabette to see the moonlight over the sea.

Attica was asleep beneath the clear night. The incommensurable murmur of the sleepless waves was audible in the distance. Closer at hand, the frogs of the Ilissos were making a rumor of shaken rattles and countless toads were playing their monotonous pipes in the little river's reeds. Above Athens, extended beneath their feet, tutelary owls flew in circles. Perfumes exhaled by invisible flowers floated up to us—perhaps from the rose-bushes hanging on to the sheer slopes of the hill, perhaps even from the city; far below, its gardens mingled their somber verdure with the black shadows of the white houses. Two or three lights were still shining in the windows of a palace. They were extinguished along with the last noises and the river's batrachian chorus. Then, nothing could any longer be distinguished but the maritime murmur, soon confused with the thousand whispers of the silence.

"Look, Kritias," Phidias said to me. "Look how the night air resembles pure water. Might we not think that the city is drowned in the depths of the moonlight, as if on the bed of a beautiful lake, more transparent than a spring and more infinite than the ocean? Look: tonight, Attica is a submarine plain, and the city of Pallas truly has the appearance of a dead woman—the appearance that time will perhaps give her, and in which the present moment is amusing itself by dressing her up."

And it was true. We had before us the submerged image of the metropolis in ruins. For one thing, the suburbs, with their hovels, have always been suggestive of dilapidation. Then again, in that era of prosperity, the rich citizens were building profusely, and Perikles had ordered the erection of temples and arches in several quarters, with the result that by the light of the facetious moon, all those half-constructed monuments seemed half-destroyed. The Parthenon itself supported the illusion. It was scarcely what it is today, and did not yet terminate the chaos of the Acropolis with serenity; its lines could scarcely be distinguished, and every vague sketch accurately described the rubble to which twenty centuries would doubtless reduce it. Phidias, along with us, was busy with its completion; scaffolding surrounded it everywhere, and, from the summit of the Lykabette, I could locate my place of work: at the level of the frieze, near the second triglyph of the western wall.

The sculptor of Immortals sighed. His eyes were dreaming, confronted by the symbolic mirage. Confronted by all those sanctuaries inhabited by his works, now simulating inundated ruins, he must have been thinking about the crumbling of marble and glory beneath the irrevocable deluge of which the minutes are the drops.

Suddenly, a sound rang out. It rose up from the city toward the moon, like the musical cry of a chimerical toad. First there was one, then another, another and another, all of them identical. It was as if a string of melodious pearls were taking flight into the silence, one by one: a sequence of sonorous bubbles, escaping from calm and dormant water, each of which seemed to be the last, bursting at the surface high above, in broad daylight.

All of us had pricked up our ears. That noise was familiar. Alkamenos said, mockingly: "What drunkard is stupid enough to sculpt at this hour?"—for it was the sound of a chisel on marble.

"I recognize the wall," said Agorakrites. "It rings cleanly."

"Let's put a drachma on it," retorted Solon. "I'll wager it's the alabaster of the Pentelique."

But Phidias was listening as the harmonious strokes were strung out, and he had put his finger to his lips, to instruct us that nothing more should be said.

After a long pause, he lowered his head and complained thoughtfully, as if he were in pain: "Phew! Phew! How far off that is! How old it is!"

"Master," I asked him, "What are you remembering so tearfully. The thought of some past misfortune is haunting you—chase it away. Savor the present moment…or, rather, remember your triumphs…"

"Kritias," he replied, after a slight pause, "although foresight can only engender fear, memory is truly the fount of tears. The Gods have chiseled a changing mask for it; according to whether the memories are joyful or sad, that mysterious Arethusan face sometimes reflects joy and sometimes misery—but it's always tears that spring up in the eyes…"

"Undoubtedly," replied the flatterer Korebos. "But to move Phidias to sobs must certainly require the memory of a famous joy or a brutal chagrin. It must bring forth within him, if not some deep regret, at least the prolongation of an excessive pain!"

Phidias replied; "It's that of my most beautiful stature."

"The most beautiful of all!" I exclaimed.

And we all pointed together, some at the Acropolis, some at Delphi, and others at the Metroon.[99]

"Is it the Guardian Athene?"

"The Apollo?"

"Is it one of the thirteen for Marathon?"

"Is it the Kypris-Urania?"

---

[99] The Metroon was the original meeting-place of the Athenian city council; when it was superseded the original building became a temple dedicated to Cybele.

"None of them. The destiny of my masterpiece was a bizarre one; it was scarcely finished when I broke it."

"Oh!"

"By Zeus, what a disaster!"

Your masterpiece—broken?"

"Oh! Oh my! A Phidias statue!"

"Was it really the most beautiful of all?"

"How did it happen?"

"When?"

"It happened in the 73rd Olympiad, under the eponymous archonate of Lykas, when I had curly blond hair. And it happened in moonlight so similar to this that one might wonder whether this is the same light that has returned, in the manner of a specter—and whether, down there, it is the shade of my youth who is carving a statue beneath phantom stars…and whether tomorrow, when the flame of dawn behind the Hymette transforms into a placid volcano, will faultlessly repeat that spring morning when the story unfolded…

"I'll tell you the story.

"In that Lykadian year, in spite of the short time that had gone by since my abjuration of painting, I was already reputed as a statue-maker, and I had a little white marble house in the Street of Hermes, with a courtyard in the middle. It was there, in that aithrion, that I worked, beneath a veil of purple, when the weather as good. I can still see my bedroom, on the May night in question. It was a white, bare room; its window darted a white beam that retreated gradually across the flagstones, following an arc from stone to stone, seemingly measuring the hours of my insomnia on a lunar dial—for I was unable to sleep.

"An obsession was keeping me awake. It reproduced in my delirium the work I had almost finished, the statue that was waiting for me and the daylight in the middle of the aithrion, in order to submit to one last session—but the marmoreal naiad evoked by my eyes had sprung forth from the bosom of an evil phantasmagoria; fever distorted her features, and I despaired of ever recovering those of my beloved model. No, that was not the swimming motion of her arms. Her smile did not laugh as much at that. It's scarcely her at all; it's no longer her...

"Who among you, my children, has not been subject to such anguish? You all know it, I'm sure! Well, strange as it might seem, one awakens less easily from that sort of insomnia than from the deepest sleep—isn't that so? To escape it, that night, it was necessary for me to deploy a superhuman effort....

"I've rescued myself from the bed, though, and here I am on the threshold, in the presence of the figure. Glory to the Gods! The resemblance is there. One might almost think that it could not be improved—for the Moon, the accomplice of my desires, completing my art with its artifice, further emphasizes the similarity of the effigy to that which we call "Naiad." Her aquatic light fills the courtyard; she has sprung from a legendary well into which some Verity must have plunged. The pale nudity of my statue is immersed in the liquid half-light, and its white hue has become the pallor of a female bather beneath the cold and crystalline surface of a basin.

"It is Naïs. For the moment, it really is Naïs. Any passerby would tell you her name, on seeing that transfigured stone. And he would think: *That really is the mistress of Phidias, Naïs the ballerina, who can dance as the Nereids swam.*

"Naïs...alas, Naïs...she's no more now than a few ashes in an urn...

"People don't know how she died—or, rather, have forgotten it. No one disappears as furtively as a little ballerina. Anyhow, they think that Naïs is still swimming her dance. Perhaps they reckon her fortunate. And if anyone imagines, behind closed doors, that some shadowy lover is gazing at him, dark and alone, undulating a lovely body with siren suppleness...he does not doubt that it is Plouton.[100]

---

[100] Plouton was the Greek god of wealth, associated with subterranean regions because mining was seen as the ultimate source of wealth (hence "plutocrat"). Renard presumably

"She's dead—and my statue is only the image of my idea of her.

"Oh, to think that I had to look inside myself in order to design her! Once—is it not true?—I had better things to do with such splendor that imitate its contours! But I spent my life admiring her, and I contemplated Naïs to such an extent that I see her today in the densest darkness. Have not my hands, which have petrified her flesh, also caressed clay into her resemblance, then given lips and eyes to the blind and taciturn rock...? That mouth possesses an echo of the stifled voice, those eyes a gleam of an extinguished gaze...Naïs! Oh, can you see me? Can you speak to me?

"But there it is: it's a pebble in the moonlight, and nothing more. It's something unfinished, to be finished as soon as possible.

"Then, seizing the mallet and the chisel, I risk my task in the light of the night, which is almost diurnal by virtue of being moonlit. And my iron vibrates, making the marble ring! Swell my throat, O dolor! And you, my solitude, complain to the Gods!

" 'The Gods! Are they so cruel? Why do they only manifest their omnipotence by ill-treatment? Why are the only generous Gods those of Fable and Comedy? Ah, we see Hekate and Kronos exercise their ravages every day! The former carries off our friends, when the latter is tried of making them grow older, and both work at the same prodigious speed, which causes them both to vanish and remain where they are—for Death and Time are eternal passers-by, running in the bed of the world like rivers; they are constantly arriving and incessantly departing, and yet they are always there—and their stream is poisonous!

---

means to refer to Hades, the god of the afterlife, but has fallen victim to a common modern confusion, which misrepresents Plouton's Roman equivalent, Pluto, as the god of the underworld, rather than Hades' Roman equivalent, Dis.

" 'O Gods! These are the most certain of your exploits: dissolving youth little by little, and melting life at a stroke. Do you compose your immortality from all our stolen childhoods and our every plundered breath? I do not know why, but you steal the wealth and virtues of humans and never give them back, except in the mouths of old women or in the theater.

" 'Am I mistaken? Does one ever encounter a new Philemon beside another Baucis? Where is the Fountain of Youth? Is there an authentic Orpheus who would descend into Hades to search for his Eurydice? And since the fictitious Alkestis, O Gods, how many dead men have come back to life?

" 'Tales, my poor Naïs, tales! Old wives' tales or mountebanks' tirades! Oi! Oi! Nothing can remove you from Persephone's cortège! One cannot cross the Styx twice, except in stories; and they are merely flatteries addressed to the Olympians!

" 'If they wished, however, what magnificent exceptions they could make to our ugly harmony! How superbly they could set aside their own laws! For they exist, undoubtedly: Zeus, because his storms emit thunder and lightning; Phoebe, whose torch is providing me with light at this very moment; Eros, since I love you, O Naïs; and Phoebus, whose imminent ascension will drive the darkness back into caves and catacombs...

" 'Phoebus Apollo...he is the handsome Musagete[101] God, the supporter of arts and the protector of sculptors...it's him that I must invoke in my misfortune. But what good will it do? He has never worked a miracle? Will he do it for me? What stupidity!

" 'If he wished, though...

---

[101] Musagete—one of Apollo's many supplementary names—mean "Muse-leading."

" 'Io Paian![102] Io, Phoebus! Io, Apollo! Helios! Helios! Hub of flame with rays of fire! O Revolving One! O Resplendent One! I implore you!

" 'O phoenix-star! The innumerable dawns are made of your resurrections, but it is not the God of rebirths that I entreat in your divinity. No, I do not beseech you to rebind that which is unbound, to re-illuminate the cinder, to make Naïs the ballerina live again...

" 'But, O Fecund One, King of germinations and child-births, Creator and Brazier, throw into my statue the spark of life! Realize, with her and Phidias, the myth of Pygmalion and his beloved! Let her be a second Galatea, in becoming a second Naïs exactly like the first!

" 'And, O Resplendant One, O Revolving One, I will raise to you on the Acropolis a statue of ivory and gold—to you, gardener of the world, who sprinkles it with heat and light! To you, Phoebus Apollo!'

"Such were the words, my children—or very nearly—that I spoke. I don't remember now whether I shouted them, or murmured them, or merely thought them, so greatly was despair disturbing my thoughts. I was also very weary from my days of labor and my restless nights; fatigue and drowsiness were wearing me out without my being aware of it. I had spoken as I worked, like a sleep-walker.

"Now, having formulated that extravagant prayer without interrupting my work, I continue it. And while I softened Naïs' face with a meticulous chisel—Oh! Oh! Io, the Gods! And io, the Cytharede![103]—a pink warm flux entered into it by degrees! Mad with joy, redoubling my efforts, from the corner of my eye, I saw it descend through the face, reach the nose and the mouth, brightening as it spread...

---

[102] Paian, the equivalent of the English word paean, could be personalized in ancient Greece, as one of Apollo's epithets.

[103] Apollo was sometimes referred to as the Cytharede [cythare-player] because he was often represented with that lyre-like instrument.

"Quickly Quickly! Don't lose any time! It's a matter of anticipating the divine task; hurry, Phidias! Finish your work! If the living woman has but one imperfection…! Quickly! Only the throat remains to be polished; quickly…!

"And I make haste.

"The chin takes on color and becomes warm…and the breasts….and the delicate globe over which I slide the sharpened blade of the tool more timidly. Finally, the block is tinted with life all the way to the feet. And suddenly, another phase of the prodigy begins: the upper body and the belly quiver with voluptuous frissons. My chisel strokes a trembling breast…

"She is emotional now. The veins of marble are the veins of her flesh. The tumult of the blood is divinable beneath the skin. I dread that I might cause it to run. The chisel seems to me to be a knife-blade, and I scarcely dare put pressure upon it…

"But the legs are now trembling in their turn…another instant, and the metamorphosis will be consummated. The portrait is being erased by the original. It's almost a woman now. Naïs is returning to life within her copy; Naïs is emerging through the marble! She is arriving…

"And her imminent presence is already becoming familiar. Still absent, she seems never to have left. When she comes down from the pedestal, in a little while, and speaks, her gait will not surprise my eyes, or her voice my ears. What will she do? What will she say? I know in advance. She will go and dress herself in her hyacinth robe, which gilds her gilded locks a little more and adds an extra flourish to her flourishing cheeks; and, with her hand on the door, she will calmly say: 'I'm going out, my darling. I'm going to Phalere, to Xantho's house.' Or even: 'My sister and I are going to see our mother.'

"Ah, the liar! I know all about these excursions, from having spied upon them! She does not even know the cul-de-sac where Xantho lives, and her mother would greet her by beating her with a stick! No, no; every time she slips away she runs straight to the same place, and that's Gnathon's den!

Every one of her escapes is an escapade in that hideous hunchback's house…and they say he uses women with ingenious brutality! She will go without delay—death of Herakles!—to console that monster for such a long separation! She will go right away…unless, however…someone told me that they had surprised her in the company of Lesbia. I didn't believe it…but there are malicious tongues that insinuate that she persists in visiting Aethiops, the African gladiator…. Ha! Ha! She will race, even today, here or there, to the side of one lover or another!

"*Today? At this very instant!* It's now! It's now! The frissons are multiplying in her being; they are great spasms that are propagating like the waves in the gulf; and so rapid is the progress of the miracle that I hesitate to raise my eyes…they will see Naïs' eyes gleam, full of lust and deceit….

"How had I forgotten them—those eyes?

"Between my fingers, though, the chisel trembles, and the uplifted breast seems to me to betray the beat of a heart. You're breathing, Naïs! And as for me, I'm going to resume my existence of jealous cuckoldry, rediscover your sarcasm, our quarrels and my abrupt desire to murder you every time you depart toward love! She's moving! She's about to get down!

"Ah! Executioner! Female! Bitch! Vicious beast! You shall not go! You shall never go again!

"Ha!

"The chisel strikes at the heart.

"I've struck hard; the mallet splits under the shock, splinters of marble leap at me from the figure, and the statue, overturned on the flagstones, makes a racket like a heavy tower collapsing.

"Stupefied, with the broken mallet in my hand and blood on my lips, doubtless looking like a madman, I'm finally able to examine her without fear. She's broken. Her head has rolled away at an angle, and her shattered body is a pile of stones. *But every one of those stones seems to be quivering still, and retains its fleshy tint…*

" 'What? What's happening?'

"Then I perceive that day has dawned. The morning breeze is blowing from the sea, and above the aithrion, the purple veil is undulating. It's projecting palpitating shadows on everything, which are propagating like the waves of the gulf, and is filtering the burning vermilion light of the aurora, so effectively that the very walls of the courtyard seem to be made of quivering and roseate flesh...

"Phoebus Apollo had granted my wish. The sun had animated Naïs' marble—and that is why I erected a chryselephantine statue to him on the Acropolis."

Thus spoke Phidias—and when he had finished, the silence saddened us.

A CHRISTIAN LEGEND OF AKTEON

To Paul Dukas[104]

In those times, men having forgotten the Lord, they worshipped inexplicable powers, the stars most of all—and among the stars, the Sun and the Moon most of all. And in spite of the objurgations of Yahveh, which no one any longer heard, they constructed numerous and magnificent temples to them, in which, in order to make the commerce of the new deities more accessible, they were represented in the forms of boys and girls—with the result that, Elohim having created humankind in his own image, the false gods resembled the True.

Thus the Moon, the female of the Sun, had a statue of a young woman for an effigy. And among the multitude of peoples, each one gave her as many names in its own language as she was supposed to have influences. Under various titles and attires, she was everywhere the goddess of virgins, the protectress of child-bearers, the guardian of vessels on the nocturnal ocean and the patroness of those who hunted animals in order to kill them. The little Romans called her Diana as they buckled their belts, and the adolescent Carthaginians, looking at the chains on the feet, named her Tanit. In the depths of the weighty palaces of Hecatompyle[105] Thebes, the shrill cries of pregnant Pharaohs' wives invoked Isis. In the

---

[104] Paul Dukas (1865-1935) was a composer, best known for *The Sorcerer's Apprentice* (to which Renard occasionally makes reference), but the original version of this particular story reproduces a few bars from his *Symphony in C* (1896) by way of a prelude.

[105] Hecatompyle means "of one hundred gates."

galleys of Tyre, the hymns of the crews were heard to rise by night to Astarte...

Akteon, being a Greek and a hunter, venerated the Moon under the name of Artemis.

But the prince was the victim of an over-excited imagination, which made him see everything as marvelous. Credulous with regard to loquacious wet-nurses, he believed that his father, King Aristeus, had engendered him with the nymph Cyrene rather than his royal spouse. He believed that his ancestor, Kadmos the Boetian, having sown the teeth of a dragon, had harvested warriors. And such was his error that he was easily—and very stupidly—persuaded that the late Chiron, his old tutor, had been a centaur when alive.

Thus, when this visionary perceived the gods modeled in imitation of men and women, nothing prevented him from imagining that these simulacra were their true semblances, and that they really populated the Earth, in the same way as mortals. From then on, Akteon recognized the tracks of satyrs in goat-paths, and divined the gestures of dryads in the supple attitudes of swaying trees.

The entire pantheon of the pagans showed itself in this manner to his indulgent eyes. He saw all the gods: one behind the lightning, in the Olympian profile of some cloud; another in the human-seeming face of a curling wave, with a beard of foam. He saw—or thought he saw—them all...except for the huntress Artemis, crowned with a crescent and shod in endromides;[106] for his errant era had informed him of the alleged modesty of the illusory goddess, and told him that she hid herself, along with her nymphs, from the libertine gaze of men.

Now, in spite of the muffled remonstrances of Elohim, alarmed by such a mortal aberration, Akteon resolved to surprise the mysterious virgin; and, while spending his days and sometimes his nights hunting, he no longer kept watch only for ferocious beasts, and sought a less brutal encounter than those with wild boar and lynxes.

---

[106] Endromides are furry boots.

One evening, he was returning to the city. With a pike and a bow on their shoulders, two friends formed his escort. In front of them, on litters of branches, the corpses of a bear and three boars were carried; and the exhausted dogs were moving as they pleased, free of collars and without being retained by servants. The hunting-party and the pack were walking slowly, following the course of a stream through a wooded gorge.

Akteon, having neither killed any game nor seen the goddess, was frowning in a sullen manner, dragging his feet.

It was already very dark at the crest of the defile. Only the birch trees, which still seemed to be impregnated with moonlight, planted their pale phosphorescent colonnettes in the obscurity of the woods. Suddenly, a silvery fish darted along the turbulent stream like a stray ray of moonlight. The princely ephebe cheered up. Someone even heard him murmur with pleasure.

At once, at a bend in the path, he whispered a command to stop and be silent. He was obeyed. The friends and the servants turned questioning faces toward him, and the motionless dogs studied him, with their ears pricked.

Then he extended his hand toward the bend in the stream and said: "Artemis!"

They looked at the place he had indicated, and simply saw a white fog in front of the dark blue of the forest. It was moving over the surface of the water, as the mist does every evening, and at that moment, its round and nonchalant swirls were vaguely simulating a group of bathers. The same caprice that had sketched them soon deformed them. Forgetfulness of the truth was so profound in those times however, that there were several fools among Akteon's retinue misguided enough to share his illusion and repeat with him: "Artemis!" And they were convinced that they had surprised her bathing.

While the companions and the servants were admiring the now-formless fog with holy respect, however, there was a furious racket in the midst of their assembly of dogs running after something—and having turned round, they saw that the prince was no longer there, and that a huge red deer, with its head tilted and its antlers upon its back, was fleeing before the enraged pack.

No one doubted the metamorphosis: Akteon had been changed into a red deer. That was immediately understood—and those less faithful in the cult of Artemis were persuaded of both her existence and her power, since the divine prude was able to avenge indiscretions so effectively.

The initial amazement having dissipated, the wisest among them shouted that it was necessary to stop the dogs—and everyone, envisaging the frightful end by which Akteon the deer was threatened, melted into the thickets raising terrible clamors.

Unfortunately, they had lost invaluable minutes in being stupefied, and soon, some distance away, the cruel barking of the hounds informed them that the chase was at an end. Powerless henceforth, out of breath and gripped by fear, they paused at the sound of the horrible scene. Some let themselves fall down in despair; others, under the spur of terror, made drunken faces and tottered; there was one who wept, on his knees, striking the ground with a rhythmic fist; one started howling, to cover the noise of the kill; another stuck the fingers of both convulsive hands in his ears.

Then, when the dogs came back, with blood on their chops and fur between their teeth, they shot them down with arrows.

The Moon illuminated their return. They claimed that it was red all over.

Now, if the queen of the night really was tinted red, it was certainly under the influence of some astronomical phenomenon, not by the effect of offended modesty or indignation, still less because of Akteon's blood. Artemis, a vain chimera of corrupted minds, was entirely innocent in the matter—and besides, the prince was still alive.

Yahveh, who manages everything, had directed all of this. In His sadness at seeing Akteon, having achieved the height of his folly, presenting the most injurious spectacle and

312

the most contagious example, He was the one who, to chastise him, had transformed him into a bounding stag—but, the dogs having launched in pursuit, God made a sign, and they took another victim instead, whose carnage bloodied their mouths, for the Eternal was keeping Akteon the deer for less short-sighted aims and higher ends.

The latter, left alone in the double darkness of the hour and the forest, heard a confused voice that seemed to come from within himself, but which was really that of Elohim. "You shall live the life of an animal," it said, in substance, "until the fall of the false gods, for as long as the pagan Artemis is the patroness of hunters."

Akteon, however, only understood half of it, never having heard mention of Yahveh, except as the idol of a distant tribe. Then again, would he have understood any more, given that Elohim's habit of always expressing himself within consciences and without naming himself would have led him astray anyway? He took the Lord's allocution for a harangue by his own soul, and was only astonished by the fact that it spoke so unclearly and so inappropriately.

Nevertheless, the Words had left their inextinguishable echo within him, and for every second of his animal existence thereafter, he felt something great and unknown weighing upon his destiny.

Its accomplishment was slow.

Nothing, to begin with, distinguished Akteon from other solitary red deer stags. The latter do not give voice during spring sunsets, and no graceful herd of hinds and fawns ever follows them. Akteon's days were monotonous. He grazed the grass, ate foliage and, leaping over mirror-like springs, measured the growth of his antlers therein. Their branches fell away and grew again every year, and every year he rubbed away the moss of his new antlers against the bark of trees.

After having been the swift young stag he was the powerful ten-pointer, then became very old and saw his coat grow pale. He attained the age at which red deer die, and surpassed it. No stiffness numbed his hocks; his eye remained piercing, his ear infallible. He wore his bifurcated diadem on a cheerful and insouciant forehead; and yet, every winter, it became one branch heavier—and that had never happened before. Woodcutters, having seen him, recounted the apparition of a gigantic stag, entirely white and triply ten-pointed—but their tale excited the covetousness of the hunters of the region. Beatings were organized. Akteon went into exile and resumed the same life further away.

He attained the age at which men die, and surpassed it—but his extraordinary presence was always denounced, and it was always necessary for him to resume his flight before the generations of humankind.

All kinds of forests sheltered his wanderings and his sojourns. Some were pierced with avenues and seemed to be parks; the sun played in the foliage there; he preferred the immense arboreal vaults, where the fresh air is subterranean, so calm and tenebrous is it. Akteon breathed in their various aromas, of gardens or caverns. He rubbed his mossy antlers on all kinds of trunks; and sometimes, circling back at hazard to a certain once-familiar wood, he saluted centenarian oaks that he had formerly known as saplings. Akteon scorned the burden of centuries.

He attained the age at which trees die, and surpassed it. In faraway Greece, the great-grandchildren of his nephews were old. Those who chased him now spoke unknown languages and dressed in baroque costumes. Everything, including nations, was modified in the course of his perpetual voyage, and he did not know whether that was the result of the time elapsed or the space covered—for he was always in flight, and traveled the world, with the footfalls of men, the gallop of horses, the baying of watchdogs or the yapping of hounds behind him. Buffalo horns, ivory oliphants or copper trumpets were sounded at his heels. The fanfare was a bellowing or an orchestra. He heard the whistle of javelins, arrows fired from bows, then bolts from crossbows. The hunting-calls changed, according to the era and the country; some resembled war-cries, others predatory roars. Ambushes were set for him; he fell into pitfalls and triggered deadfalls; he was surprised from poachers' hides—but he escaped the greatest perils without injury, only leaving his cheated enemies the booty of his enormous supernatural footprints, today in the sand and tomorrow in the snow.

For God was preserving him for a further fortune.

Akteon grasped that more clearly from one day to the next, from one year to the next, from one century to the next. Whether he was taking a rest beneath an arcade of foliage or traversing some wide estuary, breathless, with the dogs at his flanks, the Words of yore obsessed his reverie or his panic without respite. "You shall live the life of an animal until the fall of the false gods, for as long as the pagan Artemis..."

Ah! Artemis! The prince scarcely believed in her any longer, and he understood that everything was happening in accordance with the prophecy, since it was already two-third realized—and while living the life of an animal, he had doubtless surpassed the age at which gods die...

Then, having thus divined the death of the goddess, Akteon began to spy on the humans he was able to approach, in order to discern any indication in their actions of the abjuration of the old divinities, which would also signal his deliverance.

Once, already, he had followed some of them. They were vagabonds moving rapidly through the undergrowth, seemingly in running away. In their thin faces they opened feverish eyes, and raised them to the heavens, murmuring supplications. One of them, exhausted, lovingly kissed two crossed twigs, as one drinks a generous cordial, and each kiss gave him more strength than a gulp of hydromel. [107]

Another time, wandering through an abandoned town at dawn, Akteon passed close to a temple of Artemis. The monument had fallen into ruins. Nothing remained standing but

---

[107] Honey dissolved in water, usually called mead if fermented.

the colonnade of the peristyle and the fronton, whose tympanum had collapsed. That made the dawn into a great celestial triangle, through which the sun gazed like a glorious eye. The prince was deeply moved by this, given that, Phoebus being higher in his course, a cloud in the form of a cross had eclipsed him. Moved by an invincible pressure, Akteon turned to the west: diaphanous Phoebe was whitening there and a dove, motionless in its flight, seemed to be scratching her out of the heavens.

Symbolic omens.

Later on, the white deer discovered a group of huts in the middle of a clearing. Crosses surmounted them and their inhabitants, clad in monkish habits and girdled with cords, were kneeling in front of identical items of carpentry. Dolls crowned with thorns could be seen nailed to the latter.

On the strength of these episodes, Akteon became convinced that the cross ruled the world; he remained surprised, though, that it was in the capacity of a gibbet, and not as a symbol of eternal and universal geometry, as he had been willing to believe at first. In any case, it mattered little to him; these things were visibly linked to the Words; thus, the time was nigh. And he gave thanks to the new religion, and blessed the cross, for he was tired of always having to flee before hunters for having venerated the crescent excessively.

One hunt came that was persistent, and lasted three days and three nights. Its passage was the bacchanal of a typhoon. Never had the enchanted animal been harassed by such a tenacious host of hunters and dogs. One might have thought them gladiators and wild beasts. Their speed equaled his rapidity, their cunning outwitted his ruses. It did him no good to mingle with herds and strike his peers to oblige them to take his place as a martyr; it did him no good to cross roads and walk along stream-beds in order to frustrate his tormentors; the ferocious din drew ever closer.

As the dusk of the third day fell, Akteon felt fatigued for the first time, and searched instinctively for the pool where he would meet his death. Having found it, he went into it—but then his poor human soul softened, and he began to weep. Now, other than him, no red deer had ever shed tears until that moment; it is only since then, in memory of his distress, that they weep like human beings in their mortuary pools.

He waited for the end. The bloodhound emerged, then the leading dogs, and then the rest of the pack. Akteon looked down at them from the height of his prodigious stature, but on sighting him, they set out to circle him, in the water, and remained there without moving any further or giving voice. On perceiving that, the first horsemen also came to an abrupt halt at the edge of the forest, their horns to their lips or their bows flexed, without the clarion call bursting forth or the arrow being released—for the cornered animal had surprised them, dressed in the gold of the dusk against the blue darkness of snowy, colossal, haughty fir-trees, with the thorns of his antlers weaving the most sumptuous diadem.

Suddenly, there was a rustle of parting branches; a palfrey whinnied; weapons clinked, and the Huntsman himself emerged from the forest. But he, alone among them, did not seem wonderstruck. He shouted insults at the dogs and mocked the beaters, then leapt from his horse and reached into his quiver…

Then, Akteon sensed a light illuminate above his head, in the midst of his great crown of thorns; and, lowering his head toward the placid and shiny water, he saw by the reflection of its light that it was a flaming cross.

The miraculous creature knew no more than that, for he collapsed, finally dead, understanding by that fact that the Words were accomplished in full, and that henceforth, all hunters would disown their ancient patroness…but without having contemplated the Huntsman prostrated before him, and without having learned that he was Comte Hubert, who would become the bishop of Liège—and a saint.[108]

---

[108] The conversion of St. Hubert (who died in 727) as a result of a vision experienced while hunting on Good Friday became

the subject of numerous paintings, and St. Hubert was duly appointed the patron saint of huntsmen. A hunting-horn alleged to be his can be seen in the Wallace Collection in London, but as the legend was unknown before the 14th century, it is no more likely to be authentic than any other saintly relic.

Afterword

It is difficult to begin a discussion of *Un homme chez les microbes* in any other way than by wondering what the novel might have looked like if Renard had published the first version with which he was satisfied—the one completed in 1913, if not the one completed in 1908 or 1909. We can only guess what differences there would have been between that version and the one we actually have, but Renard seems to have been careful to leave us hints regarding some of the things he was obliged to leave out—most notably an account of Fléchambeau's adventures among the "known microbes," a more elaborate account of the contents of the Mandarin museum, and a much more extensive account of everyday life among the Mandarins, as observed during his 60-year sojourn in their midst.

In the story as published, the "tattoos" that enable Fléchambeau to bring a rich legacy from the worlds of the Mandarins are pointless, blown away in the cataclysm precipitated by a macrocosmic puff of breath—perhaps a sneeze born of the brief fever that animates our entire universe, in Fléchambeau's dismissive suggestion—but they would surely not be there at all had they not served some purpose in an earlier draft that did not end so dismissively. Again, in the story as published, only passing mention is made of the "surges" in Fléchambeau's affection for Kala, but it is difficult to believe that the writer who described far stranger perversities, explicitly and with a gleeful verve, in *Le Docteur Lerne* would have baulked at the task of elaborating that one until some external censor had instructed him not to yield to the temptation. Yet again, in the story as published, several striking notions are mentioned once only to be left out of account thereafter—the existence of a technology of matter transmission and the controlled use of the pressure of time itself to operate watches, to

319

name but two—and it is difficult to believe that such stubs had been left undeveloped in all four of the previous drafts.

The most surprising aspect of the novel, from the viewpoint of the modern reader, might well be its failure to live up to its title. It does not, in fact, provide any account of a man among what we would think of as "microbes"—such as is provided, for instance, by James Blish's famous science fiction story "Surface Tension"—but provides instead an account of a Utopian society that might just as easily have been set on an alien planet, or even a remote island. The source of this disappointment, however, probably lies in the 20-year gap between the novel's initial completion and its eventual publication. In the course of that interval, microbiology made vast strides, and the image of the "microscopic microcosm" provided in the original version must have become irreparably obsolete.

Something similar must have happened to the image the novel provides of the subatomic microcosm, when the Rutherford-Bohr model of the "atomic solar system" replaced Rutherford's previous model, which imagined the atom as a globe in which the electrons were contained, like beads in a child's rattle—but that shift was relatively easy to repair, or at least to gloss over. The proliferation of the number of known species of protozoa and bacteria, and the increase in what was known about them between 1907 and 1927 was not a matter that could be compensated by any simple revision. In order to retain that section—which was not, of course, the most important in the text—would have required starting again from scratch and doing further research as well as writing new text; Renard can hardly be blamed for simply cutting it out, especially as he must have been under pressure from the eventual publisher, Georges Crès, to shorten the text.

We can presume the existence of this editorial pressure not merely on the basis of the text's own references to omitted material but also from the nature of the material that survives. Unlike *Le Docteur Lerne*, which had been formulated in the image of modern fiction, as a mystery story and a thriller with horrific and erotic overtones, and could therefore be accepted easily as a work with ready-made reader appeal, *Un Homme chez les microbes* was formulated in the image of the venerable but no-longer-fashionable tradition of Utopian satire. Its prominent antecedents included such admired but no-longer-read works as Gabriel de Foigny's *La Terre australe connue* (1676; tr. as *The Southern Land, Known*), Marie-Anne Roumier's *Voyages de Mylord Céton dans les sept planètes* [Lord Seton's Journeys to the Seven Planets] (1765-66) and Restif de la Bretonne's *Le Découverte australe par un homme volant* [The Discoveries of a Flying Man in the Southern Hemisphere] (1781). Renard did attempt to compensate for that difficulty by introducing the long "second prologue," whose satirical aspect is relatively gentle, and which takes the ever-ripe form of a tale of frustrated love countered by ingenious friendship, but that could not prevent Fléchambeau's adventure from becoming, once he reached the world of the Mandarins, a travelogue whose interest depends on the reader's willingness to be fascinated by the speculative motif whose implications were being explored: the possibility of a near-human race whose dominant sense is not sight but a form of perception alien to actual human beings.

Renard knew, of course, that *contes philosophiques* had been developed before into narratives that were by no means devoid of action and excitement; he named Voltaire and Jonathan Swift as two key precursors of scientific marvel fiction in his essay on that subject, and singles them out again in his account of Doctor Prologus's favorite reading, as well as in-dentifying *Micromégas* as the principal inspiration of *Un Homme chez les microbes*. He presumably assumed, when he first set out on his own project, that the wide popularity still enjoyed by the best of Voltaire's *contes philosophiques* and by Swift's account of *Gulliver's Travels* was potentially reproducible, if only he could get the mixture right—and that was doubtless one of the reasons why he persisted in trying to do so. His account of the Mandarin apocalypse was presumably added to the original version of the story in order to pep up that section of the narrative, along with the comic-opera villain Kakos, although the analogies drawn in the published version to the Great War were obviously added at a later date. The fact remains, however that Renard had set himself a literary task that was, if not impossible of execution in 1907, so difficult as to require a prodigious effort to bring it off.

Renard probably knew, at that point in time, that Gabriel Tarde—who was one of the editorial consultants of *Le Spectateur* and must have taken an interest in Renard's essay on scientific marvel fiction—had contrived to reprint the *Fragment d'histoire future* that he had originally appeared in the *Revue sociologique* in 1896 in book form in 1904, but that could not have lent him any encouragement. Nor could he have obtained any further burst to his morale is he had been able to look into the future and see Gaston de Pawlowski's *Voyage au pays de la quatrième dimension* (tr. in a Black Coat Press edition as *A Journey to the Land of the Fourth Dimension*) reach print in 1912 and, in a revised edition, in 1923. The book that undoubtedly did give him some initial encouragement, however, was the H. G. Wells novel that he used as a template: *The First Men in the Moon*. Like Wells's novel, Renard's begins with a sequence of social comedy in which an innocent is drawn into his eccentric friend's adventurous endeavors, and in Wells's novel too, the narrative concludes with a relatively straightforward didactic account of an alien society (whose substance is briefly echoed in the passage revealing that the Mandarins have a larval stage in which they are socially engineered, in a manner similar to Wells's Selenites).

The most significant difference between *The First Men in the Moon* and *Un Homme chez les microbes* lies in the complexity of the didactic account. Wells had only to elaborate an analogy with insectile hive societies that was already fairly well understood—and had, in fact, already been dramatized and popularized by one of the many writers Renard cites in his own text, Maurice Maeterlinck—while Renard had to undertake a narrative task that was far more intense and extensive: "inventing" a new sense and extrapolating the potential social effects of its possession and its dominance. Renard might also have observed—as he certainly did at a later date—that *The First Men in the Moon* had been Wells's final venture in almost-pure scientific marvel fiction, and that his occasional uses of the "scientific marvelous" thereafter had been conspicuously subservient to other purposes. That novel's undoubted success had come at the expense of testing the limits of the genre, in a direction in which any attempt to extend them further was likely to stretch them to breaking point.

Renard had also set himself a difficult task within the context of scientific marvel fiction, in that rationalizing the kind of shrinking process that he describes in the story is direly awkward. The psychological plausibility of the idea is sufficient to have facilitated a steady flow of such stories in the twentieth century—most notably Richard Matheson's *The Shrinking Man* (1956), whose film version founded a movie subgenre—but Renard's ostensible regard for logical extrapolation should at have focused his attention on some of the problems that many later writers were simply content to ignore. What happens to Fléchambeau's mass? Does he retain it, or does he lose it? In the former case, he would be an extremely heavy object by the time he arrived in the microcosm, more of a gravitational black hole than a mere man; in the latter case, it is difficult to imagine how his reduced mass could continue to support the physiological complexity of his body as he shrinks. Difficulties will surely arise in either case when he reaches a size at which he is small relative to the molecules of the air that he is trying to breathe. How is he going to absorb oxygen into his bloodstream once it begins to arrive in packages the size of footballs? (This question is acknowledged in the text, but not answered.) How will he be able to see when the wavelength of light begins to extend measurably by comparison with the cells in his retina?

The gap in the narrative between the moment Fléchambeau becomes motionless on the microscope slide and his awakening in the world of the Mandarins leaves him unconscious of the transitional phase during which these problems and their experiential corollaries would become so acute as to seem insoluble, so he, in his capacity as narrator, is able to duck them, but it is not obvious that the author should have the same license. When it is time for Fléchambeau to return to the macrocosm, and he attempts to bring Agathos with him, he reports that his original mass must have been compacted, so that he can complete the journey while Agathos merely evaporates, but that leaves unanswered the question of how Fléchambeau and Agathos could meet and interact as if they were creatures of much the same sort, seemingly similar in organic complexity and ponderousness.

A further complication is added to this network of problems by the introduction of a different time-scheme to the microcosm, so that Fléchambeau ages sixty years while a few months pass in the microcosm. This narrative move is a simple inversion of the common folktale device by which protagonists who spend a night in fairyland discover that years have elapsed when they return home, but in the context of the "logical marvelous" it raises interesting questions of relativity that Renard makes no attempt to elaborate or answer.

Since Renard does not attempt to address these kinds of problems, perhaps they should simply be left unasked and unanswered, but it might be worth recalling the distant origin that Renard's research located for the fundamental thesis of his story, in the correspondence exchanged between Leibniz and Bernouilli. It must be remembered that Leibniz's notion of worlds within worlds would have been radically different from the crude notion that atoms are merely solar systems on a much tinier scale. Although the French version of the quote from Leibniz reproduced in the text refers to "atomes" [atoms] the terms Leibniz used to discuss the fine structure of the experienced universe are usually translated into English as "substance" and "monad." In Leibniz's philosophy, there is an infinite number of substances, which are maintained in harmonious existence by God, and the limitations on creativity imposed by their inherent nature are such that, although God has made the best of all possible worlds out of them, there are still flaws in the perceived universe that reflect the limitations of the materials. (Voltaire was not being entirely fair in the attack he launched on this notion in *Candide*).

The implications of all this, for Renard and Fléchambeau, is that the latter's "diminution" cannot be regarded simply as a quantitative process, but must be imagined as a qualitative one—a gradual change in substantial nature, to which alterations in the passage of time might well be as much a corollary and alterations in the perception of space. In visiting a world "within" Earthly matter, in a Leibnizian sense, Fléchambeau is not merely visiting a realm compounded out of "matter writ small", but a world with its own distinct substantiality, a "monad" in its own right.

Seen in this way, questions about what happens to Fléchambeau's mass, and his ability to breathe (Leibniz, writing in the seventeenth century, knew nothing about oxygen and conceived of air as a kind of thin plenum rather than a loose aggregation of various molecules) can be sidelined by the argument that he is undergoing a far more complicated metamorphosis than his initial shrinkage is intended to bring about. The period of unconsciousness he endures would then become imaginable as a kind of "intersubstantial pupation," in the course of which he trades one substance, or combination of substances, for another. Leibniz would have considered such a transition inconceivable—he imagined substances to be "windowless," incapable of combination, let alone of transformation—but Renard is not obliged to stick rigidly to Leibniz's world-view simply because he found a useful precedent therein for the idea he wanted to develop. In *Le Docteur Lerne*, he borrowed the elements of his fundamental logic from Cartesian dualism, and the metaphysics he takes for granted in *Un Homme chez les microbes* can be seen as a further expansion of Cartesian thought to take in more kinds of substance than those imagined in the simple mind/body distinction.

It would not be worth making too much of this if it were not a way of thinking that continued to affect the underlying logic of Renard's scientific marvel fiction—and, indeed, to provide a unifying component that adds a measure of coherency to his entire canon. The notion that there more kinds of substance than are dreamed of in conventional dualism, which might be related to different kinds of space, and that transitions between them might be possible, had already been sketched out in "La Singulière destinée de Bouvancourt," and was to recur again, if only tacitly, in all of Renard's longer works of scientific marvel fiction. Fléchambeau's exit from the perceived universe and entry into the microcosm is more closely akin to Bouvancourt's exit from perceived space and entry into the virtual space beyond the mirror than it is to any straightforward extrapolation of the shrinkage he undergoes within perceived space.

If the first or second version of *Un Homme chez les microbes* had been published—however unsuccessfully in a commercial sense—we would now be able to hail it as a masterpiece of imaginative fiction, even more original and adventurous than *Le Docteur Lerne* or *Le Péril bleu*. It would not only be the first microcosmic romance to have been published, but would have been published ahead of the crucial paradigm-shift that encouraged other authors to develop the idea. It would probably have been one of the earliest fictional attempts (though not the very first) to represent the microcosm revealed by microscopes, as well as locating that microcosm within a hierarchy of realms that extended upwards as well as downwards, in a fashion echoed more modestly in the hierarchy of Earthly realms proposed in the epilogue to *Le Péril bleu*. It would certainly have been the most conscientious and detailed attempt yet published to describe an alien society possessed of a sensorium significantly different from our own—and in that sense, in spite of numerous subsequent attempts by science fiction writers to offer detailed accounts of societies blessed with telepathy and other "*psi* powers," the published version still has claims to be considered unique.

It is arguable that the challenge provided by the crucial passage in *Micromégas* that equips Voltaire's Sirian giant with many more senses than his Saturnian sidekick possesses, let alone the meager five with which humans have to scrape by, has never been squarely and conscientiously met by any writer of speculative fiction. *Un Homme chez le microbes* is still part of a relatively select group of texts that at least take a tentative step in that direction; in the first half of the century it stands alongside E. V. Odle's account of *The Clockwork Man* (1923) and Muriel Jaeger's account of *The Man with Six Senses* (1927)—both of which are similarly heroic and equally underappreciated—but it attempts a much further imaginative reach than either of those endeavors. That daring, in itself, would— alas!—have constituted a disincentive to the book's publication in the commercial arena.

It seems probable that another bar to the earlier publication of *Un Homme chez les microbes* was Renard's decision to give the Mandarin species an extra sex as well as an extra sense. Some earlier works—most notably the Foigny text previously cited—had made radical modifications to human sexual physiology in setting up Utopian worlds, taking similar inspiration from the apologue in the *Symposium* credited by Plato to Aristophanes, but it had not ceased to be a touchy subject, likely to make a publisher wary. The issue is handled in the published version with considerably more decorum than the perversities paraded in *Le Docteur Lerne*, but Fléchambeau's attraction to Kala might not have been the only aspect of that situation that had to be considerably toned down as the five volumes evolved. If Renard was subjected to stern editorial pressure in this specific regard, it might help to explain why he never again felt free to express such ideas as freely as he had in his first novel, any more than he never again felt free to dabble in Voltairean satire.

Renard did not abandon his interest in the possibility of defining and describing the experience of senses other than the five to which we are accustomed when *Un Homme chez les microbes* initially failed to sell. He had already made some elementary speculations about the possible effects of experiencing the world through a modified sensorium in *Le Docteur Lerne*, when Nicolas' brain is transplanted into Jupiter's

327

body, and he went on to undertake another literary thought-experiment of a kind similar to the one undertaken in *Un Homme chez les microbes* in "L'Homme truqué," in which a blind man's eyes are replaced by substitute organs that translate a new mode of perception into visual terms. That projected novel was also published in a form that must have been truncated, although it is doubtful whether the author ever completed a longer version. The same fascination with the possibilities of perception also lies at the foundation of *Le Péril bleu*, "Le Brouillard du 26 Octobre" (tr. in volume four as "The Fog of October 26") and *Le Maître de la lumière*, although it is developed in very different ways, so there is a sense in which the greater part of Renard's scientific marvel fiction takes part of its initial inspiration from *Micromégas*.

Although *Un Homme chez les microbes* does find numerous opportunities to refer back to Earthly myth, legend and folklore, by way of analogy, it differs sharply from *Le Docteur Lerne* in that its central motif—the perpetually shrinking man—has no straightforward resonance there. Unlike *Le Docteur Lerne*, therefore, it cannot be seen as any kind of hybrid work representing a transitional evolution from the mythic version of "the marvelous" to the "scientific marvelous." Even though its scientific marvel element is submissive to the further literary purpose of Utopian satire, there remains a sense in which it is a purer item of scientific marvel fiction than its analogy-laden predecessor. If the thesis set out in the preface to *Le Voyage Immobile suivi d'autres histoires singulières* really was a precursor to the manifesto set out in the 1909 manifesto for scientific marvel fiction, therefore, it might well have been the experience of writing and evaluating *Un Homme chez les microbes* that persuaded Renard of the necessity of separating out scientific marvel fiction as a special project within the broader field of the "logical marvelous." The probability is, however that the writing of *Un Homme chez les microbes* was well advanced by the time the collection was assembled and its preface written, and that the thesis set out in that preface was merely an advertising device designed to make the collection seem more coherent.

Whatever the truth of the matter, though, the argument set out in the preface is an interesting one, which certainly refers to a real historical phenomenon and retains some relevance to the evolution of twentieth-century fantasy fiction. The realization that there are interesting ways in which to balance, combine, hybridize and contrast the marvelous and logical elements of fanciful stories, thus producing different sorts of narrative energy, was a vitally important factor in the twentieth-century development as such subgenres as comic fantasy, as it ranged from such authors as Thorne Smith and James Branch Cabell to Roald Dahl and Terry Pratchett, and "dark fantasy," as it ranged from such authors as Robert W. Chambers and Clark Ashton Smith to Tim Powers and Philip Pullman.

In becoming a propagandist for scientific marvel fiction, Renard—like many later champions of science fiction—seemed to be looking forward to a day when such fiction might be clearly demarcated from other subgenres of "the marvelous" by the purity of its logic and the particular substance of its thought experiments, but in practice that never happened. It is arguable that precious little "pure" scientific marvel fiction (or science fiction) has ever been produced, and that even if the category is estimated to be larger than it really is, it still remains, very obviously, part of a continuous spectrum that extends all the way to the purest literary nonsense— which, by no means paradoxically, tends to draw much of its own narrative energy from the scrupulous application of logic to its own quirky premises, as flamboyantly illustrated by the pioneering endeavors of Lewis Carroll. Renard, therefore, deserves credit for not only arguing that such a spectrum exists but attempting to exemplify its range with a series of samples.

Viewed as exemplars of the spectrum described in its preface, however, the stories in the collection do leave something to be desired. "Le Voyage immobile" hardly qualifies as type specimen of scientific marvel fiction, even if (as in the prior English translation) it is carefully stripped of the apologetic twist in the tail that reveals the account of the *Aerofix* to be a mere hoax. There is a hint of Lewis Carroll about the narrative anyway, encouraged by its comic tone.

"La Singulière destinée de Bouvancourt" is similar, and not merely because it features a literal journey through the looking glass. Its attempt to rationalize the concept of an accessible "virtual space" is perhaps half-hearted, and self-consciously so—and it is hardly surprising that the author, in search of a swift denouement, had to make an adjustment to the character of the story, opting for an ending suspended somewhere between the horrific and the poetic—but if the story is set alongside *Un Homme chez les microbes* it can be seen as a further exploration of the same range of exotic possibilities, and it ought not to be dismissed as trivial.

"Le Rendez-vous" is presumably placed third in the sequence because it rests its logic on the "fringe science" of hypnotism, but the reason that one of its models, "The Facts in the Case of Monsieur Valdemar" qualifies an important precursor of science fiction has more to do with the tone of its reportage—which parodies the contemporary form of scientific reportage—than the plausibility of the event that it describes. Its other model is, of course, "The Masque of the Red Death," which is one of the purest fantasies in Poe's canon, and established a cardinal example for the extended prose-poetry that Charles Baudelaire's example and Joris-Karl Huysmans' commentary were later to establish as the perfect format of the Decadent style. If one overlooks its heavy dependence on second-hand motifs, however, "Le Rendez-vous" is a fine story, and the most interesting thing about it is, indeed, the fact that it adds an extra dose of logic that is wholly appropriate to its era to its recycled materials. In its attempt to capture and describe what it might actually be like to undergo the extraordinary experience that afflicts the protagonist, it comes as close in spirit to the modern works of Stephen King as it is to the antique endeavors of Edgar Poe, and it really does represent a transitional phase in an evolutionary process that extended between the two, better than most contemporary works of the same sort.

"La Mort et le coquillage" is placed fourth in the sequence because of the analogy drawn between the seashell and a phonograph, but the analogy is only an analogy, and could never be anything more; the real interest of the story is to serve as a prologue of sorts to "Parthénope ou l'escale imprévue," which was obviously Renard's favorite within the collection, and perhaps deservedly so, although opinions generated by other viewpoints might consider "Le Voyage immobile" or "Le Rendez-vous" to be superior.

The notion that there might be a zoological basis for accounts of many legendary creatures is sufficiently commonplace for an entire quasi-science of "cryptozoology" to have grown up, so there is nothing very exceptional about the attempt to imagine a "real" siren that might somehow be slotted into conventional animal taxonomy, nor is it obvious that such an attempt ought to place the story third in the sequence rather than fifth. The literary merits of the piece are, however, by no means confined to that simple core hypothesis; the narrative works on several levels, intricately entwining the attitudes that the various characters adopt to one another with their attitudes to antiquity and its myths, and, inevitably, their attitude to the eventual brutal confusion of one such myth with a present reality that is discomfiting in more ways than one. In that respect—not excluding the component of innuendo threaded into the weave—the story is an apt precursor to the kind of sophistication that was subsequently to be integrated into late-twentieth-century hybrid and chimerical fantasies.

Although they have no relevance at all, however peripheral, to the category of scientific marvel fiction, both "La Statue ensoleillée" and "Une Légende chreétienne d'Aktéon" are hybrid works of a sort. The former belongs to a subgenre in which natural events are misconstrued as supernatural because of a combination of particular circumstances and the unusual psychological state on an observer, and therefore qualifies as an instance in which logic and the marvelous are in a special kind of tension—although it is arguable that the main interest of the story lies in its further exemplification of Renard's deeply jaundiced view of erotic relationships. The tension in the latter is not between the logical and the marvelous but between two opposed schemes of the marvelous, and its curiously sentimental account of a transition between them recalls kindred works by Anatole France and Remy de Gourmont which might be reckoned to lie close to the heart of the Decadent world-view. It is, perhaps, the nearest Renard ever came to writing an extended Symbolist prose-poem, and its placement within the sketched-out spectrum helps to explain why there is such a marked link between the Symbolist movement and early French speculative fiction, many writers having followed the examples of Edgar Poe and Villiers de l'Isle-Adam in shifting—slightly or markedly—from the former literary position to undertake significant endeavors of the latter kind.

Although the short stories reproduced here inevitably lack the depth and breadth even of the published version of *Un Homme chez les microbes*, they should not be regarded as trivial, but rather as smaller but vital components of the same great work—which was, in sum, the expansion of human thought. They cannot go as far as the microcosm, let along the macrocosm, being confined to a much narrower gutter—but, as Oscar Wilde famously observed, even viewpoints located in a gutter are capable, and fully entitled, to search for the stars, and perhaps also for worlds beyond. Were it not for the smaller steps he took, by way of experiment, Renard might never have been able to produce a text that took the giant leap contained in *Un Homme chez les microbes*: a leap whose awesome extent can now by fully appreciated, at least by connoisseurs, even though it could not find due appreciation at the time of its initial composition, and eventually appeared in a form that is probably a shadow of its earlier self.

SF & FANTASY

Guy d'Armen. *Doc Ardan: The City of Gold and Lepers*
G.-J. Arnaud. *The Ice Company*
Aloysius Bertrand. *Gaspard de la Nuit*
Félix Bodin. *The Novel of the Future*
Didier de Chousy. *Ignis*
C. I. Defontenay. *Star (Psi Cassiopeia)*
Charles Derennes. *The People of the Pole*
Harry Dickson. *The Heir of Dracula*
Sâr Dubnotal *vs. Jack the Ripper*
Alexandre Dumas. *The Return of Lord Ruthven*
J.-C. Dunyach. *The Night Orchid. The Thieves of Silence*
Paul Féval. *Anne of the Isles. Knightshade. Revenants. Vampire City. The Vampire Countess. The Wandering Jew's Daughter*
Paul Féval, *fils. Felifax, the Tiger-Man*
Arnould Galopin. *Doctor Omega*
V. Hugo, Foucher & Meurice. *The Hunchback of Notre-Dame*
O. Joncquel & Theo Varlet. *The Martian Epic*
Jean de La Hire. *Enter the Nyctalope. The Nyctalope on Mars. The Nyctalope vs. Lucifer*
G. Le Faure & H. de Graffigny. *The Extraordinary Adventures of a Russian Scientist Across the Solar System* (2 vols.)
Gustave Le Rouge. *The Vampires of Mars*
Jules Lermina. *Panic in Paris. To-Ho and the Gold Destroyers. Mysteryville*
Jean-Marc & Randy Lofficier. *Edgar Allan Poe on Mars. The Katrina Protocol. Pacifica. Robonocchio.* (anthologists) *Tales of the Shadowmen* (6 vols.) (non-fiction) *Shadowmen* (2 vols.)
Xavier Mauméjean. *The League of Heroes*
Marie Nizet. *Captain Vampire*
C. Nodier, Beraud & Toussaint-Merle. *Frankenstein*
Henri de Parville. *An Inhabitant of the Planet Mars*
Polidori, C. Nodier, E. Scribe. *Lord Ruthven the Vampire*
P.-A. Ponson du Terrail. *The Vampire and the Devil's Son*
Maurice Renard. *Doctor Lerne. A Man Among the Microbes*

Albert Robida. *The Clock of the Centuries. The Adventures of Saturnin Farandoul*

J.-H. Rosny Aîné. *The Navigators of Space*

Brian Stableford. *The Shadow of Frankenstein. Frankenstein and the Vampire Countess. The New Faust at the Tragicomique. Sherlock Holmes & The Vampires of Eternity. The Stones of Camelot. The Wayward Muse.* (anthologist) *The Germans on Venus. News from the Moon*

Kurt Steiner. *Ortog*

Villiers de l'Isle-Adam. *The Scaffold. The Vampire Soul*

Philippe Ward. *Artahe*

MYSTERIES & THRILLERS

M. Allain & P. Souvestre. *The Daughter of Fantômas*

Anicet-Bourgeois, Lucien Dabril. *Rocambole*

A. Bisson & G. Livet. *Nick Carter vs. Fantômas*

V. Darlay & H. de Gorsse. *Lupin vs. Holmes: The Stage Play*

Paul Féval. *The Black Coats: The Companions of the Treasure. Gentlemen of the Night. Heart of Steel. The Invisible Weapon. John Devil. The Parisian Jungle. 'Salem Street*

Emile Gaboriau. *Monsieur Lecoq*

Steve Leadley. *Sherlock Holmes: The Circle of Blood*

Maurice Leblanc. *Arsène Lupin: The Hollow Needle. The Blonde Phantom*

Gaston Leroux. *Chéri-Bibi. The Phantom of the Opera. Rouletabille & the Mystery of the Yellow Room*

G. Marot & L. Pericaud. *Nick Carter vs. Jack the Ripper*

William Patrick Maynard. *The Terror of Fu Manchu*

Frank J. Morlock. *Sherlock Holmes: The Grand Horizontals*

P. de Wattyne & Y. Walter. *Sherlock Holmes vs. Fantômas*

David White. *Fantômas in America*

www.ingramcontent.com/pod-product-compliance
Lightning Source LLC
Chambersburg PA
CBHW022210010726
47493CB00002B/494